WEIRD WORLD WAR: CHINA

BAEN BOOKS
edited by
SEAN PATRICK HAZLETT

Weird World War III
Weird World War IV
Weird World War: China

WEIRD WORLD WAR: CHINA

edited by
Sean Patrick Hazlett

BAEN

A Baen Books Original

Baen Publishing Enterprises
P.O. Box 1403
Riverdale, NY 10471
www.baen.com

ISBN: 978-1-9821-9314-0

Cover art by Kurt Miller

First printing, January 2024

Distributed by Simon & Schuster
1230 Avenue of the Americas
New York, NY 10020

Library of Congress Cataloging-in-Publication Data

Names: Hazlett, Sean Patrick, 1975- editor.
Title: Weird World War : China / edited by Sean Patrick Hazlett.
Description: Riverdale : Baen Publishing Enterprises, 2024.
Identifiers: LCCN 2023040408 (print) | LCCN 2023040409 (ebook) | ISBN 9781982193140 (trade paperback) | ISBN 9781625799463 (ebook)
Subjects: LCSH: Science fiction, American. | War stories, American. | China—Fiction. | Alternative histories (Fiction), American. | Speculative fiction, American.
Classification: LCC PS648.S3 W38733 2024 (print) | LCC PS648.S3 (ebook) | DDC 813/.087620806—dc23
LC record available at https://lccn.loc.gov/2023040408
LC ebook record available at https://lccn.loc.gov/2023040409

Printed in the United States of America

10 9 8 7 6 5 4 3 2 1

✪ Dedication ✪

This volume is dedicated to three people who've made a difference in my life. They aren't the only ones who've made an impact—there are far too many to list here—but they have all passed on and deserve to be remembered for their many contributions to humanity.

The first person is my brother-in-arms, Captain Ralph J. Harting III (1976–2005), who rode honorably with the Blackhorse in the sands of Mesopotamia. You sacrificed your life so others could live. One day, I will share a pint with you at Fiddler's Green where cavalrymen rest forever. *Allons!*

The second is Mike Resnick, who passed in early 2020. A legend in the genre, Mike always made a point of giving back to the science fiction and fantasy community by taking new writers and editors under his wing. I consider myself one of his "writer children" as do several of the authors in this anthology. I owe a great deal of my publishing success to his mentorship and support. Mike's advice and encouragement were instrumental in bringing this project to life. Without his guidance, this anthology and the two that preceded it would not have been possible. Fare thee well, old friend.

The third is former Secretary of Defense Ashton B. Carter (1954–2022), whom I consider to be a mentor and the smartest person I've ever met. As my thesis advisor and boss at the Stanford-Harvard Preventive Defense Project, he taught me everything I know about international security strategy. Without his keen stewardship of the Nunn-Lugar Program to denuclearize Belarus, Kazakhstan, and Ukraine, as well as to stabilize the remaining Soviet nuclear arsenal in the wake of that empire's collapse, the world would've been a far more dangerous place. He also designed and executed the DOD's strategic pivot to the Asia-Pacific region, a topic that is highly relevant to the subject matter of this volume. Farewell, my friend. The world will be a less secure place without you.

CONTENTS

★

WEIRD
WORLD WAR: CHINA

PREFACE

★

Sean Patrick Hazlett

The term "Thucydides' Trap" has often been used to characterize the evolving relationship between the United States and China. The phrase describes a situation where an emerging power threatens to displace a dominant one. It harkens back to a time when the rise of Athens and the Spartan fear of that rise made the Peloponnesian War inevitable. Whether China's ascent truly represents a Thucydides' Trap, it is fairly obvious that the United States and China are currently on a collision course.

In late October 2022, China's ruling Communist Party awarded President Xi Jinping an unprecedented third five-year term as general secretary, eschewing a tradition of a two-term limit established since the death of Mao Zedong, the last leader to rule China for more than a decade.

Xi's break with custom is an ominous sign of things to come for China. The elevation of Xi and the increased concentration of power in his hands have almost certainly increased the likelihood of future conflict. His calls for faster military development and defense of China's interests abroad, as well as retrograde notions of a return to the past "glories" of Mao's China are concerning. As I write this, the people of China are bravely resisting an oppressive lockdown in major cities like Beijing, Shanghai, Wuhan, and Chengdu, among others, to protest the country's zero COVID policy at a time when the rest of the world has long since returned to some semblance of normality.

His crackdown on Chinese entrepreneurs and shift backward

toward a state-controlled economy could be especially damaging, particularly for a country that has one of the fastest-growing ageing populations in the world. According to the World Health Organization, 28 percent of China's population—an estimated 402 million people—will be over age sixty by 2040. With a proportionally declining labor force, that rapid growth will require an adaptable approach to support this demographic shift; an approach that will challenge a China hamstrung by an inflexible and corrupt economy composed of state-controlled enterprises.

At the same time China's domestic concerns are growing increasingly unstable, the country has become progressively bellicose abroad. Chinese adventurism in the South China Sea's Spratly and Paracel Islands has involved a patient but inexorable march to steadily establish footholds on uninhabited islands claimed by multiple nations in the resource rich expanse using a strategy akin to slowly peeling away multiple layers of skin from an onion.

Not only do the Chinese employ this strategy at sea, but also on land. Since 1962, the Chinese military has been carefully creeping forward along its Indian border to seize contested land from its neighbor in the Himalayan foothills around the Line of Actual Control.

The Chinese have also ramped up military shows of force near the disputed Senkaku Islands in the East China Sea, which Japan also claims. The threat there is dire enough that Japan's ruling party has proposed doubling its defense budget as a share of GDP from one percent to two percent over the next several years.

China's military sorties into Taiwan's air defense identification zone to wear out Taiwan's air defense forces have not only been provocative, but also have dramatically increased the likelihood of a war over the island. Chinese jingoistic rhetoric prior to US Speaker Pelosi's 2022 trip to the island nation, and its simulated blockade and live-fire exercises afterward, represent yet another instance of concerning adolescent behavior by a rising power. And with more than 90 percent of the world's most advanced semiconductor manufacturing capacity concentrated on Taiwan, such an attack would force the United States to intervene, not just to protect that island nation, but to defend its vital national security interests. In fact, the US National Security Council projects that the loss of the Taiwan Semiconductor Manufacturing Company could cause a one-trillion-dollar disruption to the global economy.

Most recently, in February 2023, the Chinese government went as far as sending a surveillance balloon over the continental United States, violating US sovereignty. The situation ended with US aircraft shooting down the object over the Atlantic Ocean and the US Air Force conducting an ICBM test in the Pacific Ocean as a show of force.

The infiltration of American society by Chinese interests is also a major cause for concern. As of July 2020, the FBI was opening one new China-related counterintelligence case every ten hours, and half of the FBI's five thousand active counterintelligence cases involved China. Chinese intelligence ran an extensive operation between 2011 to 2015 to influence and compromise local, state, and national politicians, including several members of Congress. One suspected intelligence operative, Chinese national, Fang Fang or Christine Fang, targeted rising politicians in the Bay Area and nationally, like Representatives Eric Swalwell, Ro Khanna, Judy Chu, Tulsi Gabbard, and Mike Honda.

The Chinese have also established unauthorized "police stations" in numerous countries around the world to include the US and Canada, possibly to pursue influence operations, spread propaganda, and harass Chinese nationals living in these countries.

Through talent recruitment programs like the Thousand Talent Programs, the Chinese government paid scientists at American universities to secretly establish parallel research programs in China, sometimes involving US federally funded research. In fact, one estimate suggests that over the past decade, the Chinese government spent two trillion dollars on such efforts—a sum larger than its military budget over the same period.

China has also been active in the cyber realm. Beginning in 2009, Chinese hackers infiltrated US corporate networks and stole trade secrets from dozens of US companies ranging from Morgan Stanley to Google. In 2014, Chinese intelligence hacked into the Pentagon's Office of Personnel Management, stealing the personnel files of all current and former federal employees as well as all security clearance applications, affecting more than 22 million people, including the editor of this very anthology. In 2017, the Chinese military hacked Equifax and stole the sensitive personal information of 150 million Americans—nearly half the US population.

Chinese intelligence has also attempted to use its commercial technology as a Trojan horse to penetrate the telecommunications infrastructure of the United States and its allies. In 2012, Australian intelligence officials discovered malicious code in a Huawei software update that had infected that country's telecommunications systems.

Even today, the FBI warns that video-sharing app, TikTok, owned by the Beijing-headquartered ByteDance, could be used by the Chinese Communist Party to influence users, control their devices, and even spy on US federal employees by hoovering up data about their location, preferences, and salacious details about their private lives that might make them vulnerable to compromise. In November 2022 and prior to the US midterm elections, Twitter uncovered three covert Chinese operations spanning nearly two thousand user accounts to stoke partisan discord.

While the looming great power competition between the United States and China is only starting to heat up, the myriad histories of the next world war are now in your hands. What strange circumstances precipitated the Great Sino-American Conflict? Was it triggered by an ultrasecret US occult computer that hurled American soldiers backward in spacetime to thwart a Chinese-summoned eldritch horror or does an extraterrestrial intelligence spur an arms race that leads the two countries to war? Did a US military campaign in mainland China awaken a supernatural force that could move mountains and rend continents or did World War III begin with a bomb sent from the future to erase the past? To find out, gaze through the kaleidoscope of multiple realities and bear witness to the disturbing visions of World War III from today's greatest minds in science fiction, fantasy, and horror.

ELDRITCH OPS

✪

Larry Correia and Steve Diamond

Three pairs of children's shoes rested on top of a small, folded pile of clothes.

Considering the things I'd seen in various timelines, across several centuries, on more eldritch hunts than I could count, I don't know why that sight bothered me so much.

Two members of my squad stood silently beside me, each staring down at the threadbare rags on the edge of a road outside a small town in the middle of podunk China. I could tell it bothered them too. I took a deep breath and knelt down, poking the clothing with my M5's suppressor. We'd learned the hard way not to touch suspicious stuff with our hands.

"Careful there, Sarge," Lieutenant Cicero warned. He nodded his head at a barely visible swirl of black dust. "That looks like the same residue that got on—"

"Private White and melted his face in Vietnam. Yeah, I know." I heard one of the boys make a noise. "You all right, Mok?"

Specialist Mok had his eyes closed and pinched the bridge of his nose. Getting launched through time and space could be both mentally and physically degrading. "Yeah, Sergeant Cainho. Massive migraine. I feel hungover." He wiped his nose and showed me his bloodied hand. "I don't know how you down timers do this."

"Lots of practice, kid." I'd done this more times than I could remember. Mok was the new guy, on his first jump, attached to this mission as our linguist because none of my boys knew Bai, the primary Chinese dialect spoken in these parts. "You good for now?"

"Sure. I just traveled back to 2028 because the Pentagon's top-secret occult computer warned us the PRC government in this timeline was about to summon some ancient elder god, whose name no one knows how to pronounce, to start World War III so they can conquer the world . . . before I was born. Yep. Totally good. Anyone got a Snickers?"

I remembered when Snickers had been invented—1930. "They still have those?"

Cicero pulled out a small piece of glass and scrolled through strings of data. We'd been born in the same era, but unlike me, the LT had adapted to all the crazy technology people took for granted now. "Looks like Snickers bars stopped being sold in 1987 in this deviant timeline."

Mok sniffed at the light nosebleed. "This is why we can't have nice things."

I flipped over some of the clothing, revealing more shiny black dust. A lot more. There was a certain feel to the stuff. It made the hair on your arms stand up. My team knew it well.

"Elder residue." Cicero made the sign of the cross.

"All right." I checked the countdown on my watch. "We've got two hours to stop these godless heathen communists from accidentally destroying the universe. This is where the wormhole dropped us. Where the hell are we?"

Cicero tapped on his datapad. "Shengcun." Leave it to the miracles of future technology to make it so a West Point grad could actually do land nav. "It's in . . . Yunnan Province. That mean anything to you, Specialist?"

"Yes, sir," Mok answered. "It's where they speak Bai."

"No shit. Any notes on that toy of yours?" I asked Cicero.

"This area used to be known for rice terraces and markets. Some of these pictures make it look quite beautiful."

I glanced around at the abandoned houses and empty, trash-strewn streets. The place stank like oil smoke and decay. "Yeah. Real tourist trap, LT."

"That data packet say anything about, oh, I don't know . . . giant, world-killing monsters?" Mok had backed away from the children's clothes slowly as if they could explode at any moment. "This isn't how I imagined visiting the land of my heritage, but, since we're here, I suppose we should save it from being destroyed."

"That's the plan," I lied, because poor Mok wasn't cleared to know about this particular unit's standard response for this kind of threat.

"Sensors are registering huge amounts of energy from that direction." Cicero pointed. "An elder god might already be in this plane of existence."

"Just our rotten luck. It's Normandy all over again." I gave a hand signal. The rest of the squad picked it up and passed it along. Riflemen rose from their covered and concealed positions. Time to move out.

Glancing over my squad, I could see exhaustion etched on their faces. How many missions was this? Twelve? Eighteen? Fifty? They all tended to blend together. Each trip through time and space ate at our minds. Each time we died and came back, things got a little stranger.

Most of these poor bastards had been in the 101st Airborne when we'd made a fateful jump into France, stumbling across a Nazi experiment that had gotten us stuck in an endless time loop. Our world hadn't survived the unleashing of Yog-Sothoth at Mont Saint-Michel, but there were plenty of other Earths, so my squad had been plucked from the time stream and put to work. It hadn't been the first time we'd been drafted. We were in an endless war where the eldritch gods feasted on our misery and loss.

Now we were all going slightly insane from cellular degradation caused by jumping back and forth in time, but the risks were fairly well known to us. The big brains back at HQ had machines that registered anomalies across timelines. These attacks were coming more and more regularly. My squad was a nothing more than a Band-Aid. Chewing gum plugging a hole in a dam. The scientists were trying to figure out why the number of timeline-killing events was accelerating . . . but not fast enough for my liking.

We moved toward the town, quick and quiet like.

Private Lunden gave the signal to freeze. Our machine gunner was a big, quiet fella, who'd been working lobster boats in Maine before the war. He had a gift for casual violence the likes of which I'd never seen. Sometimes I figured Lunden did so well in our current assignment because he'd been a little crazy before all this weird shit had started, so he'd had to make less of an adjustment than the rest of us.

I moved up to Lunden, and he pointed at the middle of the road. "If you tilt your head so the sun hits the dirt just right, you can see a black glimmer, like something left a trail."

Signaling for Farris to check, I hunkered down to wait. Farris was a Jewish kid, who'd grown up in Idaho, guiding elk and wolf hunts. If there was a sign, Farris would find it.

Sure enough, Farris gave us the signal for tracks. Then he ran back to report to the LT. "Barefoot, and lots of them. Also, some animal tracks."

"What kind?" Cicero asked.

"Don't know, but whatever made them's got claws."

There were small, empty shoes on piles of clothing lining the path. That seemed somehow ... profane. We didn't see a single sign of life. No birds flew overhead. No squirrels fled from our approach. Even the sound of insects was absent. A light breeze caused the occasional door or window shutter to creak. The trail of black residue led through the empty town, then further through the rice terraces. The sun reflected off the water, making each of the irrigated fields look like liquid gold. In another time, in better circumstances, this place might have been as pretty as the LT's little machine claimed it was.

But now ... now I could feel anxiety and paranoia clawing at my chest. The men were no different. I could see the death-grips on their M5s, tensed shoulders, and rapid breathing. There was evil in the air. With any other squad I would have been worried, but these boys had seen some things. We'd fought everything from Roman legions to dinosaurs. We'd watched unspeakable horrors devour the stars, died, and then gone back to work the next day.

"Trail narrows ahead," I warned.

"That glare off the water is killing me. Can't see a damn thing. Anyone got better eyes than me?" When no one spoke up, Lieutenant Cicero said, "Good spot for an ambush. The sensor is showing massive energy spikes. We're heading in the right direction, in case anyone needed extra verification."

"This feel too easy to anyone?" Farris asked. "Last time things were this obvious we got jumped by that shoggoth in the Civil War."

The memory was hazy, but I remembered being dragged by tentacles into a mouth full of teeth, and then being chewed as I pulled the pins on every grenade I carried. It wasn't the worst way I'd died.

The squad moved faster than I would have liked, but time was of the essence. The future Army had issued us a whole bunch of fancy doodads and gizmos to spot landmines or lurking snipers, but there was no substitute for good old-fashioned human intuition. Too bad neither man nor machine functioned properly under the influence of the old gods.

"Hold up," Mok said. "LT, there's somebody in that field. Shit. It's just a kid. Looks like a little girl. She's in bad shape. I've gotta help her, sir."

The new guy splashed out into ankle deep water before Cicero could stop him.

"Mok, wait!" The linguist was normally smarter than this, but time travel messes with your head, especially for first timers. I rushed after him, but the kid had a lead. "Lunden, help me."

Sure enough there was somebody lying in the mud. It looked like an average Chinese child. Rail thin. Filthy clothes. Specialist Mok closed on the body and started speaking in rapid Bai. I couldn't understand a word of it.

I wasn't going to fault any of my soldiers for wanting to protect a kid. But something was off. The girl was shivering violently, like a terrified dog. No, not shivering. Vibrating. Rhythmically. "Damn it, Mok!"

The girl leapt and spun. Her body convulsed in midair, and her hands suddenly doubled in size, transforming into massive claws. She swiped at Mok, who fortunately had his rifle held before him. The girl's claws struck the barrel as Mok threw himself backward. The girl's mouth split into a wide grin exposing massive, pointed obsidian teeth. Her jaw unhinged like a giant snake as she threw herself on top of him.

I raised my M5 but didn't have a clear shot. Then Lunden tackled her the instant before her claws could rip into Mok. The monster hissed and spat, clawing at the big man. A knife appeared in Lunden's hand, and blood spattered from both of them as they rolled through the mud.

Lunden maneuvered behind the creature, then stabbed it in the throat and ripped the blade outward in a spray of arterial blood. Where it hit the ground, it landed more like tar than blood. Night black, thick, and it seemed to . . . move. The new necktie hadn't stopped the monster in child's skin, but it gave me a brief window, and I shot it in the chest repeatedly, before Lunden was back in the way, plunging his knife into the monster's right eye. When the thing continued thrashing and tearing at him, he grabbed its head and wrenched it to the side as hard as he could. We all heard the wet *crack* as the monster's neck snapped.

The creature went still.

I rushed forward and pulled the child's body off Lunden. He was covered in black blood. The thing was far heavier than I expected. From the looks of it, it shouldn't have weighed more than fifty pounds, but felt like one-fifty.

"I'm sorry, Lunden," I heard Mok saying behind me. "I didn't . . . I mean . . ."

"Don't worry about it, kid. I should've seen it coming. I . . . shit . . . I'm not feeling so good."

I knelt next to Lunden. His arms were cut to ribbons and covered in the monster's blood. As I checked his wounds, I found a hot patch of red blood under his left arm. I pressed my hand against the wound, but from the rapid flow, I knew it was too late. At some point the thing had pierced him through the armpit.

"That you Sergeant Cainho?"

"Yeah, Lunden?"

"Can you tell my sister . . . tell her . . ."

"I'll tell her," I said, even though Lunden's sister had died of lung cancer in 1967.

And then he was gone.

The LT was shouting for the squad to set up a perimeter, and sending men to help me. He was no stranger to fixing goat ropes.

"Shit, shit, shit." Mok collapsed against one of the terrace pool's retaining walls. "How could I have been so stupid? How—?"

"Get your head on straight, Mok." Where the monster's blood had got on my gloves, my hands felt suddenly heavy. I ripped the gloves off and rubbed my hands together in the irrigation water. I felt . . . unclean. Like I needed to see a priest urgently. "We only have a few minutes before the trackers in his blood transmit a flatline back to HQ. He's gonna blink back real quick here. Help me drag him."

More men had reached us, and they barely paused when they saw Lunden was dead. We'd all seen it before. "Bishop, grab the MG. Milton, help Mok drag him onto dry ground. Hurry."

Farris met me at the monster's body. He knew what to do. The thing's hands were still massive claws. They weren't covered in human skin, but rather were more like bone growths. He threw a loop of paracord around one of those claws, pulled it tight, then did the same with the other arm. We each grabbed a cord and struggled to pull the monster's body back to lay it next to Lunden's. We only had a few minutes until his body returned to HQ, and when it did, the monster's corpse would go with him now. The scientists back there would want to study the creature. The girl. I forced myself to not think of the monster as what it used to be.

As we got the monster back onto the path, Flynn, our medic, was working on Lunden, but we all knew he was just going through the motions. Farris tapped my arm. "Sarge, I think only one of the monster's legs worked."

Sure enough, he was right. One of the legs was twig thin. The knee joint was bent backward in extreme hyperextension. Given the thing's impossibly increased mass, the leg had probably given out.

"Maybe that's why it was out here alone. Whoever turned the girl into . . . *this* . . . left her behind." I thought back to the empty shoes lining the path here and had a sobering thought. A thought so sobering it made me want to drown it eternally. "Any of you see any adult shoes on the way here? Or just kids?"

Cicero turned a little green, while Farris just looked sad. The ancient gods couldn't come into a world unless they were invited. Which was why they whispered promises of power to the worst men in history, telling them all they had to do was read these forbidden tomes, brew up this ancient potion, perform this specific ceremony when the planets align, that sort of thing. I hated when they used children as guinea pigs.

"We've got to see what we can learn from this body before they blink." Cicero grabbed our medic and pulled him away from Lunden. "No surgical scars, but there's something at the base of the neck. Flynn! Get over here and help me roll it over." From their grunting and straining, the body was still impossibly heavy. Cicero gestured at the spine. "Looks like an IV port of some sort. They were giving her some kind of transfusion."

"I bet that means there's gonna be more," Farris whispered to me.

The smell of burning rubber suddenly filled the air. "Everyone get back!"

Electricity arced all over Lunden's body, then from his to the monster's. Soon they were covered in a writhing ball of the stuff, then with an audible *pop*, they vanished.

"Sir, would you kindly check your glass," I urged. "What're his odds?"

Cicero checked his device to see if any new messages from the future had passed through the wormhole. "There's not a very good connection to his last place on the timestream, so Lunden's only got a fifty-fifty chance at resurrection." The LT took a deep breath and let it out slowly. He turned the glass in the direction of a distant hill. It wasn't very big, but it was practically a mountain here. "The energy is two klicks that way and growing in magnitude. I don't like where this is headed."

It would be worse odds for all of us if we failed and this timeline fell to the enemy. I checked my watch. "We've only got an hour left."

"All right, boys, you heard the sergeant. Let's go."

Mok was staring at the scorched patch of ground where the bodies had just been. I grabbed him by the neck, pulled him close, and said, "Yeah, you fucked up. You can feel guilty or stupid about that later. Right now you've got work to do. In one hour you can do whatever you want. Until then you're not allowed to feel anything but hate and determination. Got it?"

He nodded, wide-eyed.

"Good. Now carry the machine gun."

We passed broken, immobile husks of children all along our path to the mountain. The majority lay like cast-aside dolls, dead and unblinking. Malformed limbs marked most. Some looked to have been gnawed at by some wild beast. With the teeth of the girl-thing fresh in my mind, I suspected animals weren't the cause of the half-chewed corpses.

On occasion we would stumble across one still living, but they were never in as functional a shape as the first we had encountered. They all seemed to be so burdened beneath their own impossibly dense masses that they mostly snarled at us or glared with baleful eyes. The ones that *had* eyes anyway.

We saw no other movement on the residue trail. No people. No animals or even bugs. The slight breeze we'd felt back in the village was completely gone, and the air itself had turned oppressive. None of us spoke. The terraces gave way to simple fields, and then to rocky terrain as we approached the mountain. Nightfall would be on us soon.

At the foot of the mountain, I finally noticed fresh signs that we weren't the only humans around. Tire tracks. They led to an opening in the rocky formations around us. A cave highlighted by a large, inset pair of metal doors big enough to drive trucks through. Doors that hung open in the dead air.

We scouted the area, but there was no sign of guards. The power was on, and a diesel generator was running. There were barracks, but no sign of the soldiers who'd been stationed here.

"Blood," Farris said pointing at a smeared handprint on a doorframe. The kind one would make holding on for dear life while being pulled in.

Cicero had the squad advance through the camp. Normally we'd want more time to recon the area rather than rush in, but according to the Pentagon's magic thinking machines, this universe was thirty minutes away from the apocalypse. And everybody knows timelines are like dominos.

Mok didn't say a word. Between the kid-turned-monster and Lunden's death, the new guy was barely hanging in there. In the cave, everything was carved rock except the floor, which had been smoothed down and paved. Flickering lightbulbs hung suspended from ceiling wires at regular intervals, just like in mineshafts I'd seen pictures of.

In the stuttering light, I saw the small, huddled form of a child. The walls and floor around it glistened wet whenever the light hit just right. Around the child—the monster—were misshapen clumps of whatever it had been eating.

I looked deeper into the shadows and saw the whole passageway was lined with small, human forms. All the children who had once filled those empty shoes.

Cicero tapped me on the shoulder, and when I turned to look at him, he put his hands together next to his face in the universal signal for "sleeping." I looked again at the nearest monster. The LT was right. I saw the slow, even rise-and-fall of the thing's chest. If they had been awake, we'd probably have already been dead.

We didn't have much of a choice. We had our orders, and the clock was ticking.

Every step felt like it would be the last I'd ever take. Regardless of how tiny they looked, these mutations were deadly. None of them looked as deformed as the ones that had been left behind on the road. Most had fleshy remains scattered about them. Some obviously human, some looked like other children who had been turned into the . . . things.

A monster to our left stirred, and the squad froze. Not that they would do much good. Sure, we'd smoke one creature, but we'd wake the rest.

The monster settled without waking up and murdering us all. I let out the breath I'd been holding as quietly as I could, looked over my shoulder and couldn't see the door outside anymore. The path ahead showed no sign of ending, though it did seem like we were gradually heading downward. Maybe into Hell itself.

There was an eerie light ahead, pulsing like a slow heartbeat.

Every child we passed added to the weight of my dread, and I could only assume the others were feeling the same. Farris was sweating like we were in the middle of the Sahara. Cicero had his jaw clenched so hard I could hear his teeth grinding. Mok's knuckles were white from gripping Lunden's M250 like it was the only thing keeping him sane. At any time, I was sure the things would wake up and gut us like fish.

I looked to the LT, and tapped my fingers against my chest, questioning. Cicero had a pouch on that spot of his vest, but he shook his head. We had to be closer to be sure.

When you activated a Quantum Annihilator, you only got one shot.

Still stepping carefully around the huddled, sleeping forms of the infected children, we approached the growing light. It pulsed in the gloom, fluorescent white, then a sickly green. Cicero showed me the image on his device. The energy levels were spiking higher and higher with each flare of light.

We didn't have much time.

The passageway widened ahead and emptied into a massive, open underground cavern. Steel girders lined the towering walls and crisscrossed all the space between. My eyes were drawn immediately to the center of the cavern where a slumbering god was chained to the floor. Its pose looked remarkably like the forms of the children in the passageway . . . as if those children had been mimicking their new eldritch parent.

The god wasn't the biggest I'd seen, but it was still hundreds of feet tall lying down. A malevolent aura surged off it in waves. I could see a pair of leathery wings, folded in on themselves, and when the god shifted in its restless sleep, its head turned our way. For a moment I thought it resembled a lean dog, but in the pulsing light I caught flashes of what it really was. Or had been. Or maybe what it was supposed to be. Beneath the leathery skin was the serpentine body of a perversion of a Chinese dragon. Tendrils hung below its jaw where hair normally would have been. The horns on its head curled down like a demon's. Its mouth opened in a yawn. Teeth larger than people. They were so large I could clearly see their jagged edges. Like fractals, they had their own, smaller teeth protruding off them.

I closed my eyes, squeezing them shut as hard as I could. I just needed a second. A little time for my mind to pretend it could cope. When I opened them and looked at my men, I noticed they had all done the same. This was the part where even strong men descended into gibbering insanity.

Rather than stare endlessly into the maddening visage of a corrupted dragonlike thing from beyond our time and space, I tore my gaze away and looked around the cavern. What I saw didn't make me feel any better.

The floor was completely littered with sleeping children, covered in blood and human remains. I saw torn and shredded lab coats, and military uniforms, and quite a few heads absent their bodies. A number of the creatures slumbered with clumps of flesh hanging from their open mouths. There were partially eaten hands, fingers, and entrails.

Out of the corner of my eye, I saw Cicero waving for my attention. He pointed beyond the children to the walls which were lined with open vats of liquid. The sides were made of some type of reinforced glass. I could see the ooze circulating, black as pitch. Each vat must have held tens of thousands of gallons of black fluid, and all had hoses attached to them, dozens of feet in diameter. They snaked across the floor, then up into the god's body under the wings. I'd been so focused on the terror the thing exuded, I hadn't noticed the Chinese had been tapping the god for its blood.

Up close, the god seemed even larger, somehow. Every step nearer made me feel more and more nauseated. I could almost feel the thing clawing into my head. Mok's nose was bleeding, but he kept both hands firmly on the machine gun. Cicero held up a hand and doubled over, vomiting as quietly as he could manage. Farris lifted his M5 and trained it on the nearest sleeping child-turned-monster. It stirred, then settled again. Farris let out a small sigh but kept his rifle level.

Cicero straightened up, but appeared shaky. He gave us a thumbs-up, in spite of trembling so hard I thought he would pass out.

The symptoms lessened as we passed the god and approached the back of the cavern. In the pulsing light, we discovered what had happened to all the adults in the village. Next to a line of cremation ovens were piles upon piles of misshapen corpses—adult corpses. They all bore the hallmarks of experimentation, but every one of them showed extreme deformities. I understood in an instant. The adult tests had all failed.

So they had moved on to the kids.

We went to the nearest vat of god blood. At its base, dozens of beds were arrayed. IV lines ran from the vats, to what would normally have been saline bags, down to dripping needles. I caught the LT's attention, pointed at the needles, then tapped the back of my neck. This was what the scientists had been infusing into the children through their IV ports. I knelt down and carefully lifted the end of the IV line. It should have been as light as a feather, but instead was as heavy as a barbell.

The whole scenario became clear . . . well, clear enough. How the ancient god had gotten here in the first place was a question well above my pay grade—maybe it had been buried here all along—but the PLA scientists had experimented with its blood. When it wouldn't work on adults, they had tried it on children. It had infected the kids faster and stronger than anyone had anticipated. Maybe some of the kids had escaped in the chaos and tried going home, only to succumb completely to the disease in their veins. Then maybe all the kids . . . well . . . had eaten everyone and everything. And whatever the Chinese army had been using to sedate this ancient thing was about to wear off.

I let the IV down gently, not wanting to get any of the black blood on me. I didn't know how much it took to start turning a person, but I didn't want to find out.

We had seen enough. Lieutenant Cicero slowly, quietly, and deliberately removed the Quantum Annihilator from the pouch on his chest.

The rest of the squad knew what was up. We'd all seen these things in action before. It would send us back to our main timeline as the crystalline matrix detonated, obliterating the otherworldly threat, and vaporizing everything within a hundred miles of it.

Cicero flipped the switch.

Nothing happened.

The god stirred, strained against its chains, then turned its head our way.

Six eyes—three on each side—flickered open and stared at us. Hate overwhelmed me, and I fell to my knees clutching at the sides of my head. Images flashed through my mind of horrors I didn't even know were possible. I blinked a few times, and when my eyes cleared, I noticed movement all around us. All the slumbering monsters were waking and pushing themselves to their feet.

My squad didn't need an order.

Everybody started shooting. The roar of automatic fire helped lift the fog from our brains.

"Why didn't it work?" I bellowed.

"I don't know!" Cicero shouted back, as he banged the weapon of mass destruction against a tabletop, then flipped the switch again. "Stupid future junk!"

I switched off my brain. There were only threats. Size and age didn't matter. This wasn't the first time I'd disconnected. To stay engaged that way was to invite the kind of madness only a self-administered bullet could fix.

To my left, Mok wasn't able to disconnect like I was. Tears poured down his face, but it wasn't stopping him from raking Lunden's machine gun back and forth across the cavern.

The creatures came at us slowly, still waking up from their dreams of God-knows what. I dropped a mag and slammed another home. It was probably the fastest reload of my life. I pulled one of my shots to the right, and the bullet smashed against the side of a vat.

Milton got disemboweled. Flynn got his throat clawed out. They were gone and being eaten by the malformed monsters before anyone had a chance to warn them of the threat from behind. Farris pulled a grenade, yanked the pin, and lobbed it into the thickest pack of things shambling our way.

"Cover!" Cicero screamed, and we all dived to get tanks of god blood between us and the blast.

The concussion was brutal in the cavern. I stood and rounded the edge of the tank, and realized I'd dived behind a separate tank than the others. A horde of the monsters teemed between us. There was no getting back to the squad.

The grenade blast knocked loose wires everywhere, causing showers of sparks to fly into the now-solid-green light. Nothing in the rock-walled cavern seemed all that flammable—until the sparks hit puddles of blood from the dozens of monsters we'd killed, and there was a *whoosh* as they lit up like they had gasoline in their veins.

The children—no, the *creatures* screamed as the flames consumed them. No matter how they rolled on the ground, the flames never went out. It looked like some were burning from the inside out.

A massive pack of the things shambled my squad's way. For the moment, none of the things seemed to notice me. I jumped and waved until I got Cicero's attention. I pulled an incendiary grenade from my pack and held it up.

"Do it!"

I popped the grenade and tossed it into the nearest vat. Then I ran for my life.

The vat turned into a pillar of flame fifty feet high. Fire raced up the giant IV line until it lit up one of the dragon god's wings.

Veins glowed red and orange in the green light, then burst outward in a shower of molten blood. The dragon god roared so loudly it felt like it could almost stop my heart. Almost as one, the monsters collapsed grabbing their ears. Steel scaffolding collapsed, further separating me from my team. Falling rebar rained down on my men like hot javelins. A metal shard stabbed through Cicero's eye. Another impaled him through the center of his chest, hitting hard enough to pierce the cavern floor.

Farris pulled a flare from his pack, struck it, and tossed it into the nearest vat. Molten blood splattered outward, arcing into another nearby vat which also exploded upward. Jets of fire hit the god one after another.

Some of the molten blood also hit Farris in his left arm, consuming it. His mouth opened in a scream.

Mok dropped his pack and dumped it, pulling out every flare and incendiary grenade. He ripped open Farris's pack and did the same, then slapped a grenade into Farris's good hand. Mok helped Farris up, then they began running, pausing only to toss flares and grenades into the tanks.

I ran toward the cavern's entrance and pulled out every fire accelerant from my bag. I didn't have much, just a single flare and a pack of matches.

I popped the flare, tossed it into a nearby vat. As it exploded upward, I ran to the last vat on my side of the cavern, pulled one match through the book to light the whole thing, then lobbed it over the edge of the glass.

As soon as I did, I knew I was too close. The explosion threw me back toward the entrance. My helmet hit the wall hard. For a moment, everything went black.

When I came to, I saw the eldritch god surge up and strike its head on the ceiling. Rock cracked as the cavern began to collapse. Every vein in its body glowed through its skin as its blood turned into fire. The lines of flame coursed up into its head. The six eyes exploded, and the dragon went limp, slowly falling to the ground. Directly beneath it was Mok and Farris. They hugged each other right before the god collapsed on top of them.

Few of the children were coherent in any way, but one crawled in my direction. I tried drawing my pistol, but my arms wouldn't work quite right.

The monster was only a few feet from me, face stretched and looking more and more like the unholy combination of a child and the corrupted dragon eldritch god. Electricity arced around me. Somewhere in the conflagration, the damned Annihilator must have been triggered. Finally. HQ was pulling me back, and not a moment too soon.

My vision went solid white and blue.

Head swimming, I found myself lying in a glass coffin. On the other side of the glass was HQ's launch control.

All I could do was try to breathe as my brain caught up with the journey across time. The relief of being home flooded me. My ears were still ringing from the explosions, but all I could think about was getting out of the coffin to check on my men. Hopefully they'd all been resurrected.

My eyes blurred, and for a second, I thought I was losing my vision. Then I realized it was just the lights flickering.

They dimmed, then went solid again.

Weird.

I managed to push myself up to wipe the steam from the glass. Instead of being greeted by our CO and the usual gang of scientists and doctors, all I saw was blood and body parts.

The glass of the pod next to mine was shattered and covered in black blood. Lunden's coffin. This was where he would have popped back into the main timeline. On the floor in front of it was the body of the monster we'd sent back with him.

I caught movement from the corner of the room. In the wavering light, Lunden stood up, took a bite from a bloody arm he was holding. The severed arm still had part of a shoulder loop with general's stars on it. Lunden shivered and twitched, still covered in the black blood from the kid he'd killed.

Infected.

Lunden's eyes met mine—slitted and sickly yellow like the eyes of the dragon god—and he smiled at me with a mouth full of sharp and jagged teeth.

LURKING DEATH

✪

David Drake

Breyer had never met this district commissioner before but he had no reason to be concerned. The aide who met him outside the building was a young fellow with dark blond hair. "Commissioner Erskine wanted me to warn you that you'll be meeting not only him but also some American gentlemen," the aide said.

The Indian servant was already jerking open the door. Breyer asked, "Is this about the tiger last June?"

The aide bowed at him through the door. "It may be, sir," he said.

Erskine rose from behind his desk when Breyer entered, as did the three other men in business suits sitting in chairs along the wall.

"Sir," said Breyer even as he took the commissioner's outstretched hand, "I told you exactly what happened. I had full permission from Mr. Graves"—Erskine's predecessor as commissioner. In fact, Graves had invited him to come deal with the man-eater—"and if something went wrong, it wasn't my fault."

"No, it certainly wasn't," Erskine said, seating himself again. "You've done nothing wrong, Mr. Breyer. These gentlemen just want to talk with you. They've come all the way from America to do that."

"All right," Breyer said, "but there isn't much to tell. I came to Naini because Mr. Graves told me there was a man-eater he'd like some help with. He assigned me a two-room forest bungalow near the village but in heavy scrub. I walked around the village and found no tiger markings though there was a large pugmark I couldn't identify. It had sunk into hard soil deep enough that it had to be something as big as a tiger."

The eldest of the three strangers leaned forward in his chair. "Mr. Breyer," he said, "why were you sure that the animal was a tiger?"

"I *wasn't* sure," Breyer said. "The villagers said it was a tiger, though the color was funny. It had pulled down a full-grown buffalo. Nothing but a tiger could have done that, though it had torn the buffalo's throat open with its jaws, instead of leaping on its back and using its claws. But it was the man-eater I'd been sent to shoot. It had killed a herdsman the week before and before that, a woman cutting grass for fodder.

"I know now it was a hyena, but that never crossed my mind. It was way too big for a hyena and anyway it was tan and covered with spots, not like the hyenas I'd seen in the zoo in Madras."

"What you saw in Madras were the standard Asian striped hyenas," the man who was smoking said. "The animal you shot was colored like the spotted hyena of Africa."

"We're a thousand miles from Africa here," Breyer said.

"The distance is a lot farther than that," the stranger said. "The hide color seems the same as the ordinary spotted hyena, but the museum says the bones are those of the cave hyena, which has been extinct for at least tens of thousands of years."

Breyer shook his head and went on, "Anyway, I went out to where the buffalo had been killed. A grown buff is too big for even a tiger to eat in one go. So I figured he'd be coming back to the kill site. It was rugged country. The attack had been in the open but the drag line was down into a steep narrow valley. From the precipice above I could see the buff lying just inside a patch of wild plums. Most of the body remained, so there was a good chance the tiger was coming back. There was a good-sized pine tree in the plums only twenty feet from where the buffalo lay, but to reach it without being seen by the tiger, I'd have to approach from the valley below.

"I made the long circuit to reach the lower end of the valley and started up the next morning by foot. I was only carrying my Winchester and my knapsack with a rope ladder, and a thermos of tea and a sandwich for lunch. Even so I was almost all in when I reached the base of the pine. I tossed the ladder over the lowest branch in the late afternoon and climbed with my rifle slung. There was enough breeze that the stock swung against the tree as I climbed.

"I'd judged that the lowest branch of the pine would make an adequate perch. When I got onto it, I found it was in fact a trifle less comfortable than I'd expected because the branch didn't spread immediately from the trunk, so my position was cramped. I also had trouble getting the rope ladder to lie in as broad a loop as I wanted to support my feet, but I judged it would do. Tigers can climb, but I wasn't expecting it to.

"I wasn't expecting it to come from behind me either, but that's what he did. He must have been deeper in the plums, but made a near circuit to reach the kill. I was looking down from above as the tiger slunk past. The size seemed right, but the color was dun and mottled instead of orange with black stripes. I waited for the beast to settle before I took a shot. Unfortunately, it stepped over the dead buffalo and remained half hidden as it worried out a rib with a large gobbet of meat clinging to it. I got a look at the beast in profile though, and saw it was a hyena rather than a tiger.

"He tossed the buffalo's head and then lowered it to begin crushing the bone he was holding. During the moment he was concentrating on the bone, he was still. I squeezed off my .405. The shot made a sharp crack, and the bullet hit with a dull sound like a tree limb falling to the pavement.

"The hyena twisted and snapped in the air where a man who had just kicked it would have been standing. I worked the underlever to eject the empty case, but recoil on my awkward position prevented me from laying the sight back on target in time for a follow-up shot. The beast leaped into the plums and was lost to sight.

"Villagers had been watching from the precipice and could probably see the hyena though I could not. I took my time about getting down from my perch. I'd seen the hyena's jaws snapping. They could bite a man in half. They could bite *me* in half. I told the villagers to pick up clods of dirt. The ground in this valley had no pebbles to pelt the wounded animal or stir it out of the band of trees when we located it.

"The trees weren't closely spaced, so by lying flat on the ground the men accompanying me could see quite deep into the forest. They moved out ahead of me while I remained upright in a relatively clear portion where I had clearance for my rifle if the hyena came rushing out.

"In fact the beast sprawled only fifty feet into the trees. It didn't move under a bombardment of dried clay.

"We strapped it to a litter made from a pair of saplings and dragged it back to Naini. I didn't bother skinning it, but I cleaned the skull and some of the big bones on an ant hill and shipped them back to Commissioner Graves."

"They got here fine," Erskine said. "Graves couldn't make anything of them so he forwarded them on to London. It seems they were at a loss, too, and I guess they sent it on to"—he nodded to the three strangers—"Mr. Collins here."

"You're boffins?" Breyer said doubtfully, looking again at the men.

The eldest of the three said, "Not exactly, but people in our Department of State had us tasked to look into the matter when they got a notion of what was going on."

"Wish to hell I had a notion," Breyer said. "Which I do not."

The eldest stranger exchanged glances with the colleague who'd been smoking. That man shrugged and said to Breyer, "We've gotten reports that the Soviets and Chinese Communists have been working together on time travel. The appearance here of a cave hyena suggests that their trials are more advanced than we'd dreamed. The military implications are obvious."

The other two Americans nodded in agreement, but Beyer shook his head and said, "I don't see anything obvious about it. Are you worried about the Commies invading America with hyenas? They're nasty critters, I grant you, but a .405 solves one just fine."

"Mr. Breyer," said the eldest American, "this appears to have been a very large hyena. But a principle that could undetectably move and deliver a five-hundred-pound hyena to another time would probably do the same with any similar payload."

"If the appearance of the ancient hyena was not a hoax," said the man who'd been smoking, "and you *have* convinced us that it's no hoax, Mr. Breyer. It's a weapon that can potentially penetrate any of our defenses."

"I see," said Breyer. "Then are you done with me?"

"We'll ask you to guide us around the site of the incident," said Collins. "A year after the event there probably won't be much to learn, but we can at least hope to get an inkling of how the Russians and Chinese are accomplishing this."

"Sure, I'll introduce you to people," Breyer said. He thought of the big cats, man-eaters, that were his regular quarry. Cunning, stealthy, and able to strike down a man or woman with no warning.

Compared to a tiger or leopard, a bomb twice the size of a man could strike down a whole city. And if it didn't really exist in the present time until it went off, everyone in the world would have to feel the way Breyer did when he knew that a tiger was stalking him in the darkness. It was a terrible feeling and there was no way out for anyone.

Until the bomb went off.

EMPTY YOUR CUP, OR DRY IT?

✪

Nick Mamatas

The fourth master of the Supreme Ultimate Fist was actually not terrible, not for an old man who had never sparred in his life. He didn't flinch or freeze at the jab-cross combo, had decent enough balance and almost stuffed the takedown, got in a nice straight left of his own, and even had wits sufficient to try some small joint manipulation on Pappas's right wrist on the way down to the canvas. The fourth master of the Supreme Ultimate Fist even left the ring under his own power, and without shouted excuses to his disciples or whispered complaints to the referee. Or even with the help of a stretcher, as the second master had.

"You good?" Davidson asked Pappas in the corner as he wiped the fighter down. There wasn't much sweat. Pappas looked up at Davidson and saw himself, all bulbous nose and stretched Joker lips in the chrome convexity of Davidson's 180-degree Vcord eyewear.

"How many more?" Pappas asked by way of answer. "I want lunch. Beating up these tai chi guys is making me hungry, and not for Henan cuisine."

"Looks like two more, of the last four we had signed up, are willing to take their chances," Davidson said. "One guy just slipped out the back, and another made a show of looking at his phone, waving goodbye to everyone, and taking off."

"Getting some good footage, Mr. Hoplologist?" Pappas asked.

"Yeah, but not a lot," Davidson said, smirking.

"Should I go easy on this next one, let him get in a free hit or two?"

"Absolutely not," said Davidson.

The referee called for both fighters to leave their corners and meet in the middle of the ring.

Pappas's stomach turned at the sight of the carp, complete with head and tail, resting roasted on a bed of noodles no thicker than angel hair, on the plate in front of Davidson. The restaurant had a version of American food too—a big if oddly spiced hamburger patty with sweet dipping sauce, rice, and bitter melon. Pappas got the pork chops too. Davidson wasn't looking at his food. He still wore his recorders, which looked like a pair of shiny ice-cream scoopers atop his eyes, and was reviewing the footage, first wincing, then chuckling.

"Should we get some booze?" he asked. "Baijiu?"

"Is that the stuff that tastes like Sterno?"

"It's rice vodka," said Davidson.

"So yes," said Pappas. "Too easy to hide poison in a drink that already tastes like death."

"You have the palate of a child," said Davidson. "Fists of a God, but otherwise, you are an overgrown toddler. And nobody is going to poison us. You're a viral hit."

"It's easy to score knockouts against old men with no footwork and no head movement," Pappas said. Maybe he didn't want to talk about the morning's bouts anymore. He filled his mouth with beef to have an excuse.

"We learned something, though," Davidson said.

"That kung fu is bullshit? That tai chi especially is bullshit, even for kung fu? We knew that already," said Pappas. "Masters were getting knocked out by amateur kickboxers even in the days of YouTube and the free web."

"We learned something other than that," Davidson said, his attention still on what was playing out on the inside of the shining globes attached to his face. He hadn't even touched his carp. "You know what they say: sometimes you have to empty your cup—embrace the beginner mindset."

Noise and movement erupted from one of the large round tables just behind Pappas, and as one all the men seated there sat up straight. The fourth master, surrounded by his students, raised his glass and said something celebratory that the translation earbud couldn't quite pick up thanks to the hyperlocal dialect, the drunken slurring of the words, and the master's fat lip and loose tooth. The disciples applauded and nodded and smiled at Pappas. Pappas smiled and nodded back and lifted his bottle of Coke. A waitress quickly and subtly swooped past and left two small glasses of baijiu on the table.

"They won't think you're tough if you don't drink it," said Davidson. "Of course, if you do drink it, they'll think you like it and send more."

"Of course I'm tough. I kicked all their asses. Supreme Ultimate my ass."

"You beat up a bunch of seventy-five-year-old men. And that guy, Andy Chen, gifted you a little mouse. You didn't even knock him out," said Davidson.

"Andy!" said Pappas.

"Yeah, *Steve*," said Davidson. "You don't run around calling yourself Soterios, do you?"

Pappas shrugged, shoulders rolling like boulders, then he snatched up the little glass, gestured toward Andy Chen, barked, "Yamas!" and emptied the baijiu in a gulp.

The old woman, who referred to herself only as "Mrs. Chen," had a kind of wiry strength, agricultural strength, in her thin limbs, which she was happy to show off, even smiling as Davidson recorded her the next morning. Her teenage grandkids and several nephews and nieces were watching. She sure could swing the guandao, which probably weighed fifteen pounds, said weight unevenly distributed thanks to the thick curved blade on one end. Davidson wouldn't want to be the foot soldier on the wrong side of a mounted Mrs. Chen, that's for sure.

"My yiayia could do the same, if she practiced," Pappas said. "She used to dance around with a broomstick. She loved Ginger Rogers and Fred Astaire."

"It takes a lot of gongfu to have gongfu," Mrs. Chen said sharply as she completed the steps of the form. Mrs. Chen's English was just fine. Pappas screwed up his face and peered at Davidson, who kept his own gaze on Mrs. Chen.

"How long have you been training, if I may inquire?" he asked.

"Not so long as my brothers," she said. "Maybe I was eleven when I started. My brothers, they start at six, but they play, we all play, with sticks and copying the hand forms, very early. Two, three."

Mrs. Chen offered a fist in palm salute and excused herself, balanced the guandao on her shoulder, and strolled casually down the paved road. She was the last Chen of the day. The bit of field where various village residents had demonstrated their weapons and hand forms, their pushing-hands drills and two-person sets, was well destroyed, all mud and footprints.

"I'd like to see that old lady against a jarhead with a pugil stick," said Pappas.

"Will it also be an old lady Marine?" asked Davidson.

"This is a tourist trap, like Shaolin Temple," said Pappas as he gestured in the distance at the brutalist architecture dominating the low landscape that was once farmland and dirt. "There are more white people filling these kwoons than there are at Bautista Air Base. And they're all hippies, or nerds!"

"Hippies! Where did you learn the word hippies?"

"My grandpa who ran a fruit stand in San Francisco had to deal with them," said Pappas. "They were shoplifters ... Oh, that reminds me, check this out." Pappas slipped off the stone bench he'd been sitting on then walked gingerly onto the muddied patch of ground where Mrs. Chen and her retinue had just been. "The zeibekiko!"

Pappas raised and outstretched his arms, almost like a man on a cross, and snapped his fingers, once, twice, again. He stepped, grapevined his right foot behind his left, bent his knees slightly, started to sway a bit, and then started to dance. First shuffling, then hopping, then kicking up a leg and smacking his foot. "Opa!" he cried. "Tornado kick!" Then he bent his legs, put a palm on the floor, and kicked up. "Dog-style groundfighting! Not enough for ya, Mr. D?"

Davidson stared on, or at least it looked like he did, as his huge chrome goggles sat unblinking atop his face, a bit like a very large fly contemplating an unclean kitchen.

"This one's the hapasiko," Pappas explained. "A literal military number, and a dance for a secret guild of butchers. Check out the footwork, imagine ten men marching abreast." If there were significant choreological differences between the zeibekiko and the hapasiko, the motion-analysis programs embedded in Davidson's goggles were certainly cataloging them. Pappas declaimed as he danced: "Sneak a step, leg trip and throw, diagonal throw—see, just like all these tai chi forms!" He stopped, laughed, and spit on the ground. "You're not a hoplologist, you're like an anthropologist for traditional Chinese aerobics routines. You can find 'martial arts' moves in any weird little dance. You'd be better off filming mosh pits, if you want to see some fighting skill."

"You're a good dancer," said Davidson. "Didn't know you were into ethnic folk dance. I'm amazed you aren't married."

"My grandmother made me join the church dance group when I was a kid. You know, Greek grandmothers are—"

"Settle down, Zorba," said Davidson. "You're going to go viral again, the bad way." Pappas glanced around. The kids who had been watching Mrs. Chen were back, and they all had their smartphones out and trained on him.

"Hey," one of the kids called out in English. He wasn't even the biggest of them; he wore his teen body awkwardly, like his first-ever suit and tie. "Is this where the challenge matches are, or the breakdancing?" He punctuated his joke with a little poppin' and lockin' as two others beatboxed *boots-n-cats, boots-n-cats*. Pappas stood up. The kids whooped. Pappas walked toward them. The kids switched to Chinese and moved into a semicircular formation around Pappas.

Davidson called out, "They're kids!" to Pappas, but reached up to his eyewear and depressed the record button anyway. "It's still their country," he told Pappas. "They didn't sign waivers. They're also recording this. Use your head."

Use your head meant something in particular. Feint right, dive left, ankle pick, drive head into opponent thigh for takedown. Pappas exploded at the kid, had him over his shoulders in half a second, in the dirt in another. Then Davidson lost track of Pappas, as the other kids dove atop him. One girl held what looked like a pretty sharp rock in her hand.

Davidson's war had been pretty short. Like most of the Coalition forces in the Yellow River Valley, at first it seemed easy. One town after another had offered minimal resistance, and the drones putatively controlled by Beijing had gone into business for themselves, sometimes harrying the invaders, and sometimes practically paving roads for the 14th Infantry Regiment, to which Davidson was informally attached. He'd been a debt-draftee thanks to foolishly getting a master's degree from Princeton and signing up with the sort of transnational private military company that doesn't have a website, or a logo, to pay off his loans. In peacetime, and it was never peacetime, the firm fancied itself an AI-enhanced think tank, and for whatever reason the algorithm had decided that Davidson would get a lot of thinking done in China, driving a truck full of telecommunications equipment.

Maybe it was a mistake—the whole war, of course, but also attempting to occupy the ancient capital of Kaifeng. The air base had been abandoned, the PLA refused to engage or retreat. Davidson filed some reports from his dashboard, suggesting that the war was going according to Mao's old playbook: *trade land for time*. Who read it? Who knows?

Someone, perhaps the Chinese, perhaps the Coalition, maybe some mercs, or even just an inscrutable AI for which a *Todestrieb* subroutine was either a feature or a bug, decided to level Henan University's Jinming campus, home of the engineering school and nanotechnology labs. It's not even clear what was being stored there, nanobugs or a cache of e-bombs, but observers on both sides couldn't help but notice that the smoke plume seemed more like a writhing mass of thick black tentacles, more like a slow gusher from an oil well, than soot and superheated air.

Forty-eight hours later, Davidson was affixing a bayonet to his rifle. Even had the truck still worked, the telecom equipment was just so much ballast, not even worth using as cover from enemy fire, had there been any enemy fire. Everything had been fried, on all sides, the radios, everyone's personal Vcord lenses, and even the smartrifles that both sides had invested in so heavily. Smartrifles licensed and sold exclusively by the armorer wing of the international think tank, which also owned Davidson's labor contract. Drones fell from the sky like poisoned birds. The nights were dark enough to see constellations, as though it were the twentieth century. Any bit of expendable fabric of color was repurposed to make signal flags. The PLA surged forward before trenches could be dug. Davidson got to experience the sort of battle not seen in centuries—soldiers on opposing sides lining up like a bunch of assholes and rushing across empty fields, armed with blades and spears and, almost comically, the occasional pistol or freshly unburied civilian rifle wielded by men running with arms extended and eyes squinted half shut, just hoping for the best.

The Chinese had all the advantages: they knew the terrain, enjoyed the universal support of the populace, had more experience fighting without the extended techno-umbilicus on which the Coalition force so depended, and they could fight hand to hand. The battle wasn't quite like the old wuxia movies Davidson had watched as a kid, but only because movie fights last for more than a few seconds. There were plenty of sloppy fighters on the Chinese side, and a fair share of Coalition scrappers who did well, but a small phalanx of local spear wielders from the hinterlands of Henan Province penetrated Coalition lines with ease, and when the long weapons were snapped or blunted or lost, they took down soldiers twice their size with a mix of standing grappling and dirty boxing that Davidson had never before seen.

In truth, he didn't see much of it that day either, but he felt it intensely enough when a Henan fighter grabbed his clavicle with his left hand and pulled him in all the better to eat a straight right corkscrew punch. Davidson's last thought before losing consciousness was, *I wish my Vcorder was working.*

"This is your fault," Pappas said, though his words were slurred thanks to a new gap in his teeth and a lip swollen to the size of a banana. He was lying on a cot in a small and shadowy room lit only by Davidson's Vcorder projector aimed at a bare wall.

"Let's watch it again," Davidson said. "Good takedown—"

"You told me to. You set me up to fail," Pappas said.

"So, you're saying that your central nervous system listened to me instead of to you," Davidson said.

"I should have stayed on my feet, lured the big guy out, and chin-checked him."

"The big guy? You mean the fifteen-year-old?"

"He trains," said Pappas. "I had to really go for it, just like you said to."

"Yeah," said Davidson, distracted. He was watching the footage as it rolled backward now—the kids leaping away from Pappas, Pappas crouched low and helping a teen boy to his feet, then standing up and jumping off the edge of the screen.

"All this demonstrates, Davidson, is that you shouldn't call the shots. No pun intended."

"No pun detected. You're a hothead. China is still their country.

You could have been arrested for attacking those kids. You're lucky you got away with a concussion," said Davidson.

"That's me, Mister Lucky," said Pappas. "Thanks for taking your time diving in to help, by the way. It's good you let every single Chen child have their turn kicking me before breaking it up."

"How are you feeling?" Davidson asked as he turned back to his projector. He put on some other footage, that of Pappas handling individual tai chi fighters handily. "This'll make you feel better."

"I'm concussed. I have a concussion. I'm nauseated, thirsty, and tired. And I'm not allowed to sleep or I might die. That's how I feel."

"Tough guy," muttered Davidson. He messed with his Vcorder a bit, as he spoke, then reached into the small bag at his feet for a bundle of wires and electrodes. "I have a med program in this thing. Low-field magnetic stimulation. LFMS is good for concussions, brain injury, jet lag, all sorts of things." Then he removed a half sphere of aluminum from the bag. "This only looks like a spaghetti colander. Want to give it a try?"

"I don't think I do," said Pappas.

"Too bad I outrank you," said Davidson.

"We're both civilians," said Pappas.

"You signed a contract."

Pappas sighed dramatically. It took a few minutes of messing around to get the helm on and properly attached, and several more of testing to ensure that LFMS was occurring. The process was a bit like an old-fashioned color printer booting up—Pappas reported either seeing or not seeing blue and red vertical lines, experiencing the taste of cinnamon on his tongue, and hearing the Westminster Quarters, the name of Big Ben's familiar chime he did not know until, in a flash, he did.

"Well, it works," Pappas said. "Now what?"

"Now you sleep."

"I'm concussed. I'm not supposed to—"

Davidson turned Pappas off before Pappas could say "sleep."

Now there was little for Davidson to do to upload the Vcorder data into Pappas's central nervous system, and to watch him twitch as he learned.

That, and to wait for the extended familial networks of Chen Village to do their work.

★ ★ ★

"Take it off," said Andy Chen, gesturing toward Davidson's Vcorder. Disappointing. This sort of televisual shyness was one of the problems with the Chen family martial art. Nobody ever wanted to spar on camera, not when it was for keeps, not when there was going to be an actual challenge match. Blame the Cultural Revolution. The crackdown on traditional martial arts was only a small part of Mao's master plan to remake society according to Communist principles, but for family arts it was deadly. Show your kid how to get out of a wristlock, and you could end up chucked down the village well by your heavily propagandized, or perhaps just envious, nephews. No more sparring, no more disciples to pass down the forms and the techniques which comprised the forms, no fighting classes outside of the Army, and definitely no trips to Hong Kong to make it big in the movies as a wuxia star.

"Why?" asked Pappas. He was feeling much better after a day and night of rest and magnetic field stimulation. "We've been filming beatdowns all week." The crowd of local fighters and uninvolved people eager for some midday excitement that had formed a crescent behind Andy didn't murmur or shout any insults. Most of them just watched on stoically, as though the movie featuring Pappas and Andy Chen hadn't gotten good yet. A few shuffled to the left or the right, to let a few new people through.

Davidson was sure he recognized one of them, from the war. One had a tendency to remember the face of a man standing over you, holding the tip of a short spear to your throat, even fifteen years later. The man hadn't seemed angry then, just young and enthusiastic. He was wizened now, and upset—forty pounds of leather wrapped tight around one hundred pounds of cleverly twisted rebar. Maybe the Vcorder, with its ridiculous twin bug-eyed cameras, obscured Davidson's face enough to keep the man from recognizing him.

The man said something harsh and with an accent sufficiently rare or in a dialect just local enough that the instant translators handed Davidson some random guesses, and the words "virtuous spirit," which was clearly a rendering of the fellow's first name. When neither Davidson nor Pappas responded, he said something else, and gestured toward Andy Chen.

Andy stepped forward and said in his excellent English, "Please meet my uncle, Mr. Wong. He's husband to my mother's older sister. You have annoyed him by picking a fight with his own brother's favorite grandniece and damaging her phone, and now he is here. He would like a 'free fight' with your man, Mr. Davidson."

"They've all been free fights," said Pappas, before Davidson could even say anything. "Hey, Mr. Wong, you really want your last four teeth knocked out?" Davidson hoped that Pappas hadn't chosen to say "four" on purpose, which sounded so much like the word for "death" in Mandarin, but it hardly mattered. There was going to be a fight, and Davidson would get a real field test of the Vcorder's LFMS system, and his pet theory about the Supreme Ultimate Fist.

The Chens knew their forms well, but either couldn't show their skill in a sparring match, or they refused to. Davidson had been recording the bouts, yes, but also, and more importantly for his project, recording *the crowds* that had gathered to see their relatives get pounded by Soterios Pappas. The little twitches in their arms and legs, the flinches and feints, the way they held their hands while they watched. And these Davidson had fed into Pappas's brain, after arranging for that little altercation Pappas couldn't win, either martially or socially.

Wong took three long loping strides forward, his legs and arms bowed like a wrestler's. Pappas dropped into a fighting stance, but it wasn't his typical wide stance, with his hands up in fists by his temples. He extended his arms, left out ahead of right, south of his chin, about sternum height. He loaded his weight onto his rear right leg. Wong stopped, two paces away, right outside of range, and adopted a similar stance, a looser one, with elbows down and fingers extended.

"No video," said Andy Chen. "No video!" He rushed Davidson. Pappas inhaled, then exhaled sharply, and made his move. There was a sound, bones breaking in half, then through skin. Two great palms filled Davidson's field of vision. From the ground, through tears of blood, he saw Wong feint, bury a left in Pappas's liver. Something was wrong with Pappas; he looked shorter somehow, he had an extra knee. Pappas lowered his right hand, and Wong threw a left at his jaw. Pappas was halfway to the ground when Wong hit him with a straight right, one that would have been an overhand right if not for Pappas already being asleep and claimed by gravity. The classic combo right out of Jack Dempsey's manual.

Then down came Andy Chen's foot.

★ ★ ★

Davidson couldn't help but calculate the price of all the presents the various masters of the Supreme Ultimate Fist brought him. He was sharing a semiprivate room with Pappas, who had also received many gifts—good cognac, an armload of ridiculous watches, a small cube of palladium, dumplings by the basket the smell of which was driving Davidson mad. Davidson was all right except for his jaw, and the suspicious "milkshake" that was his lunch. Pappas's legs were in traction.

"I'm going to kill you when I heal up," said Pappas. "Spiral fractures. That's what I'm going to give you. That's what Chen family style is all about. *Chán sī jìn*. Spiral energy." Pappas could even pronounce tones decently now. LMFS learning was really remarkable, but a tongue, throat, and larynx were easier to instantly train than limbs, as it had all turned out. Pappas had managed to break both his own tibiae when approaching Wong. Wong hadn't even bothered using the family fist to knock Pappas out. Plain ol' Western boxing had done that trick.

I'm going to be home in America by the time you heal up, Davidson's phone intoned after Davidson typed up that sentence with two good thumbs.

"I know kung fu now," Pappas said. "That's what I'm going to kill you with."

Your mind knows it, Davidson typed. *It'll take some long practice to build your body in a way that'll let you use it. Are you going to stay here and learn?* Davidson had selected a soothing female voice for his phone, but Pappas still seemed agitated. Hot-blooded Greek, Davidson decided.

You know what the masters say, Davidson typed, *it takes a lot of gongfu to get gongfu.* It was a little joke. Gongfu, or kung fu, could mean "hard work," or it could mean "the positive results of hard work."

Pappas had the bed by the window, which was only fair as he couldn't go outside. Some people were making a point to practice their forms and two-person sets down in the parking lot. They were the ones who had brought the gifts. "They stole your research. They stole your recordings and used it on themselves."

To be fair, I was stealing their gongfu from them, typed Davidson. *And they kind of paid us back. There's some pretty good stuff here. This phone is especially nice.*

Davidson gulped. He hadn't typed that last line. The phone was going into business for itself. He couldn't help but notice that its wallpaper was an animation of a swirling, oily, black mass. It seemed familiar somehow.

"Are the Chinese going to be unstoppable now?" asked Pappas. "Don't answer, smartass. It's a rhetorical question. And I hate your stupid phone's stupid voice."

Davidson typed up a snappy response, but the phone said something else, a hyperlocal slang expression that Davidson didn't know—maybe one of the kids had said it while they were stomping on Pappas. Pappas laughed, said something equally slangy to the phone, and then reached over and grabbed, not the phone, but one of the bottles of cognac.

He popped it open, whooped, tipped the neck toward Davidson and said, "I'll drink to that, ladyphone. Too bad your jaw's wired shut for the next four weeks, Davidson. I'll polish off the booze and the pastries for the both of us, in peace and quiet serenity. The phone agrees. *Gānbēi.*" Davidson knew that one. A toast: *dry your cup.* And Pappas did just that.

FLAWED EVOLUTION

✪

Brian Trent

They awakened her around 2 A.M. and said it was an emergency. Her first thought was that Ezekiel had come back to life—it was always trying. Throwing on her clothes, Dr. Marguerite Chapman of the National Defense Research Committee went from her trailer to the mobile command center—really, just a larger trailer on the India-China border. Adjusting her glasses, she studied the monitor array.

"What am I looking at?" she asked.

"It's the Chinese team," Colonel Andrews explained, standing at her side. "Inside Ezekiel."

Briefly, her eyes flicked to the monitor showing the downed extraterrestrial craft that lay a half mile north of their position. She would have preferred to be closer to the crash site, but that was impossible. The Himalayan valley was a bubbling, toxic landscape. It was the same with the two other vessels comprising the UFO invasion. Wherever they went, they poisoned the environment around them. No one knew how to even begin discussing cleanup.

It also meant that analyzing the alien craft was challenging. Researchers from America, India, and China rotated shifts inside Ezekiel while donning bulky hazmat suits that would slowly erode in the polluted conditions.

"I see them," Chapman said, indicating a monitor that displayed the eight-person research team from the People's Republic of China. They were busy collecting samples from Ezekiel's fleshy interior.

"What do you notice?" the colonel asked.

She studied the onscreen activity, looking for anything unusual.

Of course, the whole thing was goddamn unusual, she thought. There was nothing inside the alien craft corresponding to human notions of an aircraft or a ship. No cockpit. No engine room. No cargo bay. No crew quarters. Ezekiel was an unmanned *thing*, and despite first impressions—when it and two others entered Earth's atmosphere and began toxifying swaths of the planet like malevolent crop dusters—it didn't appear to be a machine in the traditional sense.

It was far closer to being a lifeform, she mused. And a hardy lifeform at that, since it had taken days of sustained bombardment to bring them down.

And they kept trying to heal.

Kept trying to return to the sky to resume their poisonous mission.

The only solution had been to physically restrain the UFOs with a netting of steel cables, and cutting into their bodies with industrial drilling equipment. The research teams snaked cameras into the exotic flesh. They sawed off tissue. They cracked bony protrusions to collect strange fluids in an attempt at understanding how the vessel worked.

"The Chinese researchers are taking samples," Chapman said with a shrug. "How is that unusual?"

Colonel Andrews shook his head. "Look at the guy crouching by the wall."

"What about him?"

"He's been there quite a while."

"So?"

"Everyone else is moving around like ants over a roadkill. That guy hasn't moved for at least an hour."

She felt a flash of irritation at having been awakened for this. "Maybe he's running a camera there. I still don't see why you—"

The colonel tapped the keyboard. A different view—one she'd never seen before—appeared onscreen.

"This is from a hidden camera," he said. "I had several installed around Ezekiel in secret, to keep a watchful eye on our Indian and Chinese friends. What do you see now?"

Chapman stared hard at the real-time image and adjusted her glasses. "He has both arms buried in the wall, like he's feeling around for something. So?"

"He's downloading data from Ezekiel's neural network."

"*Excuse me?*"

He indicated the diamond-patterned flesh into which the Chinese scientist was plunging his hands like a plumber working on a waterline. "This is *neural tissue* back here. You said it yourself—the challenge in learning about these ships is that they don't seem to have traditional mechanical properties. No computers or engines. No weapons array. You suggested they might really be alive. Living things should have a nervous system."

"That's one of the theories."

"It's not a theory anymore. These things have brains, and it's possible to download data from them."

Chapman rotated in her chair to face him and glared behind her glasses like an angry schoolmaster. "How the hell could you know something like that?"

He sighed with the resignation of someone about to unburden a dangerous secret. "Because *our* researchers managed to do it—three days ago—with the UFO that went down in Wichita."

Aboard the train, Dr. Chapman closed her eyes and tried to sleep. She was exhausted, going on twenty hours without sleep now, and much of that time spent hauling her equipment into a truck for the long drive to a train. Nonetheless, she couldn't sleep. Too much was happening. Finally, she turned to the window to regard the night-shrouded vista as the train rattled south to the Indian port of Haldia.

Colonel Andrews sat across from her, the lines on his face as deep as scars.

"Where are we?" she asked numbly.

"Just north of Jamshedpur."

"The bomb went off?"

He fumbled with a cigarette, lit it, and took a deep drag. "The nuke detonated two hours ago. It's the lead story on social media."

A sick feeling spread through her stomach. "Jesus Christ."

"We had no choice."

"We killed all those people! We killed our *own* people!"

"It *had* to look like a terrorist attack," he explained, the cigarette trembling between his lips. "We leaked a story that rogue elements from Myanmar smuggled a nuclear device to the site."

"Myanmar?" she scoffed.

"There's been suspicion they've had a nuclear program for some time. At any rate, Ezekiel has been destroyed."

"Our people—"

"Did you think we could just pull every American out, conveniently before the detonation? It was challenging enough getting *you* out, with Chinese satellites breathing down our necks."

She felt her anguish sharpen into rage. "I want to know why this was necessary! Those were *my* people! Ezekiel was *my* project!"

"The President didn't come to the decision easily."

"What the hell did we learn in Wichita, Colonel?"

He puffed his cigarette, the smoke moving around his mouth like tendrils. "The alien technology is centuries ahead of us. Weapons, advanced flight theory, tissue regeneration, communications... whoever learns to reverse-engineer it will decide the fate of the world. You want it to be us? Or Red China?"

She considered that. Slowly, her scientific pragmaticism pushed through her anger, and she said, "What I *want* is to understand why the aliens came here to begin with."

"Whatever their reason, they failed," he said with pride.

"Tell me how Wichita figured out how to access their UFO's biological databanks."

"Do you know what a brain-machine interface is?"

"Of course." BMIs had been discussed in scientific literature since the 1970s, and first achieved in 2008. They allowed the communication of electrical signals between an organic brain and a microchip. Successful experiments allowed monkeys to control a robotic arm with thought alone. DARPA was actively researching how BMI chips might allow paralyzed people to walk again. There were even experiments to connect a human mind and a computer...

The realization hit her like a thunderbolt.

"We connected a person to an alien vessel?" she cried.

Colonel Andrews shook ash from his cigarette, looking distinctly uncomfortable. "Our intel told us that the Chinese were preparing to attempt it. We fast-tracked our own experiments to beat them to the punch. This isn't the kind of contest where we can afford to place second. One of our researchers in Kansas volunteered to be implanted with a cutting-edge BMI..."

He explained the rest, and Chapman listened with fascination and a measure of horror. The Wichita experiment had worked. The researcher connected her own brain to the UFO. She received images. Most were meaningless, but some helped the research team understand how the alien craft could heal at such an astonishing rate. There were radial structures that directed proteins to stimulate tissue repair. It was even possible to choose what parts of the craft you wished to rebuild— which suggested it might be possible to grow one UFO off another, in the way that splitting a starfish could result in two separate organisms.

How far did that regenerative skill go? What else was possible?

"You understand why we'd want to keep this under wraps?" the colonel asked. "If it's possible to develop our own UFOs, we don't want the Chinese to know that."

Chapman adjusted her glasses and looked at him. "It would appear they already learned to do it."

He took a long drag of his cigarette. "That's why Ezekiel had to be destroyed. Whatever China learned from it is all they're going to get. We still have ours in Wichita."

"There's a third one in Kenya," she pointed out.

He shrugged. "It sank to the bottom of Lake Naivasha. That puts it a bit outside China's jurisdiction, so I think it'll be a while before they can access it."

The Boeing C-17 crossed into Kenyan airspace and was descending to Naivasha Airport when an explosion rocked the aircraft.

"We're taking fire!" the pilot shouted over the intercom. "Buckle up! It's gonna get dicey!"

Chapman strained to see outside a window in her cargo compartment, surrounded by the equipment she needed to get a new lab up and running. Black smoke vented from one of the engines. Beyond that, the city of Mombasa was a palette of orderly buildings bisected by tropical vegetation.

The plane veered sharply to the left. Another missile streaked by, so close she could see the vapor trail.

"Holy shit!" she cried.

Colonel Andrews was strapped into a nearby seat, and he touched the Bluetooth at his ear. "Shoulder-mounted missiles," he said, apparently receiving reports from the ground. "Fighting has broken out in the city."

"Fighting between *who?*"

"Officially? Chinese soldiers and Kenyan insurgents."

She was getting tired of his games—she'd received approval to set up a research base in Kenya to study the submerged UFO there, and wanted nothing more than to work in a laboratory again. The breakthrough in Wichita *proved* that alien tissue could be grown in vitro.

"And unofficially?" she demanded.

"Chinese soldiers and US contractors."

"What the hell are *either* doing in Kenya?"

The colonel explained it as the plane made a nauseating series of evasive maneuvers to avoid ground fire. The PRC had maintained a presence in several African countries since the early 2000s, looking to press its economic partnerships. This included the construction of a railway connecting Kenya with neighboring countries. To protect its investment, China had troops on the ground. Since Ezekiel's destruction, those troops had increased tenfold...

...especially around Lake Naivasha.

"We know the Chinese are running deep-submergence rescue vehicles to the lake bottom," Colonel Andrews said.

Chapman glared at him. "And we've tried sabotaging their efforts, right? No wonder they're pissed! Isn't it enough that we've got our own UFO in Kansas?"

He opened his mouth to reply when another explosion rocked the plane. This time it blew a hole in the wall, and the Boeing tilted into a screaming dive.

We're going down! she thought in horror. Crazily, she realized she was about to die without ever understanding *why* the aliens had come to Earth.

The last thing she remembered was her research papers flying around the cargo compartment like little UFOs of their own. They snapped out through the breach and into blue sky.

She didn't remember the crash.

When she opened her eyes, she found herself in a hospital bed. A nurse was removing an IV from her arm.

"Where am I?" she croaked in a paper-dry voice.

The nurse looked at her in surprise. "You're on the USS *Roosevelt*. In the Aegean. You were airlifted here three weeks ago."

Three weeks?

Thinking of her papers flying around the doomed C-17, Chapman asked, "Where's Colonel Andrews?"

The nurse began to sweat, and she recoiled from the bed as if unnerved by her patient. Something was wrong. It was in the woman's eyes. "You . . . you were the only survivor of the crash," she stammered. "To be honest, I didn't think you *would* survive, considering the extent of your injuries, but—"

Chapman sat up with a suddenness that made the nurse shrink to the other side of the room. "There was an attack!"

"Ma'am? Please take it easy."

"Tell me about the attack!"

"You were shot down in Mombasa."

But she violently shook her head. "I'm not talking about Mombasa! I mean Wichita! There was an attack there! Lots of people killed, my God!" She hesitated, realizing what she was saying. "I've never been to Wichita. How . . . how could I know there was an attack there?"

A man appeared in the doorway. He might have been handsome if not for the odd scarring on his face and neck. He wore a polo shirt and black pants. Probably a CIA spook—they had a bearing about them that was unmistakable.

"A lot's happened since your crash," he said, and as he neared her bedside she gasped. The scars on his face and neck were peculiarly diamond shaped, and from each point of the diamond a line extended to connect with other diamonds. This was not the work of shrapnel or medical surgery, but deliberate scarification.

"The Wichita lab was attacked," she said.

"The Wichita lab was nuked."

"*How?*"

"An unidentified craft invaded US airspace. It stopped over the research station. A black-ops unit rappelled out, grabbed computers and laptops, and planted a nuclear device. Wichita is a smoking and irradiated crater."

She shook her head. "I don't believe this."

"It happened. You *know* it happened."

"Where did the craft come from?"

"China."

"I don't understand. You said it was an unidentified craft. How does a Chinese aircraft penetrate American airspace then use a dozen guys to attack a high-security base—"

"It wasn't a dozen guys," he countered, his eyes oddly luminous in the dim hospital room. "It was six Chinese operatives. They grabbed what they needed and jumped back aboard—and I do mean *jumped* aboard, even though their aircraft was hovering six meters above them. They escaped before the nuke went off."

Understanding came in a flash. "China has reverse-engineered alien technology. They managed to build—or rather, *grow*—their own UFO." She thought again to her papers in the C-17. In one of them, she'd speculated about the possibilities of using alien tissue for a number of adaptive purposes. Experiments had indicated that it was *remarkably* adaptive.

Chapman closed her eyes.

She didn't remember her C-17 going down. And yet—somehow— she remembered viewing a security recording of the Kansas attack. Remembered sitting in the White House Situation Room, talking to the President! Remembered other things that she couldn't possibly have participated in.

What the hell was going on?

The memory of the Wichita attack was especially vivid.

It's 0300 on the security feed when the hangar wall collapses around the gliding shape of a particularly unusual UFO. A metal door has been added to the side of the craft. Like a silver scab. The alien flesh is swollen around it.

In the hangar, American troops converge on the craft from every direction. They unload hundreds of rounds into it. The UFO responds by emitting a circular spray of toxic chemicals from its lateral vents. Soldiers dissolve on contact, melting like novelty candles.

The metal door slides open. Six figures in full protective gear hop out of the craft. Four of them grab unscathed computers, laptops, and binders. Two carry a crate that contains the nuke. One by one, they leap back into the UFO with the ease of kangaroos jumping on the moon.

Chapman opened her eyes and regarded her mysterious visitor. "China did more than grow its own UFO."

"I know," he said.

"They enhanced some of their people with extraterrestrial DNA."

"Yes."

"Superior musculature. Lightning-fast reflexes."

He nodded.

She sighed. "Are you *certain* this attack came from China? Other countries might have learned to grow their own alien tissue by now."

His glowing stare reminded her of certain nocturnal animals. "Not only do we know it was the Chinese...but also I can tell you the names of all six men involved. I know the cities and villages where they were born."

"How?"

"In the same way *you're* going to tell me my name."

"You haven't told me your name."

"Try."

She closed her eyes.

As with her inexplicable knowledge of the Wichita recording, she became aware that an entire reservoir of outside knowledge was available to her. No, not just one reservoir, but many. At a whim, she could extend mental fingers into any one of those wellsprings. They burned softly with a suggestion of names and places.

"Your name is Daniel," she said at once, connecting with his mental presence. "You were born in Boston. Before the invasion you worked as a translator for the NSA. You saw that security feed in Kansas. You briefed the President. You've been waiting for me to recover from being paralyzed because...wait...I was *paralyzed?* The crash *paralyzed* me?"

From the back of the room, the nurse said, "Your spinal column was pulverized. You broke thirty bones throughout your body. The decision was made to—"

Terror flooded Chapman's mind. Peeling back her hospital sheets, she saw the diamond-shaped scars over her chest and arms. "You... you...*grafted that alien tissue onto me!?*"

Daniel took her hand. "It was the only way to save your life. We need you, Marguerite. You were project leader at Ezekiel. America has—"

She saw the end of his thought before he could say it, and said it for him: "—fallen dangerously behind China in this arms race. You need me, and as many of America's brightest minds as possible, to combat their efforts."

"Yes."

She ran her finger over the scars. At the same time, she became aware that one of the mysterious reservoirs in her mind was reaching out to her. Trying to connect. Trying to read her thoughts. It wasn't coming from Daniel. It was further away, but flaring close, like a shooting star trying to strike her.

"Think of a wall," Daniel said quickly.

"Excuse me?"

"Imagine a wall! Do it fast!"

"I don't understand what you—"

An image leapt to her mind of a large green wall—the Green Monster from Fenway Park in Boston. The foreign mind in her head battered uselessly against it.

"That's how we shield our thoughts from the enemy," Daniel explained. "I'm sharing with you the image that I use, when China's agents try reading us. Everyone enhanced by alien cells becomes—"

"Part of the same telepathic network," she said, reading it from his mind.

"Yes."

"We can *all* communicate with each other?"

"That's why it's imperative that we shield our minds. It isn't difficult—you just imagine a barrier. There's a guy in China who actually imagines the Great Wall." He chanced a smile, saw she wasn't sharing it with him, and said, "I know this must be difficult for you."

He said the rest through his thoughts. A new age of espionage had dawned. China's enhanced agents tried spying on America's. In turn, America tried spying on China. Day and night, the two telepathic networks attempted to snatch little bits of intel from each other. The location of labs. The progress they were making on adapting alien technology.

Through it all, Chapman struggled with how to feel about these new rules of the world. Did the aliens know their invasion would cause such chaos?

"It isn't chaos," Daniel told her. "Where they failed, we'll reap the benefits."

She stared at the diamond patterning on his face. "Did they fail?"

"We're here, and they're not."

Chapman stood from the bed, testing out her legs. She expected that her muscles would have atrophied in three weeks. To her surprise, she felt strong enough to run a marathon. Her thoughts, too, seemed bolstered by a clarity she'd never experienced.

"The toxifying clouds," she said suddenly. "Have we learned anything about *why* the aliens were poisoning our environment?"

"Only one thing so far," he said. "The poison zones aren't lifeless anymore. Plants have begun sprouting in them."

Her heart skipped a beat. "That's great news! We were afraid the UFOs had permanently sterilized those areas." She felt the grimness of his thoughts. "When you said plants . . . you didn't mean *terrestrial* plants, did you?"

"No."

"Alien vegetation is growing in them?"

"Yes."

"Is it spreading?"

"Beyond the poisonous zones? No, thank God. It appears to be strictly contained in the areas 'dusted' by the UFOs."

Chapman felt a ripple of discomfort. "The UFOs were trying to terraform our world to suit their tastes."

"If so, they failed. At the moment, we have a more pressing problem, and that's—"

"—to catch up with China."

Despite her unease, she felt a certain undeniable exhilaration at her burgeoning telepathy. And she knew—felt it in her mind—that there was an entire network of fellow telepaths, capable of instant communication that went far beyond the clunkiness of smartphones and the limitations of language.

This was communication as it should be. In this regard at least, the alien way was better.

"Come on," she said, looking around for her glasses and then realizing, to her amazement, she no longer needed them. "Let's go find it."

Daniel raised an eyebrow. "Find what?"

"The location where China is growing its own UFOs."

Twelve hundred miles from mainland China lay the Spratly Islands.

Though in international waters, since 2010 they'd been artificially expanded by the PRC to serve as naval bases. This had transformed the South China Sea into one of the most hotly contested areas in the world. It was only a matter of time, experts predicted, before war broke out there.

The war was in its fourteenth day when Dr. Chapman leapt from the American-made UFO as it made a low pass over one of the islands. She landed easily on the beach and considered her surroundings.

It was a cloudy night, and the air smelled of rain. The island was a rocky beach. Beyond it, the South China Sea presented a surreal vista: the expanse of black water stuttered in strobelike illumination as American and Chinese navies clashed, while the black sky was streaked by American and Chinese aircraft. Aircraft carriers, destroyers, and cruisers blazed like funeral pyres on the sea.

She sighed, wondering how things had gotten to this point.

"Flawed evolution," she muttered to the Network in her head.

There were some chuckles at this—it had become a running joke among America's telepaths. For them, it was obvious why the world was in such a chaotic state. The rest of humanity was cut off from each other. Communication between regular people was a pinball game of flawed linguistics and assumptions. Their isolation stunted them. Made them neurotic. Clearly, Earthly evolution had gone wrong.

From the UFO hovering above, three Navy SEALs rappelled down to the sand.

"Follow me," she told them.

Up from the beach was a rocky formation with a small alcove. It appeared to be natural, but around here, appearances were deceiving. Chapman ducked inside and found the hidden keycard scanner set into the recess.

She smiled. Even though her Network had concluded a secret base was here, it was exhilarating to be right. It had taken weeks of psychic assault on the Chinese Network to gather clues. Probing at their individual minds. Looking for cracks in their mental walls. Catching snippets of memory. Of dreams. Like trying to put together a jigsaw puzzle with only half the pieces.

Yet it had worked.

An image of a beach.

A Chinese researcher glancing at the night sky while smoking a cigarette.

A glimpse of a submarine's serial number as supplies were delivered to the lab through an undersea sub pen.

Backtracking the movements of that sub to narrow the search.

Chapman pressed her fake biometric card to the scanner. A green light blinked. There was a pressurized hiss, and the rock wall slid aside to reveal a set of stairs descending into the island's bowels.

The SEALs went in first. She followed, preparing herself for what was to come. The mission was dangerous. The odds of success—of even surviving it—were exceedingly thin.

Then again, if the war continued on its current trajectory, everyone's odds of survival were minimal.

The nuclear attack in Kansas had been followed by a nuclear strike in Kenya. The last of the alien UFOs was destroyed. Earth's victory against the invasion was complete, and there was speculation that global tensions might return to normal.

Instead, the war between America and China spread. Manmade UFOs struck military bases and laboratories alike, and as they weren't precision weapons, the damage was becoming catastrophic. Poisoned zones multiplied tenfold. Economies were crashing. The global food supply was drying up as more and more farmland was targeted in an effort to starve the enemy into submission.

At the bottom of the stairs, a short corridor opened into a cavern. The SEALs took position ahead of her. Chapman followed them, and then froze.

"Holy shit," she muttered.

It was as humid as a rainforest in the cavern. It even *looked* like a rainforest, with strange vines and bulbous vegetation filling the underground space. Less a laboratory than a greenhouse, and Chapman immediately saw why.

The lab was growing UFOs.

It called to mind a kind of nightmarish pumpkin field, with vines connecting to swollen alien craft. America's burgeoning UFO program was being conducted in more sterile environments, where engineers shaped alien growth around metal struts and prefab chambers to accommodate human occupants. China had taken it a step beyond. This discovery alone made the mission worth it.

Through Chapman's eyes, her telepathic colleagues were spreading the word.

America needed to expand its program.

Needed to develop greenhouses like these.

One of the SEALs motioned to her, indicating a Chinese researcher in a white lab coat. The woman typed at a portable computer station, unaware of the intruders.

Chapman nodded. The SEAL crept up behind the researcher. He clasped his hand around her mouth, jabbed her with a tranquilizing syringe. Quietly, wary of raising an alarm, he eased her limp body onto the ground and dragged her toward the corridor.

This was it, Chapman thought anxiously. The mission's success or failure hinged on these next few moments.

Kneeling by the woman, she looked into her dazed, barely conscious eyes.

No one had ever managed to infiltrate the Chinese Network. Likewise, no one in China had managed to breach the American one. The mission had been greenlit, therefore, to incapacitate an enemy researcher. Attempt a full breach. Steal as much as possible, learn as much as possible, before the walls came down.

Chapman pressed her hands to the diamond-shaped patterns on the woman's face. Then, with the full weight of her Network behind her, she went inside.

Into the woman's mind.

Into the enemy Network.

It was like a supernova in her thoughts. She instantly knew the woman's name—Jianmei. Knew she was from Guizhou Province. Knew what achievements had been made in the island lab . . . in all the labs.

And then, before Chapman could react, the Chinese Network looked into *her*.

Into *her* mind.

Into *her* colleagues.

There was a fleeting moment when she felt the American Network scramble to impose a wall on the intrusion—just as the Chinese were scrambling to impose their own. But then something happened in those precious seconds. The camaraderie she'd felt with her enhanced colleagues was amplified a hundredfold. The Chinese felt it too. Even the men who had attacked Wichita were plugged into that perfect moment, and all jigsaw pieces assembled . . .

Chapman began to laugh.

In locations across the United States and China and India and Kenya, others began to laugh too.

Why had the UFOs come to Earth? Chapman had sweated the question since the invasion began. China's scientists struggled with the same query. Yet now, the combined Networks realized the question was irrelevant. Maybe when the planet-seeders set out from their homeworld, Earth had yet to develop civilization. Maybe the UFOs were single-purpose drones incapable of understanding the damage they were causing to terrestrial life. Maybe they understood and didn't care; after all, a human farmer doesn't think twice about destroying an ant colony to make room for his farm.

It didn't matter why the UFOs had come.

What mattered was that humanity was a flawed product of flawed evolution. Human achievements were the crawl of an inchworm barely outpacing its own destructive habits. What were "Americans" and "Chinese" but petty enclaves of small-minded beings? Earth itself was flawed and fragile . . . but things were changing. The alien life growing in the "poisoned" zones was hardier, energy-rich, and better suited to feeding a global population, as long as that population was enhanced accordingly.

Earth itself could be enhanced.

A better world was possible.

And it was suddenly obvious how to do it.

Chapman withdrew from Jianmei and whirled to the nearest SEAL. "The Chinese are growing thousands of UFOs," she said.

He blinked at her. "*Thousands?*"

"We've fallen far behind. We need thousands of our own to match theirs."

In that same moment, American researchers across the United States were phoning Washington, telling the President the same thing. Thousands of new UFOs were needed! Thousands of people must be enhanced to operate them!

And in China, researchers phoned Beijing to report that the Americans already had a fleet of thousands. Tens of thousands of UFOs, with tens of thousands more people, were required to counter the enemy!

As quietly as they'd entered the lab, Chapman and the SEALs withdrew from it to the beach. The American craft hovered over the sand, its fleshy skin dappled by the lights of distant battle: Chinese and American forces attacking each other, like ants warring over a roadside puddle.

Chapman stared at the craft in new appreciation.

Three alien vessels had tried improving Earth, and had failed. But soon, we'll actually be able to do it. Humanity would be improved with it. The future didn't belong to—

"Flawed evolution," she murmured, and the combined Network replied in one voice:

Not for much longer.

LUNAR ASYLUM

✪

Martin L. Shoemaker

My balls itched.

I didn't tell Rita. She stared out at Tycho Crater as the hangar dome slid open for the crawler carrier hauling the transport from the Arch. Her eyes were agog. Me, I'd gotten bored with the surface a decade ago while on excavation teams. And no matter what the designers promised, my suits *always* itched.

I had transferred to the tunnel farms because I was ready for some routine; but that day I had volunteered for even more tedium: working for Bader Security, processing refugees from the Grand Nation of the Celestial Arch, also known as GNCA in these parts.

The crawler moved at a walking pace up the long stretch of regolith to the hangar. Perched atop it was a stubby Arch transport full of refugees. The last one had held sixty, packed nearly on top of each other. I wondered how many this one carried.

The crawler approached, and I gave one more visual inspection. "Crawler Five, Mosley," I said. "Clearance confirmed."

The crawler pilot transmitted, "Mosley, we have confirmation from the door sensors."

I tugged on Rita's elbow, and we backed inside the hangar. She said, "Where'll we put them?"

I had no answer. The sixty refugees from Pad Four were crammed into the quarantine center. The tram from Tycho Under had broken down, and we had no details or repair status. The refugees were about to get *really* friendly. I hoped Traffic Control would give us a break after this.

But it was no more in their hands than mine. The Arch was shipping refugees as fast as they could load them, trying to stave off famine as Skvrsky's Blight swept through their grain stores. Their entire economy rested on Pan-Asian migrant farmers. Now the farmers couldn't even feed themselves. The Arch had invoked emergency rescue protocols to send refugees to the Lunar cities, and to every station in orbit.

The crawler halted, and the hangar started shuttering. I shook my head. This would upend everything at Bader Farms. And *we* were lucky: we were already turning out kilotons of food for sale Downside. We could feed the refugees; but I wondered about some of the stations.

"We're up!" Rita said, heading to the lift. I followed to where a belt rose up and down a shaft, grabbed a loop sticking out from it, stepped into another below, and let the belt carry me up.

When I stepped off, Rita was heading down the gantry to the transport's hatch. A suited figure stepped out, checked gauges, nodded, and lifted his visor. The hangar was at forty percent pressure, sufficient for normal operations.

The man turned to Rita. "Pilot Meng reporting," he said in a thick Chinese accent. He was on the tall side. His expression betrayed nothing. "I am delivering forty-seven refugees."

Rita answered, "Lieutenant Masters, Bader Security. Welcome to Tycho." She checked her comp. "Your manifest says forty-four."

Meng nodded. "We had three late arrivals." For an instant, his professional demeanor cracked, betraying a hint of compassion. "I found room for them. They were hungry."

Rita looked back at her comp and frowned. "It's not like we have details on most of the refugees anyway. Your records leave much to be desired."

"Not my records," he answered. "I'm just the pilot. May my passengers disembark?"

"Permission granted," Rita said. Meng opened the airlock.

I expected difficulty. Gravity *always* matters. The one-sixth Lunar g is bad for a Downsider. It makes them prone to stupid errors. The Grand Nation of the Celestial Arch was a classic O'Neill design, two cylinders spinning every three minutes to produce forty percent Earth-normal gravity. Archer instincts were just as bad as a Downsider's.

Worse, they were used to Coriolis effects. On Luna, they tended to correct for spin that isn't there. I expected bruises.

But I *didn't* expect a squat, dark-haired man in dirty coveralls bursting out of the airlock. As Meng stepped back from the hatch, the man sprang into the air. "Whoa!" I reached for him.

If he was puzzled by the gravity, he didn't show it. Before I could grasp an arm, he kicked off from Meng's helmet and over the gantry rail.

Rita hit her comm. "Medic to the hangar floor!" Even on Luna, falling can be fatal. He would hit at ten meters per second.

I ran for the lift, grabbed the down belt, scrambled down the moving cable. Could I catch up with him? Catching him would mean broken bones for both of us, but he'd survive.

But when I looked up, I saw that his leap had taken him to the transport's hull. He clung to handholds and climbed down toward the crawler.

"Stop!" I shouted. He didn't stop, he just looked down at me and scurried around the hull. If I had to climb up there and get him, we *would* exchange words.

On the far side of the transport, he started straight down, fast; and as he did, he called down, "Asylum!" He was still gasping "Asylum..." when he dropped to the deck and wrapped his arms around me.

"Tycho Traffic Control, come in." I was met with silence. I looked over at the hangar chief, Hyun Sung. "How long have they been out?"

She shook her head. "I haven't had a reason to contact them." She glared at our guest. "You're making a lot of fuss for one panicked refugee."

"I'm just trying to pass the buck," I answered. "He won't talk to me, and we don't have authority to grant asylum. Let the bosses deal with this."

"I'm sorry," the man said. "Please, you must protect me."

"'Must,' nothing," I answered. "We've got a hundred people in a facility equipped for thirty. We've got communications down, transportation down, and we've got you climbing a ship like a goddamned monkey. You won't tell us your name or your problem, just that you want asylum. Maybe I'll just take you back with the others and forget I ever saw you.

His eyes widened. "No! That's where they—" But he stopped, mouth clamped tight.

"Who are 'they'?" I asked. "And why are you afraid of them?" I leaned closer. "For somebody who wants help, you're sure uncooperative." I took a deep breath, trying to calm down. "Go ahead and wait. When I get through to the bosses, you're their problem."

Just then, the control room hatch chimed. Sung tapped a button on her console, and the face of the Chinese pilot appeared. "Can I help you?" Sung said.

"You have one of my passengers," the pilot said. "I must confirm his condition."

"He's fine," Sung said. I moved to stand out of the pickup. "I'll vouch for him."

"That is not proper procedure," the pilot said. "I must inspect the man."

I nodded, and Sung said, "I'm keying you in now." I backed off to a corner.

When the hatch opened, the pilot stepped in stiffly. He walked up to the man, grabbed his arm, and shouted, "Why did you do that?" The man glared sullenly at him, but said nothing.

The pilot turned to Sung. "This man has broken seventeen safety protocols. He is under arrest."

I cleared my throat and stepped out from the corner. The pilot turned as I said, "That was in Bader Farms jurisdiction, not on the Arch."

The pilot glared at me. "Bader Farms *has* no jurisdiction. You're a corporate entity, chartered under the System Initiative. You have no authority here."

I itched to reach for my sidearm, but I restrained myself. I stood casually as I said, "Free Luna has a differing opinion on jurisdiction, but *no one* believes the Arch has authority here." I nodded to the stranger. "He'll answer to Bader Security officers."

The pilot frowned. "I don't have time for this, *Bader Security*." He looked at his comp, then turned to Sung. "How soon can you refuel my ship? We have more evacuations."

"We're working as fast as we can," Sung answered. "You'll be topped off in eighty-three minutes, and we'll tow you out as fast as the hangar can depressurize."

The pilot nodded. "Thank you, Chief. My apologies for being abrupt. I shall have to explain all of this to my superiors when I get back to the Arch." He glared at the stranger, then exited.

I turned to Sung. "That's it? He didn't even check ID?"

"He had visual pickups built into his flight suit," Sung answered. "Full facial and biometric recognition. He knows who we have here."

"No," the man said, breaking his silence at last. "If he knew, he'd have never left."

I shook my head. "You can't spoof bio-facial."

For the first time, the man didn't look grim. He gave a slight smile as he said, "With enough time and enough access, you can spoof anything."

The man had a point. Especially for someone who looked more European than Asian.

"You?" I said. "A migrant farmer?"

"I'll explain to your bosses." He seemed more assured now. "Get me to them without alerting anyone else. The risk is too high."

"The risk to whom?"

He peered closely at me. "You. Your bosses. Maybe half of Earth-Moon space."

I fumed. "Don't pull that ominous shit with me. Give me a name or I'll take you back to quarantine with the rest of the fucking refugees."

We locked eyes. He was determined, but I'm just plain stubborn. Finally he blinked. "I'm Dr. David Skvrsy, and I'm formally claiming asylum."

That made me stare. "Skvrsky? The man who sequenced the Blight?"

He slumped into the chair, burying his face in his hands. Then he looked up and said, "No. The man who *synthesized* the Blight."

I looked over at Sung, and her eyes were as wide as mine. Then I looked back to the man. "Explain."

"I can't." He winced. "Let me talk to a geneticist. I can make *them* understand."

I crossed my arms. "I told you, *Doctor*, we've got no trams or comms. Explain it to *me*. The news streams said you sequenced the Blight and are working on a retro injection."

"Of course they say that! That's the big 'surprise': the Arch will announce a miracle cure after the Blight has served its purpose."

"Purpose?"

He waved his arms, taking in the hangar. "Look around! The Arch is dumping their undesirables, and humanitarians on Luna and Earth are taking in all their problems."

"Wait . . . Go back to where you created the Blight."

Skvrsky sighed. "I designed the vector. My allele injector nanos."

I nodded. "Automated CRISPR. Precision injection of alleles into chromosomes." His eyes popped. I gave him a smug grin. "Farmers study genetics."

Skvrsky nodded. "My apologies. I assumed . . . If you know my work, you know it was controversial. Everyone feared it might be misused." He lowered his eyes. "They were right. They were *all* right."

"All but the Arch."

He nodded. "They offered me a microgravity lab, funding, and personnel. I was so blinded by my vision. I believed they had the perfect containment mechanism. I needed to insert detectable base pairs at precise points in specific gene sequences. Their suggestion was to work with wheat, which they had in abundance, and to inject genes that would prevent germination."

My jaw dropped. "The Blight." Skvrsy nodded somberly. "And it accidentally leaked?"

He slammed his fist on the desk. "It *intentionally* leaked. I told you: this was deliberate. They wanted to devastate their wheat crop."

"That's crazy!" I said. "Their whole economy depends on wheat."

"Bah. The Blight let them purge most of their itinerant farmers, make them your problem. They've upended the agriculture industry, putting the Earth-Lunar economy into a spiral. And they made secret market investments to take advantage of that.

"And look at the other effects! Since no one understands the Blight, *all* orbital crops are taking a beating. Grain markets are being manipulated. Those exports they certify as clean all go to China. People are hungry across Asia, but not in the Central Kingdom."

"They still have to feed themselves."

"They can," Skvrsky answered. "They have enough stores for their reduced population—a much more homogeneous one, all Chinese immigrants—and enough robot farmers to maintain the crops. Any time they need more food, all they have to do is stop spreading the allele injectors."

"This is crazy..." I said. I looked over at Sung. She was busy punching at her console, but she glanced up at me and frowned. "No one could plan a conspiracy this big and keep it secret."

"Big?" Skvrsky chuckled darkly. "The Arch has a population of millions. They maintain air and water down to the milliliter and segment each individual into a specific societal niche. Big is what they do." He glanced at the hatch. "And they plug leaks. Like they're trying to plug me."

"So you fled."

"At first I played along. When the Blight was revealed, it was obviously my injectors loaded with mitosis inhibitors. They didn't try to hide it. They explained: they would use the Blight to reduce the food supply then promote me as the lead investigator for a cure; and when time was right, I would become a hero for eliminating Skvrsky's Blight. I could retire in luxury."

"You went along with that? Fucker!"

He leaned forward and glared at me. "I could go along or I could have an 'accident.' You don't know what it's like there. Official Truth is not to be questioned, no matter what you remember, what you see. The only way to stay alive is to accept the Truth unquestioningly. Learn to be part of it."

"To be complicit."

"To stay alive! Corpses can't fight back."

I looked quizzically at him. "You're fighting back?"

"I'm here, aren't I?" He took a breath. "I accessed systems they didn't realize I was aware of. There's always an underground, if you know where to look."

I eyed him. "How did you escape?"

He shook his head. "You don't need details. Records were altered so the automated systems wouldn't recognize me. I acquired forged credentials and got on a refugee transport. But... I was followed, I think. Arch authorities scanned the identification chips of every refugee on the transport. That's why I'm begging you to get me out of here!"

I glanced over at Sung, but she shook her head. I answered, "We'll get you out as fast as we can. With no comms and no trams—"

"You think that's a coincidence?"

"What else could it be?"

"Saboteurs! Use your head! You think all those refugees have been properly vetted, and there were no Arch spies among them?"

I wanted to answer confidently, to reassure him that no one would slip through our screening.

But then I remembered Meng, the Chinese pilot, saying that three refugees had boarded at the last minute, without time to vet them. The authorities had checked identities on the transport, yet they hadn't turned up these stragglers? Impossible . . . unless they weren't *supposed to* turn them up.

He had a point. Who might be prowling the Free Cities right now, hacking into communications, spying on operations? Maybe spreading the Blight?

I rose. "All right, I'll get you to the bosses."

At that moment, an eerie squeal echoed from the ventilation shaft, like a machine screaming in pain. That ended in a loud *clank*, then silence. No soft whisper of the air management system in the background. Real *silence*.

Then with a distant *boom*, the lights went out.

"What the hell?" I drew my pistol and backed away from the desk. Skvrsky had made me paranoid, and I didn't want to be an easy target.

The darkness lasted only a second before dim emergency lights came on. I looked to the control console and saw Hyun Sung frantically working. "Sung?"

"Busy!" she said, never taking her eyes off her console and her flashing fingers. "Internal comms are down," she said. "Look around, report back to me. Make it fast."

I turned to Skvrsky. "Doctor, let's get you to cover." The control room was tiny, just the console, a couple of desks, and a lavatory. I grabbed his arm and pulled him to the lavatory hatch. "Lock the hatch, cycle it, and stay put." I opened the hatch—like all Lunar hatches, it had a dedicated power cell precisely for emergencies like this—and pointed to a viewscreen. "If you see anyone but Sung or me, don't acknowledge you're here."

"Understood," Skvrsky said. He stepped in and cycled the hatch.

That left me to do some reconnaissance. I headed toward the exit hatch, asking Sung, "Anything specific?"

She shook her head. "Eddie, it's not good. Videos, motion sensors, comms . . . They're all down. This wasn't accidental, too many simultaneous failures. They probably shut down the air to kill Skvrsky by asphyxiating everyone. But they didn't consider that when the air shuts down, nearly every hatch in the facility becomes a pressure seal. They're as trapped as we are."

"They'll die right along with us."

"They just might be fanatical enough to do that, Eddie. Skvrsky's right, you don't understand the culture. But they may have an escape plan. They had time to prepare. Be ready for surprises."

I nodded. Most of the hangar facilities were subsurface. The control center was on Level I. The refugees were on II.

Somebody had attacked power and air on III. They would be hard to reach—and would have a hard time getting up here.

That assumed there was only one operative. I couldn't know, so I crouched low as I cycled the hatch open.

But not low enough. I felt the round rip through my left bicep before I heard the shot. I cried out in pain and fell backward, trying to roll; but the agonizing fire in my arm wouldn't take weight. I flopped flat on my right side, pistol arm pinned. I needed to get to cover. But I couldn't think, not with the agony . . . and the pressure of my suit's automatic tourniquet constricting. I pushed over onto my back, and the pain in my arm intensified. My eyes got blurry, spots fading in and out. I stared at the hatch and saw it sliding closed.

But not fast enough. A figure stood in it, pistol out. I raised my weapon and fired. The kick knocked me into unconsciousness . . .

Sung leaned over me. "Eddie, can you hear me?" I managed a moan. "Eddie, the tourniquet's holding. I'm pumping in null plasma."

She shouldn't worry about me. "Console . . ."

"Locked up. I've got my AIgents working on it, but there's nothing I can do right now. Besides, you asshole, you were bleeding out."

"Bleed . . . suffocate . . . What's the diff?"

"Bleeding's a hell of a lot faster. Now wake up. The null-P should be hitting you soon."

And it was. My head was clearing. I rose up on my right elbow, but my left arm was useless and numb from the tourniquet. Sung had zipped off my sleeve and was applying a pressure bandage to my bicep, replacing one sopped through with red. "Wow . . . I bled a lot . . ." Then I remembered why. "Did I get him?"

"From that angle? In shock? Hell, no!" Then she smiled. "But you made him retreat, gave me time to draw my piece. I got him."

"Nice work...Who was he?"

"He wore a farmer's coveralls."

I nodded. Even that hurt. "Son of a bitch!"

"Sorry," Sung answered. "Need some painkillers?"

"No. The null-P is doing its job. I want to stay clearheaded so I can get these bastards."

"Eddie, you can't! Your—"

"No choice. Can you reach anybody else?" She shook her head. "I can't run your AIgents, so you have to stay on that. Somebody's gotta stop these fuckers, and I don't see another choice."

She frowned. "Eddie..."

"I don't like it either." I glanced at the lavatory. "But if Skvrsky's right, we're at war, and only the three of us know it. This is bigger than you and me, even bigger than Skvrsky. The bosses have to know. With the patching you did, I'll live, right?" She nodded. "Well, I ain't waiting around. I'm taking the fight to them."

This time as the hatch slid open, I stayed beside the opening, hunched low. I glanced out to see a pool of blood seeping from a corpse. I edged my pistol around the corner and peered through the comp scope on my wrist. There was no one in sight. The man had been strong and fit. The bullet had shattered his lower right ribs. Not immediately fatal. Any compatriot could've saved him, but they hadn't. He was alone.

I checked the scope again before I reached out and tugged on his sleeve.

I swear the shriek I uttered, as the strain aggravated the bicep wound, was manly. Manly or not, I got the corpse inside, swiftly sliding the hatch shut. I switched my scope to X-ray and swept it over the body.

For a farmer, the man had a lot of subcutaneous implants: three comps, a camera, and a magnetometer. Also two ident chips, one in each palm, allowing him a different identity scan for each hand.

From his pockets, I pulled out four knives and two pistols. The man had been loaded for trouble. If Sung hadn't acted fast, we'd all be dead now.

He should've set off every metal detector in the ship. The authorities *had to* know he was on board. And the pilot...But Meng had *told* me about three unidentified refugees on board. If he was part of some conspiracy, he could've kept his mouth shut. Wouldn't that have made more sense?

Skvrsky's story rang true, the accidents were too coincidental, and the hole in my arm was persuasive. I was worried. I was a former miner turned tunnel farmer turned rent-a-cop. I could handle myself in a fight, but I was in over my head.

I turned back to Sung. "Could someone have sabotaged power and air remotely?"

She shook her head, pointing at her console. "The indicators say physical sabotage, not hacking. Somebody had to go down there."

"And it all happened too fast for that man to get back up here. He couldn't have done that *and* shot me."

Sung stared at her screen and said, "No, not even through the construction shafts."

"The shafts? I should've thought of those." The main shaft ran directly from the control center down to the air and power plants; but there was no power to the belt, and I had no functioning left arm. I would have to scale the ladder, which was normally easy in one-sixth gravity. One-armed, in pain, it would be torture.

Sung had managed to zip my sleeve over the pressure bandage (with only a few screams from me). With air recirculation still offline, I wanted a reliable source of oxygen, and that meant my suit. She had over-pressurized the sleeve and sealed it at the shoulder, turning it into a makeshift splint that mostly immobilized my arm.

I jounced down the ladder to the air plant's hatch. Then I activated the display panel and looked out.

Three technicians lay on the floor. Two had been shot in the head. The third looked like she'd taken a double gut shot. There was no one in the immediate vicinity, but I couldn't see the rest of the air plant, nor the power plant next door.

I wasn't going to solve any problems sitting there. I cycled the hatch open and thrust my pistol in to search the angles.

The machines in the adjacent chamber were beyond hope. Rent shards of metal were strewn around. Giant, twisted vanes lay on the floor. Air recirculation was dead. CO_2 would build up, and eventually everyone would get massive headaches before drifting to sleep. Permanently.

But I still believed the assassins would try to escape. One had come hunting Skvrsky in the control center. This one had disappeared. Were there others? I was still thinking about Meng's three . . .

I hurried under a nearby desk. Now my scope could see the hatch to the outer corridor. It was open. The saboteur had left.

I cautiously made my way to the hatch. The control panel had been forced open, and someone had jumpered the lines. The saboteur was somewhere beyond.

I stuck my pistol through the hatch, waved it left, waved it right—and stopped. Almost beyond the curve of the corridor was a lift hatch. A man with his back to me, working on the panel.

I was weak, and I was hurting; and although undeclared, we were in a goddamned war. I wasn't stupid. I sighted in the pistol, let its computer lock onto his center of mass, and squeezed the trigger three times in rapid succession. The man fell. If he wasn't dead, it wasn't for my lack of trying.

I needed rest. I backed against the wall, turned, and scanned with my weapon, activating its motion detector. Unless I stopped it, it would fire upon anything that moved. Then I leaned back, breathing heavily. The suit showed my pulse running high but steady. I was keyed up, but I wasn't going into shock again.

Nothing came around the curve. The man in the corridor never moved. I was, briefly, safe. It was time to get moving.

I cautiously walked out to the body and bent down to inspect it. Besides the same gear as his partner, the corpse carried a toolkit in a pouch, as well as some sort of electronic device with a button and two lights: one blinked steadily, the other flickered.

I pushed the button, and the two lights went solid green. I heard a comms carrier and saw my helmet status lights indicating messages. But that lasted only a moment before the first light went back to flashing green, and the second resumed its flicker. As soon as the flickering resumed, comms traffic stopped again.

I held the button down, but nothing changed: some sort of reset cycle, and then comms cut out.

It would take all day to figure out how the box worked; but it took only seconds to drop it on the floor and kick the shit out of it until it was nothing but splinters.

The comms came back on for good. The first signal I heard was Sung. "Eddie, you got comms back up!"

I sighed. "That's the only good news. Three air techs are dead, and the air plant's useless."

"Damn!" she said. "CO_2 is already climbing. I can release emergency O_2, but we won't have enough air for a hundred for long."

"You have surveillance back online?"

"I can try emergency power, but most internal surveillance is still down."

"Can you cycle through the cameras?"

"Checking..." She paused. "I can route power to one camera at a time. Where should I check?"

I looked at the elevator hatch beside me. The man had been going up. But to where?

"They'll need suits. Check the suit lockers on I."

A few seconds later, Sung shouted, "Yes! One's breaking into the lockers now, getting three suit boxes."

"Three in his team. I've accounted for two. He's the last. I don't suppose we have power to the lifts?"

She paused. "Damn!"

"What?"

"I switched to the power plant. Two techs dead, the system wrecked. The generator was fast work, an explosive."

"Shit! That's not coming back online."

"Nope. Not—Damn! While I was checking the power plant, number three disappeared."

"Follow him!"

"Stop distracting me! There he is! Pushing a cart to V-Lock 3."

"V-Lock 3. Got it." The vertical locks let personnel cycle up into the hangar when it was depressurized.

I pushed the button on the elevator hatch. Again I had to climb. If I thought climbing down was a challenge, up was a nightmare. Each rung I had to lean forward, let go, reach up as fast as I could, and grab the next rung before I tumbled backward. Several times I had to wrap my good arm around a rung so I could "rest." The whole time, my left arm bounced stiffly out like a heavy balloon. Every third or fourth bounce would go wrong, and I would wince from the pain.

It seemed like hours to reach Sub-Level I. My comp said it had been a little over seven minutes, but that wasn't how it felt.

When I reached the top, I cycled the hatch; but my useless left arm wouldn't let me pull myself into the corridor beyond. If the pain made me let go, I would fall two stories. I might not break a bone, but I'd have to start the ascent all over again. Even more injured.

I had to make the leap. If Skvrsky could make the leap *he* did, I could do this. I was a Loonie.

I turned sideways on the rungs, bent my legs, and held on with my good arm. Then I leaped across the gap and through the hatch, tumbling. My flopping arm smacked the hatch frame, and I yelled, but I was through.

V-Lock 3 was visible from the elevator shaft, and vice versa. I had to keep moving. I scrambled awkwardly into a crouch, and I scrabbled around the curve, away from the V-Lock.

No shots rang out. I leaned against the wall and breathed heavily as I stuck my pistol around the corner for a check.

The corridor was empty save for two sealed suit boxes—plus one unsealed and empty. The saboteur was already in the V-Lock.

I chose V-Lock 5 to stay out of sight of 3. The big dome was divided into storage pads. A half dozen transports could park there, a dozen if they were small. Each pad had a complicated gantry and lift system to let the crawler pull in a spacecraft and then roll back as the craft was lifted and berthed.

The hangar was still pressurized. Sound waves would propagate. I clung to the legs of a local hopper as I worked toward the center of the hangar. There was a saboteur in there somewhere—unless he'd already made his way out onto the surface.

I boosted my audio gain, hoping to hear movement; but I hadn't expected two voices arguing in Mandarin. One was Meng. I couldn't place the other.

As Sung had promised, the Arch transport was still on the crawler for refueling. I saw the pilot standing on the gantry near the hatch, looking down toward an unseen voice near the base of the craft. Despite the language barrier, I could clearly tell the second voice was barking commands. He expected to be obeyed.

The pilot, on the other hand, was stubborn. He was resistant, and the commands just smashed upon and flowed around him like a rock.

And he was a great distraction. While the argument preoccupied the saboteur, I maneuvered between the berths and toward the transport.

Suddenly the pilot shouted, "Bader Security, he's coming your way!" I ducked behind a service cabinet as gunfire rang out; but it wasn't aimed at me. I heard a cry from the gantry, followed by a thud as the pilot fell to the metal platform.

The next few minutes were tense but silent: two men carefully positioning to kill each other. I caught a flash of metal once, followed immediately by three shots as I pulled my hand back to safety; and I darted in a new direction, behind the hull of an ore carrier.

Then I looked up at the carrier and remembered Skvrsky's climbing act. Even with my lame arm, I could scale the hull, take myself off the playing field to where I could see what was going on. Easy, right?

It was *torment!* My left arm flopped uselessly, and it was all I could do to keep from banging the hull and drawing attention to myself. But eventually I reached a safe perch ten meters up, where I could look down.

And more importantly, my *pistol* could look down. I turned it to motion sensor mode, trusting that the saboteur and I were the only remaining motion in the hangar.

I didn't even realize when my pistol locked on target. I saw the motion of the man just before I felt the kick of my sidearm and heard the *crack*, followed by the splintering sound of a helmet shattering, and a skull exploding inside it.

Meng leaned back against his hatch, a wrench in his hand. He managed a weak smile. "Bader Security . . . How do you say? 'Took you long enough.'"

"I had to find a first aid kit. Hold still."

There were no diagnostics in his suit. I had to strip him out of it with my good hand to get to the big spreading shoulder wound. I slipped on a portable autodoc, and it fed me readings and instructions.

Meng would live. "Let's get some pressure on that," I said. "It's going to hurt."

"What about . . . bullet . . . ?"

I shook my head. "It was a soft round, meant to fragment. I don't have the skill to get the pieces out. Let's just stop the bleeding and get you some null plasma." I started to work as I continued, "What were you arguing about?"

"Wanted me to launch . . . He would drive crawler to the pad, and we would leave."

"You thought he was crazy, so you refused."

"I thought he was GNCA security, and I told him to fuck himself." My eyes widened, and he grinned through the pain. "We are not blind, Bader Security. We see the preparations. We see through Official Truth. The leaders want war, and us behind it. You can find the *real* truth if you know where to look. They prepare for war, and some of us want nothing to do with it."

"So you didn't know what he was up to, but you still said no."

"He was state security. That was enough. I decided to take a stand." Then his grin widened. "I should make an asylum claim. Will your people accept it? I can throw an Arch transport into the deal."

I grinned back, and then tightened his pressure bandage. "I'll put in a good word for you. But first we need to get help. A hundred people need air and water. And I've got news to deliver."

"Good news?"

I shook my head. "Awful news. The war has begun."

And my balls still itched.

RICOCHET

✪

Blaine L. Pardoe

Lieutenant David "Grumpy" Covington, knew something was up the moment he came into the pilot briefing room aboard the USS *Nimitz*. Since the war had broken out, he had been in and out of the room many times before going on strikes against Chinese-held Taiwan. This time was different. Usually the room was cramped and tense. The tension remained but there was only one other pilot in the room, Lieutenant Walter "Werewolf" Kraaier. Whereas David's call sign stemmed from his scowl, Werewolf's came from his perpetual five o'clock shadow. Glancing over at Werewolf, he saw the man's jaw locked and his muscles tensed.

Commander Holmes stood at the front of the room, gesturing to the seat next to Kraaier. Sweat stained Holmes's armpits far more than usual, a testament to the warmth in the briefing room. Covington slid into the seat, noting the beads of sweat on the brow of the air operations officer standing in front of him.

This isn't just the AC not keeping the room cool—he's nervous. I don't think I've ever seen him like this before.

"Gentlemen," Holmes said slowly. "I'm not going to sugarcoat this. As you are well aware, as of two hours ago, there's been a nuclear detonation over Pearl Harbor. Honolulu's destroyed, and there's nothing left of our naval and air bases there."

Rumors of the attack had spread throughout the ship, and they had been at general quarters ever since. This was the first that he had heard confirmation of the devastation though. The Chinese assault on

Taiwan had been sudden and swift. At the onset of the invasion, they had destroyed Clark Air Force Base in the Philippines in a preemptive strike—as well as Kadena Air Base on Okinawa and three airfields the US used in Japan. A wave of missile strikes had neutralized Big Navy, the forward naval base on Guam. In a matter of a few hours, the ability of the United States to honor its commitments to defend Taiwan had been effectively hamstrung.

Everything in the Pacific seemed to be turning to shit and fast. The North Koreans, no doubt at the prodding of the Chinese, had crossed the DMZ and had seized half of Seoul. As if that wasn't bad enough, the new allies of the Chinese, the Russians, had begun to position troops and transports in the Bering Straits—clearly locking their gaze on Alaska. Not since 1941 had the United States been caught so flatfooted on so many fronts. While America reeled under the sudden and violent shift of power in the region, China had fired missiles, artillery, and rockets into Taiwan, covering their massive assault fleet's invasion.

The invasion had been vicious for two days or so, before the weight of China's numbers overwhelmed the tiny republic. Sabotage by deeply planted Chinese agents further enabled the aggressors. Parts of Taiwan still clung to their freedom, if only by their fingernails.

With the Army preparing for an invasion in Alaska and coping with a North Korean assault, and the Air Force losing so many aircraft and air fields, it had fallen to the Navy to assist the beleaguered nation. Hypersonic missiles had taken out the USS *Gerald Ford* and three cruisers, leaving the *Nimitz* alone as the only carrier within distance of the island. There had been an attack by Chinese jets three days ago, but US naval aviators had shot them down—one by Covington himself in his first real dogfight. Word was the Navy had been assembling a task force at Pearl—but now Pearl and that task force were gone in a nuclear strike . . .

. . . a nuclear strike!

No one had expected China to use nukes in its opening salvo. In a cold calculating way, it made sense. Covington's years at the Academy had taught him that to hold strategic initiative, bold strikes to disable the enemy were almost textbook. The use of nuclear weapons was unprecedented though.

Just like the Japanese in 1941, the Chinese have awakened a slumbering giant. Hopefully we can set aside our differences and unite against this threat.

In the meantime, defiant Taiwan fought to hold onto the tiny pockets of the island still under its control. China was paying dearly for every meter of ground taken.

Commander Holmes continued. "Your F-18s normally aren't equipped for a nuclear exchange. Covington, you have experience piloting FB-111s. We've rigged the nuclear arming switch from those aircraft to your F-18 airframe. We've adjusted the weapons mount as well and have armed you with a B61 nuclear weapon. Kraaier, your mission will be to ensure Covington gets to his target unmolested. Your designation for this operation is Sledgehammer Strike." He paused for a moment. "Gentlemen, you two are going to be delivering the first nuclear attack by the United States since Nagasaki. By order of the Commander in Chief, you will avenge what they did to us at Pearl."

His words were far from arrogant—they were solemn.

For the next thirty minutes, Holmes went over the strike plans. Covington was numb, drinking in the details but at times feeling as if he were having an out-of-body experience. Their target was Fuzhou just off the coast. Covington would deliver the nuclear payload while Kraaier would cover him. After a coordinated attack on Fuzhou Airbase with cruise missiles and ECM and armed drones and decoys to neutralize and confuse Chinese air defenses and interceptors, Covington and Kraaier would go in together, coming in low, then break north some twenty miles off the coast and head for their target. A low-altitude airburst with Wuta Tower as the designated target, would obliterate the city. On paper, it was simple enough, but Covington doubted the Chinese would allow it to be a cake walk. Commander Holmes clearly felt the same way. "They have to be expecting us to retaliate after Pearl. You should anticipate an aggressive air defense, even after we shape the battlefield. Coming in low will help, but to deliver your payload, you're going to need to climb to avoid any surviving SAMs and enemy fighters." The words were not just cautionary, they spoke for the need to be fast and agile.

When they were dismissed, Kraaier came over to him. "This is some serious end-of-the-world shit."

"It's a hell of a responsibility," Covington responded, running his hand back through his cropped blonde hair, already slick with sweat.

"Ya think? You always were the master of understatement," Werewolf replied, shaking his head as he marched out of the room.

Covington's takeoff from the carrier was almost routine, though he could feel some handling changes with his F/A-18F Super Hornet's slightly sluggish tanks to the unusual payload slung under him. Covington formed up on Werewolf's right with Werewolf slightly in the lead. The sky was bright blue, no hint of clouds except on the far western horizon.

They hung low, below one thousand feet. As he glanced out of the side of his cramped cockpit, Covington saw the ocean was almost a blur at that altitude—only the occasional white cap was visible. Covington twisted his head to crack his neck. It was then that he realized just how tense his muscles were.

Of course I'm tense. I've got a 340 kiloton nuke under me.

He tried not to think about the mission's implications. Millions of people were going to die if they were successful with their strike. Many would die instantly, but those who lingered would suffer far more from radiation sickness. The only thing that kept his focus was the knowledge that the Chinese had started this—*they dropped a nuke on Pearl Harbor. How many innocent people died in that blast?* How many of his fellow Academy graduates had perished in that explosion? *They upped the ante and deserve what they are going to get.*

Toggling his radio channel, he spoke. "Comms check Werewolf."

"I read you five-by-five, Grumpy."

Covington could hear the tension in his wingman's voice.

"Same here," he replied. "Stay sharp. We're ten minutes out from Waypoint Alpha. They won't pick us up for a while still—if at all. And even if they do, it'll take a while for them to scramble intercepts."

"Roger that."

For ten minutes neither man said anything. Covington thought about his family back home in Valparaiso. His dad was a Navy man. He would be proud of this mission, especially in retribution for the loss of Pearl.

His mother, however, would feel very differently. She would quote the Bible to him, warning him against mass slaughter. In his mind he could hear her words, *"Make sure that nobody pays back wrong for wrong, but always strive to do what is good for each other and for everyone else." Mom always believed the world to be a better place than it really was.*

A squelching sound came into his ears. "CVAN-68 is declaring an emergency. Repeat—CVAN-68 is declaring an emergency! Sledgehammer Strike leader, respond on tactical three."

The Nimitz! Hearing their code name made him instantly start to sweat. Covington switched to the air boss's channel. "This is Sledgehammer Strike group, Grumpy calling—go CVAN-68."

"This is Zeus," the air boss, Commander Sheryl Hart, replied. "Grumpy, be advised, we have been hit by missiles . . . most likely hypersonics. We are unable to recover aircraft. The task force is turning about. Aircraft landing will be impossible. You will need to intercept with us and eject near the ships for recovery." Beyond her voice, he could hear panic, warning alarms, and terror.

"Roger," Covington said. It had to be bad if the ship was unable to recover aircraft.

"Be advised we are transferring air control to the *Spruance*."

He gulped his breath at those words.

They are abandoning ship!

Suddenly, Werewolf's voice cut in. "What in the hell is that?"

Several miles out, there was a white light. A nuclear burst would have blinded him, but this seemed very different. It was slow like a long wall of light. It rushed right at them.

"Werewolf, emergency climb!" he barked, pulling back on his joystick and throttling the engines. *Maybe we can clear it.*

"Roger, Grumpy," came back the strained voice of his wingman.

The g-forces pushing him back and down were impossible to ignore as the F-18 angled skyward. He watched his rate of climb, his airspeed, mentally calculating the g's he was feeling as well as assessing the performance of the fighter. A darting glance showed the wall of light rising as it got closer.

Shit! We aren't going to beat it.

"Bank hard and around, maybe we can outrun it," he said, angling hard to starboard.

Werewolf's voice came back—filled with stunned wonder. "Who or what is that?" His wingman screamed—not in terror, but in agony.

Everything went bright white, and Covington's consciousness disappeared...

When Covington jerked awake, he floated in an unending white void. His aircraft was gone, but he could still feel the contour of his ejection seat under his butt. The air was cool, he could feel it on his cheeks. There was no source to the bright whiteness, yet it was everywhere. There was no smell, it was as if he were in a white void.

I'm dead... that's it!

Looking down, his body was still in his flight gear. He removed his mask, and the air felt fresh in his lungs.

I'm breathing, maybe I'm not dead. What in the hell was that?

His mind tried to process what he assumed he had collided with.

Was it a tidal wave from a nuclear blast?

It was impossible to know for sure. All he could tell was that his F-18 was no longer around him.

Then he saw it, a figure. It was dark in the distance, a bit greenish. Starting as a tiny dot, it moved closer to him in the whiteness. Its arms were extended, like a scarecrow—or perhaps Jesus on the cross, though he could not see anything behind the arms.

It was a flight suit, sans the helmet. Rivulets of blood soaked the dull green flight suit maroon. As it grew and got closer, he made it out. The face was that of his wingman, but was horribly disfigured. It looked as if someone had removed his skin and was wearing it, floating in the void closer to him. It drifted close enough that he could smell the stench of rotting flesh as if it were a breath coming from the ghostlike apparition wearing the skin of his wingman. The arms moved down, but not *humanlike*—more like a marionette.

Panic set in. A part of him wanted to move, but couldn't. Paralysis gripped him and fought every muscle he tried to flex. As the bloody visage of Walter Kraaier got closer, he could see that the skin sagged in the cheeks. There was something behind it, something glowing blue. Through the eye holes of Kraaier's flesh, he saw some kind of shimmering blue energy.

It paused in front of him, its arms moving awkwardly down to its side as the bright blue eyes glared at him. "What are you?" he managed.

"I am Huapigui," a voice said in a low growl through the lifeless lips of his wingman.

"What have you done to my wingman?"

"I am borrowing his skin to provide me a form you would be familiar with," the floating image said.

"You killed him?" A cocktail of shock, anger, rage, and fear overwhelmed him all at once.

"His destiny was to die before finishing his mission. You were to be successful. A decision had to be made. He has already gone onto the afterlife. You, however, still possess a chance."

A chance? A chance to what?

"Where is this?"

"You are at the end of time, the only safe place for us to speak."

"I don't understand."

"It is my role to protect my people. If I had not interceded, you would have dropped your infernal weapon. It would set into motion a chain of events that would be unstoppable, even for me. My people would respond with brute force, as would yours and others. The air would burn and millions of souls would perish. I seek to avert that from happening."

Covington didn't trust the flesh-wearing apparition, but it was his only link to reality. "So you prevented me from dropping my bomb."

"No, I pulled you out of time. I lack the power to interfere more than I already have. The future still may unfold, but I seek to prevent it."

"How?"

"I will send you back before all of this. If you do not make this flight, do not ignite the world, then we are all saved."

"Someone else will fly the mission if I don't. You're just prolonging the inevitable."

"That may or may not be the case. I only see your role in these matters David Covington. Killing you would be easy, but I see a role for you in this game being played. Sending you back, is something I can do ... something I am compelled to do."

"How can you do that?" He felt his heart pounding in his ears.

"I am divine. My people have been under my protection for centuries." There was a hint of pride in the specter's voice.

This must be some kind of Chinese ghost. What if this is all a ruse? How can I trust it—it's wearing Werewolf's skin?

"I don't believe you," he finally managed to spit out.

"I do not require your belief, only your willingness to attempt to avert what your bombing will set in motion. I can tell you are not a heartless murderer. There is guilt in you, a fear of what you have been asked to do. I ask only for your permission to try and save the world." The meat suit continued to drip thick drizzles of coagulating blood onto Kraaier's flight gear as it drifted in front of him.

Huapigui was right about him not wanting to complete the attack. Covington didn't know how he'd cope with the guilt of causing millions of deaths. It was a nagging silent thought that had torn into him since getting his strike orders.

"How do you know that my going back will change anything?"

"How can it not?" the skin-wearing spirit replied.

What are my options? It could keep me here forever for all I know. Maybe I can change the game somehow. For long minutes he said nothing as he wrestled with his thoughts.

"What say you, David Covington?" Huapigui asked.

He nodded quickly. "This is insane. But so is being here. You're probably nothing more than some fragment of a nightmare in my head. I may already be dead—maybe this is my purgatory. If it will get me out of here, then I will do it."

His wingman's grizzly skin face cracked a disturbing smile. "So shall it be!"

A wave of vertigo washed over him, complete with a ripple of heat and a dizziness that made him swallow the bile in his mouth. Covington's cockpit suddenly was around him, an alarm blaring in his ear. Struggling to focus, he saw a familiar sight in the distance—the *Nimitz*!

". . . repeat, you are violating restricted air space. Divert immediately or you will be fired upon," the terse voice of air-boss Commander Hart commanded.

This is impossible . . . the Nimitz *was abandoned!*

"Negative Zeus, this is Grumpy." His eyes darted to the warning lights, and he saw he was low on fuel.

How is this possible? That ghost somehow put me here. And if that's the Nimitz, *then I have gone back in time.*

"I don't know who you are, but if you don't divert away from us, we will shoot you down. This is our last warning." Commander Hart's words offered little solace to his confusion.

He juked the joystick over, banking away from his flight path toward the *Nimitz*.

"Zeus, be advised, I am low on fuel." His eyes drifted down, and he saw that the B61 was still on the belly of his F-18. "I am also carrying nuclear ordinance."

While there was no chance of the bomb detonating—it had not been armed yet—the loss of such a weapon was not something the Navy was likely to support.

For a few seconds, there was no response. He continued to put distance away from the task force surrounding the carrier, watching the remaining fuel dwindle even further. A soft landing in a jet on the churning ocean was not likely survivable, and he wanted to live. *Best to punch out now.* His left hand drifted down to the ejection ring between his legs.

With a stern pull, the canopy blew off, and a wall of air slapped his face as the ejection seat cleared the aircraft. The jerking of the chute was hard, the straps cutting into his crotch as he watched his jet angle over and splash into the ocean.

After long hours of interrogation, all Lieutenant Covington had left was frustration and exhaustion. "I told you, I don't know how this Huapigui did it—but it somehow sent me back in time." Despite two bottles of water, his mouth was parched. Licking his dried lips, he could still taste the sea salt.

"We heard you the first dozen times," the *Nimitz*'s intelligence officer said. "That doesn't make it any more believable. So, Mr. Manchurian Candidate, why don't you tell us who you really are?"

The reference was lost on him. He tipped his head back and rolled his sleep-deprived eyes. He had been questioned for hours after being rescued from the East China Sea. He had been allowed to dry off, but his skin now had grit from the sea salt in his joints. "You saw my aircraft, you've checked my fingerprints—I am Lieutenant David Covington, serial number N567222."

The ship's grim-faced XO shook his head from across the table. "Sorry but we already have one. He's in the next room until we sort this out."

It was a strange feeling, knowing that his past self was still on the ship—in the next room. They had not told him much other than the date and time. He was aboard the *Nimitz* before it was attacked, a full eighteen hours before Pearl Harbor was blasted by a Chinese nuke. Despite that, no one was willing to accept what he had to say. The lack of food and sleep was gnawing at the edges of his nerves, as it was intended to do.

"Look," he said in exasperation. "I don't know how I came back, but I can tell you what is going to happen. The Chinese will attack Pearl Harbor in a few hours, and you're going to send me and Lieutenant Kraaier to drop nukes on the Chinese coast. You've got to warn the people at the base and Honolulu that they are targets. Get the fleet out of the harbor before it's too late."

The intelligence officer rubbed his hand back through his short-cropped hair. "Is that what your handlers want, us to move the fleet out of the protection of Pearl? Why? Do you have subs out there waiting to sink them?"

"I don't have any handlers," Covington fired back. "I'm a member of VFA-22 damn it! If you don't listen to me, it will lead to nuclear war. Millions are going to die, including a lot of people on this ship." He had relayed the story of the *Nimitz* sinking, which had gone over like a lead balloon with the men interrogating him.

"Look," the ship's XO said coolly. "Even if we did believe you, the Navy won't act on the word of someone who claims he has magically been sent back in time by some Chinese ghost. Topping that off, *we* don't believe you."

"You have to. If you send me on that mission, the war will escalate," he pleaded. He knew that the executive officer was probably right.

"That isn't your concern," the XO assured him. Before he could speak, the XO nodded to the intelligence officer, and they left the room.

Long minutes passed as he was left with the room's dull silence and his own dark thoughts. He could feel the cameras there, watching him. They were outside, no doubt coming up with some strategy to break him.

I'm already broken—I've told them everything. They just refuse to believe it.

Maybe this was what Huapigui wanted, his frustration and despair. Perhaps this was all some sort of twisted prank—an attempt to drive him insane. He knew nothing about the skin-wearing apparition, only that it had somehow sent him back in time.

It hasn't helped at all! They won't even warn Pearl that they will die. I haven't prevented anything.

Exhaustion swept over him as he waited. David crossed his arms on the cold metal table, using them as a pillow. He lowered his head down and leaned forward. Every joint on him ached, either from the ejection or exhaustion. Sleep came fast and hard despite his desire to remain awake.

The klaxon sounded, jarring him awake. "General quarters, all hands, general quarters!" Sitting up, he realized he did not know how much time had passed. Shuffling through the jumble of his memoires from the events that had transpired, a sinking feeling hit his stomach. *It's Pearl . . . it has to be.* The warning blared over the speakers again every five minutes for nearly an hour. Then he saw something unexpected as the door opened.

Stepping into the room was himself—David Covington—the version from this timeline. It was an eerie feeling, seeing himself standing before him. The other-David shut the door and seemed to study him with suspicion, a bit of awe, and a dose of something else—wonder.

"It's happened, hasn't it?" he asked his mirror image.

The other-David nodded, crossing his arms. "Word is Pearl just got nuked. No one knows how bad it is yet."

"I do." *They refused to listen to me!* Shaking his head he held back the tears of frustration. "It could have been averted."

"How did you know?"

"I'm you," he said glaring at the other-David. "I was sent back to try and change things. It looks like I failed."

"How can I be sure you are really me?"

It was a valid question. David thought for a moment. "Back in third grade. The handlebars of your bike scraped the paint on Dad's Pontiac, the blue one. You blamed Jimmy Bishop up the street for it."

The words made the other-David step forward to him. "I never told anyone about that."

"I know."

"So what happens next?"

"You and Werewolf get the assignment to bomb the coast with nukes. They are probably outfitting your plane on the hangar deck right now."

The words seemed to make the other David stagger for a moment—a gut punch only he could understand. "You'll take off, and the *Nimitz* will be hit, and I assume, sunk. This ghost-thing will intercept you and Werewolf and send you back in time. You'll become me."

"This can't happen, not this way," his counterpart said. "If you are telling the truth, I—we can't let this happen."

"It's like a bullet that's already been fired," he said grimly, with an icy resolve. "Everything is set in motion all over again."

"I'm not going to spend eternity reliving this," the other-David resolved. "If we can't prevent it, maybe we can deflect that bullet. We can change what happens. We're the only ones who can change history."

"How?"

His other-self pulled out his survival knife. The two men looked at each other and grimly nodded in unison.

The executive officer of the *Nimitz* stood over the comingled gore of the room, looking down at the dead men sprawled on the floor. He was angry and frustrated. This day had not gone at all as he had envisioned. "I want that guard brought up on charges. He never should have let him in here, let alone with a weapon."

The intel officer nodded. "Already done. Dereliction of duty. Jesus . . . I never expected this to happen. I mean this was strange enough as it was—how in the hell are we going to report this? They will lock us up as madmen."

"I've briefed the captain. He's ordered us to proceed with the strike. Covington's being replaced with Howler. He lacks experience with the arming system, but the air boss is going to walk him through it."

"Those bastards have to pay for what they did to Pearl."

"They will," he said. Suddenly the ship rocked and throbbed deeply, and the lights flickered off. A heartbeat later, another explosion tore through the ship, and in a flash, the two men died in a torrent of fire.

Shu gui, a spirit of water, rose through the whiteness of the void in front of the Huapigui. Her body was flowing, rippling with the purest of water, undulating and calming. They rarely spoke.

No doubt she will have harsh words for me.

Shu gui's shimmery watery form hovered before him. "I assume you are proud of yourself."

"After all of these centuries, I'm entitled to some fun." *Especially at the expense of our enemies.*

"Millions will still die. What have you averted?"

"Millions of *our* people dying."

"There were other ways, Huapigui. You simply could have killed the two Americans. Sending one back in time was not necessary."

"But it was," he insisted. He stirred under the American aviator's dead skin he wore as his own. "Simple killing is easy. Making your enemies kill themselves in your name, that is something that requires finesse. Even you must admit, it was a masterstroke—a piece of art."

"The Americans will strike back, you have seen it."

"Not today," he reminded her. "And by the time they do, our submarines will have set their coast ablaze."

"All you have prolonged is the inevitable."

"What I have done is what is best for our people," he said with a grisly resolve.

"Perhaps. It is reckless to treat time as a child's toy. You should not enjoy your interference so much."

The dead man's mouth grinned. "What fun is power if you do not savor its use, Shu gui?"

THE GREYHOUND'S GAMBIT

✪

Kevin Andrew Murphy

Saturday, June 14, 1997: Aberdeen, Scotland

The White Greyhound of Richmond loved to run, for King and Country, or as there had been again for almost half a century now, for Queen. It was her birthday today, Elizabeth II's seventy-first—the official one, at least, since her actual birthday had been back on the twenty-first of April—and as one of the Queen's Beasts, he had been running and fighting for her ever since her Ascension to Queen in 1952, a year before her Coronation. So had the other Beasts of her House—the Lion of England, the Unicorn of Scotland, the Red Dragon of Wales, the Yale of Beaufort, the White Lion of Mortimer, the White Horse of Hanover, the Black Bull of Clarence, the Falcon of the Plantagenets, and the Griffin of Edward III—but of the Ten Beasts, the White Greyhound was almost the fiercest and always the fastest.

Elizabeth I had had greyhounds, as had Henry VIII before her, and all the White Greyhound's Henrys before that. Even Victoria and Albert—of the Hanoverians descended from the White Horse's first George, who the White Horse had brought over to replenish the English royal line after Anne had been so thoughtless as to produce only one heir (William, who died of smallpox when he was eleven) and then died herself—had had greyhounds, bitches both, Albert's beloved black parti-color Eos and Victoria's white greyhound Swan, who was one of the White Greyhound of Richmond's distant granddaughters. The White Greyhound had bred them both on and

85

off while helping Victoria forge an empire that spanned the globe, and while the empire building had worked, the breeding had sadly failed to produce a true faerie heir. But this was always the trouble with faeries and mortals. It did not help that the British Empire was now falling apart as well.

The White Greyhound took it as a small personal affront that Elizabeth II favored corgis—those stubby-legged little freaks—rather than the royal greyhounds who had been pets of the Crown since King Canute's day. But, of course, Elizabeth II being busy with her corgis gave the White Greyhound freedom to race around as he willed, doing what was best for the Crown, as decided by himself and the other nine in the Nobility of Beasts. Just so was it today, a desperate secret errand in need of his speed, like Alice in the Red Queen's race, where you had to run as fast as you could to stay in one place, and you had to run twice as fast as that to get anywhere.

Fortunately, the White Greyhound was up to the task. A few moments ago, he had been in London, parading with the other Nine Beasts in the Trooping of the Colours for the Queen's birthday celebration, all disguised in one way or another by means of faerie glamour, for, as the old rime went:

> *Glamour*
> *Could make a lady seem a knight,*
> *A nutshell seem a gilded barge,*
> *A shieling seem a palace large,*
> *A youth seem age and age seem youth,*
> *But all is lie and naught is truth*

Well, almost all disguised with faerie glamour. The White Horse of Hanover had insinuated himself as yet another white parade stallion, hiding in plain sight, a horse-sized and horse-shaped thimble in a game of *Hide the Thimble*. He had taken the role of Elizabeth's white stallion Columbus before and Sir Winston Churchill's white stallion Colonist before that, but the White Greyhound knew that the White Horse's true name was *Hengest,* having won it from him after beating him in a race back during the reign of George III.

So, when one of London's ubiquitous pigeons fluttered down to the Queen's open carriage and cooed something in the perpetually perked ear of one of the Queen's myriad corgis, none recognized that the pigeon was in fact a bird of prey and a faerie one at that, and not just any faerie raptor, but the Falcon of the Plantagenets. Nor did anyone notice that the corgi was in fact the White Greyhound of Richmond, tall and lanky beglamoured as short and stubby as the little beast barked, leapt from the carriage, and raced off as fast as his little legs could carry him, outracing the white stallion in front with an insouciant yap and blurring as he disappeared into the throng of royal admirers, glamour shifting as he went.

The White Greyhound, like the White Queen in *Through the Looking Glass*, was faster than a bandersnatch, which was very fast indeed. He could race to put a girdle around the globe, like Puck in *A Midsummer Night's Dream*, for Robin Goodfellow was his father, having taken the shape of a hound as that merry sprite was sometimes known to do and, in that form, found a pretty white greyhound bitch, a princess of her breed, descended in an unbroken line from the royal greyhounds of King Canute, in the kennels of Edward III, who in 1343 was King of England and trying to be King of France too.

Puck had his way with her as hounds do, which incidentally was six years into what would come to be called the Hundred Years' War, so folk had cause to be distracted. Nine weeks later, in 1344, and seven years in, she whelped a dozen pups. The next month, which was March, on the sixth, which was a Sunday, Edward asked his third son, John of Gaunt, who had been granted the Honour of Richmond and made its earl at his birth, what of all of Edward's kingly possessions the young prince would like best as a present for this, his fourth birthday.

John considered solemnly then asked for one particular greyhound puppy he had seen in the white bitch's litter in the royal kennel when he got to watch the birth—the seventh born, the little white boy with the bright eyes. This was considered an extremely modest request as kingly boons go but was in fact the most valuable of all of Edward's many possessions, lands, and titles put together—all except for a falcon named Finist that the King had in his mews, which he had once liked to hunt with, but had now mostly forgotten about because of the busy business of being a king and the war and all that.

But Finist the falcon had not forgotten about Edward III.

John named his new puppy *Mathe*, which meant *Gift of God*. All the courtiers agreed that this was a very clever and diplomatic thing for a four-year-old to say, given that he had been given the pup as gift by his papa, the King. It could have also been that John had a childish lisp, but they were too diplomatic to point this out, especially given the way the Castilian ambassador at court lisped Spanish and the extra trouble of the second war in Castile, which John's birthday celebration had been meant to be a pleasant distraction from.

The Siege of Algeciras had been going on for two years now, bloody and brutal as wars were, then made even bloodier and more brutal with the addition of gunpowder from the East, with no obvious end in sight, part of the Reconquista to retake Spain for Christendom in general and Algeciras for the Kingdom of Castile in specific. But then a courtier—also, oddly enough, named Finist—arrived from Spain, so swiftly that some wags jested he must have flown rather than journeyed by ship and horse, bringing news that the forces of Abu al-Hasan Ali ibn Othman, the Marinid Sultan of Morocco, had been dealt a devastating blow and that the battle for Algeciras was almost won.

Finist, sharp-eyed as a falcon, then took note of the pup that John of Gaunt had chosen as his birthday gift and, seated above the salt as Finist was—the salt here being a gilded silver saltcellar in the shape of a boat, called a *nef* in the French fashion, which was a necessary ostentation for any royal table in the Middle Ages—and at the King's right hand as well, given the import and honor of the news, he suggested that such a beast as the White Greyhound might be meet as a supporter for John's heraldic arms as the Earl of Richmond, much as Edward III had the Falcon of the Plantagenets as one of his Royal Beasts and his personal Griffin as another. A second courtier—strangely enough named Griffin, and a great favorite of the King—seconded this advice, so Edward III agreed and told his heralds to make it so.

Mathe did not know any of this yet, nor did he know he was a true faerie hound, the only one in the litter, not at first. All he knew was that he was very clever and very fast, and he loved his little boy with all his heart, placing his paws on his shoulders and licking his face so John would know too.

John grew up and Mathe did too, listening to the tales of the bards and jongleurs who entertained the court, and through them learning the ways of faeries and faerie wars. The Marinid Sultan was tricky, for unlike the forces of Christendom, the Muslims eschewed having any beasts, fabulous or otherwise, on their heraldry, for such was heresy to their religion, despite their prophet, Muhammed—peace be upon him!—flitting about on a maiden-headed beast called the Buraq who had the body of a donkey and the wings and tail of a peacock and was clearly a faerie, though of course the Muslims called their faeries peris when they did not call them djinn. As for their heraldry, they favored the fanciful floral forms that foreigners called arabesques, and so their courtly faeries were gathered from the flowers, usually desert roses and the like.

But the Marinid Sultan and his flowery fées were not the problem. The true threat lay far off in distant Cathay, which was what China was called in those days, and the court of Toghon Temür, Emperor of the Yuan Dynasty, and his second empress Bayan Khutugh, and their respective faerie sponsors, the Dragon Emperor and the Phoenix Empress, who had been the faerie powers behind the mortal throne since Cathay's dynasties began. Moreover, aside from the Dragon Emperor and his Nine Sons, who were fabulous beasts spawned from his dalliances with the Black Tortoise of the North and other notable Cathayan faerie beasts, and his crab soldiers and lobster generals, too numerous to count, there were the other eleven Beasts of the Chinese zodiac to contend with, about whom there were many scurrilous stories that had made it over the Silk Road, notable among which was the time the Dragon Emperor tricked the Rooster into lending him his beautiful horns—which he never gave back—but most important of which was how they organized their order and precedence, running a race to go meet the Buddha. Mathe, the White Greyhound of Richmond, could respect this, but not the fact that the Dog of the Cathayan faeries was a ridiculous little Pekinese, so had come in second to last in the race, only followed by the Pig, or that the Ox would have come in first except that the Rat, at the last second, had jumped on the Ox's nose and won by a whisker.

The minstrel bringing this faraway tale of exotic Cathay also said that this is why the Cat hated the Rat, for the Rat straight up lied about the day of the race, and the Cat missed it, leading to the Cat not getting a place in the zodiac at all, and with it losing a chance of dominion over a twelfth of the mortals in Cathay, for that was how the heavens were arranged in the East.

The enmity between the Cat and the Rat of Cathay sounded legendary, even worse than the French faerie tales about Reynard the Fox and Chanticleer the Rooster, notable faerie beasts both.

But the Rat was still the problem, for while faeries did not breed easily, rats bred frequently, and, moreover, rats, faerie, and mortal alike, carried the Black Death. Trade ships brought rats who ran into European towns and once there, the faerie rats took the form of crook-backed crones with ragged brooms, mothers with black books, or maidens beautiful as the faeries they were, who danced about, waving red silk handkerchiefs which the Dragon Emperor had infused with the Plague brewed up with the same Taoist alchemy he had used to make the gunpowder that had proved so deadly in Algeciras.

The Black Death swept over Europe, killing half the French but only a third of the English due to Mathe's diligence, the White Greyhound of Richmond able to smell a rat leagues away, rushing off in the blink of an eye with faerie speed, seizing one faerie maiden or another by the neck, and shaking her till she turned back into the faerie rat she was, as he snapped her neck. He then pissed on the ensorcelled silk handkerchiefs, ending their spell, and rushed back to John's side, laying the dead rat at his Prince's feet. John praised Mathe for killing the rat, telling him he was a "good boy!" unknowing that Mathe had run as far north as Scotland or south as Wales to fell a faerie rat, the source of the Plague.

Fifteen years later, at John's wedding to his cousin, Blanche of Lancaster, the courtier Finist—who like many courtiers only appeared for momentous occasions such as weddings, funerals, significant birthdays, and wars—offered to take Mathe for a walk in the royal gardens. Mathe perked up his ears at this excitedly, for like most hounds he knew the word *walk*, and not just in English and French but Spanish too, as John and his courtiers had discovered.

Regardless, Finist was allowed to take Mathe for a walk in the gardens, and while so doing, Finist told Mathe that he was quite aware that Mathe understood human speech, and not just certain words either, like some clever dogs, but all of it, for Finist knew that Mathe was a faerie hound, and not just any faerie hound, but the son of Puck, which was quite the pedigree, at least for England. He then commended him for his efforts to deal with the Plague Maidens, who were faerie rats in service of the Dragon Emperor of Cathay and wished he could have had his aid in France. Finist then revealed that he was also a faerie beast and a French one at that, by the simple expedient of shifting his form from Finist the courtier to Finist the falcon, who was one and the same as the Falcon of the Plantagenets, child of the faerie princess Melusine, mother of the Merovingian Dynasty and also a dragoness on Saturdays. Speaking then with such enunciation and elocution as to put all birds save faerie ravens and parrots to shame, in exquisitely inflected medieval French, the Falcon of the Plantagenets told Mathe in no uncertain terms that while Edward III's Griffin might be lax about such matters, the Falcon outranked him, and it was high time for Mathe to not just speak human speech but take human form, for fifteen was very old for a greyhound, even if the White Greyhound did not show any grey, and people were beginning to talk.

So Mathe had, taking the seeming of an enormously tall but equally narrow youth with a remarkably long nose, deep chest, and blond hair so pale it was almost white, very much like the form he wore now, no longer a stubby-legged corgi escaped into the crowd at Elizabeth II's seventy-first birthday parade in London, but a man, and a lanky one at that, jogging down the coast of Aberdeen, from the River Don toward the River Dee, tracing one of the old paths England was famous for and warming up for a proper run. London to Aberdeen in the blink of an eye had been a mere sprint, a necessary warm-up before the race.

Of course, today he had used his faerie glamour to shift his seeming to appear garbed in white shorts, shirt, and trainers unremarkable for a jogger in Scotland in June of 1997, rather than the pageboy's livery he had conjured in 1359 to take the role of Mathe, the new kennel boy, who somehow was never seen at the same time as Mathe, the White Greyhound of Richmond. Then two years later, when John was distracted by the death of his father-in-law, the Duke of Lancaster, and being made Earl of Lancaster himself, Mathe informed John that his beloved greyhound Mathe had perished at the astonishing age of seventeen, but he should fear not, for there was another white greyhound in the kennels, one of Mathe's sons, who was almost a twin for his beloved companion.

John had cried for the death of his old friend but rejoiced to have another hound so like him he seemed to be Mathe restored, no longer aged and limping as Mathe had feigned for the past two years with faerie glamour and ordinary acting. Mathe rejoiced being able to give up the ruse and accompanied John throughout his life and military campaigns, first to France, where they faced Philip the Bold of Burgundy, who was aided by his own faerie beast, the Red Lion of Burgundy, as well as the Black Lion of Flanders who protected Philip's new wife Margaret. But on John's side was the Lion of England, who was gold like natural lions, not that Mathe saw him much then.

Mathe dealt more with the Griffin of Edward III, who as near as he could tell was the chick or cub of the Lion of England and the Falcon of the Plantagenets. Mathe had thought that Finist was male, but then again, with faeries it was often hard to tell, and doubly so with birds. The Griffin might also have been the child of one of the various faerie eagles flapping about, patron of this royal house or the other, and the Black Lion of Flanders, for Ghent was in Flanders, and back then, Ghent was Gaunt, where John was born, and Finist was just the Griffin's foster father. Mother? In any case, the Lion of England and Edward III's Griffin were more concerned with guarding John's older brother, Edward, the Black Prince, so Mathe did not care. Mathe's first loyalty was to John.

But loyalties change and families were odd, especially with royalty, and John was too busy with wars and trying to become King of Castile—and so far as Mathe was concerned, the less said about the Gold Dragon of Castile and the Peacock of Navarre the better. The Dragon would simply not shut up about this ruby which his favorite king, Don Pedro the Cruel, had murdered the Sultan Muhammad for, then paid Edward the Black Prince with to help him not, in turn, be murdered by his half-brother, Enrique. Enrique succeeded in murdering Pedro two years later anyway. As for the Peacock, he was the most disagreeably proud screechy boastful bird Mathe had ever met, even for a faerie and a Spanish one at that. Indeed, Mathe suspected the Peacock of Navarre was the father of the Buraq, sired on some faerie donkey in Arabia as part of a dalliance a thousand years before when the Peacock had moved from India. But that was before Mathe's time and mere supposition.

As for John, the next time Mathe thought it prudent to reintroduce himself as a new greyhound, he found himself given as a present, not to John's nine-year-old son Henry Bolingbroke, whom he loved and had looked after since Henry was a baby, but to John's nephew Richard who was the same age, in 1376, to console him for the death of his papa, Edward, the Black Prince, after he was so rude as to die of dysentery.

Mathe liked Richard well enough, and even better when he became King as Richard II the next year after Edward III died. Richard got to wear the Black Prince's blood ruby on his crown, where it looked very nice, and it would have been a lovely coronation except Edward's Griffin of uncertain parentage screeched loudly enough to rival the insufferable Peacock, even taking his natural form as a fantastic beast, with the body, haunches, and tail of a golden lion and the wings, beaked head, and taloned forelegs of a golden falcon or eagle—which should really properly have been hind legs—and two pointy ears like a startled greyhound might have, though Mathe knew for certain he was not the Griffin's father. The Griffin also had a little tufted goatee, both in his Griffin and human seeming—suspiciously identical to the one sported by the Unicorn of Scotland—and he flapped and screeched around Sheen Palace to the wonderment and horror of all the mortals who were used to seeing fabulous beasts painted on shields and embroidered on banners, not flying around in real life and screeching their grief at the death of the King. But it was the Middle Ages, well before the invention of photography, and people were slightly more used to miraculous signs and portents.

The White Greyhound of Richmond, both as Mathe the kennel master and as Mathe, the eavesdropping and occasionally talking greyhound, did everything in his power to help Richard II, especially with the Peasants' Revolt and its revolting peasants in 1381. But some ten years on, Mathe got to see Henry again, now a grown man. It was too much. Mathe threw himself on him and licked his face just like he had with Richard.

Richard II bewailed this change of affections but accepted it, at least on the surface. But when he not only banished Henry but tried to disinherit him after the death of John in 1399? That was too much. Mathe took his greyhound form and howled as only a faerie hound could, a keening cry the sum and total of his grief for John and his hatred for Richard, a faerie curse of doom. Richard II was soon overthrown, to die in the dungeons as he deserved. And Henry? He was on the throne as Henry IV, first of the House of Lancaster, thanks to Mathe, with more than a little help from Rose Red, a faerie maiden who was one and the same as the Red Rose of Lancaster.

Henry IV was followed by Henry V, who wore the ruby on an extremely gaudy helmet to the Battle of Agincourt where it saved him from getting his head smashed in with an axe, and then Henry VI, and while Mathe had not meant to start the War of the Roses, he was not sorry for it either. Hounds were nothing if not loyal, and with John dead, he had to look after his Henrys, especially when dealing with Rose Red's prickly twin sister, Eglantine, also known as the White Rose of York. Eglantine warred to put her pair of Edwards on the throne, one after the other, and then Richard III, who was far worse than Richard II ever had been.

But then Richard III died at the Battle of Bosworth, with Mathe taking a direct part in the fight as Henry Tudor's greyhound, hounding Richard from his horse as Henry bashed his head in. While it took a few more centuries, the White Greyhound of Richmond saw to it that Grey Friars church where Richard III was buried got torn down, forgotten, and then finally replaced with a car park, so Mathe could go and piss on his grave whenever he felt like it, usually on Fridays after tea.

Rose Red and Eglantine made up, combining as only flower faeries could to become the Tudor Rose, and Henry Tudor married Elizabeth of York, and the ugly mess of the War of the Roses was over, with Henry VII on the throne and his wife immortalized as all four queens in playing cards ever on. Henry VII was followed by Henry VIII, who was lovely so far as Mathe was concerned, since Henry VIII loved sports and always dropped plenty of scraps under the table, which was perfect for a greyhound. Then everything went pear-shaped, with Edward VI reigning for six short years, then Bloody Mary killing Lady Jane Grey and anyone else who got in her way. Then finally the throne went to Elizabeth I, who loved greyhounds, and everything was wonderful until Elizabeth died and things went pear-shaped again.

Mathe would not fail his new Elizabeth, even if she did have her weird thing for corgis.

He raced past the Girdleness Lighthouse, feeling the faerie power beneath his feet, and fell forward, shifting as he did, letting his glamour strip away and taking his true form as the White Greyhound of Richmond, born to run, and run he did. The old straight paths of England were called ley lines, lines of power running from faerie site to faerie site, but in the East, as he had learned, they were called dragon paths, which was just as fair a description and just as true, for they were tread by the dragons of the earth and sky, fire and water, and all the faerie elements in between, little atomies such as drew Queen Mab's nutshell carriage, to transmute from faerie flesh to faerie glamour, pure as light and just as fast, and in a flash, leap along the Silk Road in a gossamer thread of light connecting Aberdeen, Scotland, to the Aberdeen Docks in Hong Kong where the British had arrived in 1841.

Mathe considered for a fraction of an instant, then chose to forego all glamour, appearing on the promenade as an elegant white greyhound bearing no collar nor insignia save himself. If hiding in plain sight was good for the White Horse of Hanover, it was good for the White Greyhound of Richmond, especially since in the intervening 156 years Hong Kong had become far more cosmopolitan than the quaint fishing village it had been, and a white greyhound would stick out far less than an unusually lanky long-nosed white man, no matter how Mathe chose to glamour his attire. Hong Kong was also seven hours ahead of Scotland, so appearing in the precise second as the green flash at sunset just as the sun sank below the horizon on the south China sea was style points. But then again, Mathe was a faerie, and style was always important.

The White Greyhound of Richmond trotted down the docks, past lovers out for a stroll in the evening and tourists trying to snap the perfect picture. A handsome greyhound striding purposefully past seemed only slightly out of the ordinary, and Mathe glanced about, taking in the lay of the land and, more importantly, the sea.

Taking China had been hard, but also comparatively easy, given what he had learned in the War of the Roses and the battle between Rose Red and Eglantine. China was the same, caught in a dance between Dragon and Phoenix, Emperor and Empress, Yin and Yang. But there were cracks in their eternal harmony, troubles with their courtiers, problems that the right European ambassadors might exploit.

Rooster, for example, had never forgiven the Dragon Emperor for the theft of his beautiful horns. Chanticleer had spoken with him about that. Cat still hated Rat for being tricked into missing a chance at a seat in the zodiac, something which Tybalt, the King of the Cats, at least in the West, wished to speak with him about. And the Fox? The Queen of the Asian Fox Faeries, who styled herself Tamamo-no-

Mae, had been in China during the rulership of King Zhou and again during the rule of King You, before being exposed and driven out. After Reynard freed her from the Sessho-seki stone in Japan, she had been more than amenable to helping the British Empire take a piece of China, with Hong Kong becoming a Crown Colony.

Of course, it had taken two Opium Wars—the poppy faeries were highly useful for that—and another outbreak of the Black Death in 1894, with more of the Rat's plague-bearing daughters for the White Greyhound of Richmond to death shake, and finally Sun Yat-sen's revolution in 1911 to fully break the bond between Dragon and Phoenix, with the Dragon Emperor accepting exile to the Isle of Formosa, now known as Taiwan, promising to never again set claws on mainland China.

But faeries were ever creatures of the letter of the law, and the Dragon Emperor no less, for floating just a few feet away from the dock was an immense Chinese imperial palace, gilded and glistening. A helpful neon sign proclaimed it **JUMBO KINGDOM FLOATING RESTAURANT**. A smaller sign by the gangplank read **Dragon Court: reserved for private banquet**.

It was a dangerous gambit, going to beard a dragon in his den, but Mathe had done it before with the Gold Dragon of Castile, the Red Dragon of Wales, and the Dragon Emperor of China, so it was not his first time in a dragon's den. The doorman opened the door for an opulently dressed couple and Mathe darted past at a speed startlingly fast for a mortal greyhound but an elegant stroll for a faerie hound, trotting down the hall and coming into a large room decorated with a mix of Ming dynasty and modern Chinese décor set up for a grand banquet with two dozen guests in attendance. A dignified Chinese businessman seated in the throne of honor in the center rose to greet him. "Ah, Mathe. Always punctual. I am honored."

The doorman and a half dozen waiters ran into the room after Mathe, but stopped at an imperious gesture from the businessman. "Leave us and shut the door. My guest here is expected."

The waiters and doorman did not question this order, they merely bowed and exited.

Mathe did not bother with a human seeming and simply spoke with the jaws he had been born with. "Dragon Emperor."

The businessman nodded in assent. "Since you are dispensing with illusions, we shall do the same." His glamour melted away, revealing a great imperial Dragon coiled around the room, only his whiskered head where the businessman had been. An elegant pair of antlers graced his brow, ones that would have looked well on the large Rooster who perched atop the chair ten seats down on his left. On the same side, arrayed in the order of their place in the race eons ago, including the fifth seat where the Dragon Emperor rested the sun disk at the tip of his tail, were all the Beasts of the Chinese zodiac, from the sly Rat in the first seat to the fat Pig in the twelfth seat, eagerly eyeing the covered dish before him.

To the Dragon Emperor's right sat the beautiful Phoenix Empress, then the Nine Sons of the Dragon Emperor ranging from Bixi, the Dragon Tortoise, child of the Dragon Emperor and the Black Tortoise of the North, to Pixiu, the one-horned Dragon Lion, the Dragon Emperor's spoiled youngest son, who if rumor had it, ate only gold, silver, and precious jewels. Next to him sat a smaller golden dragon and a resplendent peacock.

"Castile," Mathe said in surprise. "Navarre."

"I believe we may dispense with further introductions," said the Dragon Emperor, "and get straight to negotiations. You have taken much from me, O Mathe, White Greyhound of Richmond. You saw me banished from my kingdom and stole my most precious treasure from me, my last emperor, Pu Yi. You even made him ask to be called 'Henry.'"

"I loved my Henrys," Mathe told him. "I always wanted to have another. I promised I would raise him as my own, and I did. If I'd disliked him, I would have called him 'Richard.'"

"Just so," said the Dragon Emperor, "and you glamoured yourself as Sir Reginald Johnson, his tutor, rather than dealing with your George V. Was one King not enough?"

"I am good at being two places at once," Mathe told him. "No one missed me in England, for I was there too. I'm fast. But this is old history. Let us cut to the point. You wish to return to mainland China. We can release you from your exile, on behalf of myself and the other Queen's Beasts. But in return, Britain wishes to retain its Crown Colony here in Hong Kong. I know it is set to go back next month, but eleventh-hour politics are always in play, so you can give us this in exchange. Win-win."

"A possibility I have considered," he allowed, "but before we talk such business, I am a bit peckish, so let us first consider everything we have on our plates." The sun disk at the tip of his tail in the fifth chair to his left blazed, and its rays dispelled more of the faerie glamour, removing the silver domes before each of his guests, revealing their plates. Before Pig there was a great mound of slop. Before Dog was a dainty pile of dogfood fit for a Pekinese. But before Pixiu at the other end of the high table was the Imperial State Crown from the Tower of London with the Black Prince's ruby right in the center.

"It smells delicious, Father," said Pixiu in what had to be a rehearsed line but no less chilling for all that. "May I eat it now?"

"Not yet, Pixiu..."

"How...?" Mathe's head pointed to the ninth seat to the Dragon Emperor's left where Monkey sat before a plate of peaches, nonchalantly polishing his fingernails. "Hanuman. Of course...."

"Just so," admitted the Dragon Emperor. "I'm certain you're considering whether your legendary speed is faster than Pixiu's equally legendary hunger for gold and jewels. There's also the possibility of a fight, and while you are fierce and have slain many of Rat's daughters over the years, O Mathe, White Greyhound of Richmond, you are far outnumbered, and I daresay, outpowered. Besides, there are others here who desire these jewels."

"The Black Prince's ruby rightfully belongs to Castile," snarled the Gold Dragon.

"And the Koh-i-Noor," the Peacock of Navarre pronounced, dropping his Spanish for a Hindi accent, "is properly part of the Peacock Throne...."

Mathe considered. Empires had been toppled for less, and a Crown Colony was not much good without a Crown.

"Done," he agreed. "You may return to China when I have returned the Crown to England."

Saturday, June 14, 1997: London, England

Elizabeth Windsor had had a long and tiring day. Birthdays were like that, and doubly so when you were a Queen, and old. She had thought the worst thing was when one of her corgis broke loose and ran off into the crowd. A reward was offered, of course, and it was all the talk of the news. But then came private news that there had been a break-in at the Jewel House at the Tower of London while it had been closed for the day for her birthday festivities. There was also the stranger news that the thief was apparently a trained monkey.

Did it make her a bad Queen that she was more concerned about her dog? Or a bad woman that she was still concerned about her Crown?

Then, all at once, her missing corgi leapt onto the bed out of nowhere and dropped the missing crown onto her pillow. He barked once for attention.

She stared, then gasped, agog and aghast. "Oh Mathe!" she cried. "Good boy!"

Mathe wagged his tail happily. He was getting to like Elizabeth II after all.

PROJECT BLACKWORM

✪

Julian Michael Carver

150 Kilometers Northwest of Chengde, China
Near the China-Mongolian border
20 August 2037

Phew! Smells like bear shit.

Trying to ignore the liquefying sensation of swamp crud soaking into his boots, Private Zane Kennedy of the United States Marine Corps glanced back at the AAPV-7A1 amphibious armored vehicle.

Wedged between two gnarled trees that jutted out from the swamp, the amtrac had become a permanent fixture of the Northern Chinese swampland. The treacherous night trek ahead beckoned, as Zane observed the eerie environment through the ghostly green glow of his night-vision goggles.

Caught below the swamp by some unseen obstacle—possibly a leftover from the war—the vehicle had thrown track and become utterly inoperative. The Marines' comms equipment had also been fried after a Chinese computer virus had infected the network during the Tianjin Offensive, ruining any chances of signaling their position.

Eager to begin the journey to the runway on foot, Zane was the first one out of the hatch and into the water. With similar enthusiasm, the vehicle's five other occupants followed.

The delay caused by the amtrac's immobility would almost certainly mark them as the last squad out of China. With the war having come to a close months earlier, and the Pentagon ordering the last of the Old Breed's battalions out of the war zone, Zane was relieved to *finally* be going home. When he wasn't holed up in the amtrac, his tenure in China had been spent storming bombed-out cities and manning foxholes. The amtrac had been their shelter, guarding them from the shrapnel from cluster munitions dropped from Shenyang J-11 aircraft as well as small-arms fire from waves of Chinese infantry. Leaving the sunken vehicle behind was bittersweet, but buoyed by the dream of returning to the world, Zane eagerly splashed through the swamp, letting the wetlands swallow the vehicle's remains.

Beats the hell out of waiting to get rescued. Wading through fetid water, he shuddered. *I can't believe we're in this mess! Thanks for that, Sarge.*

To save time, Sergeant Connor Ford, known for his discreet, unauthorized excursions, decided to take a little detour to the extraction point: a shortcut through a swamp just shy of the Great Wall of China's ruins. His rationale: one last joyride to reminisce on their time overseas and a chance to push the aging amtrac to its limits. Unfortunately for Ford, the vehicle failed his moronic test, marooning the six of them in a bleak wasteland miles south of the extraction point.

"Quit your belly-aching, Kennedy," Zane recalled the sergeant bellowing when questioned about the last-minute route. "This vehicle hasn't done us wrong yet. Don't worry; your whining ass will be sittin' pretty on a C-47 fappin' to centerfolds before you know it. Now chin up, and drive us through that forest!"

Zane—the amtrac's driver—complied, and about an hour after leaving the main road and pushing through the wetland, the vehicle had gotten stuck in a shallow pond, becoming an enduring monument to the prolonged Sino-American War. He had tried to move the machine through the muck, but the steaming water had told him a story he hadn't wanted to hear. Once he'd heard a buckling sound near the vehicle's treads, he'd known the machine was toast. Not only had the vehicle thrown track, but also the worn treads had snapped, leaving nothing but the wheel assembly to churn helplessly in pond silt.

Carrying part of the blame for their ill-fated journey, Zane was tasked with scouting ahead of the five other Marines, plotting a course through the swamp toward their long-awaited salvation.

"Eyes ahead, Kennedy," grumbled Corporal Lonnie Hackett,

waving his M5 through a cloud of cantankerous mosquitoes. "I'd hate to get greased by a sniper just a few klicks from the extraction point."

"*If* they wait for us," Private Dwight Simms grumbled from the tail end of the small group. "They might label us MIA and leave us for dead."

"Now why would you say that?" Private First Class Wyatt Mayfield frowned, channeling his thick Brooklyn accent. "You'll jinx us, Simms!"

"Relax, Mayfield," Dwight groaned, tripping on a sunken log. "War's over—no one's gonna snipe you. Besides, you think they'd have snipers defending a hellhole like this? This isn't some lush bamboo forest; it's a *swamp!* Hell, half of it's underwater."

Following a compass needle and Sergeant Ford's pure intuition, the convoy maneuvered five miles inland, praying for signs of the US runway. When hours passed and no one spotted a C-47, Zane couldn't help but groan in defeat.

Since abandoning the amtrac, all he could do was pray for a swift arrival at the tarmac. Now, he found himself hoping a pit viper wouldn't clamp down on his kneecap.

Finally, after passing endless pools, scorched trees, and obsolete military equipment from years gone by, the Marines found a patch of dry land. Mayfield was the first to touch down, falling on his face and kissing the mud. Spitting the sordid soil from his parched lips prompted ridicule from his peers.

"Probably a mix of snake shit and twenty-year-old diesel!" Dwight chuckled, pulling his companion back to his feet. "You might grow a second head now with all the crap they've dumped here! How'd that taste, Mayfield?"

"A little better than your mother's moldy *snat*—"

"Sergeant, with all due respect," Zane interrupted, eyeing the oncoming terrain, "shouldn't we be approaching the extraction point? I figured we would've heard a C-47 by now. But nothing. Not even perimeter lights."

And that awful swamp ambiance. I won't miss this place one bit.

"You think you could do better, Private Kennedy?" Sergeant Ford grunted, scraping swamp residue off his boot with his knife.

"No, Sergeant," Zane replied immediately. "Not at all. The compass doesn't lie. I just wonder if we might have estimated that the extraction point may have been a little ... *uh* ... farther away than we had originally thought."

"I could try the radio again," Mayfield suggested, unzipping his backpack. "Got a little banged up after Tianjin, but I salvaged what I could. I reckon if I fiddle around with it, we could—"

"Save it, Private Mayfield," Sergeant Ford went on, eyeing Zane. "Admit it, Private Kennedy. You just want to bitch about my shortcut!"

"No, Sergeant! *I*—"

Before Zane could defend himself, the sergeant did something he never had.

"I fucked up," Ford said, slamming his fist into a gnarled tree. "Okay? I was *wrong!* There, happy, Kennedy? It's bad enough that I'll have to report to the CO that I cost the battalion an amtrac. Now I gotta worry about gettin' you four assholes back home safe and sound."

"*Four? Uh*, Sarge—shouldn't there be five of us?"

Corporal Lonnie Hackett's haunting words hung in the air, sending a chill up Zane's spine as he turned back to the ghastly swamp. When they had left the mired amtrac, there had been six Marines. Now, as they regrouped on the dark, desolate island in the swamp, Zane had counted five, including him and Ford. Between the sunken amtrac miles to the south, and their current coordinates, someone had gone missing.

Reybitz.

"Where's Trey?" Mayfield shrieked, instinctively clicking off the safety of his M5. "Hey, Trey! *Trey Reybi*—"

"Simmer down, Mayfield," Sergeant Ford snapped, veins bulging from stress. "And put that safety back on! The swamp's got everyone on edge, is all. If a snake or sniper would've plugged him, we woulda heard somethin'!"

"We gotta go back," Zane insisted, even though he recoiled at the idea of retracing his steps through the swamp.

"No shit, Kennedy!" Ford snapped, straightening his helmet. "You think I was gonna leave him?"

"No, Sergeant. Of course *not*—"

"Okay, spread out. If he drowned, we'll find him. Swamp's only a few feet deep. Damn, we're already runnin' late! They're gonna give me shit on the runway for this. Fan out! Let's get this over with!"

Zane cringed as his boot sunk back into the gunk, vanishing under a green film of leech-infested swamp. Finding himself on the edge of the search party, he scanned through the mist with the grainy green light of his night-vision goggles. It was nearly two in the morning, four hours after they had been scheduled to depart for the States. If they were fortunate enough to set foot on the tarmac, Zane feared their plane may have already departed, postponing their homecoming in Camp Pendleton.

Damn, Reybitz! Where the hell did you get to?

Private Trey Reybitz—who had been at the rear of the group—had disappeared suddenly and inconspicuously. Retracing his steps, Zane pieced together the squad's path since they'd abandoned the amtrac. He had last recalled hearing the plainspoken Texan about two klicks beyond their starting position, when Zane had asked how deep the swamp water was. After a few guesses from the others, Reybitz had responded. That was the last time anyone had heard from him.

How the hell did he just disappear? You mean no one else noticed him missing? How far could we have possibly gone since he vanished? This is too surreal.

"Seriously, Reybitz," Corporal Hackett yelled, wading through a deeper section of swamp. "I better not get any more leeches. This is the *last* thing I wanted to do."

"Especially when I saw myself seeing Beijing shrinking from a plane window," Private Simms added, swatting mosquitoes and patting his brow with his shirt collar.

"See anythin'?" Sergeant Ford shouted from the opposite end of the search party.

"Nothing yet, Sarge!" Mayfield replied.

Trying not to gag on the rancid swamp's stench, Zane waded timidly through the frothy pools. Twenty meters to his left, Simms was barely visible, obscured by bramble patches. The other members of his company remained concealed behind a wall of fog, apparent only by their constant bitching.

I can't wait to get out of here, Zane thought, trying to imagine the calming rustle of leaves in smalltown America. *Come on, Reybitz, where the—*

Something intruded on his thoughts; something that didn't belong. Ahead, the shadowy silhouette of a Marine, stood rigid in swamp water two feet deep.

Splashing a few steps, Zane arrived within fifteen meters of the man.

Trey Reybitz.

Oh, thank God!

"Trey!" Zane yelled, hardly believing his eyes. "Hey, guys! I found him. Hey, Reybi—"

Trey Reybitz was unresponsive. At first, Zane wasn't sure how to approach his comrade. Was Trey suffering from a PTSD episode?

"Trey, what the hell man?" Zane called, wading toward his comrade. "You lookin' to get court-martialed?"

"Hey Reybitz!" Ford yelled as the other Marines came splashing through the fog. "Hey, why don't *you—?*"

"*Holy shit!*" Hackett screamed, raising his rifle. "His arm! Where's his fucking arm!?!"

Arm? Hackett, what are you talkin'—

As Zane circumnavigated Reybitz, he witnessed the bloodcurdling truth; a reality so obscure and horrific it made the battle of Beijing look like a luxury cruise. The unsettling sight nearly knocked him back into the festering swamp. Nothing in basic training could've prepared him for what came next.

Something pushed Trey sideways. Clamped onto his left arm were the jaws of a shadowy biped, covered in hair, wreathed in shredded leaves and swamp matter.

At first, Zane thought it was a man in a ghillie suit, but the figure's glowing eyes suggested otherwise. Zane stood in stunned silence, watching in horror as the figure feasted on Trey's right arm, now a mangled stub of blood drizzling flesh. The creature, seemingly unaware it was being observed, kept one hand planted on Trey's pale forehead, as if using it for leverage, while Trey stared blankly into space.

"*Dammit!*" Corporal Hackett cursed. "The *hell* is that thing?"

"Our next target," Ford replied, switching the safety off his M5. "Light 'em up, boys!"

"No, Reybitz is still breathing!" Zane howled. "*Don't—*"

A torrent of small arms fire lit up the dark swamp. Rounds raced toward the skunk-ape-thing at three thousand feet per second. The barrage ripped apart Reybitz, snapping the incoherent Marine out of his stupor only to be eviscerated by a hail of bullets. The creature caught one in the shoulder, dropping the shredded Marine. Now, with a clean shot, the Marines sent round after round into the beast's gut, chest, and head. The animal remained upright for over a minute, before collapsing on the fallen Marine in a splash of mud and water.

At least these fuckers can be killed!

Zane unloaded his magazine into the ape-thing's back, before turning around and facing his squad.

"Sarge, Trey was still alive! *Sarge?!*"

Sergeant Connor Ford froze in place. With a smack of his lips, his mouth hung open. He dropped his M5. Corporal Hackett, Private Simms, and Private Mayfield seemed equally catatonic, their weapons splashing into the water.

Swamp sludge curdling around their kneecaps, the four men stood stone still, bewitched by the same powerful spell that had overtaken Reybitz.

Jamming another mag into his weapon, Zane charged his M5, then aimed in the direction opposite their transfixed gazes.

There you are!

It took only a moment to identify the creatures in the shadows about twenty meters away; four of them, one for each spellbound Marine.

Zane aimed center of mass, then fired his M5, sweeping from left to right in disciplined three-round bursts.

Three creatures dropped in quick succession, but the fourth...where...?

The hairs on the back of Zane's neck prickled. A brilliant aura of fluorescent light washed over him; a kaleidoscopic experience of colors unknown in an endless vortex. From a world away, he felt the grip of his spent M5 slip from his hands, rattling off rounds until it splashed into the swamp. His consciousness departing and his short-term memory a blur, Zane couldn't help but succumb to the monster's cerebral voodoo.

Unable to control his own body, his kneecaps gave way, slamming him into the foul swamp water.

And there, in the festering pool, he witnessed a kaleidoscope of madness.

Fragments of the past few hours jumbled or forgotten, Zane couldn't look away from the light. Or rather, the glow radiating from the outstretched hand of a central figure. The entity reached into Zane's mind, sorting out his thoughts, fears, and desires.

A wave of images invaded Zane's consciousness. Soon, Zane came to understand the strange, sordid history of the swamp.

Through an alien awareness, Zane glimpsed the swamp years earlier as a calm prairie on the Mongolian border, farmed and tilled under the long shadow of the Great Wall of China.

The vision jolted into darkness when the American warplanes arrived. Cluster munitions mixed with white phosphorus as the topography of the prairie churned and burned. Impact craters from the blasts desecrated the land, leaving it vulnerable to rainfall that flooded the landscape.

The wildlife adapted to the new environment or perished. But one species evolved at an exponential rate, elevating their consciousness to a higher level.

After the United States Army and Marine Corps took the fight inland, the swamp's proximity to the runway made it a convenient dumping ground for toxic and radioactive waste—a festering cauldron of the horrific byproducts of the Sino-American War. From this caustic cocktail, these things emerged with the power to hijack human consciousness.

Able to remotely influence unsuspecting humans.

One such telepathic nudge had convinced Sergeant Connor Ford that there was a shortcut through the swamp. Zane then saw a vision of the actual route they had taken, a convoluted maze, twisted with miles upon miles of mangled trees and submerged bomb craters. Having seen the true nature of the swamp, Zane realized his squad had had no hope of traveling through it without stumbling into the strange colony.

Their entire excursion had been a ruse; lured into a human abattoir by a species of irradiated, but genetically enhanced mutants.

And these unnatural abominations had only two goals; to breed and to consume.

No! Break free! Fight it! Fight it and break—

Free.

Reality blurred around Zane as the hallucinogenic haze wore off. The ground rushed at him, as the moist muddy floor smeared his face.

"Ugh!"

It took everything in him to move; his brain, having traded energy with his captor, fought to communicate with his body. With great effort, he willed his head to tilt and take in his new surroundings.

Suffering from missing time, Zane last placed their position ten feet from the amtrac, beginning their trek through the swamp. Now he found himself in a crudely dug, subterranean warren. American and Chinese artifacts of war were strewn about the dark domain, illuminated by moonlight shining through the carved windows of the muddy walls. Skeletal human remains littered the area, their faces wedged in the muddied walls like rebar. The stench of death and decay was everywhere. It was a place of complete despair and lost hope, a testament to years of brutality, contamination, and war.

Uncle Sam's own outhouse right in Beijing's backyard.

Zane's memories returned in fragmented, blurry pieces. He now remembered what had transpired after departing the amtrac.

The swamp trek. Reybitz going AWOL. The creatures.

Suddenly it was clear; he had been abducted by the strange beings and taken to their lair where they planned to digest his remains, just like they were doing with Reybitz after their hypnotic possession of his physical—

"*Hey, Zane!* Get up! It's coming back, man!"

He turned to the left, where Private First Class Wyatt Mayfield stood ten feet away, fused to the wall with translucent swamp goo.

Zane followed Mayfield's awkward head-bobbing to the floor. One of the creatures was struggling to get up. Somehow during their duel of consciousness, Zane had managed to subdue the being long enough to break free of its spell. Using its hairy, mud-caked arms to lift itself back up, the beast regained its stance, towering over him by at least a foot.

"*Dude!*" Mayfield shrieked, gyrating his head—his only free appendage—toward his feet. "My rifle's right *there!* Quit dickin' around and nail that sucker!"

Snapping out of his daze, Zane dove toward the sloppy ground where the weapon rested. The creature, fighting off what Zane judged had been a telepathic hangover, approached with a sluggish gait. With a desperate tug, Zane freed the barrel from the goop. He spun toward the creature and filled it with lead.

The barrage knocked the thing against the wall, then through it, and into the swamp beyond. The putrid stench outside permeated the chamber as swamp water flooded into the cavity. Zane watched in disbelief as the creature's corpse sank into a vortex of frothing swamp water.

"Get me out of here!"

"I'm *trying*, Mayfield! Pipe down! They'll hear us!"

It took all his remaining strength to free his comrade from the syrupy residue. The substance, whether some fecal matter left behind by the creatures or radioactive residue from the swamp, was extremely sticky. Having grafted to Mayfield's palms, the material had to be pried off. After freeing Mayfield, Zane spent another minute scrubbing the slop off, allowing time for his comrade to retrieve a weapon; a dented but operational Chinese QJS-161 light machine gun.

"No time to waste." Mayfield rushed past him. "Let's jet!"

As they turned to leave, Zane vomited on the wall. When he looked back up, he saw eight more ape-things fifty yards down the corridor, feasting on the remains of his fellow Marines—their bodies infused to the wall. Corporal Lonnie Hackett was being devoured from the waist down, with one creature munching on the man's thighs as it worked its way down toward the kneecaps. Private Dwight Simms hung diagonally, while a creature chewed out his throat. Sergeant Connor Ford, his face contorted in a rictus, had two of the wretched things latched on one arm. Private Trey Reybitz was almost unrecognizable; a corpse defiled by the ravenous beasts.

"They're *dead* man!" Mayfield squealed, ducking out the escape hole. "I can hear a C-47 from here! *Come on! Come o—*"

Mayfield's pleas faded into the background. Zane had become entranced by the creatures down the corridor, devouring men who over the past three years he had come to regard as brothers. They had bonded, talked about returning home together. He knew their families, their spouses, and their children.

Hell, they had even *killed* together.

Now they would rest here for all time, their bones entombed into this accursed charnel house until the ages rendered their remains into dust.

It wasn't until Mayfield grabbed Zane by the collar and yanked him out from the tunnel that he broke free of the disturbing scene and back into the swamp's nauseating atmosphere.

Zane stumbled forward into a mad dash through the swamp. The terrain outside the lair was lined with narrow paths above water, weaving between odorous pools and rusted out military hardware. Here and there, Zane caught glimpses of the creatures, feeding on bloated remains from other soldiers lured into the slaughterhouse, both American and Chinese. Now, in the full light of the moon, Zane took in their sinister appearance.

They were vile, wretched things, some six to seven feet tall, covered in matted mangy hair. Yellowed claws curled from their fingers like tendrils that reminded him of ancient ground sloths. Their feet were flat and webbed, powerful and adapted for efficient swimming. They resembled a bizarre perversion of bear and reptile; an accident of nature infused with biohazardous waste; a truly terrifying creation.

Part bear? Part snake? Part man?

Some of the mutants turned to pursue Zane as he struggled to keep up with Mayfield's chaotic sprint. The creatures lumbered slowly at first, before increasing their pace to a calm lurch through the wetland.

The distinct rumble of a C-47 Pratt & Whitney engine interrupted his hectic, helter-skelter thoughts. Ahead, the swamps emptied into a prairie, beyond which stood a rusty chain link fence. And beyond that—the beautiful mortar-cracked pavement of the American tarmac.

The runway! We've made it!

As both Marines trudged out of the swamp and into the grassland, something peculiar stood in the shrubs ahead. Instantly, Zane recognized it as a soldier, dressed in dark tactical attire and shining a laser sight on both Marines as they fled the thicket. Mayfield saw him too, raising both arms as if to flag him down.

Thank God! We're saved!

"Hey! Help us!"

The man in the shrubs nodded as if he understood Mayfield's woeful cries—before peppering the Marine with a burst from his HK416.

"Whoa! Stop! St—"

Hundreds of rounds joined the volley from the surrounding forest, shredding Mayfield into a geyser of blood, bone fragments, and hamburger. Before he could process Mayfield's death, Zane felt a powerful stabbing sensation rip into his shoulder. More hot lead riddled his midsection, knocking him flat on his back with the sting of a thousand yellow jackets.

Coughing up blood, Zane wept as he gazed up at the starry sky and watched the C-47 rise to the heavens.

Those two sons of bitches don't know how close they came to salvation . . .

Special Operations Group Commander Caleb Elliott peered through his night-vision goggles. Among the foliage just beyond the field, eight glowing forms on infrared stood at the edge of the swamp. Standing erect and undaunted by the presence of the covert operators, the strange colony eyed the prairie, likely calculating whether to attack.

Ten feet away lay two members of the missing squad. One of the men had already died, while the other was hacking up blood, his chest slowly rising and falling as he stared up at the sky. Elliott assumed they were the only survivors of the mutants' savagery.

Raising the infrared scope of his HK, Elliott centered the glowing cross hairs on the middle biped fifty meters away. Around him, he could feel the nine other members of his strike team do the same, carefully selecting their own targets.

Ten of the CIA's elite paramilitary operators versus eight powerfully psychic beings, Elliott thought, weighing the odds. *It would be a battle for the ages, but in the end, good ol' firepower would win out . . .*

Or at least he hoped.

After another minute of tension, the mutants slowly retreated into the swamp. One by one, Elliott watched their heat signatures fade away, until any trace of the strange race had been engulfed by the darkness.

Elliott, relieved the creatures hadn't infested his mind, lowered the barrel of his HK. Around him, the other strike team members relaxed, chattering about the standoff. After all the rumors, they had finally caught a firsthand glimpse of the elusive race.

Close call. Damn things must be gettin' bold to venture this close to the runway.

"One of these days, they're gonna wander out into the prairie," a young operator named Hawkins noted.

"China's problem," Elliott said, eyeing the dying man on the grass. "Do me a favor and put one in his dome. He's a US Marine. I can't stand to see him suffer like that."

"Wilco," Hawkins said, walking calmly over to the Marine slumped on the grass.

An orange muzzle flash and pistol shot followed. The deed was done. Hawkins returned to the shrubs, holstering his sidearm with the callous affect of a dead-eyed killer.

"Lee. Murph. Bury them closer to the tree line," Elliott said to two operators. "Everybody else man the perimeter. After we bury these Marines, we'll depart for extraction. I'll call it in. And congrats; looks like we'll live to see another day."

Grunts of acknowledgement followed as members of the strike team set out to complete their assigned tasks. Elliott pulled out an Iridium satellite phone from his ruck and dialed a number from his recent call log. On the blue digital screen, a dialing icon blinked to life before connecting him with a government official on the other end.

Elliott had never met the officials that tasked him and his team to the Chinese forest, but had been briefed on the objective. Needless to say, it was the hairiest mission he'd ever been assigned—both figuratively and literally.

"It's finished," Elliott said bluntly, eyes trained on the wetlands.

"Excellent," replied a brusque male voice from the other end. "Now you can appreciate the months you've been deployed to Chengde. We didn't anticipate any military personnel moving through the swamp. In fact, strict orders were delegated to the appropriate authorities to ensure it would never happen. I guess these enlisted boys got cute and decided to go exploring. It cost them dearly. How many made it out?"

"Just two," Elliott replied, glancing at the pair of corpses on the tarmac lawn.

"But no survivors, right?" the government official said.

Elliott tried not to let his voice betray his guilt. "Correct. Witnesses have been neutralized."

"Congratulations, Commander," the government official went on. "You've done your country a great service. The secrecy of Project Blackworm is of the utmost priority to the United States. We cannot risk any leaks about the existence of this species. We simply cannot have another Giant of Kandahar moment."

"Understood," Elliott said. "But if you don't mind me asking, *uh*, what are those things?"

The man on the other end seemed to ignore the question. For a moment, Elliott wondered if he had overstepped a boundary by asking the question. After all, the motto of the CIA's Special Activities Center was *Tertia Optio*—Third Option. When diplomacy and war wouldn't do, the President came to them for more covert methods of imposing the nation's will—no questions asked. Fearing that he had just become another liability or loose end, Elliott prepared to apologize. After all, all information on this species was classified at above top secret.

"We first came in contact with them a little over two years ago," the voice suddenly admitted. "We believe they were genetically engineered by some other organization, but I'm not authorized to share anything more on that specific point. During the height of the Battle of Tianjin. Similar scenario. Some boys got a little slaphappy when they were called home and took a detour. By the time they showed up on the other end of the swamp, their forces had been winnowed down to a handful. The survivors told strange stories about demons in the dark and mind control. After these witnesses were ... dealt with ... the administration sought fit to prevent knowledge of this species from ever reaching the general public. Get a good look at 'em did you?"

"Roger," Elliott answered, casting a weary look back at the swamp on the edge of which Lee and Murph were still digging two graves. Elliott had worked in black ops long enough to know not to ask which organization it was.

"We've had spies from Beijing to Wuhan since before the outbreak of the war. The swampy areas the Blackworm species calls home weren't swamps back then. Air raids and missile strikes tore apart that entire region, creating the cesspool you see today. Waste crews dumped chemicals and biological waste in the area. From what I've been briefed on, this species is some kind of scientific anomaly, kind of like nature's antibody to a human virus."

Cleaning up some fucked-up bureaucrat's mistakes once again, Elliott fumed, gritting his teeth. *Now six good Marines lay dead because some twisted bastard decided to play God.*

"Any other questions, Commander?" the voice asked impatiently.

"Negative."

The line went dead.

Elliott turned back to the wetlands. Shoveling quickly before the mutants returned, the two operators had finished digging one of the graves. Lee and Murph approached one of the Marine corpses. Taking one leg under each arm, they swiftly dragged the cadaver over to the grave. Elliot turned away as they cast the corpse into the hole and buried it.

As the two started digging the second grave, Elliott finished packing for evacuation. Somewhere over the clouds, the hum of a C-47 roared toward the tarmac, beginning its descent over the wetlands. A mile downhill, a chain link fence beckoned, guarded by the last contingent of American troops stationed in China.

A Lockheed C-5 Galaxy transport aircraft would be landing shortly on a hidden runway several klicks to the west.

"Ready to pull out?" Hawkins asked. "It's just a hop, skip, and a jump to the extraction point."

"Have them wrap it up on that last grave," Elliott said, eager to get the hell away from here. "Tell the others to start heading for the trail."

"Caleb?"

"Yeah, Hawkins?"

"I heard you ask that intelligence officer what these things were," his subordinate asked speculatively, "but I didn't hear the answer. I apologize for eavesdropping, but, if you don't mind me asking: What the hell are these things?"

"Another American boo-boo," Elliott replied, looking back at the wetlands. "They're our little goodbye kiss to China, Hawkins. Now, hurry up. I want my boots snug on that plane's riveted floor within the hour."

"You got it, boss."

As Hawkins shuffled away, Elliott gave one last look at the swamp before shouldering his ruck and departing, hoping to catch the sunrise somewhere over the Philippine Sea.

THE VIRUS DUET

✪

D.J. Butler

Captain Li Qiang sat in a black Nissan Paladin sedan across the street from Tokyo's Marunouchi DoubleTree Hotel and Convention Center. The upper-middle-class sedan would pass unnoticed in any business district in the world, even with its privacy-tinted windows. This particular Paladin was the off-catalog XE model, which featured: self-driving, so Captain Li could sit unobserved by human eyes; electronic surveillance scrambling, so he could ensure no enemies of any secular or mortal nature could observe him; and bulletproof glass and a hardened chassis, in case any planning missteps led to a shootout.

A joss stick smoldering in the Paladin's ash tray protected him against observation by supernatural enemies. The demons, for instance. The Soul Eaters clamored for release—could they be watching Li? And perhaps it was fanciful, but he liked to imagine that the name of the car itself, the Paladin, brought him luck. A paladin was a warrior with a sacred cause, protected by the benevolent powers of heaven. Just like him.

A meticulous planner, Li was very careful about avoiding exposure.

Captain Li wore street clothes, unremarkable gray slacks, a black jacket, and running shoes. His service-issue pistol lay on the Paladin's shotgun seat.

The DoubleTree crawled with businesspeople and engineers, some Westerners, but many from the eastern and southern Pacific Rim like Australia, Korea, Japan, Indonesia, and others. The DoubleTree hosted this year's J.P. Morgan Aerospace and Defense Conference. The executives and engineers—Li could tell them apart because the executives dressed like Taiwanese pimps and the engineers dressed like they still needed a mother's care—were from aerospace manufacturers, but also software engineering firms, semiconductor companies, telemetry innovators, and a host of other industries that lived adjacent to the production of jet airplanes, like the pest-eating birds on the back of a rhinoceros.

Captain Li served as an intelligence officer with the People's Liberation Army. In other years, he might have attended the conference himself, posing as, say, the bodyguard of an executive from a compliant Chinese firm participating in the three days of product demos, presentations, sales pitches, and schmoozing. During his career, he'd used such disguises to harvest technologies stolen by hundreds of agents embedded in as many technology companies all over the world. He might attend a conference and come away with a dozen new schematics, passwords, and samples tucked into his travel bag.

Today, his interest was considerably narrower. He was after one man and the secrets that man carried—secrets that would determine the success or failure of the demonic forces the PLA would soon unleash on the world.

The secrets of Alex Chen.

Named Chen Jun by his parents—both now imprisoned—Alex had adopted a western name in school, and had used it in his work at Microconductor Trading Company. The giant chip manufacturer was ostensibly Korean, but dominated by its acquired American subsidiaries, to the extent that half its VPs and directors were Americans. MTC's American culture and personnel were what allowed it to do US government and security work, including supplying the processor chips for the state-of-the-art F-29.

Day two of the conference was just beginning to wind into motion. Attendees staying at other hotels were starting to straggle in. They wore sunglasses or held hands over their eyes against the light, and they sucked at water bottles or black coffee, trying to take the edge off their hangovers. Alex Chen had a room at the Marriott Ultra across the street, and Captain Li sat watching the ground between the two hotels.

Autobikes, electric rickshaws, and buses dominated the scene. Conference attendees shuffled through like the walking dead, serviced by a host of bodegas, kiosks, and cart-mounted vendors sandwiched between the district's premier banks and four-star hotels. Li saw plenty of cars, but at this, the ground level of the district, they were mostly parked, or looking for parking. Cars that passed through tended to move on one of the three elevated roadways, colloquially known as the Knee Road, the Waist Road, and the Shoulder Road. Crystal assemblies gathered light at the tops of the buildings and then gently diffused it all the way down to these three elevated roadways.

Alex Chen emerged from the Marriott Ultra. His white shirt was not completely tucked in, and might have been the shirt he had worn the day before. His hair was unkempt, and he had one trouser leg tucked into a white sock.

Alex was, of course, an engineer.

Captain Li did nothing. It wasn't his job to do anything at this moment, other than observe.

Alex stumbled to a coffee vendor, a cart on the sidewalk that mounted four different coffee machines and a spring-loaded dispenser of cups, lids, sugar packets, and stirrers. Two men stood in line in front of him. Alex rubbed his eyes blearily, fumbled thick spectacles into place, and tried to read the prices printed on the green side of the cart.

He hadn't finished reading yet when the two customers both turned toward him. They grabbed Alex by his arms, one on each side, and pulled him back. A black van stopped, its side door rolled smoothly open. The men threw Alex inside and jumped in. Before the door shut, Li saw one of the men pull a black hood over Alex's head.

Captain Lie didn't follow the van. He knew another route to get where it was going.

Operation Duet was coming to an end.

Captain Li stood at ease with Colonel Xu Longwei in the observation area, separated from the interrogation room by a one-way mirror. Both rooms were painted drab green, floors, walls, and ceilings, and lit with archaic fluorescent tubes. Alex Chen stood in the interrogation room, furnished only with two simple wooden chairs and a table between them. At the direction of a soldier and under the muzzle of a rifle, Alex slowly stripped off his clothing.

The colonel wore fatigues. He had no rank insignia and wore his sidearm openly. An older man, he was burly with a hard slab for a face.

Captain Li was still dressed in street clothing, though now he carried his pistol in a concealed holster at his hip.

Three hours had passed since the abduction. The extraction team had flown Alex back to the mainland in a capacious Xian Y-21 cargo jet, with him hooded the entire time. On the flight, he had delivered a memorized string of characters to the extraction team's leader.

Li had flown in the same Y-21. He'd sat quietly in the corner, never taken off his sunglasses, and avoided all conversation. He'd watched Alex carefully during the entire flight. Upon landing, he'd followed Alex and his handlers to this facility.

Alex hesitated when he was down to his undershirt and briefs. He was doughy, showing how soft a man became when he worked too long behind a desk. "This seems unnecessary."

"My orders are to shoot you if you fail to comply," the soldier said.

A tinny one-way intercom carried the voices into the observation room. This was an old facility, an abandoned secret military base. Not all of its infrastructure had been modernized.

"Reports indicate the extraction was a success," Colonel Xu grunted.

"No shots fired." Captain Li nodded at Alex. "And we have him back."

"Good job." Colonel Xu nodded. "What will MTC think of his disappearance?"

"Maybe that he was kidnapped by a competitor," Captain Li said. "Sometimes that's the cheapest industrial espionage there is. Or maybe that he was kidnapped for personal reasons. We planted evidence of gambling debts in his hotel room."

"It won't matter what they think for long," the colonel grunted.

Captain Li nodded. How long? Days? Hours?

"After we hear Chen Jun's story," Colonel Xu said, "what shall we do with him?"

"He will be expecting us to release him," Li said. "I would recommend that we hold him until nothing he can say will jeopardize the operation. In isolation."

"Ah, Army intelligence." Colonel Xu smiled without humor. "So humane."

"The most humane thing will be a quick war," Li said, "with a prompt American surrender. This is the humaneness I favor." He hesitated, then tried an indirect approach. "You say that it won't matter for long what MTC thinks?"

"Yes, yes." Xu chuckled. "You are impatient. So am I. The time is upon us."

Upon us? How soon?

But it wouldn't do to show too much curiosity. Li nodded.

"I am thinking," Colonel Xu said, "of bestowing a singular honor upon Chen Jun. Speaking of the time being upon us."

"Yes?" Li asked.

"Unique," Xu said. "An honor reserved only for one man."

Alex had finished undressing and stood totally naked. He turned, and the soldier conducted a body cavity search with brutal mechanical efficiency. While Alex had nothing concealed on his person, a distinctive series of tattooed glyphs ran from his right shoulder blade straight down to his hip in a line. They looked Chinese in style and form, but none of them amounted to an actual Chinese character, and they were unreadable.

"You may put your pants back on," the soldier said.

"Only my pants?" Alex asked.

The soldier nodded and stepped to the door. Alex pulled his pants on and sat facing the door, his back to the mirror.

The soldier left, and an interrogator carrying an electronic tablet came in and sat across from Alex. Captain Li didn't know her name, but he'd seen her before; she was a hard-faced, needle-eyed woman dressed in green fatigues. Her hair was cropped short and streaked with white.

"You were contacted by Falun Gong," the interrogator said.

"No," Alex said.

The interrogator raised her tablet and showed Alex a recorded video. Li couldn't see the images from where he stood, but he knew what they showed: Falun Gong approaching Alex at Mission Dolores Park in San Francisco, where they'd invited him to undertake exercises with them, and he'd declined.

Captain Li had studied the video extensively.

"I had forgotten this moment," Alex said. "But they didn't contact me. I was walking in a park and had a chance encounter."

"Why did you hesitate when the two women approached you?" the interrogator asked.

"I don't believe I did hesitate," Alex said. "But you certainly know that some of my family members are imprisoned because of their attachment to the subversive Falun Gong sect. If I hesitated, perhaps it's because I saw those women and thought of my own family's behavior, and felt shame."

"You sympathize with the Falun Gong," the interrogator said. "Admit it."

"I deny it," Alex said. "I am a materialist. I believe in science and the will of the people."

"Even if the people were not to choose scientific materialism?" the interrogator asked. "Do you believe in the will of the people if the people choose capitalism? Do you believe in the will of the foolish American people?"

"The people, properly informed, will always believe in scientific materialism," Alex said. "And the people, properly informed, will always choose socialism and the revolution."

"You have Falun Gong tattoos," the interrogator said.

Alex chuckled slowly. "Is that what they are? I can't read them."

"No one can read them," the interrogator said. "They're incomplete."

"Perhaps they are Korean," Alex suggested. "You're aware that Korean businessmen drink heavily."

"Like Russians," the interrogator said. "They're not sophisticated people and they engage in unsophisticated, unscientific practices."

"That's true," Alex said. "And when you meet the engineers or the negotiators of another Korean company, after the meetings, you have to prove yourself by drinking as much as they do."

"Soju," the interrogator said.

"And hongju," Alex added, "and rice wine. And recently, when I experienced this ... unscientific practice ... I woke up with the tattoo on my back."

The interrogator sniffed and stared into Alex's face.

Li had already read the analyses of the tattoos. The Army had made Alex strip here, to reveal the tattoos as well as to humiliate him, but they'd captured surveillance footage of the tattoos months earlier. They could make nothing of the characters, which seemed to be a row of partial glyphs, as if the tattoo artist had been working from a column of text which had been half erased.

"You accomplished your mission," the interrogator said.

Alex nodded. "I gave the codes to the extraction team."

"These will ground the American F-29 fighter jets?" the interrogator asked.

"All of them," Alex said. "It's a failsafe to prevent theft and sabotage."

"Ironic."

Alex shrugged.

"Why was your mission called Operation Duet?" the interrogator asked. "I thought you planted a computer virus, but 'Duet' sounds as if you sang a song."

"I planted half of a virus," Alex said. "Hardwired into the microprocessors I designed for the F-29's navigation system. This is why I infiltrated MTC. This is what I have been working on for almost a decade."

"Half of a virus?"

"There is a second agent, who built the other half into the F-29's navigation software. Upon installation, the virus assembled itself into a whole and began transmitting data."

"Including the grounding code."

Alex nodded.

"And this other agent?" the interrogator asked.

"I never met him," Alex said. "Or perhaps the other agent is a woman. The individual works at the software engineering firm assigned to the project. I suppose if you haven't met him, he may still be embedded there."

"With more missions to carry out?"

Alex shrugged.

"This is a heroic task you have accomplished," the interrogator said. "When our demon army is unleashed on California tonight, America's principal fighting jet will be unable to launch, and we will achieve both total surprise and complete supremacy."

"Tonight?" Alex asked.

Tonight?

"Or soon. This victory will be thanks to your efforts. You should have a parade and a medal. You should be given a luxury apartment. Your name should be taught to schoolchildren everywhere."

"I am happy to serve the revolution," Alex said.

"Do you not resent this interrogation?" the interrogator asked. "You did as you were asked, but instead of a hero's welcome, we kidnapped you off the street. Instead of a feast, we forced you to strip in an interrogation cell."

"In a time of war," Alex said, "one must make extraordinary sacrifices."

"What if the sacrifice required is to wait out the war in a cell?" the interrogator pressed. "To be released only after the war is over and your secrets can be told?"

"I'm happy to serve," Alex said. "Soldiers will die on the battlefield. I cannot do any less."

Colonel Xu chuckled.

Captain Li kept his face expressionless. He noticed Xu checking his watch.

"Shall I have Chen Jun escorted to a cell?" Li suggested, his voice carefully flat and neutral.

"Come with us, Captain. You too shall have your reward for your excellent work on this operation."

"The same reward that Chen Jun gets?" Li smiled faintly.

Xu chuckled. "Oh no, not that special. But maybe more enjoyable." He chuckled again. "In the long run."

They opened the interrogation room and the interrogator left. Alex was shrugging back into his shirt and shoes. He had a studied look of humility on his face, and not a hint of recognition as he met the two officers.

"Chen Jun," Xu said. "I am Colonel Xu Longwei, and this is Captain Li Qiang. Though you did not know it, you were undertaking Operation Duet under our direction."

Alex bowed.

"Do not trouble yourself with what the interrogator suggested. You will not wait out the war in solitary confinement. Indeed, you are to receive a special treat, a reward just for you. I will take you now and show you the great engine of our imminent victory over the Americans."

A look of delight crossed Alex's face. "Is it true that we shall ride to war behind a horde of Soul Eaters?"

Xu frowned at Li. "After our victory tonight, we must examine our organization to see who leaked this information."

Li nodded.

Tonight.

But then Xu frowned. "It doesn't matter for the moment. Come, Chen Jun." He wrapped his arm around Alex's shoulders. Then he directed the engineer through wide corridors and down several flights of stairs toward the center of the facility.

"Yes," the colonel explained as they walked, "tonight we release the Soul Eaters. The Americans are not expecting such an attack and will be surprised in any case. The Soul Eaters ride the sky faster than sound, many times faster. Before dawn, the Americans on the West Coast will hear their thunder. And, thanks to you, the Americans will scramble their great war jets and find them inert. America will surrender within twenty-four hours. And if she doesn't, then she will fall."

"It is what we worked for," Alex said.

The colonel led them onto an iron-latticed observation deck. Li would have guessed that they were already below ground level by now, but a shaft descended from here, dropping beneath the observation deck into visual infinity. There was no handrail. Ducts ran up the shaft. Looking upward toward the opening at the top, Li saw a hint of twinkle that he took to be stars in the night sky.

Along the ducts were painted elaborate characters, some in scripts Li could not read. Those he could were spells. Some were amulets defending the building from attack; others gave direction and willed the targets of the spell to race across the Pacific Ocean to California. A flat slab of stone, the size of a child's mattress, lay on the observation deck. It too was marked with characters across its upper surface and around its sides, but Li couldn't read these.

The center of the shaft was filled with light that pulsed to a two-second beat. It was green, like a lightning bolt that had fallen ill and been bottled up in a tube. As it expanded, it nearly touched the deck; at its maximum point of contraction, it was a thin column, thirty feet from the platform.

"This looks like an energy weapon," Li said. He had meant to keep his mouth shut, but felt astonished and overwhelmed at what he saw.

"Ghostbusters," Alex said.

"Yes." Colonel Xu harrumphed. "And as with the Ghostbusters, the stream of energy traps the devils. We have been awaiting only the result of Operation Duet. With your codes in hand and ready to broadcast, we will now release the Soul Eaters. The people's sorcerers have prepared this shaft like the barrel of a gun, which will launch these demons at our enemies."

Li searched the shaft and saw no other human beings.

"Very interesting," Alex said. "I am honored beyond my expectation that I am permitted to see this weapon. May I also be so honored as to see the demons themselves?"

"You will have more honor than that." Xu drew his pistol and shot Alex Chen in the belly.

Alex dropped to the iron grate, blood streaming down his legs. His glasses slid over the platform's edge and disappeared. He clasped his wound with both hands and gasped.

"I am happy that I can die for my people," he gasped.

"*The* people," Xu said.

Alex only grunted.

"Look." Colonel Xu gestured with his pistol at the column of light. Its pulsing had stopped, and it was swollen to its maximum extent, a green lightning bolt fixed in the center of the shaft. It hovered only centimeters from the observation deck—

And there were faces inside it.

The faces looked human, but they were too large. Some had multiple rows of teeth, like sharks. Others had two pairs of eyes, one set above the other. Some had slit-shaped pupils like those of a cat; others had the hourglass pupils of goats. Some had snakes for hair, some lacked noses, one had a scorpion's tail for a tongue.

They pressed against the edge of the lightning bolt like trapped animals clawing against the walls of the cage. Captain Li thought he could hear their voices, wailing, whispering, cajoling, and threatening, but he couldn't make out any words.

"A sacrifice is necessary to release the Soul Eaters," Colonel Xu told Alex. "You have the great honor of being that sacrifice. I shall see it recorded in history that you volunteered for this privilege, the bravest of the brave."

"Why?" Alex gasped.

"Your family is undependable," Xu said. "Untrustworthy. Un-Chinese. Nonscientific. Believers in ghosts. You are not to be trusted any more than necessary."

Alex squeezed out a rattling laugh. "Believers in ghosts? And what about demons, Colonel? Are these demons scientific materialists?"

Xu frowned. "That is different. And in any case, I am not going to argue with you." The colonel holstered his sidearm. "Captain, help me get the sacrifice up onto the altar."

The colonel bent down to grab and lift Alex.

Captain Li drew his pistol and shot the colonel. He aimed for the shoulder, and not center of mass as dictated in training—he wanted to incapacitate the man. When the colonel fell back, Li shot him in the other shoulder, and then once through each knee.

The shots, mingled with the colonel's bellows of pain and rage, echoed through the shaft.

The devils pressed harder against the edge of the light. Their faces swelled up and bulged, like balloons inflated to the point of distortion.

Li removed the colonel's pistol and threw it into the shaft. He patted the officer down and found no other weapons.

"Traitor," Colonel Xu growled.

"Can you stand unaided?" Li asked Alex.

"No," Alex grunted. "And I am dying." But a light of understanding and hope dawned in his eyes.

Li nodded. He stripped off all his own clothing, setting it in a neat pile out of the colonel's reach, with his pistol on top.

He turned to show both Alex and Colonel Xu his back. "As you can see, I have tattoos of my own."

"They match the traitor Chen's," Xu said.

"No. They *complement* Alex's tattoos. Together, our tattoos form a single vertical line of glyphs. A spell, in fact."

"Did you go drinking with Korean businessmen as well?" Xu spat.

"On his way home from that drinking contest, Alex met me," Li explained. "Though he never saw my face. We were tattooed then, in great secrecy. I have been very careful, naturally, to keep my own tattoos a secret, knowing that Alex's would inevitably be revealed."

"What is this?" Xu snarled.

Li knelt and carefully helped Alex undress. Alex's skin was clammy and cold to the touch; he had very little time.

The devil faces bounced around in the light, raving and slobbering.

Li helped Alex stand. He wrapped his arm under Alex's shoulder and around his back, lining up the two columns of half-glyphs, merging them into a single vertical line.

"Why, Colonel," Captain Li said. "You are slow and dense. Alex has already explained to you exactly what this is."

"It is a virus," the colonel said slowly. "In two halves reuniting to form a spell."

"Yes," Alex said. "I knew there was another infiltrator, but I did not know who he was. And, to be honest, I thought he might not find me in time."

"I was with you all along," Li said, "brother."

"I am dying," Alex said. "We must make the sacrifice quickly."

"The sacrifice?" Xu thrashed in pain, but he was intent and focused. "Will you unleash the demons, then?"

"No," Li said. "We will destroy them."

"And the grounding code?" Xu asked.

"It is real," Alex said. "But that doesn't matter, because you won't be able to use it. You will have no Soul Eaters for the invasion."

"Ironic," Li said.

"I am slipping," Alex said.

"Stay." Li took a took breath. Locked chest to chest with Alex Chen, he led the man through the First Exercise. Xu hissed and sputtered, but to no avail. The motions, the controlled breathing, and the stretching of the exercise, also called Buddha Showing a Thousand Hands, calmed and strengthened Li.

Alex's breathing also became more regular. He could only raise one arm above his head, but he did so in synchronization with Li's movements, stretching, relaxing, and breathing. The clammy feeling of his skin faded. Was it Li's imagination or did the bleeding also stop?

As they showed the thousand hands, the green light slipped from the observation deck to the edge of the stone slab. The beam of the light seemed thinner, somehow, in an arc above the line where it contacted the stone. Had a door opened? The Soul Eaters withdrew a meter and waited, surprise and confusion on their faces.

With the First Exercise completed, they separated and stood next to each other, then stepped onto the stone. Li could feel the light as a faint warmth on his naked skin. He looked down at Xu; the colonel was dead. His face was twisted into a rictus of rage.

"When we step through," Alex said, "the demons will be destroyed. But so will we."

"In a time of war," Li said, "one makes extraordinary sacrifices. Are you ready?"

"Yes, brother," Alex said.

Li gripped the other man tight again, bringing their glyphs into alignment.

They stepped into the light.

THE MIDNIGHT HORDE

✪

David J. West

I never should have been here. I never should have come back to the lands of my forebears, but desperation leads to foolhardy, even irrational actions. Who can say how it will all play out?

How did I get here? Some said it was the once-in-a-lifetime rains that finally broke the dam, others said our own super weather machines like HAARP did it.

I never heard the truth.

A month and a half back feels like an eternity ago. I remember the rainstorms flooded and finally overwhelmed the Three Gorges Dam, utterly devastating everything in the Yangtze River's path. This crippled China economically and pushed it far beyond what it could bear. Chinese forces hungry for vengeance attacked Taiwan, and after a hell of a fight, it fell. But there was no gain in Taipei's destruction, no plunder left after the Pyrrhic victory.

In the chaotic aftermath, a great fracture shattered China into a host of warring states that competed for resources and supremacy. At least six different general secretaries wrested control of the government. None lasted a week. When those warring factions reunited again after a brutal civil war, China directed its attention north, invading Siberia to reclaim the land Russia had stolen from it during its imperial decline.

Doing the weekend warrior thing to pay for college had seemed like a pretty darn good idea until I had been mobilized for active duty. World War Three had never been on my bingo card.

My name is Baatar Evans. And even though I'm half Mongolian, I had never really thought I'd ever see the country where my great-grandparents had been born. It just hadn't been in the cards. There were so many other places I'd wanted to see. Because I could still speak half-ass Mongolian, my recruiter had told me not to worry. He'd assured me my language skills would guarantee I'd stay behind a desk as a human-intelligence collector, translating voice intercepts out of Mongolia. Then before I knew it, I was being sent as an interpreter, attached to a Special Forces A Team on the ground in Mongolia. I didn't know anyone else on the flight. I skimmed my dossier. We were heading for Damansky in Russian or Zhenbao in Chinese, an island in the Ussuri river, astride the border between Chinese Heilongjiang and Siberian Primorye, where already over a thousand soldiers had died, mainly on the Chinese side. My arrival coincided with the brutal aftermath of a head-to-head clash between twenty-one Russian and twenty-eight Chinese brigades on the longest border on the face of the planet: 2,670 miles. A lot more people were going to die here. They had to cut fat from somewhere.

I landed in what was left of Osan Air Force Base about sixty-four klicks south of the Korean DMZ and then boarded an old retrofitted C-141 for a one-way trip to the Transbaikal where our Russian allies planned to halt the Chinese advance. I couldn't believe it, the Russians hadn't been our allies in almost a hundred years. I'm not sure where we were when we took some flak, but the aircraft came down hard. Credit to the pilot for getting us to the ground in most of one piece.

I'll not burden you any further with how I'd managed to survive that first night in the burning wreckage, nor how my Russian allies had nearly killed me when I'd stumbled into one of their ambushes while crossing a frozen field. The gods alone know how I'd survived that night run. Later I'd been captured by the Chinese and had escaped thanks to the timely intervention of Mongol rebels. That's what's important, that is where my story really begins.

Now I traversed the lands of my ancestors with a motley band of Mongols, lost Russians, and even a few Japanese to fight the invading Chinese. I remember my great-granddad mentioning forces like this that he had heard about when he was still a kid in Ulaanbaatar. Way back before the Maoists took over. All the stories I had learned when I was six or seven years old came flooding back to me now. Tales of blood and thunder out on the open steppe.

This is the story of the old gods and how they remain...

We camped in a ravine and dared light a small fire to cook a sheep that one of the Mongols found lost in a crevasse.

Chinggis, one of my inadvertent rescuers, recounted what happened back at the river the day prior. "Several of the Russians were burnt by flamethrowers, and no longer had faces, just blistered bundles of flesh. A bullet had taken away the lower jaw of one man. The meat patching the wound did not fully cover his trachea. I could see his breath escaping in wheezing bubbles. Machine-gun rounds had threshed into pulp the shoulder and arm of another man, who was also without any bandages. I've been on five overseas deployments, but I have never seen anything like this.

"Not a cry, not a moan escaped the lips of these wounded, who were almost all seated on the grass. Hardly had the distribution of supplies begun than the Russians, even the dying, rose and flung themselves forward. The man without a jaw could scarcely stand upright. The one-armed man clung to a tree trunk, the burnt men advanced as quickly as possible. A half dozen of them lying on the frozen earth also rose, holding in their entrails with one hand and stretching out the other with a gesture of supplication. Each left behind a stream of blood which flowed into an ever-increasing river."

"That's enough," said the eldest Mongol. "It will do no good to dwell on such misery while we eat."

"We need to know what we're up against," protested another.

The first speaker continued despite the old man's warning, "As I was saying, the most horrifying opponents encountered on the modern mechanized atomic battlefield are the *gyonshi*. We need to find a way to counter them before they overrun our entire land."

"*Gyonshi*? What's that?" I foolishly asked.

"Walking atrocities," spat a grim man at the edge of the firelight.

The look on my face made it clear I did not understand.

The old Mongol answered, "They are the unclean dead, who will not rest. War creates them as much as anything. The fields where men have fallen in wrath and fear spawn them. It is unwise to speak of them."

"Bad feng shui," added another man.

Nothing more was said, but I remained as puzzled as ever. Later that night on watch, young Ganzorig, who was the friendliest to me, said, "Rumors persist that *gyonshi* are almost as dangerous to their side's own troops as they are to us. I've heard that evidence was collected in the field allegedly proving that *gyonshi* are not animated corpses. I think they are chemically altered."

"How did you hear that?"

"Before everything went to hell, and we were on the run like this, I worked in intelligence, like you. My commander, Khasar, said they were manmade. Like zombies. But the enemy wants to play upon our fears and superstitions."

"So, it's all a PSYOP?"

He shook his head. "I don't know. I'm not sure what to trust. I've seen things out here that still make me wonder. Rumors persist that anyone wounded by *gyonshi* is susceptible to the 'gyonshi disease' and may become one."

"That does sound like a zombie."

"The *gyonshi* are unable to use any kind of firearm, much less drive a vehicle, they rely on their hands and crude close-combat implements."

"So we can shoot them in the head?"

"If you can. *Gyonshi* can wear body armor. They're clumsy and slow, and tend to walk into obstacles before going around them."

"How many are there?"

"We saw more the last few days before we attacked that outpost where we found you. But *gyonshi* tactics are simple: once they are driven away from their release point—usually by judicious application of cattle prods or bayonets—they head in a mob in a straight line in that direction until they stumble into people, which they immediately attack regardless of affiliation. You cannot surrender to the *gyonshi*. If you are cornered, you'll be torn apart. When attacked by *gyonshi*, most of our units panic unless the unit is elite or highly disciplined."

"What about what Chinggis was saying?"

Ganzorig shook his head. "It takes a lot to put the *gyonshi* down, and we're running low on ammo."

The next day our group split up, judging we'd be harder to track down by the advancing Chinese forces. Our three Russian comrades headed northwest, our two Japanese companions went east, and the Mongols and I trekked eastward into the mountains where we hoped to evade the drones flying on the edge of the horizon. While I was supposed to be attached to the Russians, in my heart, I didn't believe any but the Mongols would survive the coming days.

By late the next day, our small group moved northward through a small river valley that wound through the mist-shrouded mountains. The road was rocky and covered with snow. We tread carefully, passing the ruins of a burnt-out fortress, which swung around the shoulder of a ridge. After fording several streams, we began to ascend the mountain. Bound together by a single length of rope, climbing was hard and dangerous. The trail snaked through mountain ravines and passed over jagged ridges before slipping back down into shallow valleys, and then climbing ever upward. One of the peaks ripped through the fog-laden ridges, and we witnessed a vast expanse of snow dotted with black spots.

"What are those?" I asked.

"Those are the obo. Sacred signs and altars to appease the demons who guard this pass," said the eldest Mongol. "This pass is called Jagasstai. Many old tales about it have been passed from one traveler to the next for eons."

Eager for something to break the monotony, I asked him to share some of these tales.

As he spoke, he uprooted several long, peppered gray hairs from his head and cast them into the wind as an offering. He rocked on his feet for a moment and looked around tentatively before beginning his story. "Very long ago, the grandson of the great Genghis Khan ruled all of Asia from a Chinese throne. Through treachery, Chinese usurpers killed our Khan and vowed to sever any right of succession by slaying his kin.

"A wise old lama secreted the favored wife, Tah Sin Lo, and the heir out of the palace. They left on swift camels, which carried them beyond the Great Wall and out to our rolling desert plains. The Chinese usurpers searched for the trail of the refugees and ultimately discovered it. They sent a detachment on horseback to capture and slay them. When the Chinese had nearly caught up with the Khan's fleeing heir, the lama called down a blizzard from the heavens. The snow was so deep only the camels could pass through it. This lama was from a distant monastery and knew the old ways of the land. He knew they were not yet safe and had to get beyond Jagasstai Pass. And it was here that the old lama suddenly became ill. He was struck down with the foulest of Chinese sorcery. He rocked in his saddle and fell dead upon the cold ground. Witnessing her rescuer's death, Tah Sin Lo, the widow of the great Khan, burst into tears.

"Pressing towards the frigid pass, the Chinese were drawing ever closer. Tah Sin Lo's camels were tired and could run no farther. The widow did not know how to drive them on. The Chinese drew nearer. Their bloodthirsty cries echoed in the valley, taunting her that they'd take their heads back to Peking to be desecrated by the masses. In desperation, the widow lifted her tiny son towards the heavens and cried out to the earth and the gods of Mongolia to protect this descendent of the mighty *Genghis Khan*.

"She then noticed a tiny white mouse sitting upon a stone nearby. It jumped to her knees and spoke: *Fear not, I am here to help you. The lives of your son's enemies have come to an end.*

"The widow did not understand how a small mouse could hold back more than three hundred men screaming for blood. The rodent jumped back and said, *I am the demon of Jagasstai, but because you've doubted my power, from this day, Jagasstai will be dangerous for both the righteous and the wicked.*

"The Khan's widow and son were saved by the demon, their pursuers perished in blood and fire, but Jagasstai has remained a merciless and dangerous pass, and during the journey, one must always be on guard. For the demon of the mountain is ever watchful and vigilant. One false move, and it will bring the very might of the mountain down upon you."

The top of the ridge was thick with uplifts of rock and gnarled branches. We passed an altar of towering stone, left by some wayward traveler to appease the gods for the doubts of the widow.

Evidently the demon expected us.

When we began our ascent, the cold wind assailed our faces. Whistling and roaring, it threatened to cause an avalanche from above. We couldn't distinguish anything around us and were scarcely able to see one another.

The ground gave way beneath me. I dropped like a stone. Faster than thought, I stopped. I looked around. Nothing was visible. Dangling between two stones over a deep crevasse, my feet swayed in the empty air. The only thing separating me from life and certain death was the rope securing me to my companions above. I had slipped and fallen in a crevasse while the bags slung over my back had caught on a rock and arrested my fall.

This time the demon of Jagasstai had only played a joke. But soon he showed more displays of anger. With furious gusts of wind, he almost dragged us off our feet and nearly knocked us over the cliff's edge. He blinded us with freezing snow, preventing us from finding shelter. At last we entered a small valley where the wind whistled and roared with a thousand voices.

It was dark.

The elder Mongol wandered around searching for the trail. He returned, waving his arms. "We must stop here. The path is lost, and we are snow blind."

Against howling winds and blistering snow, we struggled in the cold to pitch our tent. With frozen hands, we stowed our weapons and equipment, and packed the outside of the tent firmly with snow to insulate it from the cold.

And yet being without fuel, we shivered. Some had begun to show the signs of frostbite and hypothermia. While a fire might give away our position, without one, many would die in the night.

Saying nothing, Chinggis grabbed an axe and ventured into the darkness. He returned an hour later with a big wooden cylinder.

"What the heck is that?" I said.

"An old telegraph pole." He pointed outside the tent to his left. "There's more out there, but you'll have to cut them down yourselves. I paid respects to the demon of the mountain, and he showed me where to find them."

And so we ventured out into the night to find the ruins of a once great Russian telegraph network that had connected Irkutsk with Uliassutai long before the Bolsheviks had befouled the land. These abandoned poles were our salvation. Now we could rest in peace and cook hot chow beside the warmth of a fire.

Early the next morning we found the road not more than two or three hundred paces from our tent and continued our hard journey over the pass.

It caused me to wonder about how ancient the powers that held sway over this land really were. Were they gods? Nature spirits? Whoever they might be, the land was theirs long before any of the invaders had ever dreamed of venturing across the steppe.

At the head of the valley, a flock of Mongolian crows with carmine beaks circled the rocks. There, we discovered the fresh bodies of a horse and rider. They lay close together, the bridle wound around the man's neck. His Mongolian coat was splayed open. Chiseled into his chest was a strange script. The Mongols had a Cyrillic alphabet; this was anything but that.

Our Mongol elder bowed his head and whispered, "It is a warning. The message on his chest is carved in traditional Mongolian script, used in the days of Genghis Khan. The traveler did not sacrifice to the southern obo, so the demon claimed both rider and horse."

At long last, we exited that infernal pass, which emptied into the valley of the Adair. We followed a serpentine riverbed through towering mountains carpeted with rich grass. Broken telegraph poles of varying lengths lay on both sides of the riverbed. In the far distance, billowing smoke testified to the destructiveness of China's Mongolian campaign.

Ever wary, we continued through this land of vengeful demons and hungry ghosts.

In many places we came across sheep carcasses with the flesh stripped from the bone.

"The work of wolves," said the Mongol elder.

To bivouac for the night, we sheltered beneath a great stone overhang jutting from the mountain near the shore of a frozen stream. With our stove, we had a fire and a kettle to boil water for tea. Our tent was warm and cozy. We were quietly resting with pleasant thoughts to soothe us when raucous and infernal howling exploded from just outside the tent.

"Wolves," said the Mongol elder, who took a revolver and went out into the night. He did not return for some time. A single shot heralded his return.

"I gave 'em a little scare," he said. "They were gathered around an antelope carcass."

"Will they return?"

"We'll make a bonfire behind our tent, then they won't bother us," he said with an air of confidence.

After talk of demons, *gyonshi*, and now wolves, I was no longer sure what to expect.

After supper, we turned in, but I lay awake for a long time listening to the wood crackle in the fire, the snoring of my sleeping companions, and the distant howling of the wolves. But finally, despite the noise, I fell asleep. How long I had slept, I did not know, but suddenly I was awakened by a strong blow to the back of my head. I was lying at the very edge of the tent, and something was outside pushing against me. I thought it was one of the sheep chewing the tent's felt. I took my pistol and struck the wall. A sharp yelp was followed by the sound of quick footfalls running over pebbles.

In the morning, we discovered the telltale tracks of wolves and followed them to a half-dug burrow under the tent wall.

The old man spoke, "Wolves and eagles serve the demon, Jagasstai. However, this does not prevent us from hunting wolves. But we don't touch eagles and hawks. We even feed them. When we slaughter animals, we cast bits of meat into the air for the hawks and eagles to catch in flight, just as we might throw them to a dog. The birds of prey fight and drive away the magpies and crows, which are dangerous for cattle and horses because these pests scratch and peck at the smallest wounds until the animals become sick with disease. So, they do us a service, and we, in turn, grant them respect. Always remember to pay your respects."

"Why are you telling me this?" I asked.

"Your blood is from the steppe, but your flesh is American. You have not learned our ways. But you have come back and must return to them. That is the only way for our people to survive what is coming."

"What is coming? Beyond the obvious? We need tech and firepower, not stories."

"How could you know you could defeat the enemy if you never heard stories that it could be done?" The old man didn't wait for an answer, but shrugged at my silence and continued down the path. What could I do but follow?

Over the course of another day and night and another day, we crossed bitter fields of snow and ice. We made camp in the late afternoon and could hear the Chinese advance before we could see it.

Chinggis scouted ahead. "They're just over those hills. Tanks and armored personnel carriers. There must be thousands."

"And the Russians?" I asked hopefully.

Chinggis shook his head. "They're not coming. This valley would have been the place to face them."

The old man said, "We can't fight them like they fight us. Bullets and blades aren't enough, we must ask for the help of our ancestors. The blood of the land will help us overcome, just as it always has."

"What are you talking about?" I asked.

Ganzorig spoke excitedly, "The blood of the Khan flows through our veins. We have beaten them before in ages past. The Great Khan trod them under the hooves of his warhorse hundreds of years of ago, and we shall do so again!"

"How? We don't even have any good rifles, let alone a Golden Horde."

The old man poked me in the chest as he answered. "I told you, we ask the ancestors."

"Ghosts? How?"

"We speak through the blood, we make sacrifice and commune with those beyond our world, those above and below the open steppe." Seeing that I didn't fully comprehend his words, he withdrew his knife and sliced across his hand, letting the scarlet drops fall to the icy ground.

"That is how. We perform a communion tonight under the full moon and let the spirits know our hearts. They will answer and help us. But we must be in the right place."

"Where is that?"

"The obo of the god of war. It is near."

I was dubious. Of course, I had heard all the old stories of Genghis Khan and the Mongol hordes, but how could that help us now? What could ancestor spirits really do today against an unstoppable foe that had already defeated the Russians?

The rising moon cast a cold light that bleached the steppe in a bone-white luster.

We approached a small monastery within a square of large buildings. These structures were surrounded by high palisades. Each side had a wall with a gate leading to the temple's four entrances at the center of the square. The temple was built with round lacquered columns with the Chinese-style roofs that dominated the surrounding low dwellings of the lamas. An old Chinese trading post stood on the opposite side of the road. Like all old Chinese trading posts, it appeared more like a fortress with double walls for protection. But the post had long since been abandoned by the Chinese more than a hundred years ago, and all that was left was this scar in the Mongolian landscape.

There was a peculiar din, where I could hear murmuring voices and an irregular drumbeat. I looked at my companions in alarm, but they assured me not to worry. Despite these assurances, I was beginning to question their sanity in such manners.

Several triangular flags flapped in the breeze. The old man said this was a sign of the curse of disease. Near some yurts, high poles were lodged in the ground and capped with Mongolian shepherd hats—a marker that the host of that yurt had died. Packs of wild dogs in the area suggested that the corpses lay somewhere nearby, perhaps in a ravine or along a riverbank.

The frantic beating of drums, the mournful sounds of the flute, and the wailing quickened as we approached the camp. The old Mongol went forward to investigate and spoke with an old woman. After several minutes, he returned and said, "Several Mongolian families have come here to the monastery seeking medical attention from a Peace Corps aid station that had once operated in one of the buildings near the temple. These poor souls had traversed vast distances only to find that the aid station had been abandoned many years ago, just before the war."

"So who's treating these people then?" I asked.

"Shamans," he said. "The people had no choice. They were dying one after another. They have already lost more than two dozen."

"Shamans?" I asked incredulous.

As we were speaking, a shaman emerged from a yurt. The old Mongolian had a scar that cleaved his face from chin to forehead. His eyes were vacant and troubling. His blue tongue flickered from his mouth in the involuntary manner of a snake. He wore a tattered Russian Army uniform, likely stripped from the back of a fallen soldier. With drum and flute in hand, he began to whirl like a dervish, then stumble into an irregular and chaotic writhing, beating his drum, playing the flute, or shrieking into the darkness. He gesticulated until his face went ashen; his eyes, bloodshot; and he collapsed upon the snow where he writhed and wailed in some long forgotten and inhuman tongue.

It was utter madness.

The old Mongol said that the shaman treated his patients in this manner, using his madness to frighten the disease-carrying demons away. A second shaman treated his patients with a muddy brownish water which I later learned was opium.

While the shamans railed against the unclean spirits spreading disease, the ill were left to fend for themselves. They lay huddled together under heaps of sheepskins, shaking in delirium and coughing up bloody phlegm. Beside a burning brazier, the remaining adults and children squatted. Seemingly oblivious to the suffering, they chatted, drank tea, and smoked, as if the horror around them was perfectly normal. Within the yurts, the diseased suffered with such misery that I shuddered at the reality of its cruelty.

On the one hand, the old man was telling me to respect the old ways, that it would be the salvation of the people, but on the other, I saw this, the madness of crazed healers and the lives they destroyed. I saw this camp of the dead, and I was ready to explode as I heard the groans and ravings of these dying men and women. Somewhere in the distance, the wolves howled and the shaman's drum boomed with a discordant beat.

The old man watched and he knew my anger and frustration. He shouted aloud, "O great Genghis Khan, why with all your might have you forsaken your people? Why after they preserved the memory of your customs and traditions for generations have you denied them the peace they deserve? Why in your vast knowledge of warfare have you not returned to rescue them from the enemies that prey upon them in their multitudes? Your withering bones, secreted in some ancient charnel house in the anonymous hills and valleys of your homeland, never to be found, but only to be honored in the mausoleum of Karakorum, must lament the eradication of a once mighty people who held sway over half the civilized world!"

I can't explain it, but my anger ebbed as I listened to the old man.

I could no longer witness this depraved horror. I could not shake the thought that some horrible apparition was stalking us. The devils of disease? The souls of men who've been sacrificed on the altar of darkness in Mongolia? An inexplicable fear haunted my consciousness. Only when we had turned from the road, passed over a timbered ridge into a bowl of mountains, and escaped from the sound of the drums, could we breathe easy again. It was here beside a large lake that we discovered yet another village.

On a cowhide, by a burnt-out fire sat a young girl, drowned in tears. She was inconsolable and did not respond to questions. The people in the village told us her tragic tale. Her father had been slain by the invaders. He lay now beside the war god's obo, which we were informed was perilously close to a Chinese forward operating base.

"Is that where we must call to the ancestors?" I asked.

The old man nodded. "Deep magic from beneath the steppe is there. The war god himself consecrated that obo, and we shall reach his ear from across the void."

"I will show you the way." The crying girl had heard our talk. She was now standing and dusting herself off.

I still wasn't sure what I believed anymore, but I couldn't deny that I was here now. For whatever reason it seemed destiny or fate had placed me in the path of this desperate ritual. None of it made sense to my logical American sentimentality, but another part of me heard my ancestors calling.

We followed the girl down a winding trail through birch and fir trees until we reached the dark cedars. The icy wind whipped through the pass. Ganzorig twirled his beaded necklace, and the girl looked around anxiously.

There lay the obo, a tall pyramid of piled cedar trunks hung with innumerable ribbons, bleached and whipped to rags by the blasting wind. Figures carved in wood hung everywhere, and at the foot of the shrine lay caravan tea, corn, frozen butter, and other provisions. We deposited our sacrifices beside the sacred altar. Blood from our sliced hands, our hair, most of our meager food provisions, and even an old bronze knife.

The old man began to build a small fire.

"What if Chinese scouts see our heat signature. They could have drones."

He shook his head. "The flame must be here to light the way for the spirits to see us. Besides, if this doesn't work, it won't matter, and *gyonshi* will devour us." He began to softly beat upon an old skin drum, which I wondered briefly if he had taken it from one of the shamans.

I thought it was all a bad joke; a joke I didn't find funny at all.

The old man began reciting the old chant of prayers to the ancestors, and the girl joined in. Soon both Chinggis and Ganzorig were also praying. I alone was silent as the snow that swirled around us.

Shadows danced on the fringes of the firelight, and in my peripheral vision, I thought I saw movement. A trick of the light in the dancing snowflakes? The very air seemed to vibrate with strange energy. Hungry wolves daring to see how close they might approach? Or terrible Chinese *gyonshi* waiting to pounce and feed upon us like ghouls?

The old man continued his chant, his voice growing hoarse with effort. The girl looked expectantly at me as the coals flared with the vengeful wind.

At her, I silently mouthed, "What can I do?"

"Sacrifice," she said.

What more did I have to give? Everything I had left was thousands of miles across the sea. When I was captured, all my equipment had been taken except my ACUs which were now in a wretched state. Everything I had left, the rebels had given me. It had no real value. What did I have left of any worth? What could I give up? What must I sacrifice?

I took a deep breath. I opened my mind to the possibilities of my ancestors' beliefs. I put aside my fear and my logic, my assumptions and my scientific beliefs. I laid it all bare in my mind's eye and let it go in the moment. I was open to anything, that everything they said could be true, no, that it *was* true. I caught myself shouting along with their sacred chant, almost singing it despite not knowing the words. I chanted it with them as loudly as I could.

A form materialized from within the obo and stepped forward.

The wraith did not look like a Mongol despite his red silk coat; he had blonde hair and a bristling red mustache along with the piercing eyes of a tiger.

I looked to the others and asked mutely, "The war god?"

In unison, they nodded.

"Did you wake me from my slumber?" he asked, and though his words were neither English nor Mongolian I could understand them as if they were spoken inside my mind.

"I did," I stammered, but drew up some courage.

"Do you know me? I do not know of you, though I can see this land is in your blood."

"I am Baatar Evans. I'm an American, though my grandparents hailed from the Mongolian steppe."

"A prodigal returns," the wraith said with a grim chuckle. "I am the Baron."

"Von Ungern-Sternburg?" I gasped.

"I am he," said the wraith.

In that ethereal haze, I understood every word, as if the wraith's growing aura of power granted me a kind of clairvoyance and clairaudience.

The old man's drum came to an end; I had almost forgotten it beside my own throbbing heartbeat. "The god of war has come and will light the way with sword and fire, to turn back the enemies of our land and prepare the way for the great Khan!"

The wraith rendered a salute, like a commanding general might a respected staff sergeant.

"What would you have us do?" asked Ganzorig, kneeling in the snow.

"Alert the nation. Let them know the Horde has returned and awaits the new Khan," spoke the Baron as he raised his hand and reached toward the steppe. A twinkle like stars or tinder catching sparks spread over the steppe in ever widening ripples, and from each starlike glow, another form rose from the earth. Had I not seen it for myself, I would not have believed it. Countless figures pale as snow, bedecked in every manner of weapon and armor, raised their rusted accoutrements to the sky, and cried out like thunder, cried out in unison for battle. "Shoog! Shoog!" They would face the enemy of their land and drive the invader into the sea. Who could face such a force, who could stand against the dead and gaunt, the specter and the lich? Who could resist the bloody Baron, herald of the Great Khan to come?

Spectral horses appeared, and their corpse riders mounted them. Wreathed in ghostly light, they required neither sun nor moon, for their own phantom glow illuminated the way. The Horde formed up in units of law and chaos and rode forth.

An ebon mount appeared beside us. The Baron mounted the ghostly mare and rode to the head of the midnight Horde. Riding at unimaginable speed, they smashed against the Chinese defenses like a wave of death.

We pursued the Chinese soldiers, leaving bloody prints in the snow where our shoes had been cut to ribbons by the jagged ice as we scaled the ridge, I looked down and saw the mighty divisions of the Chinese host, firing blindly at their ghostly attackers. I heard their curses on the wind, their dying breaths caught in ice.

Science would say that madness had taken them, had robbed them of their faculties, and that they had turned upon one another. But I knew the truth of it. The ghostly Baron had swarmed over them with his undead army and laid waste to those who deign to forget the power of the midnight Horde and respect the steppe from which they had come.

From where would this new Khan emerge and to what frontiers would he lead this Horde of the dead? I did not know, but I was sure he would be coming very soon.

RADIOAKTIVITÄT

✪

Sean Patrick Hazlett

In a secluded corner of Fort Meade, Major Julian Skaggs made his way across an open, snowy field. A crisp wind howled as it swept in from the west. Ahead, a massive evergreen flanked two nondescript single-story white buildings hidden behind a threadbare screen of oak. Built during World War II, the structures were stained with the soot of age. Testaments to the military's focus on function over form, the buildings had one primary purpose: not to draw attention to the people or activity inside them.

With mangy black hair, jeans, and a bulky Members Only jacket, Skaggs looked like any old schlep off the street, unless the observer knew what to look for. His wiry frame and careful movements would have told them that he was anything but ordinary.

Skaggs covered the distance quickly, anxious to get his next assignment. Finding Muammar Gaddafi's location in support of Operation El Dorado Canyon had been a bust. Something had blocked Skaggs's perception, and on several subsequent targets, he'd been off. He needed a win and fast. Otherwise, the DIA's Directorate for Science and Technology would probably send him back to the Army where the green machine would shove him into some Regimental S-2 shop. There he'd waste away moving plastic North Koreans on a giant map or get skull-fucked by the big green weenie for incorrectly analyzing a boot print in a pile of DMZ night soil.

No. Fuck that, he thought.

He was gonna get a win, and he would do whatever it took to make that happen.

147

He headed toward the larger building on his left, the headquarters of the Defense Intelligence Agency's DS-T remote viewing unit.

He typed in his access code at the front door, and entered the facility. To his chagrin, his civilian boss, Dr. Alvin Nowak, was waiting for him in the hallway.

Nowak's expressionless demeanor betrayed nothing about what the man was thinking. For a remote viewing unit, it was maddening. The man adjusted his glasses on the bridge of his nose and said, "Major Skaggs, I have a very special project for you today." Then he turned and started walking toward his office.

The man's matter-of-fact delivery betrayed nothing. Meant nothing. Suggested nothing. Major Skaggs could find himself doing anything from a coffee run to a short-term field assignment in Nicaragua supporting Operational Detachment Delta. He couldn't read a damn thing from the man's humorless face.

So like a good officer, Skaggs just nodded, and followed his boss. When Skaggs entered the room, he immediately noticed it was much dimmer than usual.

Dr. Nowak sat down, adjusted his blood-red tie, and said, "Close the door." He motioned for Skaggs to take a seat in front of Nowak's mahogany desk. The good doctor folded his hands, then stared directly into Skaggs's eyes for ten uncomfortable seconds.

To fill the awkward silence, Skaggs felt a nearly insurmountable urge to speak. But he knew better than that. Nowak would most certainly use anything Skaggs said against him. So it was best to stay silent, especially given all the rumors about the man's involvement in several CIA black projects associated with the occult stretching all the way back to the '60s and '70s. Some whispered that Nowak had worked closely with members of the Thule Society who the Army had extracted from Germany as part of Operation Paperclip. The scuttlebutt was Nowak had conducted disturbing experiments on unsuspecting American citizens—experiments so unnerving he'd allegedly gotten thrown out of the agency after the infamous Church Committee hearings in the mid '70s.

"Major Skaggs," Dr. Nowak said, carefully enunciating each word. "Your results are less than satisfactory."

Skaggs felt a lump in his throat. "Well, yes, sir. About that . . ."

Dr. Nowak held up his right index finger. "Hold on. I'm not finished. And it's Doctor, not sir."

Skaggs shut his mouth and meekly nodded.

"I was going to send you back to a Regular Army unit, but another government agency requested you by name for a very specific mission."

The major desperately wanted to know which agency, but Skaggs knew better than to speak unless Dr. Nowak specifically invited him to. So he waited for the doctor to finish.

Dr. Nowak glanced over his right shoulder, then his left, then back again at Skaggs.

Skaggs was surprised to see two tall men dressed in black suits and wearing fedoras. Cloaked in shadow, they had been standing there the entire time. Even in the darkness, they wore shades.

"These two gentlemen have an assignment for you," Nowak said. "This Special Access Program is separate from Project SUN STREAK, and you are not, under any circumstances, to share the mission's details with any of your colleagues."

"Understood," Skaggs said. Out of the corner of his eye, he caught a glimpse of one of the men's faces. It was pale and skeletal. For a brief instant, Skaggs felt nauseated, but couldn't quite figure out why.

Dr. Nowak snapped his fingers in Skaggs face. "Major, look at me. Ignore them. Your assignment will involve a mixture of remote viewing as well as some limited fieldwork. This assignment is of the most sensitive nature. There are very few men and women alive who have knowledge of this Special Access Program. You could count the bigot list on the fingers of one hand."

The bigot list included the personnel who were read in on a particular program. Some say the term had emerged during World War II, prior to the Allied invasion of North Africa. It was a reversal of the codewords "TO GIB," meaning "To Gibraltar."

Skaggs nodded, keeping his eyes fixed on Dr. Nowak.

One of the men handed Nowak a smooth, cylindrical, ivory container with a lid. The doctor accepted the item from the man's gloved hand without looking back. Figures adorned in togas and other regalia reminiscent of ancient Greece decorated the container. The impressions were painted in red and black. But it was the image on the lid that caught Skaggs's eye. It was like gazing into a mirror, only it wasn't a mirror, it was a face that could have been Skaggs's twin.

"Before he left for Thermopylae, Leonidas gifted this *pyxis* to his wife," Nowak said matter-of-factly.

"It looks as if it were made yesterday," Skaggs said.

Nowak stared directly into Skaggs's eyes. "That's because it was."

"What do you mean?" Skaggs asked, now deeply curious.

Ignoring the question, Nowak pulled a slip of parchment from the artifact. A series of eight Arabic numerals—a number system that didn't exist in Ancient Greece—were scrawled onto its surface.

"These are your coordinates," Nowak said. "Put everything else aside, and provide me with a full write up of what you see by tomorrow afternoon."

Skaggs nodded. It was protocol to receive nothing but an eight-digit number for a target. Providing any other detail about it would make it more difficult for a remote viewer to objectively describe it. Any scrap of information beyond the coordinates might tempt that viewer to pull everything he or she knew about the target from their mental Rolodex or imagination, which could negatively impact results. The best way to work with the subconscious was to know as little as possible about the target other than the coordinates that represented that target's *gestalt*.

What was odd though was the presence of the strange artifact. So strange, in fact, that despite Dr. Nowak's apparent limited tolerance for questions, Skaggs felt compelled to ask another question: "Is there anything significant about that artifact I should know for my session?"

"No," Dr. Nowak said. "More information will be forthcoming once you complete this initial assignment."

"Got it," Skaggs replied. "Thank you, Doctor."

As Skaggs rose and turned to leave, Nowak interrupted him. "Oh, and Skaggs?"

"Yes, Doctor?"

"After you repeat the eight digits at the beginning of your first session, I want you to say the following: 'Tune into the memory.'"

Before he could stop himself, Skaggs said, "What?"

"Tune. Into. The memory," Nowak repeated as if to hammer home the point.

"Tune into the memory," Skaggs said. "Got it."

Skaggs left, now more confused than ever.

★ ★ ★

Tune into the memory...

In the building adjacent to the one where he'd received his coordinates, Skaggs sat at a rectangular table in a dimly lit room. He grabbed a single sheet of blank paper from an inch-thick stack on his left. He read the target's coordinates aloud, then recited Dr. Nowak's peculiar mantra: "Tune into the memory." On the left side of the page, Skaggs quickly jotted down the target's coordinates and let his subconscious push his pen across the sheet to form a signal line.

A series of images buffeted his thoughts. He'd never had perceptions this crisp or clear.

He felt chaotic motion as if the ground were shifting violently beneath his feet. He could smell smoke and burning meat. He heard screams.

His perceptions came at him so fast, he struggled to record them all. A majestic red structure collapsed into the ocean. It gave him a strong impression of the Golden Gate Bridge. He quickly classified the vision as an analytical overlay to ensure his mental interpretation didn't corrupt his session. He continued to watch buildings and other structures quake and crumble.

Without warning, there was a dark stillness. His perception telescoped upward into the stratosphere. When he looked down, he saw the unmistakable contours of California as it shattered and flooded moments after a tsunami had claimed its fractured ruins.

Then his consciousness was flung further forward in time.

An Asian man of relatively advanced age in a black suit with red tie and wearing a jade half-mask covering the right side of his face, sat at the front of a large auditorium where he held court among half-starved masses. A cordon of Chinese soldiers kept him a safe distance from the desperate crowd. Behind him, a Chinese flag stood above that of California's Bear Flag Republic.

With dizzying speed, Skaggs's vision catapulted forward again. A family of barely animated and shivering cadavers shambled forward through an ash-covered mountain pass. Skaggs's gut grumbled in sympathy with their intense hunger. Two emaciated children and their desperate parents struggled uphill through mountains peppered with smoldering fires. The melted hulks of tanks and armored personnel carriers littered their path. In the smoky distance, soldiers wearing helmets and gas masks, and dressed in gray environmental suits, ushered the refugees toward a shimmering pale blue light into which they disappeared. And beside these men stood a single metallic sign rattling in the cold wind that said: *Radioaktivität*.

Skaggs immediately ended his session. His heart pounded. His face was slick with sweat.

What the hell was that?

To center himself, he took a deep breath, then set about writing up his session summary.

In his analytical mind, his visions made no logical sense. They were all over the place. But one thing was constant: an oppressive cloud of hopelessness overshadowed everything.

Deep in his gut, he knew what he'd seen had been quite real. Yet he would prefer to lose his billet here than for those visions to become true.

"Dr. Nowak, I'd like to offer an apology," Skaggs said, placing his session notes on his boss's desk. "But I don't think I had such a great session."

Nowak adjusted his spectacles. "Is that so?" He grabbed the session notes and leafed through the material. He stopped and looked back up at Skaggs, giving the major an inscrutable look, then said, "In that notion, Major Skaggs, you are most assuredly mistaken."

"Huh?" Skaggs said.

"Because the scroll with your target coordinates mentioned you by name and described what you would see. You saw your face on its lid, did you not?"

"Wait. What?" Skaggs tried to keep his comments to a minimum. "Why?" The experience seemed so surreal that it could only be a test.

"Reality is not precisely linear," Nowak said cryptically. "So you see, you are not only the right man for this job, but also you are the exact man."

"Do you have a sense of what I'm supposed to be looking for?" Skaggs ventured.

"Yes," Nowak replied, then stared at Skaggs from across the mahogany desk.

Skaggs stood there and waited for Nowak to say more.

"Now that you've confirmed what this scroll predicted," Nowak continued, "you are to proceed to the next coordinates."

"Okay?"

"I would like you to do another session this evening. Then leave your write-up on my desk before tomorrow morning. Time, however flexible it might be, is of the essence."

Skaggs tightened his jaw. Nowak's apparent refusal to share information along with his order to do a double shift were aggravating.

"Yes, sir," Skaggs said, then dutifully wrote down the coordinates.

As Skaggs turned to leave, Nowak said, "Yes, *Doctor*. And don't forget to repeat the mantra."

Skaggs again faced Nowak, "Tune into the memory."

"Exactly," Nowak said, all business.

A single Asian man stood in the way of a tank column moving through a massive concrete square. The lead tank attempted to drive around him, but the civilian moved with it, denying it access to the plaza beyond.

Then it was night. Battalions of soldiers arrived on armored personnel carriers and streamed into the square. A crowd of unarmed civilians, many barely older than adolescents, opposed them. The massacre that followed was difficult to observe. It was even tougher when Skaggs felt the protestors fear and despair. They reeked of death.

Again, his visions were clearer than they'd ever been. He was certain this was China in the near future, but where, he could not guess.

Before he could catch his breath, his consciousness was yanked backward in time.

It was a misty morning over a dense primeval forest. Its mountainous highlands were lush with fir and pine, while birch, oak, and beech peppered the lowland's undulating hills.

Skaggs could feel a slight chill in the air.

As if waking from a dream, something flashed in the gray morning sky. The clouds glowed as if they'd been bombarded with white phosphorus.

Then Skaggs saw it: a silvery disk streaking across the heavens at an unimaginable speed. An explosion followed, burning a hole into the hitherto peaceful forest.

An unseen force nudged Skaggs slightly forward in time. A group of soldiers stood around a silvery disk, their mouths agape in wonder. They pointed at the object and spoke to one another in German.

Skaggs consciousness shifted again still. This time he estimated he'd moved ahead several years. The same silver craft rested in a massive hangar. Regiments of German soldiers stood in review as two very young men in World War II–era SS uniforms entered the object. Moments later, the craft began to wobble, then levitate. Slowly it floated out of the hangar, then zipped into the atmosphere.

In an instant it was gone.

A moment later, the craft hovered back into the hangar. The soldiers remained at attention. From a place with no discernable seams on the craft, a cavity opened and two men exited.

In his mind's eye, Skaggs looked deeper. He noticed these were not the same men who had entered the craft minutes earlier. They seemed at least one or two generations older. One man's hair was white with age. The other was completely bald. But as Skaggs peered closer still, he noticed similarities between the men who had entered the craft and the two who now stood before the German regiment.

Then the realization of what he saw crashed down upon him like a demolition of the Empire State Building:

These were the same men, only creaking with the disease of age.

How was that possible?

Skaggs frantically scribbled down his impressions. Filled with words, he pushed the sheet aside, grabbed another, and continued to furiously capture what he experienced.

He shifted in space, but curiously, not in time, and found himself amongst the smoldering remains of a 1940s New York, then Chicago, then Los Angeles, San Francisco, Dallas, Kansas City, Las Vegas, and on and on and on.

His consciousness spiraled backward in time in what felt like an impossible stretch of infinity.

From space, Skaggs beheld a beautiful blue and green world that looked hauntingly similar to Earth, only instead of seven continents, a single massive landmass coiled around the globe like a serpent. On its dark side, a vast array of lights dotted the planet's surface.

Something drew him downward.

In moments, he found himself among great dark green columns that spiraled upward in counterrotating sinuous patterns that reminded him of a double-helix structure. Thousands of cloaked saurian bipeds passed between the columns. The reptilians hummed an eerie melody that made the very air vibrate in sympathy. Then came thunder and lightning. The earth quaked, and the columns wobbled until they collapsed into dust. The very air burned with the intensity of a supernova.

Skaggs winked back into outer space where he witnessed a great pillar of light atomize the once great civilization. And again, some hidden power propelled him far forward in time as the mighty continent sundered and churned. Tectonic plates crashed upon one another, giving rise to a massive tsunami that swept across the continent, destroying all in its wake. The scarred wound of the lizard people's annihilated city remained fixed in his vision as a shimmering eye of concentric circles. As the passage of time seemed to decelerate, the vast rings of West Africa's Richat Structure were all that remained of that shining city.

His mind's eye narrowed its focus onto a hidden cavern nestled in the folds of the encroaching desert. And in that cavern, was a translucent diamond tablet. And chiseled on that tablet, was a set of coordinates—coordinates Skaggs could not read through remote viewing.

A week later, Skaggs was on a flight to Nouakchott, the Mauritanian capital. It was that country's largest city and deep-water port on the eastern Atlantic rim.

As Skaggs stepped out of the plane, the Western Sahara's simmering heat washed over him. All around, through a kaleidoscopic prism of floating grains of sand, stood the great tent city of Nouakchott. Not a single building rose higher than one story.

Skaggs sighed in relief that he and the four Delta operators wouldn't be spending much time among those desperate masses of humanity. Instead, the team would trek northeast through the western desert for over six hundred klicks in three Land Rovers carrying nothing but water and fuel. The Delta operators had also arranged for three Berber guides to smooth their passage through any tribes they might encounter on their journey to the Eye of the Sahara.

As dangerous as the expedition might be, operating in the city would've been far worse, especially since it had only been two years since Colonel Maaouya Ould Sid'Ahmed Taya had deposed his rival, Colonel Mohamed Khouna Ould Haidallah. The new boss was very keen on maintaining his tenuous control over his sparse desert nation. Mauritania was the last nation on Earth to abolish slavery in 1981, but according to US intelligence, the slavers were still very much active. Running into them was something Skaggs was very keen to avoid.

All but one Delta operator drove each of the three Land Rovers, while the fourth, a chiseled man of medium height who went by the name "Bill" sat shotgun in the lead vehicle. From there, he directed their infiltration into the lonely Sahel. A Berber guide also accompanied each vehicle. In the second Land Rover, Skaggs sat next to the driver, a laconic Southerner who went by the name "Lance."

The trucks rattled through the late afternoon and into the evening. The temperature dropped quickly, and Skaggs shivered in the approaching darkness.

At twilight, Lance quickly powered up his AN/PVS-5 night-vision goggles to avoid switching on his headlights and drawing any unwanted attention.

As the covert caravan meandered through the open desert, Skaggs was struck by how quiet it was. At the same time, there was so little ambient light, he could clearly see an infinity of stars above.

The long, lonely journey gave Skaggs time to think; time to reflect on why he had traveled across the Atlantic to acquire an artifact he'd seen only in his mind's eye. And based on that fragment of trained intuition, the US military was willing to gamble on Skaggs's impressions and support the mission by sending four of the US military's most lethal operators.

And yet, Skaggs had this strange but utter certainty that his hunch was anything but one. The artifact was the key; a key to a gate he had yet to uncover.

Navigating through the empty desert illuminated by the eerie green light of his NVGs, Lance slowed the Land Rover to a near crawl, then stopped. He turned to Skaggs and said, "Wait here." Lance grabbed his CAR-15 rifle and left the truck, running forward to the lead vehicle.

The Berber guide behind him just stared blankly at Skaggs, as if oblivious to the sense of danger Skaggs felt rising in the distance.

Moments later, Lance returned to the Land Rover and whispered something in Arabic to the Berber. The Berber replied, shaking his head emphatically. Lance paused for an instant, then pointed at Skaggs. "Grab your rifle. Someone else is camped about a klick from here who shouldn't be."

Skaggs stared at Lance, dumbfounded. "Wait, we're going to assault these people? How do we know it isn't a Berber encampment?"

Lance jerked his thumb toward the guide. "Because our friend here insists none of his people are in the area."

"But how do we know they aren't just a bunch of unlucky tourists?" Skaggs pressed.

"Because our intel—intel no one shared with you—indicates the Chinese are operating in this region."

"The Chinese? I thought you were gonna say the Soviets. Why the hell would they be all the way out here?"

"That's need to know. And all you need to know is they're hostile." Again, Lance pointed at Skaggs's rifle.

Skaggs had been in this game long enough to know not to push any further. So he grabbed his weapon and NVGs, then crept out into the night.

The encampment was a modest affair. About ten men crowded around a solitary fire. On the perimeter, four more clutched AK-47s and stared into the darkness.

Skaggs felt incredibly uneasy being part of this effort. As far as he knew, these people had done nothing to him. But he simply had to resign himself to trusting that Bill had good reason to kill these men. And that was something that was very hard to do.

The mathematics of conflict dictated that he and the four Delta commandos were outnumbered by nearly three to one—and they would be on the attack, not the defense. Any soldier in the conventional Army would tell you that anything outside a three-to-one advantage was a suicide mission.

But not Delta.

The operators crawled into position and silently slit the throats of the four men watching the perimeter. Blinded by the light of the fire, it would have been difficult for the men sitting there to see anything in the blackness.

Bill had insisted that Skaggs remain at a distance until the killing was done. A mercy for which Skaggs was thankful. Impersonally liquidating strangers just wasn't his bag.

Skaggs heard and witnessed three flashes of precisely aimed and synchronized shots. In under three seconds, there were nine bodies lying in the sand. The lone survivor, a rail-thin Asian man sat serenely, gazing into the fire.

In accented English, he said, "None of you is Major Skaggs."

Bill paused, as if the man's words had been unexpected. "Skaggs! Get over here!" he yelled.

A sense of foreboding electrified Skaggs's skin like a fractalized aura. He steeled himself, then headed toward the scene.

Bill grabbed a walking stick from one of the bodies, ripped a strip off a dead man's clothing, tied it around the stick's edge, then lit the rag with a Zippo. He pushed it in the man's face, not quite touching it, but close enough to make the man scream. Withdrawing it, Bill said, "Where is it?"

At that instant, Skaggs walked in from the outer darkness. The man's eyes glowed in apparent recognition. "Major Skaggs. You are as you appeared in my vision."

There was something oddly familiar about the man, but Skaggs couldn't quite place him.

Burning the right side of the man's face with the torch, Bill repeated, "Where is it?"

The man's screams echoed in the darkness.

As the man's face bubbled and smoldered, he cackled. "It's in the cave. We did not come for that. We came for Skaggs."

Skaggs stepped forward and pushed the torch away from the prisoner's smoking face, which smelled like a seared steak. "Why did you come for me?"

"Only to relay a message," the Asian man said. "It is thus: I serve the Manchurian; you serve the Tibetan. Your nation and my nation compete in this space and timeline. But our masters play the great game in all space and all time, and in every permutation of reality. The quickening is coming. Soon. Very soon."

Bill lifted his rifle and aimed at the man's chest. Skaggs pushed the rifle aside. "No. Leave him be. He'll never make it out of the desert alive anyway. Let's recover the artifact and then get the fuck out of here."

Hesitating for a moment, Bill then quietly nodded. "Lance and Zed, watch the prisoner and maintain far-side security. Mike and I will take Skaggs to the cave to retrieve the package."

And before he knew it, Skaggs and the two Delta operators were racing through the desert to a cave on the outer rim of the mysterious Richat Structure.

Mike and Bill entered the cavern first, creeping silently and guided by only the dim green light of their night-vision goggles.

"Clear!" Bill shouted, signaling Skaggs to enter the cavern.

Through his night vision, Skaggs could see that the cave was no deeper than the inside of a CONEX. Painted on the walls were images of warriors and elephants and lions, and half a dozen other flora and fauna no longer found in the desolation of the Western Sahara.

"Where is it?" Bill said impatiently.

Skaggs held out his hand. "Give me a moment."

Closing his eyes, Skaggs took in impressions from the chamber around him. He observed the distant memory of saurians blasting a hole in the rock. They appeared to him like superimposed images overlayed on his reality. He watched as they placed a glimmering clear tablet into the hole. Then one of the shades looked directly at him across the gaping chasm of time and space, as if to indicate that some grand design beyond all human comprehension had reached a decisive point. The being then sealed the hole with some kind of energy device just before Skaggs's mental projection faded into oblivion.

"There!" Skaggs said, pointing to the far back corner of the cave. He scampered over to the area and reached into and through what appeared to be the mirage of a solid rock wall.

The two operators watched in awe as Skaggs retrieved a clear diamond tablet. To his surprise, the tablet had nothing more than a series of eight Arabic numerals.

How could a nonhuman civilization that existed hundreds of millions of years ago possibly know about Arabic numerals? Skaggs thought.

"I need to do a remote viewing session," Skaggs said.

"Okay," said Bill, "but not until we get back to our vehicles."

At a gut level, Skaggs was certain what he had to do.

"No," he said. "I need to do the session right here. In this cave. Now."

Bill approached Skaggs and grabbed his shoulder, but the glare Skaggs gave him convinced him to step back. "Okay," he said. "But be quick. We need to be on the move before dawn. Otherwise, Lance and Zed could be compromised."

"Understood," Skaggs said.

Skaggs pulled out a pen and a small notebook from his hip pocket. He closed his eyes and took several deep breaths to lower his heart rate. He repeated the eight digits out loud.

A flurry of images blasted into his consciousness. He again saw the man with the jade half-mask giving orders to a military man. His vision shifted to watching that same officer giving orders to fire on a group of protestors at a place called Tiananmen Square.

And with the vision, Skaggs had a horrifying realization: it was the same man that the Delta operators were holding back at the camp.

Another image appeared in Skaggs's vision—CONEX boxes filled with weapons and soldiers unloading at night in a port on the southwestern tip of a narrow island separated from the mainland by a narrow strait.

Moving forward a day, a vast armada of aircraft bombarded a large industrial facility. Skaggs's vision shifted west in space. He saw flashing red as the NASDAQ collapsed in sympathy to the loss of ninety percent of the globe's advanced semiconductor capacity.

Moving months forward, he watched in horror as a manmade genetically engineered pandemic infected the unborn of non-Han Chinese parents, birthing a generation of children with a crippling skin disease that prevented them from ever feeling the sun's warmth. Weeping mothers cursed the Sun Sickness that consigned a generation to darkness.

And then as if drawn in by the dark ethereal tendrils of some otherworldly entity, Skaggs felt himself descend into the depths of self-loathing in a dark pool hidden somewhere in the Kunlun Shan Mountains.

Stuck like a fly in a spider's web, Skaggs felt helpless. The dark silhouette of a man shaped like a human slug, unable to move, but gifted with tremendous mental and psychic power, gazed into his soul, greedy to pry away its secrets.

In a sort of knowing, the entity, which Skaggs sensed was a hybrid being, warped by decades of Frankensteinian genetic manipulation, inundated Skaggs's mind with a warning: *The Tibetan's cure is far worse than my disease.*

Again, Skaggs saw the devastation he'd witnessed in his visions of the 1940s: the alternative timeline where the Nazis had acquired a crashed device and bent it to their twisted will.

You must be the Manchurian, Skaggs thought.

Without answering, the entity replied: *This will be your future if my disciple does not return.* An image of the man in the jade half-mask appeared.

But my country is destroyed by the Chinese in your future, Skaggs replied.

Only a portion, not the main. America will still exist, albeit in a diminished capacity, and the Thule Society will save some of the survivors by pulling them through a rift in spacetime, only to enslave them on the other side. In the other reality, the Tibetan's reality, America will cease to exist entirely.

Skaggs snapped out of his fugue. He was lathered in sweat.

What the fuck am I supposed to do?

The sound of small-arms fire in the camp spurred Bill and Mike into action. Bill grabbed Skaggs and pulled him along.

In the distance, Skaggs saw two rail-thin men in black suits and fedoras silhouetted against the rising sun—the same men who had been standing behind Dr. Nowak's desk.

"Wait!" Skaggs yelled. "They're friendlies!"

Just as the words passed through his lips, Skaggs sensed something wasn't right.

After having unloaded rounds into the two men, Lance and Zed ceased fire. Their eyes were wide with shock as the two men-in-black calmly marched forward, past them, and toward their Chinese prisoner.

"No!" Skaggs yelled. "Don't touch him!"

The enigmatic men still strode forward.

Panicked, Skaggs took off in a sprint. He needed to close the gap. If only they knew the stakes.

As Skaggs drew closer, he could more clearly see the men's gaunt and skeletal features. Their skin was a pale beyond white marble. Their eyes, black as solid orbs.

"No!" Skaggs yelled.

One of the men reached for the Chinese agent and grabbed him by the throat. The agent screamed. His face was drained of all color as his body shriveled like a prune.

By the time Skaggs arrived, the Chinese agent dropped to the ground, his body nothing more than a wrinkled and desiccated husk.

"You had no right to do that," Skaggs said to the men. "You've condemned us to a horrible fate."

"No," the murderer replied in a thick German accent. "We have merely restored the proper timeline. Tune into the memory. You will see that the world is already returning to its correct course."

Tune into the memory.

Skaggs fell to his knees. A wave of melancholy overcame him. He had failed, and now the world would suffer.

"What should we do?" Bill said as he and his men wavered, their rifles trained on the dark strangers.

But Skaggs was too lost in his own despair to reply. And then he remembered. The men-in-black had cut the Manchurian's thread by executing his totem, the man in the jade half-mask. What if the only place that timeline existed was in Skaggs's memory—a timeline that required Skaggs's continued existence.

What if I didn't exist? Skaggs thought. *What future may come of it?*

He had no choice. He had to do it now before he changed his mind.

Skaggs turned to Bill. "Shoot me."

"What?... Why?"

The two men-in-black raced toward Skaggs at almost supernatural grace and speed.

"Shoot me!" Skaggs yelled.

Bill hesitated.

The men-in-black were seconds away from grabbing Skaggs.

Aiming his rifle at Skaggs, Bill fired.

"Major Skaggs," Dr. Nowak said, carefully enunciating each word. "Your results are less than satisfactory."

Skaggs felt a lump in his throat. "Well, yes, sir. About that..."

Dr. Nowak held up his right index finger. "Hold on. I'm not finished. And it's Doctor, not sir."

Skaggs shut his mouth and meekly nodded.

"I'm going to send you back to a Regular Army unit. This just isn't working out."

Skaggs shrugged. It figured. But he wasn't surprised. Failing to find the location of Muammar Gaddafi in support of Operation El Dorado Canyon seemed enough of an excuse to shitcan him. Oh, well. He supposed it was time to take another one for the big green weenie. And if Skaggs were truly honest with himself, he was never cut out for this kind of work anyway.

SP1K3

✪

Deborah A. Wolf

Lifting his muzzle into the grit and smoke, Spike thrilled at the wind riffling the hair on his face. The scents shifted, and he lolled his tongue, wagged his tail a little, very much like a real dog. His claws dug into the rubble, sending small bits of concrete and dirt rolling. Straining forward he snuffled and chuffed, sifting through the delightful chaos of information.

Static burst through his skull. Spike stiffened and emitted a high-pitch whine of pain from between his clenched teeth as the wind shattered into exabytes of data. He snarled and snapped at the wind, trying to recapture the moment, but it was lost.

In the combat information center of the USS *Nancy Pelosi*, slicing through the waters of the Taiwan Strait, a team of officers and DOD civilians cheered as a black screen flared into polychromic life. Spike's neural processes were laid bare for them all to see like a frog pinned open upon the dissecting table. Spike growled low in his throat, knowing that these people would assume his aggression was directed outward toward the hidden PLA holdouts, never toward themselves. Loyalty was coded into his DNA as surely as obedience was programmed into his circuitry.

Faraway fingers tapped a series of commands directly into his mind, demanding information they already had, wanting to show him off for the civilians.

: : :

<LOCATION CHECK>

: : :

Latitude & longitude
     24.05415705, 120.436165556056
Arc-Minutes
     144324942, 722616993
DDD.MM.SS
     24.3.15,120.26.10
NMEA (DDDMM.MMMM)
     2403.2494,N,12026.1699,E

: : :

<MISSION QUERY>

Spike growled again. His stomach rumbled in answer; he was hungry. In their eagerness to launch his pod that morning, the team had forgotten to feed him.

<MISSION QUERY>

: : :

Mission: Chase a rabbit. Lick my balls.

: : :

The link dropped. Spike's head and tail drooped, knowing his handler would be coming online to take command. He would be punished for this. He'd been a Bad Dog.

His nostrils twitched involuntarily as the wind shifted again, bringing the usual savors of smoke, ruin, and death. He searched his bio-memory for the scent of rabbit, the sensation of running through grass, the taste of clean wind after rain. A full belly. A kind touch. But his queries came back null; they must have swept his database again while he slept.

In another corner of his mind, a door slid open as his handler typed in a series of passwords.

: : :

<Hey, Spike.>

Spike lay down in the rubble and rested his head on his paws. He closed his eyes and imagined that he was in a room, in a house, with his friend.

Hello, Jerry.

<Are you okay?>

Hungry. He sighed deeply. *Lonely.*

<Sorry. I should have made sure they fed you before launch.>

You should have let me know they were going to open a link. It's rude to break into someone's mind like that.

<It is. You're right. I'm sorry.>

I am not a machine.

<You are not. You are a dog. A good dog.>

Not anymore, Spike thought, but decided not to send. None of this was Jerry's fault: not the war, not the things that had been done to make him into this—this thing—not even their link had been the man's choice.

Yes, Spike sent instead, and waited. There would be a command. There was always a command.

<MISSION QUERY>

Spike imagined that he could feel reluctance in the communication, which was of course ridiculous. It was the same query, the same pattern of keystrokes, no matter which fingers pressed the keys. Jerry was as human as the rest of them, just as invested in this war.

Mission: Seek the PLA holdouts. Destroy their position.

Spike raised his head and perked his ears as a frisson of excitement caused his hackles to rise. Hunting enemy troops was a little like chasing rabbits. He pulled himself up to all fours, shaking dust from his fur and titanium plating. He could do this. It was what he was made for.

<HUNT>

Once more Spike raised his head, drawing in long breaths and letting his tongue loll like a real dog might. A feast of information rolled across his palate, more savory than meat. Sweeter than the pup cups Jerry had used to buy for him, before—

He stiffened. His hackles rose stiff as spikes from ruff to tail.

The wind had shifted again, bringing with it the tail end of a scent cone. The oils and shed skin flakes of a dozen people uncoiled before him in a ribbon of odor, taste, and data. Men had come through here not three hours before, armed and armored and shot full of synthetic hormones. Soldiers. Enemy soldiers.

An embarrassing series of yips and whines escaped Spike's throat, and for a moment he was glad that Jerry wasn't there to witness his lack of control.

Enemy Scented, he spelled out. *Triangulation In Progress.* But he hesitated, lifting his head higher, flaring his nostrils wider.

Intermingled with the markers of metal and oil and induced rage was a pair of strange, soft scents that made Spike's ears perk up and his tail wag a little. Something strange, something wonderful and familiar, tickled the back of the meager brain scraps the augmentors had left when they had butchered his flesh.

Spike took a long draft of air and held it in his mouth, sifting through the tastes of death to seek out the bright note of new life. Female, he thought. Young. Unarmed. Unaugmented. And with her, a child.

A memory came to him then, like the aftertaste of summer during a winter storm. Buried deep in what little brain stem they hadn't scraped out and thrown away. A light touch. The smell of soiled diapers, and of milk. A woman's voice, soft and full of laughter, calling him by name.

"Good boy," she had said. *"Good boy, Hero."*

Hero.

He closed his eyes and moaned.

<STATUS REPORT>

Spike crouched low, tail tucked between his legs, trembling.

<STATUS REPORT>

Spike could feel Jerry's anxiety. The other humans in the control room could see inside his mind, but none of them would understand what it was they were seeing. None of them would know that he had scented the PLA soldiers. That his augmented brain had already triangulated the enemy's position, that he could call in an air strike and the mission would be a success.

Or that a woman and child would die along with the soldiers.

Jerry would know. Jerry was peering straight into his mind and wondering why he was not sending the coordinates. Spike could no more hide from his handler than the enemy could hide from Spike.

Hero. Not Spike. Hero.

He deleted *Enemy Scented*, replaced it with *Enemy Not Found*, and sent.

He crouched in the dirt, trembling and miserable. Jerry knew. Jerry must know. They had been a team for three years now, had trained together since they day Jerry had brought him out of the shelter and into the bright, cruel world of war.

There was a long pause, and then:

: : :

<MISSION COMPLETE. RETURN TO POD FOR RETRIEVAL>

Affirmative, Spike replied, almost staggering with relief as he turned twenty degrees south-southeast and fired up both engines for the return flight.

Another query tapped at a door in his mind, a private channel shared only with Jerry, one they hadn't used in years.

: : :

Open.

<Spike>

His tail drooped, and Spike braced for the pain. But a new sensation rippled through his body, starting at the titanium plate that shone through the fur on his forehead, continuing between his ears and down the back of his neck. Like a hand, stroking him.

<Good boy, Spike. Good dog.>

The connection broke.

Spike stood for a minute, wagging his tail uncertainly. Then he lifted from the ground and burned toward home.

THE KEEPER

✪

Stephen Lawson

Beside a stretch of forgotten highway stood a forgotten gas station, its roof and windows repaired with scrap metal and its structure reinforced with pressure-treated lumber and railroad steel. There was a diner in the gas station, which its new inhabitants used as a kitchen, chemical laboratory, and sometimes as a hospital. They repurposed what had once been a detached automotive garage to manufacture tools and weapons.

A series of greenhouses made of PVC and sheets of transparent plastic occupied the area near the gas station. In several clearings they had set up deer blinds to harvest meat. There was a windmill up the hill that they had used to generate a bit of electricity a decade ago, before Ma Kelty and Rusty Wilcox had managed to cobble together the reactor.

There was little danger of an overseer sending troops to raid the compound, as its residents weren't telepathically linked to the Party. There were no resources here that the Party wanted—what had once been a nearby mining town with a depleted mine had evolved into a last stop for supplies for hikers on their way into the backcountry, and no one in the new world hiked in the backcountry for pleasure.

There were no rare earth metals here, nor oil, nor large bodies of water. The gas station stood on what couldn't even be considered an afterthought of a place, because no one thought of it after anything else. It didn't even exist on the Party's maps. And even if they *had* known about it, the Party likely wouldn't have cared. What were a couple of deer stands and greenhouses when the rest of the planet was theirs?

People had changed from what they were before; more accurately, they had *been* changed. The Party bought real estate companies and corporate debt. It purchased critical infrastructure. To control information, it acquired media conglomerates and politicians. Because the Party had ignored the global moratorium on germ-line CRISPR experimentation in the beginning of the twenty-first century, it had an advantage over backwaters like the United States in pharmaceutical development. The Party cured diseases, and people paid to be cured. Then the Party gained a monopoly over the pharmaceutical industry, and thus dictated what went into every antidepressant, erectile-dysfunction pill, and vaccine. The Party's products were perfect because they'd undergone extensive testing on disposable test subjects—Uyghurs, Christians, Falun Gong practitioners. When one product failed, a dozen new "volunteers" were always available for the next clinical trial.

Genetics changed on a global scale. Within a decade, people behaved more like a massive ant colony than individuals with unique hopes and dreams. They became compliant and susceptible to telepathic suggestion from the Party's overseers—abominations who shared most of the DNA of their worker counterparts, but with five times the brain mass. With that greater cerebral capacity came not an arithmetic increase in psionic output, but an exponential one. Yet even the overseers were engineered for compliance to the great mind, the one referred to behind closed doors as The Emperor. There was no need for obedience rituals as in ancient empires—no golden statue of Nebuchadnezzar looming over his subjects and demanding that they bow or be cast into a furnace. All people everywhere bowed with their minds and were happy to do so. Together, they could accomplish so much more.

They were all in it together.

China won the Third World War without ever firing a shot. They'd simply used slave labor to extract riches from the rest of the world, then used those riches to tunnel under the walls of the last refuge of human freedom—the mind.

Five genetically unaltered human specimens remained in what had once been a gas station. Their colony had once grown as large as twenty, but things had happened that often happen to small groups of isolated humans, and now there were only five.

They referred to themselves as the United States of America. Ma Kelty had been in her grave two years now, but she'd told them all that America was something you carried in your heart. It wasn't a geographic border—America had been America when it was thirteen colonies, and still was when there were fifty states. It wasn't people in buildings in Washington, D.C.—those had sold their country to the Party without any illusions about China's endgame, all to be first in line for luxuries that never came.

"I think," Ma had told them, "that there must be some way to fight the Party, but I don't know what it is. No one wants to join us. We don't have anybody to liberate. Their brains are all mush now, and they're happy they're mush. We'd have to destroy the whole rest of the world to save it, and I don't think that'd be the right thing, even if we could. It's like a nightmare I want to wake up from, but I don't know how.

"I won't wake up until I see my Earl again. I won't wake up until my feet don't hurt anymore and I'm not cold all the time. I won't wake up until you've shoveled dirt over me. Plant a tree in my ribs to get some use out of me at least. I ain't been much help to you since we moved here."

Rusty had laughed. He'd poured a bit of the grain alcohol he'd made into a tin cup for her and she'd drunk it. She'd coughed, as she always did, and for a few minutes he'd known her feet wouldn't hurt, and that she wouldn't be cold, and that life wouldn't feel quite so much like a nightmare. A few minutes of relief had been all he could give her.

Grace had been thirteen when they'd had this conversation, and she'd sat in the corner grinding black cumin seeds while she'd listened.

"You've been our doc for—" Rusty had said.

"Fifteen years," she'd said. "Long time."

Ma had shrugged and looked down at the cup.

"You miss Earl," Rusty had said, and patted her hand. "I remember he used to know when something was bothering you from across the compound and he'd get that look on his face, and how you woke up in the middle of the night and knew he'd broke his leg falling out of the deer stand."

"Telepathy," Ma had said. She'd frowned. "Like the Party. Like their monsters—the overseers. We could all probably do it, I guess. For me and Earl it's just a fluke of being soul mates. The Party understood it better, like the Wright Brothers figured out the best way to build a wing."

"It doesn't mean we can't build a wing too," Grace had said. She rarely spoke up when Rusty was in the room, save when she thought she might impress him with an idea. "We could do gene editing in the kitchen if we wanted to."

Grace was the one Ma had taught to sew up lacerations and make salves and cure fevers, but Grace had never been content with just medicine. She'd wanted to understand everything, as Ma had, and it all had come easily to her. She'd read every book they'd ever found—dusty books with covers falling off salvaged from the small town's abandoned library, paperbacks they'd found in a couple of cars, magazines from the gas station's rack. Then Tomas had managed to access a Party Internet Service Provider via satellite, and Grace had begun downloading books to read on a tablet computer.

When Grace was fifteen, she told Rusty she was in love with him despite his being thirty-five. Though he did his best to gently dissuade her, his face stayed in her mind constantly until she nearly went mad one winter. She distracted herself by building a CRISPR gene-editing lab in a corner of the diner's kitchen. Then she began to experiment on herself.

When a pack of coyotes attacked Rusty, she'd known exactly where to find him, and known exactly how to stop the bleeding and the pain.

"I knew where you were because I love you," she whispered as she disinfected a wound—her voice quiet enough so the others wouldn't hear. He'd been kind enough with her feelings to say nothing to the rest, despite what any of them might've noticed, and she knew it. "It's like Ma and Earl."

"I know what you've been up to," Rusty said. With a finger, he brushed aside the bangs she'd grown to hide the swelling of her frontal lobe. "I know you've been getting headaches too."

"Why won't you love me back?" she whispered, and glanced up to see if his eyes would tell her something his lips wouldn't.

He swallowed.

"Can't you tell what I'm thinking?" he asked.

"It's not like that," she said. "It's like your mind was screaming before. It was much louder; now it's quiet. I guess I need a way to focus my perception. The overseers were born with their enhancements—that kind of growth would kill me at this point."

She looked back down to her forceps and pulled the first suture tight.

"The overseers use psionic fields, right?" Rusty said. "It's like a high-power radio station broadcasting in all directions. Maybe you wouldn't get so much signal loss if you made a directional antenna."

She considered this as she tied the next suture, and the one after that.

"It's possible," she said. "Would you help me build it?"

"I—" he said. "Of course I'll help you."

"Then maybe that'll be enough for me," she said.

She worked beside his bed while his wounds healed and started experimenting with reading his thoughts when she deemed it safe to do so. They began with her identifying which playing card he was looking at and moved to her verbalizing words he was reading on a page. But if she tried to suggest anything to him, she found that his will was still his own. She couldn't do what the overseers could. Was it because he was too strong, or because she wasn't strong enough?

When he was back on his feet, he joined her in the shop. Together, they built a larger power supply and a more powerful antenna, but the psionic signal boost still gave her no power over him.

A day had passed since Grace had stitched Rusty's wounds, and he came into the diner from the greenhouse. When he walked in, Grace was lying on a table staring at the ceiling.

"You okay, kid?" he asked.

"There's still so much noise from outside," she said. "Outside my head. Other sounds; other smells. I need to go inward. I need to shut down everything but the sixth sense."

"Like meditation?"

"Maybe."

Then she looked at the basket of vegetables and herbs he was carrying, got up, and without another word she disappeared until nightfall.

He found her again after a successful hunt, this time with a boar across his shoulders. Rather than building a larger machine or changing her genetic code though, she sat with a basket of herbs, some of which she ground with a mortar and pestle.

"There was a formula," she said without looking up, "in a book about European witches. It was supposed to be used for mind control. It's called Keeper's Draught. It has some overlap with their traditional flying ointment."

"Flying ointment?"

"They used to go on drug trips and think they were flying to a Witches' Sabbath, and they could share hallucinations—see the same things—which added some credibility to their belief that they'd gone to the same place. This one's a tea though, which is great because it's less messy than smearing fat on your . . . um . . . face."

Rusty peered into the basket. It was filled with green leaves, purple flowers, and a few mushroom caps.

"What's in this recipe exactly?"

"Psilocybin, wolfsbane—"

Rusty's eyes widened at the mention of aconite.

"Never mind," he said. "I don't think I want to know, actually."

"Whatever they believed they were doing, they had a few things figured out. Modern attempts to re-create flying ointment almost always resulted in fatal poisoning. They at least had the chemistry down, and apparently the shared altered state of consciousness."

"Do I have to drink this stuff too for it to work?"

"No," Grace said. "I won't be able to hand an overseer a cup of tea."

"If it's not taking us both down some collective subconscious road together, how will it let you affect me?"

"I think," she said, "there's something underneath all our minds. A connected space. There was a drawing of a man in all the books I read about astral projection and ESP and all that. He's called the Keeper. No matter what culture the people were from or what time, the Keeper is always drawn the same. So either they communicated across vast distances before such things were possible, or he's some remnant in everyone's subconscious, or—"

"Or he's real and resides in a place you can only access in an altered state of consciousness."

"Which necessitates such a place existing and that's accessible to people who can return from it. Like Tomas hacking the Party's ISP. It's a tunnel into the collective they don't know about. This is just psionic instead of electronic. And—"

"And?"

"And it's a relatively new technology, which means security gaps will exist. To my knowledge, no one's ever tried to hack the psionic network, so security is probably nonexistent."

Rusty cocked his head to one side.

She realized it was a fringe, paranormal idea that bordered on lunacy, but the same could've been said for Chinese Communists devolving the human race into an ant colony using vaccines and controlling people through enhanced overseers. Until that actually happened.

"Interesting," Rusty said.

"Now you're caught up," Grace said. "We'll test in the morning."

Grace was in the midst of setting up the psionic antenna when Rusty walked in. She adjusted the thing so it pointed toward the middle of the floor. She placed a cushion in the dish's focal point, and then put another cushion next to the machine.

"Could you sit on that cushion please?" she asked.

"We have chairs."

"This could be disorienting. I don't want either of us to fall out of a chair. If you fall, I'll probably have to redo your stitches, and you don't want me sticking a needle in you while I'm on my trip."

They sat, and Grace donned the headset with its evenly spaced sensors on the front. She took a sip from her teacup, then a bigger swallow.

"We'll start with something simple," she said. "Just relax."

She closed her eyes.

"What if—"

"Hush," she said, without opening her eyes. "I won't die."

Rusty sat and waited in silence.

"Do you—"

"I said hush."

At just the moment he was about to give up on what was obviously a farce, Rusty felt an irresistible urge to raise his right arm. He tried to fight it, but his arm simply lifted into the air.

Grace opened her eyes, but they didn't quite focus on Rusty's arm, or on any one thing at all. There was a strange light in them he hadn't seen before.

"Is your arm in the air?" she asked.

"Yeah," Rusty said. "You can still see, right?"

"So far. Just wanted to make sure that wasn't part of the hallucination. It looks kind of like a floppy tentacle from here. I just reached over and lifted it with my hand, but my hand's still—"

She looked down and a wiggled her hand as if to verify it was still attached to her body.

She reached for the cup.

"Maybe you should—"

Grace tipped the cup back and downed the rest of the tea.

"Grace—"

"Do you want me?" she asked. She wiped her mouth with her sleeve. Her eyes settled on his face, but they still didn't quite focus on any one point.

"Grace."

"It's a simple question," she said.

Rusty swallowed.

"I've known you since you were ten," he said. "Your folks were wonderful people, and I hate what happened to . . . You're . . . you're like a daughter to me. Or at least a little sister."

"All right," she said and closed her eyes again. "Good. That's good."

He waited for a moment.

"Just please don't bring that up again," he said quietly. "It makes me a bit—"

Rusty lost a moment of time. When he regained awareness, he was on top of Grace, who still wore her headset. His lips were pressed against hers. She tasted like strange spices and poison. He jerked away from her.

"Grace!"

"I had to know it would work if you were resisting me," she said flatly. "The overseer certainly isn't going to cooperate. This is science. We're doing an experiment."

"I'm—"

"Don't hate me," she said. "I didn't take it any further." She paused before adding quietly, "But I wanted to."

Rusty's face flushed.

"I'll need to map coordinates to the nearest overseer," Grace said. Her heart was racing now, and she pressed her hand against it. Was it from the drugs, or from what had just happened? Aconite could cause a slow or fast heart rate, and cardiac arrest. How close was she to a heart attack right now?

Rusty walked out without another word, leaving Grace alone with her proof of concept, and with the smell of his sweat on her. She sniffed her shirt, half smiled, and got to her feet.

"I love you, you stupid man," she whispered, and put her cup back on the tool cart. Then, light-headed, Grace dropped to her knees and retched violently on the floor. She lay there for some time, alone, with the cool cement against her cheek.

Rusty would not come back, and for a moment she hated herself for what she'd done to him. The others were out tending to the greenhouses, the reactor, and the deer blinds. Her heart could stop, and no one would know for hours. By then she'd be as cold as the cement.

Grace closed her eyes tightly, like she did when she was having a nightmare and wanted to wake up.

When she opened them, she found herself in a cave. The cement's coolness against her cheek was gone, and the gas station's smells were replaced by those of plant life and dampness. Her vision adjusted slowly to the darkness, and she sat up. Before her lay water in every direction. Glowing lights under the surface swam and darted about. In the distance, perhaps half a mile away, she could make out what looked like a tree on a small island. It had a white trunk and white branches that hung down like those of a weeping willow. The branches stirred, but she couldn't feel the breeze that moved them. Nor did they all sway in the same direction. It was almost as though they were feeling for something in the cave's darkness, and were doing so under their own power.

Something brushed past her shoulder, and Grace yipped as she leaped to her feet. She spun and found another tree, this one much closer, with one of its willowy branch-tentacles reaching past her toward the water. It was thicker, she saw now, than a willow branch. Though thinner and longer, it looked almost like an elephant's trunk. The thing twisted and began to curl around her leg, but she stepped free of it, taking notice only now of the shifting sand beneath her feet. The branch groped blindly in the darkness, and its tip passed within an inch of her face. At its end were three openings that could only be described as nostrils, and nearly touching her, it exhaled. Strange images flashed in her mind—a man driving in a car to pick up a Party auditor; the Chinese flag above the US Capitol billowing in the wind; a woman who wasn't keen on children deciding now was the best time to have one.

The branch-thing gave up its search and reached back into the water. One of the lights swam close and attached to the branch's end momentarily, then swam away. Other branches reached into the water around the tiny island. Lights came near, then swam away. With her eyes fully dark-adapted now, Grace could see that the other islands in this vast subterranean sea each held one of these trees with its elephant trunk-branches. Lights came close to the islands, transferred thoughts, then swam away.

It reminded her of a creation myth she'd read—the first god arising from the chaos of water. The first amphibious creature crawling onto land from the primordial soup of chaos—life in its first trial-and-error states of success and death. The conscious mind arising from a vast collective unconscious full of Jungian archetypes and the stuff of common nightmares. The space in panentheism where Krishna became a separate thing from the source. She was standing in the space beneath her mind, and beneath all minds. It was a thing she'd suspected but hadn't wholly prepared herself to see.

Grace walked to the place where the water met the sand. She put her hand into the water and a light swam near. She touched the thing, and an image flashed in her mind. A boy was studying American history from before the modern evolutionary stage—from before the collective mind. The world was so disordered, so chaotic. People voted in rigged elections, wasting billions of dollars and man-hours in the process. The outcomes had always been certain, but the ruse of choice was necessary for some reason the child didn't understand.

The people of the world before had paid high-tech corporations to make devices to observe them.

They went on hikes in the wilderness just to observe nature rather than to collect resources or do research for the Party.

Such waste.

The simplicity of progress was obvious—a place for everything, and everything in its place. No one voted, so those dollars and man-hours were no longer wasted. The Party governed directly through the mind, which was really the most benevolent and efficient route to the greater good.

Monitoring software was unnecessary because all observation came directly through thought to the overseers. There was no more need for subversion or ruses. Mankind was one entity under the practical guiding hand of the Party and its Emperor.

The child scoffed at how stupid everyone had been to fight the forward march of progress. They were all in it together.

Grace attempted communication, as she had when she'd made Rusty raise his arm. She willed the child to be free, to think for himself, to detach from the overseer's suggestions and simply do what he wanted.

She felt a stinging sensation in her hand and she recoiled. The light swam away. Her suggestion had been as unwelcome to him as the thought of using toxic psychedelic flying ointment might be to a modern doctor. Perhaps her ability to influence was weakening here, or perhaps Rusty hadn't resisted the suggestion to kiss her as much as he'd put on.

Grace grasped another light that swam close to the island.

It was a man of perhaps eighty. From the first contact, Grace sensed that depression and guilt were his dominant emotions. He was a learned man, a scientist.

The overseer's nearest branch slipped into the water, and she pulled her hand away long enough for the nostrils to connect to the glowing consciousness. When they were joined, though, she put two of her fingers and a thumb to the surface of the man's mind.

The man had lived most of his life in a time before the engineering, in a time when minds had boundaries. Guilt coursed through him for not stopping the great unification, though she couldn't tell why he felt personally responsible. His altering had come late in his life, so its effects were not as complete as they had been in the younger generations.

Drink. You have money. I give you money. You need not work any longer. Drink vodka, smile for my cameras, and live out your days in oblivious peace. Your only task now is to reaffirm the plan.

The suggestion resonated in Grace's mind, though she knew it wasn't meant for her.

The branch detached from the old man, but Grace slipped her other hand around the mind before it could swim away.

"Who are you?" she whispered.

An image of a name badge flashed in her mind—Li Shu-hui—and of a face. He was wearing a lab coat. Then he was wearing an expensive suit, and Xi Jinping was shaking his hand. The man was a scientist—an important one. He lived in Washington, D.C., now, where he could be consulted by the Party's officials.

She let go of Li Shu-hui's mind, and he swam away.

"Why do you think you're not swimming down there in the chaos with the rest of them?" a voice asked from behind her.

Grace turned, and a figure appeared between the overseer's branches.

"Probably part of the hallucination," Grace said.

"This is no hallucination, Grace," the figure said. "Your mind has simply traveled downward to its lowest levels, where all sentient minds connect. In the chaos swim the devolved minds, the lesser mortals. On the islands, like the first gods birthed by Nammu, are the Givers—the overseers. They bring order to the world. They guide the ones who've willingly crawled back into the primordial soup of semiconscious existence."

"Who are you?" Grace asked, but she recognized the figure from the pictures.

"Your universe will continue its expansion until gravity can no longer hold the atoms together," the figure said, "and all that will be left is a thin gas of hydrogen and helium—not enough to support interactive life. It could support a single disembodied mind, perhaps, but only that. You're not far from that return to chaos, whether you realize it or not. A state of higher order exists when there are many liberated minds. With entropy comes the reduction of consciousness to the single Boltzmann brain—the single will—alone in the void. It is the return to Nammu."

Suddenly the name she'd seen in the books didn't seem quite right.

"Are you Death?" Grace asked.

"Most call me the Keeper," he said. "Death is just a doorway." He looked down to the shoreline. "This place didn't have so much water in it before."

Grace followed his gaze to the water. The Keeper didn't warn her when one of the overseer's appendages flexed toward her. When she looked back toward the Keeper, the overseer's nostrils pressed against her face.

Grace Elizabeth Holloway.

The thought rippled through her mind when the thing exhaled. She recoiled, but the appendage followed her.

The Giver exhaled: *Where are you?*

It inhaled, and she felt information leave her body.

It exhaled: *You're—interesting. A settlement of disconnected nodes. Five of you, no less. Why did you come here?*

The thing was blind but it could sense things about her with close contact. Its telepathy seemed more akin to smell than the sights and sounds she was experiencing. She couldn't let it get more information out of her, but its reach extended to the boundaries of the island and into the water. She grabbed the appendage and wrestled it away from her face. A second appendage whipped down and knocked her off her feet. The first, which she'd released, returned to her face.

You wish to—fight—the Party? This would be like staring at the sun and expecting it to blink.

She struggled to pull away but the thing was powerful.

As you will. Burn.

The appendage retracted, indifferent to her presence once more.

"It's not wrong," the Keeper said. "Five humans against the unified swarm of what was once their race is a bit like holding a staring contest with a star."

"It knows where we are now. They'll send troops to exterminate us."

"Also not wrong," the Keeper said.

"Can't you—can't you kill them?"

"Not my place. I have a role to fulfill—as a custodian, not an executioner. The God that made this place gave me my abilities, and the proper use of them, as He did for you."

"What does that mean?" Grace asked.

"Not many mortals have ever come down this far and returned to the surface of consciousness alive. It could be He has a plan for you."

"How do I get back then? I have to warn the others."

"You can walk on the water if you like," the Keeper said. "You're just a mind here. You're massless, so you won't sink. You'll find the way from there."

Grace stepped onto the water. Ahead, she saw the outline of a familiar form and walked toward it.

She woke in the diner with her head cradled against Rusty's chest.

"Grace," he said, then looked to someone else nearby. "She's awake." He looked back down into her eyes and smiled. "Thought I'd lost you."

"Li Shu-hui," Grace whispered.

"What's that?"

"Chinese scientist," Grace said. "Primordial soup. We're devolving back into a single consciousness . . . entropy taking over . . . think the universe itself might cease to exist but I wasn't quite clear on that part."

"That was some drug trip," Rusty said. "Did you see God while you were out?"

"The Keeper," Grace said. "I think he's like upper management. Said I was massless as just a mind. Seemed like that might—"

She stared at the ceiling for a moment.

"Might what?" Rusty asked.

"I had it, I think, but I lost it again. One of the overseers read my mind. It knows where we are. They'll be coming for us."

"Grace, it was a hallucination. It wasn't—"

"I raised your hand," Grace said. "That was real. So is this."

Rusty sighed. "You need water and bed rest until the toxins are out of your system. Looks like we're going to trade places."

Grace woke in the middle of the night to find that Rusty had strung up a hammock on the other side of the room, and had a computer set up on a table nearby to monitor her vitals. She picked up a glass of water from the bedside table, and Rusty's hammock rocked as he jerked awake. He was vigilant—worried about her rather than simply performing a task. That meant something—perhaps something he didn't understand or didn't want to admit. The dim light in the room reflected off a notebook in his hand as he kicked his feet over the side of the hammock and stood.

"What's that you were reading?" she asked.

"One of Ma's old notebooks."

"What about?"

"Something you said jogged my memory, so I went looking for her notes from that time. She'd gotten hung up on the fine barriers between physics and metaphysics. Mind/Matter/Math was what she wrote in big letters at the top of the page."

"Hm?"

"There was a physicist named Roger Penrose who said reality is broken down into mind, matter, and math. Math describes all matter but the numbers aren't truly part of it. They arise from the mind. The mind may interact with the brain and the body, but consciousness is massless and weightless—dimensionless, in fact, like the numbers. A mind exists outside of spacetime even if the two realms interact through psionic fields."

"How does that help us?" she asked.

"I'm not sure yet. I—"

The back door of the gas station swung open. Tomas hurried into the room.

"Sensor net picked up a convoy three miles from the bridge," Tomas said. "From the looks of it, they're heavily armed. We'll blow the bridge once they're on it, but they'll have their own bridging assets. They might have boots on the ground here sooner if they decide to air assault."

Grace and Rusty exchanged a glance.

"I can try to control the convoy commander," Grace said, "with the psi antenna. It's clear that it works."

"If you drink more of that stuff now, you're dead for sure," Rusty said.

"We're all dead for sure if I don't."

"And there'll be another convoy if you take out this one," he said. "And another. And you'll still be dead."

"Li Shu-hui—" she said.

"—lives in Washington, D.C." Rusty said.

"I saw him before, and the distance wasn't a problem."

"In a vast sea of minds? Can you be sure you'll arrive at the same place, or that he'll be near the same overseer?"

"I think I traveled to *that* overseer because it was putting out the strongest psionic field for our location. Must be the same for Li Shu-hui. We were listening to the same radio station."

"This is insane."

"It's this or use up a stockpile of ammo fighting the entire planet. What's the use of going down in a blaze of glory if there aren't any liberated minds after us? We'd just be snuffing the candle out."

"What is one scientist even going to do for you?"

"The whole problem with approaching faster-than-light travel and theoretical time travel is the energy required to accelerate the mass,"

Grace said. "The mind is massless. So if it actually moves in relation to a point in spacetime, it can do so at any speed with zero energy to accelerate it. Maybe 'moves' isn't quite the right word, but—"

"Aren't psionic fields energy though?"

"They're just the detectable ripples of the mind in spacetime where a consciousness has an effect. The ripples happen instantaneously—faster than light—at any distance. It's been proven, like quantum entanglement. Which makes me think time travel is possible too. Telepathy's not the only psionic phenomenon; precognition is another. How do we sometimes see future events as though we're remembering them, or get a sense of dread before something bad happens? If mass and acceleration aren't issues, then time isn't an issue. If I have the means to do one, I can probably do the other."

"See the future?"

"No," she said. "Make the past see me."

Rusty helped Grace—who was still a bit wobbly—through the hatch onto the gas station's roof. They set up the antenna, and Grace brewed her tea. Then Rusty locked the hatch and piled several cinder blocks on it.

"Tomas and Maggie are going to snipe the convoy from the tree line to try to divert them and buy time," Rusty said. "Ollie's on explosives. I'm only going to start shooting if they make it onto the roof, so let's try not to let them know we're up here."

He looked at the antenna, which she was aiming at the Moon.

"Grace?"

"Yeah."

"You can't do Earth-Moon-Earth if mass won't affect your psionic field. It won't bounce like a radio wave. Just aim it direct and it'll go through the mass between you and Li."

"Oh right. Duh."

She loosened the mount and started recalibrating.

"I wonder," Grace said, "if the Keeper appears down there because you're having a near-death experience."

"I'd say you came pretty close to not coming back last time," Rusty said. "Guess that's how he got his name."

"Hit me with the epinephrine if I flatline for more than three minutes," she said.

Rusty smiled wearily and nodded.

"It's probably a one-way trip regardless," she said. "Won't have a body to come back to. The epinephrine just means I don't have to say good-bye right now. Gives us that nasty little bit of hope of seeing each other again."

She turned on the antenna, donned her headset, and drank her tea. Then Grace lay on the cool roof of an abandoned gas station—the sovereign territory of the last group that would call themselves the United States of America—the last five free minds that would ever exist.

She heard helicopters in the distance as the toxic substances in her tea began to take hold. It'd be an advance recon element. They'd see Tomas and Maggie in the woods with FLIR, and they'd see Rusty and her on the roof. They'd gun down Ollie before he could set off a single bomb.

Through poison or bullets, neither of them would be leaving the roof alive.

Li Shu-hui stood in his lab in China's Hubei Province. He had just been promoted to lead researcher for the Party's genetic weapons program. Their first trial run was planned to eliminate a large percentage of the Xinjiang Uyghur Autonomous Region's population.

Li Shu-hui had, however, awoken that morning from the most vivid dream of his life. He saw a future where his work had been used to reduce the entirety of the human race to an ant colony—collective, subservient to one master, simple. The girl who'd appeared in his dream with an older version of himself had explained step by step how that future had unfolded.

His future self—world-weary, filled with regret and vodka—had mentioned that on that particular day, a three-legged feral dog would bite a woman on the train platform when Li Shu-hui got off. The dog had obliged old Li Shu-hui as an authenticator to his younger self, and the younger man began pondering how to avoid becoming that regretful, world-weary old man.

Li Shu-hui, as one of the Party's most trusted genetic scientists, had been entrusted with auditing the President's DNA for indicators of disease or early-onset mental illness and with making repairs if needed. He also had access to the DNA of several key Inner Party members.

Rather than targeting an unwanted minority in the Xinjiang Uyghur Autonomous Region, Li Shu-hui engineered a fairly unpleasant flu strain that only became symptomatic in key Party members.

The secret police launched an investigation. Contact tracing was performed, and evidence was collected. Several researchers in Li Shu-hui's lab, including Li Shu-hui, were sent to labor camps on suspicion of a conspiracy against the Chinese Communist Party.

But Li Shu-hui regretted nothing.

With their most talented researchers in labor camps, the CCP's genetic weapons program faltered. After a fruitless period under a new administration, its facilities were repurposed. The Party's strategy reverted to purchasing real estate, controlling politicians, and acquiring media conglomerates with American money extracted through Chinese slave labor to influence the world beyond its borders, and maintaining a stringent social credit policy and a harsh penal system within China rather than using telepathic overlords to dominate everyone. The United States of America remained a nation far larger than five people living in an abandoned gas station with a population slightly less subservient than it might otherwise have been.

Grace sat at the shoreline of a tiny island. The Giver behind her had withered, and bits of it were falling off. The water receded, and the minds that previously swam began to float in the air again, effortlessly. They grew larger, more vibrant, and more colorful as she watched. They connected not to an overseer, but to each other.

"You did well," the Keeper said as he approached. He sat next to Grace on the beach.

"I guess we drastically changed time," Grace said. "Rusty and Ma and the others had lives before they went into hiding. But my parents..."

"They'll never meet."

"So I'll never exist?"

"You're here now aren't you?" the Keeper asked. "Existing."

"But in a body? I assume you've come to take me through the door. You're the Keeper. One-way ticket, right?"

"I think you may be misunderstanding my name," the Keeper said. "It's 'keep' in the sense of a custodian, or a gardener, rather than one who takes and never gives back. I'm just the gardener here, Grace."

"Oh," she said. "Ohhh. Then—"

"He doesn't do this for everyone," the Keeper said, "but sometimes He gives people another cycle. It's not everybody, and you don't have to if you don't want to. But it's not like any religion's going to come enforce rules on Him anyway. He just does what He wants to do, and what He said was that you can go again if you're ready."

"Will I remember this place, or what happened?"

"No," the Keeper said. "Not on a conscious level. You'll be happier that way honestly. You can live a life without constant reminders of the human race's near extinction. I have an ideal point to take you back to—a miscarriage that doesn't have to be one."

"All right."

"And Grace?"

"Yeah."

"He said to tell you to stay away from witchcraft and hallucinogenic drugs this time."

Rusty Wilcox sat on a stool in a gas station diner on a stretch of much-used highway. There was a wilderness area about a half hour down the road, and though he wanted to take a day to do some hiking, he only had until tomorrow to get his haul to Cincinnati. He didn't like every aspect of being an owner-operator, but it was mostly honest work and sometimes he liked the scenery. Speaking of—

"You make up your mind yet?" she asked. Her name tag said she was Grace, and she was a lovely creature, perhaps a couple years younger than he was. She caught him studying her face, and a smile tugged at her lips. She let him look for a moment, and Rusty felt something change in his eyes—a nonverbal signal he didn't quite understand. But she saw it, and the smile spread on her face. It was almost like telepathy, but not quite, and it was like the sun coming out from behind a cloud. "Maybe I should give you more time?"

He fumbled with the menu, but managed to point to a sandwich and indicate that he'd like to buy one from her. Then he watched as she walked away with the order, and he thought that Grace was a fitting descriptor for her.

"Is your route going to bring you through again?" she asked when she returned. Her gaze flitted from his pupils to his curly hair, which he needed to get cut. But she seemed to like it. She just studied him, and he knew most of the conversation they were having wasn't with words. It was innocent, the way she looked at him—like they were children who'd met on a playground. There wasn't a hint of world-weariness or cynicism in her.

"It, um—" he said. "Yeah. In a couple of days with a return haul."

"Good," she said. "And I know this sounds weird, but there's something very familiar about your face. I feel like we've met before."

Rusty slipped his hands under his thighs so she wouldn't see them shaking. Women weren't like this with him.

"I think I'd remember meeting you," he said.

"Hm," she said. "Maybe in another life. Make sure you have hiking shoes when you come back. There's a trail I want to show you."

TUNNEL VISION

★

Erica L. Satifka and Rob McMonigal

"Captain Chen," the MP says to the American Army officer, "I'd like to introduce you to Afzat Kamnen. The, uh, diplomat."

Even without the introduction, Captain Paul Chen would have identified the man on sight. His grayish, angular face is topped by a beehivelike mass of dark red hair, and he's dressed in a caftan embroidered with a multitude of unfamiliar flowers. A pair of silver shoes like ballerina slippers completes the ensemble. The man's appearance is both comical and otherworldly, but Chen supposes there's a better-than-even chance it's the height of formal attire in Afzat's branch of the military.

This is the man who killed ten thousand people in rural China? Chen thinks. Or at least, Afzat had been part of the group that had carried out the attack. Chen finds it hard to believe, although that could be said for this entire situation.

Chen's colleague, Colonel Iris Fikowski, is already there, sitting across from the strange man. Chen slides in beside her. They'd been tasked with this man's interrogation until their replacements could arrive from Washington. Protocol was off the table, at least for now.

"Well, does he talk?" As Chen speaks, a small silver device in front of Fikowski sings out in a tinny electronic voice, a language like nothing he's ever heard before. It reminds him of the agitation cycle of a washing machine. The noise gives Chen an even bigger headache than he started with.

Afzat Kamnen, the diplomat-slash-potential war criminal, makes a face that isn't quite a smile. "Yes, I can talk," says the translating device in highly accented but intelligible English. Chen barely pays attention, though, because he can't stop thinking of Afzat's teeth. Though the rest of the diplomat looks human enough, his entirely too-white chompers are sharp and pointed like a shark's. Chen represses a shiver. Military men aren't supposed to show fear.

"Diplomat Kamnen, thank you for your patience," Fikowski says. "Now, let's begin. I'll start with the big question: did your people orchestrate the attack in Shaanxi Province at 0800 hours this morning?"

"Yes," Afzat replies through the device. "You know we did. Why do you ask?"

"Then we have no choice but to—" Chen starts, only to be cut off by Fikowski.

"Review the situation carefully," she finishes.

In fairness, it's quite the situation. And, Chen thinks, it's above his pay grade. He supposes that's why Fikowski is here, even if she has a reputation for impulsiveness.

Five years ago, Chinese scientists had found a way into another world, an alternate Earth supposedly devoid of intelligent life. Their military kept the discovery a secret as long as they could, but it wasn't hard to figure out that something strange was going on. The resource droughts of the 2040s hadn't affected China as much as the United States, the Afrizone, or any other nation-state on the rapidly depleting Earth, and the Chinese could only claim to have made a discovery of new deposits within their own borders so often. And space mining had been a dead end for every country that had attempted it.

Eventually, an American spy had located the clandestine mining operation deep in the heart of Shaanxi Province, hundreds of miles from the closest village. She'd managed to film it, at the cost of her life. The spy's video circulated for days, hitting every content provider. The Chinese government couldn't deny it, so they didn't, and they continued to mine tangible resources from thin air.

Then, this morning, there'd been an attack in rural China, an explosion no official or unofficial enemy of China took credit for. Information was scarce, but the blast didn't even appear to have originated on Earth. Hours later, US Army officials had found Afzat Kamnen wandering around the Sierra Army Depot, taking responsibility for the attack. He'd claimed to be from the world beyond

the Chinese mining portal. The story—and the diplomat himself—
were too outlandish *not* to be believed.

"How did you get here?" Chen asks, directing his question at the
device instead of Afzat. "You didn't walk from China."

Afzat gives Chen and Fikowski another one of his not-smiles. The
pointed teeth shine like beacons. "I emerged here using a device I
brought with me, which is now in your care."

"As far as we can tell, it's not a weapon," Fikowski says to Chen, "but
we still didn't think he should be allowed to have it. It's with our
technology exploitation team."

Chen runs his hand over his face, then addresses Afzat. "You're
saying you can open these—"

"Tunnels," Afzat's translator says, though the man's actual words
sound more like a broken furnace coughing.

Chen's not sure he believes the guy, but keeps his thoughts to
himself. Yet. "So, you're from another world. But that doesn't explain
why you killed all those people." He considers adding the words *you've
made things very difficult for us*, but leaves them out for now.

Afzat spouts out another staccato sentence, then another. The talk-
box waits until he's completely finished speaking before translating his
words, as if the device knew this would be a long one.

"When these people plundered our world, their crude effort at
tunneling caused a destabilizing effect that has ravaged the local
environment. We tried to collapse the tunnel with a wormhole
annihilator, but the risk to our world was too great. The land is totally
unfit for habitation, by either your people or mine." He doesn't
express any regret over killing ten thousand Chinese citizens, but if
Chen was in Afzat's silver slippers that wouldn't be the first thought
on his mind either.

"So why come to the United States?" Chen asks. "We didn't tunnel
into *your* world."

Afzat's strange face takes on a somber cast as he launches into
another staccato speech. "We have watched your nation, and despite
vast business dealings with the Chinese, you are not their allies. With
your cooperation, we wish to end the threat of our common enemy
for good. It will, of course, require many of our people to come here,
to use this continent to stage our forces."

Oh, hell no, Chen thinks.

Afzat continues, and so does his translator. "This translocation is required to maintain our global security. You understand that concept, I trust? We would, of course, provide you with certain knowledge, in exchange for your generosity."

Chen exchanges a glance with Fikowski. He can almost tell what she's thinking: This technology isn't the end of it. This could be the key to putting the United States back on top.

"We'll see what we can do, Diplomat," Fikowski says. "While we wait, why don't we go over some of the technology you brought with you? After all, as you've pointed out many times, it's far in advance of our own."

Later that night, after the interrogation, Fikowski invites Chen into her office for a discussion.

"An entire new technology, all our own! This is going to be bigger than the A-bomb." Fikowski beams behind her drink, clearly dreaming of endless possibilities.

Chen takes a sip from the glass of bourbon Fikowski had poured for him. "Doesn't that strike you as a bit too convenient?"

"Wouldn't it be nice to get lucky for a change? For our entire lives, Chen, we've been living in the decline of a once-great empire. America saw an opportunity after World War Two and took it. Could have kept it, too, but we squandered our lead. This time it will be different."

"If they're so advanced, how was China able to plunder their world and why do Afzat and his people need our help?" Chen wasn't letting go of this so easily.

Fikowski pulls a face. "You're a smart guy, Paul, but you have to stop being so paranoid. They need a place to stage their war with China, and we need their tech and the resources China tapped into. Afzat's people may have the weapons, but we have the numbers and the hometown advantage. I'd say that makes us even."

"If you say so. And anyway, it's pointless to continue deliberations. Congress is *not* going to allow immigrants of any kind into the United States, Fik. It's against the law now." Chen swirls his own liquor in the cut-glass tumbler. "Not even for access to tunnel technology."

"We need to figure out how to present this to the President," Fikowski says. "Exceptions can always be made. This may be our last chance, Chen. Caution is what screwed us in the first place."

Chen narrows his eyes. "So we do . . . what? Announce we're partners with a shark-man who promises America a way out of our decades-long depression? All that's gonna do is piss China off even more and spark a war we might not win." After officially acknowledging that the Chinese had indeed opened a wormhole into another world, the head of China's military, stodgy old General Yang Haoyu, had called on the international community for assistance in tracking down the "terrorists" and their accomplices.

At the moment, Afzat has no accomplices. But depending on the advice that Chen and Fikowski give to the incoming brass, that can change quickly.

"Think bigger. Maybe we can find a way to colonize their world safely, despite what Afzat said. Manifest Destiny, right?"

Chen runs a hand through his hair. "This is all so sudden," he says, "and it smells rotten to me. Did you read General Yang's statement? He said they didn't know the world was inhabited because there was no material evidence of human life. And now there's a creature with magic tech who just wants to help us? I'm not buying it."

"You will assist me with this mission or else, *Captain*. Don't look a gift horse in the mouth."

"That's what they said at Troy, *Colonel*."

"Dismissed," says Fikowski, icily, a vague smirk on her lips. Chen nods and leaves his superior officer to her bombast and bourbon.

The next morning, Chen and Fik, a DOD scientist, an MP, and Afzat take a shuttle to the post's outskirts. *Can't let too many people know this tech exists*, Chen thinks. *At least, not yet.*

Fikowski had plowed ahead and asked for this demonstration of the tunnel tech. And of course, the diplomat was more than pleased to provide it.

"You know a lot about us, Diplomat Kamnen," Chen says, picking up a thread he hadn't quite been satisfied at dropping yesterday. "How is that possible?"

"We have watched you through our tunnels for many years," Afzat says.

A shiver traces its way down Chen's spine. How long have Afzat's people been aware of this world and, if he were to give the Chinese the benefit of the doubt, why hadn't they observed Afzat's people? He can't imagine they remained completely passive. Had the visitors played a part in the Disinformation Wars of 2033, or the silicon riots? "The Chinese only started tapping your resources five years ago. You should have made contact before then. Maybe we could have helped you."

"We saw what you do to each other. We wanted no part of it. But the destabilization of our world makes our alliance a necessity." His tone through the talk-box is matter-of-fact.

After half an hour, the shuttle stops in a desolate location. Afzat walks the team far from the vehicle. Chen feels the hairs on the back of his neck rise.

The diplomat speaks into his talk-box. "In my world, these coordinates are at the center of a major settlement. You will be able to see past the barrier, and some of my people may be able to see you."

"Now, hold on," Chen says. "You didn't tell us that—"

Afzat barrels ahead as if he's trying to forestall Chen's words. "The fact that I am here is common knowledge among them. It is possible that some of them may ask to come through this tunnel. Will you permit this, my friends?" The artificial voice sounds almost plaintive.

He's taking advantage of us, Chen thinks with growing anger. But before he can answer, Fikowski leans in close to him so Afzat's translator can't pick up her words.

"Let him bring someone else in," she whispers. "We'll see if their stories match."

Chen sighs. Maybe it *would* be useful to interview more than one solitary individual. "You can bring in one more person, Diplomat Kamnen. No more."

Afzat makes that weird little not-a-smile with his sharp teeth and presses buttons on his box in a certain sequence. There's no noise, but the light show is like a thousand rockets being set off at once. Chen and the others are blinded, unable to tell what's happening, and he feels sicker than he's ever been before. It's terrible, and when it's all over, three strangers dressed in garb similar to Afzat's are standing in the field. Their teeth gleam in the sunlight, dozens of mini-razors. The other three are bigger and bulkier, as if they have extra muscles under their skin. Their eyes are more reptilian than human. They look *hungry.*

Chen finds it hard to keep from puking, and when he looks at Fikowski he sees she's lost whatever breakfast she'd had that morning.

"Did anyone look through the tunnel? Was anyone recording?" He glares at Afzat. "And why are there *three* of them when we said *one*?"

The scientist checks the video recorder on her tablet. "There's just a bright flash. You can't see anything." She pulls out a keyboard and begins tapping, her lower lip bitten between her teeth.

Chen stalks over to Afzat, who's chatting away with his compatriots. From the easy tone of their conversation, Chen gets the feeling these three visitors weren't chosen at random. "Damn it, you opened this tunnel *knowing* we wouldn't be able to see anything. Secure them now," Chen orders the MP, his voice shriller than he'd like. Fikowski doesn't react because she's still doubled over, vomit soiling her fatigues.

Afzat listens to Chen's words through the translator with a sour expression. "As far as I am concerned, the test went perfectly fine. Perhaps your mind is too closed to the opportunity our friendship offers, Captain Chen."

"I'll call for backup," the MP says. He appears cowed by the newcomers.

"You do that," Fikowski says to the MP as she holds her phone out to Chen, preventing him from interrogating Afzat. "We need to go back to base now, Chen. General Martinez is here, and he says there's been another incident in Shaanxi."

As soon as Chen and Fikowski arrive back on post, they're whisked into a secure briefing room by General Martinez, chairman of the Joint Chiefs of Staff. He's alone. *They're really keeping things small,* Chen notes.

Fikowski steps forward first. "We heard about the second explosion. Could you provide us with more detail, sir?"

"As far as we can tell," he says, "the Chinese attempted to open another resource extraction portal—"

"The people from the other side call them tunnels," Chen says. "At least, that's what it translates to in English."

"The . . . tunnel exploded. It's worse this time. Approximate Chinese losses number fifty-six thousand. China's going to find out about our little friend, if they don't already know. We need answers. You've been interrogating the visitor, so tell us: Is he a threat to American national security or an asset?"

This explosion occurred around the same time the new visitors came through Afzat's tunnel, Chen thinks, checking the fact sheet Martinez had handed him. *That can't be a coincidence.*

Fikowski clears her throat. "There's a situation on our end, too. The diplomat brought three others through a tunnel."

That's one way to dodge the question, Chen thinks.

Martinez scowls. "How did *that* happen?"

Fikowski feigns nonchalance. At least, Chen is pretty sure it's a feint. "They're in custody, being processed. I feel that all these people, and especially the original diplomat who made contact with us yesterday morning, can be persuaded to give us a clearer picture of what just happened. I'll force them myself, if I have to."

Chen studies Fikowski. She'd always been more proactive than him, a fireball of ambition in a military that's still a bit of a man's world.

"I don't think any radical steps will be necessary," Chen says, his words rushed. "The diplomat has been very forthcoming."

"But can we *trust* them? That's the issue here, Colonel. Find out. Fast," Martinez says.

Well, Fik? What brash thing are you going to say this time? But she doesn't say a word, and Chen finally mutters, "We'll do our best."

While Chen and Fikowski were at the meeting with Martinez, Afzat, and the newcomers had been driven back to post and confined to separate rooms, each sporting heavy restraints. Afzat's talk-box had been taken away, and Chen borrows it from the officer on duty as the two of them enter Afzat's cell.

Chen starts, beating Fikowski to the punch. "The Chinese attempted to open another tunnel, and it exploded on them. This body count is headed for six figures fast. You wouldn't know anything about that, would you?"

Afzat blows air through his thin lips, a gesture that Chen has come to think of as a chuckle. "It sounds as if our common enemy has made an unfortunate error."

Fikowski leans forward, fury on her face. "'Error' my ass, Diplomat Kamnen. I wonder what your friends in the other cells have to say about all this. Maybe we should ask them, hmm?"

"An unfortunate error," Afzat repeats.

She jabs a finger at him. "I think you tried to attack China again, out of revenge."

Chen agrees with her. How long will it be before the United States becomes the target of China's retaliation? He and Fikowski need to tread lightly here. Chen isn't sure she's capable of it.

Another enigmatic look from Afzat.

"You killed them," Chen says, "just admit it."

"There would have been no issue if the Chinese—our common enemy—had not tried to reopen the barrier between our worlds with their crude efforts." Afzat holds himself straighter despite his restraints. "We put up a line of defense in that part of our world. This latest attack just makes our home even less stable. Now we *must* have a way to fight back on this side of the barrier or we'll lose that world forever."

Booby-trapping a piece of land like that, without any warning to the Chinese, is an act of war. Chen and his country are being backed into a corner here. He changes the subject. "Those three others you brought over, who are they?"

"Some of my countrymen."

"We'll be talking to them," Chen says.

"I hope you do," Afzat replies. "They're all rather fascinating people." Chen tries not to read tone into the translation device, but he gets the feeling that Afzat is toying with them. Maybe that's been the case all along.

They continue on like this for some time, with Afzat speaking vaguely and Fikowski making excuses for the diplomat. So much for her bold statement to General Martinez.

They're friends now, he thinks, and tries to hide a frown from the other two "people" in the room.

The other visitors, who'd each arrived with nothing but poor clothing choices and bulging biceps, corroborated Afzat's story about booby-trapping the barrier between their world and Shaanxi. Talking to them, Chen's nearly certain they're all government officials, but none will disclose their rank or position.

"They were just protecting their world," Fikowski says after finishing the last interview. "Don't you believe in national sovereignty, Chen?"

"But setting a trap...it's *wrong*," he says.

"It's what they had to do," she says, "and it sounds like this trap hurt them almost as much as the Chinese."

"Afzat said it hurt their land. He didn't say it had killed anyone."

Fikowski gestures back at the cells which hold the beefy visitors. "They seem hardier than us. Besides, land's important too."

Chen decides to leave it alone. She isn't wrong.

After the four fruitless interrogations, Chen heads back into his office and puts on some light jazz. Just as he's about to doze off, he hears the secure line ring. He picks it up.

"This is General Yang Haoyu," the voice says in barely accented English. "You know why I'm calling."

Chen is shocked to hear the Chinese general's voice. "How did you get this number?"

Yang doesn't answer. "Sixty-six thousand, two hundred and eight people," the Chinese general says. "That is how many people your allies from another world have murdered in two days."

"What allies?" Chen asks.

"Don't play dumb with me. We know you have some of these terrorists in custody, out there in the California desert."

Don't engage too far with him, Chen tells himself. "Your intelligence hasn't been too good lately, General Yang. Neither has your military."

"We have told you many times that world is uninhabited. Or so we believed. We were wrong."

It wouldn't matter if you knew or not, Chen thinks, *you still would have taken their resources. And so would we, if we'd developed the technology first.*

"Let's stop lying to each other for a second and try to prevent a goddamn war. These hypothetical visitors—if we were to host them, which I am neither confirming nor denying—are fixated on what your country did to them. China is in trouble, General Yang."

"America will be too, in time."

No, because we're going to ally with them, Chen thinks, *because power and politics gives us no choice. What, are we going to partner with China instead?* "We can't offer you any assistance. And we're not giving you access to any visitors we may or may not have. That's off the table."

General Yang sneers. "You'd rather join forces with these *creatures* than with your own kind?"

"They aren't creatures," Chen says, dropping all pretenses. "They're human beings, just like us. They look a little different, sure, but they have feelings, emotions, needs. And your tunnels have ruined their land, the eastern half of it anyway. It's far worse than anything America's done, and we've done *plenty*."

"So you just believed him?" General Yang laughs. "You really believe that just going into his world caused all that destruction and made it unlivable? Did he even show you any proof?"

Chen thinks back to the diplomat's line from earlier: The land is totally unfit for habitation. "I have no reason to doubt him and a hundred reasons to doubt *you*, General Yang. I'm just grateful they don't want to destroy *everyone* who lives on this planet."

Another chuckle. "Not yet. Good luck with your new allies, Captain. You're going to need it." The line goes dead.

Chen barely makes it back to his apartment on post that night. At 0700 the next day, a private transport arrives to take him to a sensitive compartmented information facility, and Chen settles in, his head pounding.

Fikowski is already there on the other side of the passenger seat. "General Martinez and I met with Afzat alone last night after you left. I think he likes me. We've decided to ally with Afzat's people. They're in a crisis right now, and they need help. He's on his way back to Washington now to present our findings to the President."

I guess I'm the only one who's wary of trusting people we just met from beyond the psychic barrier, Chen thinks. It's then that he notices the transport isn't heading to post but to some point outside of it. "Where are we going?"

"Afzat asked us to meet him at the place where we brought the others through."

"Did Martinez say we should listen to Afzat?" Even if he's now an official ally of the United States, this is a lot of leeway to give the visitor.

"Chen, this decision is way above both our pay grades," she says. "More listening, less talking. Follow orders."

Chen shuts his mouth.

They pull up to the deserted field a little while later. Afzat is there, a green parka awkwardly layered over his official diplomat's uniform.

"My friends, welcome to this historic day," Afzat says in not-too-bad English, without his device. Chen guesses he'd been practicing.

Chen looks around. It's the same group as last time, but with more MPs and a few extra scientists. The need for secrecy is almost moot anyway, he guesses. Camera equipment is set up everywhere. Chen wonders if they'll catch anything this time. He guesses they won't.

"I hear we have decided to ally with you," Chen says.

"And a good thing too, my friend. A very good thing."

Everyone here is so damn sure this is the right path. Well, I'd already decided to ally with them myself last night, Chen thinks. *Didn't I?*

"Why are we here, Afzat?"

Suddenly, everyone's secure lines and electronic alerts all go off at once. Chen fumbles for his own clunky military phone.

China Goes Dark after Wave of Explosions, reads the first headline he sees. The second reads *Freak Event Leads to China Devastation.* He scans through page after page of results with mounting horror. *Countless Dead in China's Largest Cities.* Then he drops his phone. "You did this," he says. It's not a question, and he doesn't need to clarify what he's talking about.

"A most ingenious solution, is it not? Colonel Fikowski seemed to think so. We worked out the details last night, while you were committing treason." Afzat's demeanor can be accurately described as chipper.

"You used your tunnels to kill millions?" Chen can barely stand. "At once?"

"We'd hoped for more, but don't worry. We'll eliminate the rest on the next wave, if they don't immediately capitulate," the diplomat says with a wide, goofy grin.

"You killed them," Chen repeats, in shock.

"Absolutely. Kill or be killed. Your country has a long history of it, from what I understand." He blows air through his lips on the last sentence.

I should have shot you on sight, Chen thinks. Afzat's people are monsters. Or at least Afzat is. "You destroyed a country with no thought of the cost, not even a hint of remorse."

"Did the Chinese think of the cost when they attempted to tunnel into our world, when they stole our resources? No, they did not. We're being fairer with you Americans, partially because we like you, but also because we really need this hemisphere to remain unsullied, and well, you come along with the package. But a fair and equitable package it will be, you won't even notice our peacekeeping forces. A bargain well struck, don't you think?"

Chen can't help himself; he lunges at Afzat. Fikowski intercedes, but he manages to land a blow on the diplomat's temple first, which the man seems unfazed by. How strong are they? Could he have overpowered them at any time? It hardly seems to matter now, anyway. "You *murderers*! Why did you even ask for our help if you're so goddamned powerful?"

Afzat straightens his parka. "I never asked for help, not once. I asked for cooperation, and your general granted it. You're a military man, Captain. Surely you understand the concept of ensuring the battle never touches your own shores?" He holds up his black box. "The only issue left is Congress. Your general said they might not agree to our permanent occupation. But I think we can be *very* persuasive. It would be a shame for you if our alliance has to end, and we were forced to write this world off entirely."

It's a veiled threat. Fikowski releases her grip on Chen and freezes. *Too late now, Fik,* thinks Chen. He looks back at Fikowski. *Is she chastened? Does she even realize what she's done?* Then again, was there ever any way to stop this?

His oddness was only ever a put-on, Chen thinks. *In the end, they're exactly like us.*

Chen straightens up. "Kill me too, then. I don't want to be part of any world that contains the likes of you. Or any of *you*, for that matter," he says, glaring at Fikowski and the others.

Afzat beams. "I think we'll keep you around, Captain Chen. You two are our oldest friends here, on this side of the tunnel." He winks, and Chen has to repress the urge to punch him again.

Instead, he forces a laugh. "Joke's on you, Afzat," Chen says. "The Chinese drilled into your world in the first place because we're running out of everything. Our environment is trashed. Both our hemispheres are worthless."

The diplomat shrugs. "Then we will go elsewhere. This isn't the first world we've invaded. It's merely the most recent one to annoy us." He puts his talk-box into the pocket of the parka. Apparently he doesn't need it anymore, and maybe never did.

"You won't get away with this," Chen yells stupidly. Afzat ignores him.

"Now, I think it's time to meet with your President. How does that saying go, take me to your leader?" Afzat blows more air through his lips and links arms with Fikowski. She seems disgusted, but doesn't slap the diplomat away. "And since we'll be meeting *your* leader, it's only fair you should make contact with some of ours."

All at once, there's a sickening tear in the air. Chen trembles as tunnels open all around him, and a few of the rank and file scream. Then the ground begins to shake as dozens, maybe hundreds, of Afzat's people stream through them, many of them carrying the same flat black box as the diplomat. They chatter to one another in their otherworldly language, scarcely noticing the officers or other military personnel. One of them jostles Chen to the desert floor by accident, and Chen can't even bring himself to get up.

DO DRAGONS TEXT?

✪

Brenda W. Clough

Old Grandfather Cho had a phone. Everybody did—it was mandated by the Central Committee in Beijing. But in this season, scarce gasoline for the generator was better used to run the pump that lifted the water from the canal into the rice paddies at the foot of the mountain.

No one in Huanggangxin was interested in how the war with the United States was going. In addition to farming, Grandfather Cho was the village feng shui master. Analyzing the unseen movements of Lung, the earth dragon, kept Grandfather fully occupied whenever he wasn't plowing, sowing, or transplanting young rice stalks.

But Grandfather was one of the most important men in the village, because the passage of the dragon under the earth generated feng shui, the unseen currents of chi that ran along and under the land. Only this past year, Lung had turned over in his sleep, deep under the mountain. This had made a bit of bank on the Fenghe River crumble, forcing the villagers to dig the mouth of the canal out again. Would it be necessary to cut a new access channel to the river's water? Not only did every villager's livelihood depended upon the rice crop fed by that water, but also the Central Committee was demanding more and more of the harvest for the troops.

It was a crucial decision, fully occupying Grandfather's mind. So his phone was kept in his kitchen cupboard, behind the two chipped porcelain rice bowls and the single tin cooking pot. He never thought about it. The battery had flatlined last season.

Even when the tremendous noise woke the entire village one night, Grandfather merely ran out into the dirt lane with everyone else. It was pitch dark, but the glow from the mountain lit Huanggangxin bright as day. The pattering sound all around them was debris, dust falling from the night sky. "Gods, look at it," Madam Liang yelled. "Half the mountain is gone!"

The top of the mountain glowed like iron in the forge. And it was visibly shorter, planed off flat. It couldn't have been a bomb. Something had sliced off the tip of the entire peak. "Oh gods," Madam Liang groaned. "What if it had hit us?"

"It's the Americans," Fengfeng said. Everything bad was the fault of the Americans. "Grandfather! Do you think Lung is hurt?"

"I'm certain he's fine," Grandfather Cho said, even though he wasn't certain of anything. "Earth dragons are magical, remember. Mortal weapons don't bother them." But it was worrying. In the end the villagers agreed that the prudent thing to do would be to go up onto the mountain tomorrow, and make a small offering. A rice cake and an incense stick, just to show Lung that the village had nothing to do with it.

"And of course, Grandfather, you'll be the one to make the prayer," Fengfeng said.

"Knowing how the feng shui currents run doesn't mean dragons listen to me," Grandfather protested. But there was no one else. Grandfather Cho was the oldest man in Huanggangxin. And he knew how to sense the currents in the earth, close enough.

In the morning, the villagers set out. It had never been a big mountain, not like the big karst cliffs on the Li River. But now it was sadly diminished. The road wound back and forth up the wooded slope, and abruptly ended. Beyond, where the peak used to be, was flat as noodle dough. There were no trees, no birds or bugs. The very stone had been blasted and smoothed. Cautiously, Madam Liang patted the surface with her callused bare foot. "Ow! It's hot! Like a baking stone, you could fry a scallion cake on it."

"Melted away!"

"The Americans have a new and terrible weapon," Fengfeng said. "A torch, or a bomb, or something. This is very serious."

"We must inform the Central Committee," Grandfather Cho said. "Right away!"

No one wanted to loiter on this fearsomely deformed mountain. Grandfather wasn't easy about it either, but he felt that Lung must be equally upset, having his roof pounded like that. Perhaps a rice cake and a stick of incense would be a comfort. He took the basket from Madam Liang and said, "Hurry back and phone Beijing. I'll make the offering."

"Don't delay," Madam warned.

When they were gone, Grandfather Cho retreated into the fringe of forest. There was a sharp demarcation between the blasted bare rock and the trees. Branches had been severed, even trunks split where the line of destruction had passed. The very precision was frightening.

Finally Grandfather found a flat rock, not too far from the edge but not nerve-rackingly close. He set the rice cake on it and stuck the incense stick upright into the dirt beside it. With a cheap cigarette lighter he lit the stick. The sweet smoke twirled away on the breeze and was lofted upward by the heat from the blasted stone.

Grandfather Cho had never addressed the earth dragon before, but it was always wise to be deferential. "Lord Dragon," he prayed aloud. "Mighty under the earth. Remember that we, your subjects, have always respected you. Accept these humble offerings—"

He was staring down, at the rock and the rice cake. And suddenly the rock became real. It snapped into a powerful focus that Grandfather recognized, even though he had never seen it before. The rock became far more real than the rice cake, so that the rice cake looked like a smear of flour, the vapor from a sneeze.

Grandfather Cho reeled back a step. Oh gods, the path was doing the same thing. The ground under his bare feet was more than solid, assuming more dimensions, more reality, than a mortal could tolerate. His own feet looked thin and shadowy. He didn't deliberately fall flat on his face. He had no choice, any more than the incense smoke did. Powerful currents were pushing at him.

YOU

The words reverberated through his body. Grandfather Cho clapped his hands over his ears but the voice reverberated through him anyway.

YOU, MORTAL

"Great lord," Grandfather Cho choked.

HOW DARE YOU DESTROY MY MOUNTAIN ·

"It wasn't us, your humble subjects. It was the Americans!"

Grandfather Cho dared to peer between his fingers. The earth dragon was there. It was so real that Grandfather Cho could not see it properly. He dimly discerned a long body, miles of it, undulating in and out of the solid rock as if it were smoke. But it really was smoke. The earth dragon was so much more real. Solid matter was no more than vapor to it. Its head was the size of a cliff. And the eyes—there were six, eight, twenty of them, the hot color of the sun at noon, all of them glaring at him. The ground under his belly was losing its substance. The dragon was so terrifyingly real that Grandfather Cho could feel himself melting.

THEN THEY MUST STOP

"Mighty Lung, they are using space weapons that we cannot—"

SEE TO IT

"It shall be as you command, great lord." There was really no other reply to make. Grandfather lay trembling and sweating, silently praying he would survive this. Men were not meant to look at gods. Lung might have heard him, because the ground beneath him firmed up a little, like a jelly cooling and setting. The dragon must be moving away, deeper down into the ground. Removed from the presence of divine reality, the world gradually subsided into solidity again. Trembling, Grandfather Cho staggered to his feet and ran.

When he tottered back to Huanggangxin, however, the villagers were skeptical. "What does Lung think the Chinese Space Force is doing?" Fengfeng demanded. "They're trying as hard as they can to defeat the Americans."

"Did you phone the Central Committee?"

"I got a recording. Left a message."

"We have to do something," Grandfather insisted. "Or Lung will be even more angry."

"It must have hurt, to lose the top of the mountain," Madam Liang said. "But we're farmers. What can we do?"

Nobody knew. But under the lash of desperation Grandfather Cho had an idea. "Let me charge up my phone," he said. "I'll call Ah Mei."

"Good, good! Your smart granddaughter."

"They know everything in Shanghai," Madam Liang said.

Grandfather was confident. "She'll know what to do."

He took the phone out from behind the rice bowls. Then he had to search for the cable before he could plug it in. The battery had run all the way down, so it took all night to charge up. Ah Mei had put her number into the Saved Contacts, so that was no problem. But then there was the difficulty of actually reaching her. Ah Mei had a job with a game-design business in Shanghai. "Online multiplayer," she'd said, words that meant nothing to Grandfather Cho, though it involved working even longer hours than farming.

But after several attempts he got through. "Hello, BaBa!" she cried, small and distant in his ear. Madam Liang helped him put the phone into speaker mode. Everyone nodded approvingly at her dutiful words. "Is your health good? How is the rice crop?"

"Fine, fine. But I have a different problem, Ah Mei. A big one. Maybe you can help me, huh?"

He was sitting on Fengfeng's porch, where the signal was best, and the entire village eavesdropped without embarrassment as he described again his encounter with Lung. Ah Mei didn't come home now except at New Year. She had become a city girl, with an office job and an apartment in a tower. "Come on, BaBa," she said. "There aren't any dragons under the earth. How could we have subways or underground fiber optics if there were?"

"Perhaps they don't have any in the cities," Madam Liang suggested, but the others hushed her.

"I saw him, Ah Mei. You have to help us. He's mad about his mountain being bombed. Who can blame him? If we don't do something, he'll swim under the village and make the earth shake. He could destroy Huanggangxin in two minutes."

She sighed so loudly that he could imagine her rolling her eyes. "Okay, I'll play the game . . . how about you try this. Since Lung can swim through the earth, he could swim to America, right? Send him over there to shake apart Washington and New York."

"He's a local dragon," Grandfather pointed out. "He's lived in this valley all my life, and the life of my father before me. I don't think earth dragons travel. Besides, what about the ocean?"

"Then what about text?"

"What?"

"There are earth dragons everywhere, right? Not just in the Fenghe River valley."

"I don't know."

"There are earthquakes in the West. You say that earth dragons cause earthquakes. So there must be earth dragons in America."

"That's very smart," Fengfeng whispered.

"And there's a good chance that Lung has a way to talk to them. Like the way we have phones so I can talk to you. He has a phone, a magical internet, some way to communicate with his dragon friends."

"That makes sense," Grandfather admitted.

"Good! So go back, and ask Lung to contact the earth dragons in America. They can help. And, ooh, another brainstorm. Tell Lung there's an earth dragon in the US named San Andreas."

"Agh, a foreign name," Grandfather Cho grumbled. "Fengfeng, do you have a pen? Okay, Ah Mei, spell it slowly ... What is this San Andreas?"

"If there are earth dragons in the United States, this will be the biggest one," Ah Mei said with confidence. "Tell Lung to ask San Andreas to roll over and wiggle a little. I bet he could push California right into the Pacific Ocean."

"Oh, that would be very nice," Grandfather Cho said. "The Americans would leave Lung alone after that."

"They'd be way too busy to bother us," Ah Mei said. "Look, I gotta run, BaBa. My boss is messaging me. Let me know what happens, okay?"

"You're a good girl, Ah Mei." And blip, she was gone.

"Wow, you have one smart girl there," Madam Liang said. "She should get married."

"Does anyone study feng shui in America?" Fengfeng asked.

On this point Grandfather Cho could speak. "Only in a minor way. Maybe arranging their restaurants or moving the furniture around. They don't know anything about how the earth dragons cause the currents to flow. I'll go back up the mountain and tell Lung. And, Fengfeng. Will we know if there's an earthquake in California?"

"Oh sure." Fengfeng grinned and held up his own phone.

"Good. If this works, I think we should tell the Central Committee." Grandfather Cho looked out across the fields at the truncated mountain. "Lung could win us this war."

"I'll say that in my message," Fengfeng said. "Bet you they'll return my call."

SCION OF THE SOUTHERN CROSS

✪

Kevin Ikenberry

Falling. Twisting. Wind buffeting. Spinning. Stomach reeling. Blurry.
I'm falling.
Falling.
Wake up, Mason. Janine's voice. *Wake up.*

The parachute snapped opened. The jolt cleared the disorienting fog in my head. My chute's deployment tightened the combat harness painfully under my arms and squeezed my crotch. The straps eased as the chute's sensors determined I was condition one—good to go. A split second later, I felt my Vigilante's ejection seat fall away. From pilot school at Perth, I knew to look up and make sure my canopy was good; I thought it was. There was no moon, and clouds covered more than half the sky. At ten thousand meters, grey clouds swallowed me. I'd break through into clear air at about four thousand meters, but there wouldn't be anything more to see in the black. "Darker than a coal mine," my wingman Jimmy Brooks liked to say. Brooksy died on the way into the target.

High-speed aerial reconnaissance was supposed to be a thing of the past. Once the War for Space had taken out every satellite system inside the geo-belt, imagery had become a hot commodity again. We'd flown a high-altitude ingress from Pearl Harbor, dropped low just west of Kwajalein Atoll and caught an autonomous drone tanker before sweeping west with every sensor we had. The bastards were waiting for us on the way out and forced us into the NEZ—the Nuclear Exclusion Zone.

Why?

Can't think about that now. I opened my helmet's faceplate, and the cold, dry air of altitude rushed inside. The shock of it on my skin cleared the rest of the post-ejection fog. Under my parachute canopy, the sky was dark. I blinked several times trying to get my bearings. Damned hard to do when ya can't see anything.

Last I'd checked, the Spratlys were about eighty kilometers southeast. The Brits had a base there, but there were a thousand little islands and atolls around me. Behind enemy lines? Hell, there were no lines in the NEZ. Five years ago, great fleets tangled here and nuked themselves, and everything around them, into oblivion. Much of the South Pacific islands south and west of the Philippines were abandoned because of the radiation. There'd been some unexplained phenomena and activity in the area—surface ships no one claimed operated within the waters. More troubling were the really strange sonar readings from our hardened subs slinking around beneath the surface.

Below me the ocean was so dark I almost couldn't make out the horizon, except to the north where a sliver of clear sky let me see the stars. North, toward Okinawa, where I should've been heading instead of descending under canopy. So much for the Vigilante being the fastest reconnaissance aircraft since the Blackbird.

"You can't outrun fate, son." I said the words out loud in the gravelly voice of my last check ride instructor, Commander Raymond. The guy's mustache somehow fit under his faceplate with the same magic his rotund frame fit into a pressure suit. Some kinda miracle. The man had a saying for everything. More than once, his admonitions and commentary had saved my arse. I might not have outrun fate, or the SA-55 long-range SAM, but I had bigger problems now than surface-to-air missiles. There was no telling what was below in the NEZ, and I had to survive long enough to get rescued. I shook off the thoughts and got about it.

In an instant, the grey mist cleared, and I fell silently toward the blackness. Automatically, the drogue chutes rippled into full deployment and slowed my descent to a placid twenty meters per second. I was low enough to breathe without the suit now. The benefits of the automated system made me wonder how many poor blokes died during a slow descent from high altitude. I wasn't going to do that, but I had more work to do.

My suit had watertight dams at the neck and wrists, so I took a minute to twist off my gloves and drop them in the ocean. After a half second, I lost sight of them. I worked my helmet off my head and also dropped it into the water. Maybe I'd see a splash? No such luck. I was pretty high up, still, but at least it wasn't cold. Like it ever truly got cold in the South China Sea. If anything, the temperature seemed to rise with every second I descended toward the black water.

Not wearing the gloves made it easier to pull out my personal dosimeter and attach it to the survival harness where I could see it. This far away from the center of the NEZ, the chance for fatal radiation levels was low, but there wasn't any way to be sure. Next, I patted the survival radio on my harness. Yeah, it was still there. I almost turned it on, but SOP said not to do so until I hit the water. So I waited. Standard operating procedures seemed pointless until needed and then they turned to gold. From training, I knew my suit would inflate a survival raft around me, and once I cut my way out the chute and its shroud lines, I could reach out and touch someone. At least in theory. I checked the watertight holster for my .45 pistol, too. Precautions were necessary when flying over the NEZ. I would need a miracle to survive it.

We had a lot of theories about the NEZ and not much else. The enemy hadn't put together a naval force of any kind in five years, but every time we investigated the NEZ strange shit seemed to happen. In the days before the war, what the generals referred to as the shaping stage, the Chinese had surprised everyone with multiple nuclear strikes in and around the South China Sea. Our intel pukes said they'd attempted to irradiate nearby landmasses of all types to prohibit allied forces from gaining a foothold. They hadn't bothered hitting the Philippines or Okinawa. Nothing that far out had concerned them, and they'd believed we wouldn't move in since Taiwan had been nuked into a smoldering, radioactive slag heap. Still, we'd sent the ships in and turned the sea to a watery hell. Hard to believe that was fifteen years ago. When the war was aggressive, and our objectives were clear. We'd slipped beyond that now. Aggression always turned into stagnation. At least it had until recently.

One of their bases, on an unnamed island that hadn't been on any pre-war map, activated. Flickers of power came first. Once the lights came on, our ISR assets concentrated on the island. Anything in the air met stiff resistance from multiple batteries of hypersonic antiaircraft missiles. We didn't have the satellite networks anymore, so General Whitney said it was time we returned to harm's way. Wars needed to be fought face-to-face and not behind our autonomous vehicles and space assets. Our Vigilantes were designed and built to fulfill that mission. They drafted every pilot they could scrounge. Hauled me right out of transpacific passenger flights for Qantas and into a tighter cockpit. I fared better than the poor blokes who got fighters and attack aircraft. Many of them didn't last two weeks. I'd made it five years without incident. I could've gone home two years ago, but home wasn't there anymore. The hole in my heart wouldn't let me try.

The clouds above showed signs of breaking: the clearer weather we'd tried to take advantage of as it moved east. Hadn't really mattered, though. I didn't see a damned thing with my Vigilante's optical systems. Infrared and my synthetic aperture radar caught some stuff, but I had no idea what it was. They have analysts and artificial intelligence for data interpretation. I was just a damned pilot sent to take pictures. Without an aircraft, I was nothing but a frightened bagman with a pistol and a bright fucking orange life raft. For a second, I wondered if command had received my download before I'd punched out. I'd made it to the target and snapped the pictures required. Maybe they'd gotten them. Wasn't really my problem anymore, right? On the exfiltration from enemy airspace, I'd relaxed for a moment. The kind of mistake seasoned pilots make when things became routine. The kind of mistake some don't walk away from.

Fucking SAMs. From somewhere nearby, I knew, but I hadn't seen a thing until I was on top of them. For all I knew, the buggers were right below me waiting to fish my arse out of the water like a prize black marlin. I stared at the horizon and thought how it looked a little different from the way it had a couple minutes before and—

SPLASH!

My boots hit the surface and then I was underwater, completely submerged. My suit raft inflated as advertised with a little more force than I was expecting. My ribs took the brunt of it. Next thing I knew, I was on the surface under my orange, white, and green canopy and entangled in shroud lines like I'd lain down in a nest of angry death adders.

From the inside of my suit's right thigh, I grabbed my shroud cutter and quickly separated myself from them. I wasn't worried about them pulling me down with the raft around me, but I needed to get away from the chute in case friendlies came to the rescue. Trying to haul the wet mass in and use it for anything was a stupid idea. Cut a line, toss it away, move on to the next. A couple minutes later, I was free and moving to the next point of my internal checklist.

I saw a full white rectangle on my dosimeter. On closer inspection, there was a tiny amount of black indicator on the sensor's edges, but the remainder hadn't been spoiled. From a pocket on my harness, I withdrew the chewable anti-radiation tablets. The medicine tasted like rancid cherries, but it was far better than the alternative. I choked them down and managed not to gag as I grabbed the survival radio and toggled the switch to On. Next, I pressed the emergency beacon button and held it for ten seconds before releasing it. I prayed, but that wasn't on the checklist. All I could do now was wait and hope someone had picked up my—

Something moved to my left, snapping the placid water. I turned my head that way. Dark eddies curled the surface. My brain almost overloaded. My raft and pressure suit were supposedly bite proof, but I wasn't taking a fucking chance. The shark repellent packets were stowed by my left thigh. Grabbing one while wearing a pressure suit was hard, even with the gloves off, but I fetched one and slid the water-soluble packet into the sea.

There was no odor, and I couldn't see anything in the dark water. I didn't know if it was working or not. I sat there, tense and waiting for something to happen for a good long time. Nothing did.

See? Even gear from the lowest bidder works.

Satisfied for the moment, I patted the pouches on my harness until I found a small bottle of water. My instructors had said to conserve as much as possible. I almost laughed at the thought. Water surrounded me. I had a portable desalination kit in the raft, too. If I was out here that long, no amount of shark repellent or luck was going to help if the stories about the NEZ were true. I screwed off the cap and gulped the fluid before slipping the empty bottle back into its pouch. Training taught us garbage left a trail and to leave nothing behind, so I didn't.

If what we knew about the NEZ was true, though, garbage was the least of our concerns. Twelve months ago, the USS *Wohlrab* steamed into the NEZ on a reconnaissance mission and went down with all two thousand souls aboard. Rescue sorties uncovered "an unprecedented swarm of emergent biologics." Bullshit. The intel pukes loved making up inoffensive terms for everything. These...things weren't new species or something dredged up from the depths of the Mariana Trench. They were mutants, pure and simple. Sharks with two heads? No? Godzilla? No, but close. Megafauna. Another intel word. Mutants. The kind who'd just as soon eat you if they found you. There were images captured by some of my mates, and they were the stuff of fucking nightmares. Whatever they did in the NEZ, our enemies hadn't just purged the islands to protect themselves inside an irradiated bubble—they'd unleashed hell incarnate.

I glanced at the water and wondered if the shark repellent would attract them. My panic rose and fell in a matter of seconds. It was too late to do anything about it now. One side of my mouth curled under, amused. Five years ago, as a nugget flying my first combat sorties, I'd been scared shitless most of the time. Every noise and groan the Vigilante made brought countless fears to mind, and I'd probably taken years off my life worrying about them when, in reality, I couldn't do a thing. At my altitudes and speeds, if things went wrong I'd be dead in a couple of heartbeats. Better to relax and be present. The only thing I could do was sit still, be quiet, and do my job. Right now, that meant following the checklist and hoping like hell somebody'd brave the NEZ to fetch me.

I sighed, moved to a better seat in the raft, and yelped. A vaguely human face peered from just above the height of the inflated raft. Large, dark eyes stared at me, though there wasn't much of a nose over the wide, dark mouth. The skin looked more like a dolphin's than a human's, and its color was similar. I didn't see any hair or ears or anything, but my brain was already ahead of me.

A fucking siren.

I froze. So did it. We looked at each other for a good fifteen or twenty seconds until my radio squawked. The siren trilled in shock and disappeared beneath the waves.

"Rooster Five One, Watchtower. Got your beacon. Advise status."

I shook so hard it took a second for me to press the transmit button. "Watchtower, Rooster Five One. Condition One. Over." I managed to sound calm. We pilots have that knack. The wing could have fallen off the fucking plane and we'd still sound smooth and confident.

"Authenticate X-ray Seven Holden Fiat."

Still shaking, I turned on the low-wattage lamp on my TAC-TAB strapped to my left thigh. I'd written the authentication response in grease pencil on the bottom portion of the tablet's screen. In the Vigilante I controlled all the sensors from the TAC-TAB. Out here, it was pretty useless. In case of capture, though, it was the first thing I had to destroy. I wiped off the markings and sent, "I authenticate Bravo Mustang Niner."

"Copy all. Sit tight, Rooster Five One. Maintain radio silence. We know where you are and we're vectoring assets to you."

"Roger," I said just as the face emerged again from the water. It rose up and placed two clawed... hands on the left side of my raft. Each had two large fingers and what I thought was a thumb. It stared at the radio and then at me with an emotion I'd seen before.

Little Benny's face appeared from the shrouds of my memory. His watery blue eyes staring up at me in wonder, curiosity, and awe. The creature at my side was so similar; I wondered if it was a baby. A scar along one side of its head said otherwise. I wondered if I should smile or stay silent. A part of me wanted to scream bloody murder, but I did nothing. The siren—whatever it was, I went with my brain's designation—looked at my face and then to the left shoulder of my suit. The Australian flag with its depiction of the Southern Cross appeared to catch the creature's attention. It raised a black claw and gently scraped and traced the stars with a sort of reverence before it looked to the south.

To my shock, it pointed in a very human way and made a low hooting sound like nothing I'd ever heard before. A melody of tones that somehow conveyed both awe and confusion. I looked over my shoulder and saw the Southern Cross visible through the breaking clouds.

"That's right." I nodded. It nodded in return and stared at my shoulder. The claw touched my shoulder again. Below the flag was a white strip with black lettering that read "Mason." I watched the siren's claw trace each of the embroidered letters one by one.

The siren cocked its head to one side like a confused puppy. My brain flashed to how Benny used to do the same. A deep breath cleared the memory—I needed to focus. I raised my right hand slowly and pointed at my chest.

"That's me. Mason." I pointed to my name and again at my chest. "Mason."

The creature trilled again. After a moment, it pursed its lips and tried a different sound. All I heard was a hum. The hum broke into two parts. High and low. Two syllables almost as clear as when I'd said them. I blinked in recognition and nodded before scolding myself for moving.

"Yes. Mason."

Again, it hummed for a moment and stared at me. I took a deep breath and realized I wasn't shaking as much as before. My fright became curiosity. I took in everything about its strangely human/porpoise features and appendages. I saw gills moving on its neck, but from what I could observe it suffered no distress at being above the surface. Its shoulders were narrow and sleek, as if built for swimming fast.

I wanted to laugh. My training hadn't covered this. What was I even supposed to do? I was afraid of scaring it. Afraid of it leaving me alone in the darkest night imaginable. Wide dark eyes stared at me in the same manner, silently asking questions. Remaining still grew more difficult with every passing second. Again, the creature's claw touched the stars on my shoulder and looked into the distance. I didn't follow its gaze. Looking south would only hurt. I'd lost everything when the Chinese had nuked Cairns, finally dragging us into the war along with the rest of the damned world.

Janine. Benny. Jennifer. Their faces came up again in my memory and lingered on Janine. Her smiling at me as we walked the Gold Coast after our wedding, her dress billowing in the onshore breeze. My heart ached. Over time, the images became less clear, but the feelings remained. They'd been my entire world and then they were gone. Gone because the politicians decided the global economy needed a war. We got something so much worse—just like we always did.

I wasn't sure who'd won or lost anymore. I watched the creature staring at the stars and wondered what it might be thinking. Its behavior seemed to suggest a sense of awe. Perhaps a quest for understanding or knowledge. As fast as I thought it, I discounted it. Who was I to even know what something so . . . alien might be thinking or experiencing? I was just a pilot. Flying was all I had. My sense of wonder had died in Cairns with my family. Until this moment.

I summoned my courage along with every first contact scenario I'd ever seen from movies—good and bad. The siren snapped its head to the left, stared into the darkness for a moment, and then it was gone. I caught the tip of a fin heading north just as I heard the roar of an approaching engine. Was it something I'd done? My heart raced for a second, and I wanted to call out for it to come back, but I didn't.

"You ain't outta danger yet, mate."

Damn you, Brooksy.

Instinctively, I reached for the sidearm strapped to my lower chest, but I didn't pull it out. With my pressure suit and built-in raft, I was an easy target. There would be no submerging under the water and sneakily playing commando. If I tried any of that, I'd be dead. I released the pistol's grip and opened the pouch next to it. Inside were five Bitcoin, a silk Australian flag with a translated chit asking for my safe return to Australia, and some candy. I decided to leave those, too. I put my hands on the sides of the raft and stared toward the low, rumbling engine when I heard it whine suddenly, as if the propeller had come out of the water. Then, there was a *whump* before it shut off and silence fell.

The dosimeter caught my eye. Almost half of it was black. As if I didn't have enough on my mind, the radiation had risen to dangerous levels.

Gunfire erupted in the distance, snapping my attention back to the more immediate threat. I saw orange light from the muzzle flashes milliseconds before the staccato reports arrived. There was an awful scream. More gunfire—this time multiple weapons. Another scream. A thunderous splash. Down to one rifle. A few shots. A scream. Another lone report. I ripped the TAC-TAB off my thigh and dropped it into the ocean without turning my eyes away from the fight's general direction. A few seconds passed, then a moan wafted toward me on the breeze before I heard a violent splash and then nothing. Another boat engine revved and screamed before racing away in the distance. I sucked in a deep, slow breath and listened until I heard nothing but the breeze.

Silence.

The raft suddenly buckled from back to front, and the sea bubbled and frothed around me. I turned my head and saw the slick conning tower of a British attack submarine emerging thirty meters away.

Before my eyes, the hull appeared, and the starlight illuminated the water cascading off it like a surreal waterfall. Quickly, the entire hull breached the surface, and I saw a hatch midway toward the stern open in the starlight.

Silhouetted sailors in hazardous exposure suits came up through the hatch, and two of them waddled toward the edge and dove in headfirst—toward me.

I looked in the direction of the earlier skirmish. Voices called behind me. I heard an amplified voice over speakers calling to the rescue team. And then, I heard it.

Tones. Trilled tones followed by a distinct, low hum broken into two distinct syllables.

I heard the hum again. Calling. Calling *me.*

"I'm here! It's okay!" I yelled over the sudden noise surrounding me. Men appeared at the raft. Several threw an arm over the side, grabbed fistfuls of my pressure suit, and towed me toward the submarine. "I'm here!"

"We've got you, sir," one of the men said. "Stay quiet. This sector's crawlin' with boats."

A white light shined down on us from the tower, and I shielded my eyes with one hand. In the distance, right at the edge of the light, I saw the siren bobbing in the water. Those dark eyes stared at me, and I saw a large dark smear around its mouth and realized what had happened. Inexplicably, the siren had stopped the patrol and...fed on them. It had saved me.

"You don't understand!" I said, but none of my rescuers paid any attention. I kept looking out to sea.

I didn't know how it was possible or if it was even real. The raft hit the side of the submarine and more hands grabbed at me and pulled me up by my armpits. I heard the survival raft get punctured followed by the tearing of the strong fabric as the holes widened and the suit deflated. The suit's weight became enormous. There were far too many voices in my ears. I didn't hear them. I stared into the distance.

The hum came again. No one seemed to notice it but me. I raised a hand with my fingers spread. The siren mimicked it perfectly. A goodbye wave.

"Contact! Contact, two o'clock!" someone called. The light flashed up and illuminated the creature for a fraction of a second before it submerged. A cannon from the tower opened fire. Rounds splashed around where the siren had been and then stopped. The water stilled.

"No! Wait!" I screamed. "Cease fire!"

A deep voice growled in my ear. "Shut up, goddammit. You wanna get killed? We've got you and your gear. Now, get below, sir."

They didn't understand. I struggled against them. Flailing. They assumed I had panicked. More hands clutched at me. Adrenaline crashed through my body, but there was nothing I could do but stare into the abyss and hope it stared back. There was nothing. My resolve gave way.

A half dozen submariners dragged me up the hull and placed me on my feet. The decontamination team sprayed me from head to toe with a warm solution that smelled like sweaty feet and then wiped down my exposed skin twice. One of them plucked the dosimeter away from my suit. The whole thing was black. Had I not taken the pills, I might've been dead.

A frogman with a darkened face scanned my left wrist with a device, nodded, and motioned me to the hatch before I realized he'd checked my identity with a pistol in his opposite hand. We took no prisoners anymore.

"He's clean, sir. Class-three exposure. I'll alert sick bay."

A burly, mustachioed man in standard naval coveralls appeared at my side. His bald head reflected the light in the humid air. "Squadron Leader Mason, I'm Leftenant Kernot. Welcome aboard the *Adelaide*. Let's get below, sir. The enemy's about."

I moved where he pointed and looked again toward where the siren had been. The dark sea rolled gently and blanketed its secrets for another time. As I climbed down the ladder into the boat, I glanced at the Southern Cross and closed my eyes. My body went down the ladder simply from the weight of my suit and my suddenly fatigued limbs, but my mind heard nothing but the siren's trill.

Another decon team approached with noxious smelling wipes. Four sailors wiped down my exposed skin and started the process of getting the heavy exposure suit off my exhausted frame. As they worked, I opened my eyes and looked at Kernot. "What's our position?"

He squinted at me. "Twenty-six nautical miles northeast of RAF Spratly Bravo, sir. We've been in the area conducting sweep-and-clear operations. Are you hurt?"

I shook my head but noted the position, intent on returning once the war ended, if I managed to survive. "I'm fine."

The hell you are, Mason. You're thinking about sirens and all kinds of crazy shit. A laugh threatened to erupt from my chest. Instead, I clenched my jaw and fought the smile away. For the first time in years, I was thinking about the end of the war. About something besides dying.

Old Raymond had another saying: "You think beyond the end of the war, ya might as well not think beyond the end o' the fuckin day. They don't call it harm's way for nothin', mate."

Bullshit. A man has to have something to live for to make dying worth the cost. I'd be back. I had to know. The rest of the suit came off, and the cool air of the submarine's atmosphere chilled me almost as much as the steady, cautious gaze of Leftenant Kernot.

"Let's get you to sick bay, sir."

"I'm fine, Leftenant." My voice was soft under the dive alarm as the submarine slid beneath the surface and turned hard for the Spratlys. I tremored as the adrenaline burned out of my system. With a sigh, I said, "Just damn glad to be aboard and off of that raft."

Kernot stepped closer, as if he couldn't hear me. He smiled, but it was more from concern. For the first time, I noticed the intelligence insignia on his coveralls. "There were multiple small boats near you. Sonar reported gunfire at the surface inside a thousand meters. Did you see anything?"

I turned to Kernot and shrugged. "Heard it. Yeah, somebody squeezed off some rounds to the north but nothing close to me."

"Did you see anything strange, sir? You were in the NEZ, you know."

The truth might end my war, but I'd rather spend my service obligation in a cockpit than the brig. I knew, and the secret was mine and mine alone. Between every heartbeat, I heard it trill my name.

I met Kernot's eyes. "Not a thing. Black as a coal mine out there."

THE LAST OHIO

✪

Brad R. Torgersen

It was daylight on the Taiwan Strait.

The sky was partly cloudy with great broad bands of sunlight dancing across the surface of the blue ocean. Commander Evelyn Coombs, the USS *Nevada*'s captain; her executive officer, Lieutenant Commander Mike Whitford; and Master Chief Kruger stood on the Ohio-class submarine's tower deck and gazed through three identical sets of long-range binoculars at the island of green that lay five miles off their bow.

"That's it, Skipper," Whitford said with conviction as he brought his binos down and replaced them with his customary set of aviation sunglasses.

"Doesn't look like much," Kruger commented as he continued to watch through his binoculars.

Kruger was a grizzled old sailor at least twice as old as Coombs, and as tall as he was wide. He knew more about ships and the people who sailed them than any other crewmember. The running joke onboard was that Kruger had sailed the original submarines of two prior world wars, and Evelyn could almost believe it as she watched the ancient man's deeply lined face squint against the bright sunshine. Many of the younger sailors on the *Nevada* had lovingly resorted to calling him Grandpa Ben.

Whitford was an opposite of the hoary old Kruger in every way save competency. Tall, relatively young for his rank, sculpted like a bodybuilder, and possessing a chiseled face that any girl could fall for. The man was what Commander Coombs often considered to be the

223

glue that held the ship together. When the crew needed a pep rally, he was there for them. And when the ship itself showed signs of suffering, he managed to pull the necessary parts from *somewhere,* or at least come up with an adequate improvisation.

Right now Coombs needed both their opinions as she tried to figure out how to best approach their rendezvous. Up ahead was their point of interest: one of the many small islands belonging to the chain once known as the Pescadores. On this specific island was a world leader who had been missing—or so Coombs thought—for over two years. Did President Wester have any idea what had happened since the bombs fell? What the world powers had done to each other? Why had he suddenly come up for air, now, and in this particular place?

"Opinions, gentlemen," Evelyn ordered softly.

The old man and the young one screwed their faces up into thoughtful expressions as they watched the wave tops lap across the ship's bow. Mike took a long time in considering, and his answer had the slowness of thought still being formed.

"I'm not sure what to think," Whitford said, frowning. "It's been a while since we answered to any authority besides yours, Skipper, and I'm not sure I want to go back to the way things were. The secretary of defense, the Joint Chiefs, you remember how they bungled Afghanistan. Then came Russia in Ukraine. And the stand-off with Beijing, over Taiwan supposedly having nukes. I can't say Washington, D.C., particularly distinguished itself navigating any of that mess. If this *is* the President we're dealing with, I've got half a mind to tell him to go fuck himself."

Evelyn smiled slightly as Whitford blushed at his own audacity. There had been a time when the young executive officer would have followed any of the Joint Chiefs into the maw of Hell itself.

The hard lesson—during and since the nukes had launched—had changed him.

"Gramps?" Evelyn asked as she regarded her second man.

Kruger chuckled once and turned to snort and spit a massive loogie into the water, and then faced his commander.

"Is that a show of disapproval?" Coombs asked.

"Take it as you want, ma'am," Kruger deadpanned. "But I'm inclined to agree with the XO. I'm in no hurry to subject myself to a chain of command that blew the civilized world to pieces."

"I see," Evelyn replied, then turned to face the island once more. As far as she could tell, they were the only surface ship in the area. If the sonar arrays hadn't been permanently fouled a year earlier, she could have checked for other subs. But not even the ingenious Whitford had found a way to replace those incredibly complex parts, so the *Nevada* was about as effective as a bat with its eardrums removed.

"Guys," Evelyn said hesitantly, "I'm not too hot, either, on the idea of getting called back in by the boss—not after such a long absence. And I know how we all feel about the way the world died. But we *did* take an oath that predates the war. I think we're obliged to heed the President's call. If it is in fact him. And there's really only one way to be sure."

Kruger and Whitford nodded a few times, and then silently stared across the water.

"It's just weird as hell that Whitford is *here*," Kruger remarked. "Last we knew, Air Force One went down over the Arctic."

"It could have been Air Force Two," Coombs said. "We never verified any of those final transmissions."

"So, the President makes an emergency landing," Whitford said. "If true, why not on Taiwan proper?"

"Too many mushroom clouds making it obvious it was a bad idea," Kruger speculated.

"Maybe," Coombs said. "Have the radio guys work up a coded response."

The three turned from their watch and strode back down into the depths of the ship. Several minutes later, an encrypted call was made to the island for identification and clearance to approach. This signal was followed by an equally encrypted reply which welcomed the *Nevada* and her crew, and asked them to circle to the far side of the island where they could pull up to a dock and disembark. The President would meet them there.

The lengthy pier that stretched from the small island's southern tip looked new. The girders that made up its mass had not had time enough in the water to corrode.

Commander Coombs, flanked by Kruger and Whitford, stood at the head of that pier and watched solemnly as a horde of sharp-looking officers wearing uniforms from every US military branch came toward the moored *Nevada*. Their steps resounded on the dock like the shuffling of cattle hooves, and their smiles sparkled in the late afternoon sun whose light was cascading across the ocean.

"Ahoy there, Commander Coombs!" said a well-built man who walked to the front of the crowd. He wore no uniform, but instead sported a stylish cotton oxford shirt and a pair of relaxed-fit denim pants. His teeth sparkled brightest of all, and his toned and muscled figure spoke of impeccable self-maintenance. Evelyn was surprised to see that President Ray Wester hadn't changed a bit from his pre-war interviews. As the entourage came to a stop just short of Evelyn, Wester extended a large palm toward her.

"Commander?" he said, his deep, solid voice resonating with a power all its own.

"Mister President," she said, shaking his hand. "It really is you."

He gave her a few quick pumps before he let her palm go and shoved both of his mitts into his jeans pockets.

"In the flesh," Wester said jovially, then his eyes proceeded to scan the length of the *Nevada*. As he drank in the sight of the world's last— perhaps?—nuclear missile sub, he leaned forward and gave off a low whistle. For many moments, Coombs and her men just looked about them, trying to think of official-sounding things to say, then Wester tore himself away from the image of the ship and got handshakes from Whitford and Kruger.

"Damned marvelous to see you folks after all this time!" Wester said enthusiastically. "There aren't too many of you left in the world, and our country needs every one of you if she's going to get back on top where she belongs."

Evelyn and her two chaperones nodded, but inside, the skipper had mixed feelings. It seemed that the president was at least aware that the US military had been all but wiped out. But did he know the country they all remembered—the America of their youth—was a radioactive blast zone?

Evelyn wanted to probe him with questions, but decided against it as she was engaged in a flurry of new handshakes with the men and women making up the president's entourage. They were all Admiral this or General that. Some faces were dimly recognizable from the few high-level meetings Coombs had been privy to before the war. Most were no more familiar to her than Adam. But they all knew exactly who she was and had nothing but good things to say about her and the *Nevada*.

The president invited Coombs, Kruger, and Whitford back to the shore, but Grandpa Ben stopped them short and addressed the president bluntly.

"I don't mind if we come have an exclusive visit, but we've got boys and girls on that tub who ain't seen liberty in many a long moon. Would I be pissin' on the welcome mat if I asked permission to have them stretch their legs?"

The brass behind Wester looked silently from one to the other and then back at the master chief. Wester, however, took the old man's vernacular in stride and slapped the old sailor on the back, telling him that the island was the crew's oyster. The men and women of the mighty *Nevada* could have whatever they wanted on the island.

"Ma'am," Kruger said to Coombs, detaching himself from the party that was heading back to shore, "if you don't mind?"

Evelyn looked back at her ship and then into the old man's eyes.

"Sure, Master Chief," the commander said with a smile, and then turned to walk away.

After a few steps she stopped and turned and looked at Kruger again.

"Just make sure they don't get into *too* much trouble?"

"Aye, ma'am."

Kruger saluted her sharply. She returned the salute. The old master chief made his way back to the foredeck of his craft and dropped down an open hatch.

Coombs and Whitford were left to silently make their way behind the brass and the President as they walked to the beach. Then they followed a winding path that led up into the large hills of the green island. Half of Evelyn's mind concentrated on Wester. The man engaged in animated conversation about how much work was to be done and how miraculous it was to have Coombs and her ship arrive in one piece. The other half of Evelyn's mind was focused on the intense green leaves of the tropical plants that surrounded her and the calls from birds that drifted from branch to branch. On too many a seashore since the nukes had fallen, Evelyn had found nothing but blasted, irradiated ashes where mighty forests had once stood. She soaked up the essence of life as much as she could. Somehow, this little speck of land had been spared.

The trail stopped abruptly at a huge, armored door set into the face of a boulder. There was a hand-scan identifier to one side, and one of the brass placed her fingertips on the scanner's surface and gave a mumbled voice-identifier code. The door beeped happily at her and then slid noiselessly up into the rock to reveal a spotless and well-lit tunnel that spiraled down into the island's depths.

For many minutes they went downward, their steps echoing all around. The stairs below blocked all view of the spiral that might have lain beyond, giving the sensation that the stairs would go on forever. But the trip eventually ended in a great, high-ceilinged cave that appeared to have been fashioned by human hands. The cave was littered with office cubicles and computerlike boxes. Everything was illuminated by hundreds of bright lights on wire-suspended racks that dangled a few feet from the upper surface of the cave.

The computerlike boxes beeped and whirred happily, while an occasional voice could be heard from one of the cubicles.

"My holy of holies," Wester said, motioning with a flourish.

Coombs and her XO were taken aback by the sight of all the high technology and people that milled about the office space. She hadn't seen such a sight since before the war.

"Where did all of this *come* from?" Mike Whitford asked in a soft voice as he looked around him. "I don't remember ever hearing about a stronghold such as this. Not off the coast of mainland China, anyway."

"Ancient Chinese secret, my boy," Wester said with a wink. "But I forget, you're probably too young to remember that commercial. Hell, *I* am almost too young. Anyway, this was Taiwan's, but I worked up a supersecret lease with them before the war. Built it all myself with the black-project money I was able to skim off the Pentagon. I always had a feeling something like this would come in handy. And when the missiles launched, I was right."

Wester almost glowed with the pride of having outwitted the holocaust. Then he seemed to remember who he was talking to— seeing the expression on Coombs's and Whitford's faces—and assumed a more somber attitude.

Coombs regarded the president and found herself remembering

why the man had been elected to office. He was good. He had an actor's handsomeness as well as charm. Plus, he exuded the kind of manly aura some had once attributed to President Clinton, long ago.

"Impressive," Coombs said, motioning at all the cubicle and computer equipment. "I would assume these people are the ones who reestablished a link with the communications satellite you used to call us?"

"Yes, and much more," Wester said, smiling again. "These are some of the brightest boys and girls I could sift out of the government, before the end. They've been putting all kinds of our orbiting toys back to use. Survey satellites, weather satellites, even a telescope or three."

"What about the lunar colony?" Whitford asked.

Coombs felt her heart flutter slightly at that question. She knew the moon settlers who'd gone with Musk included Whitford's sister.

The president frowned—if just for an instant—and then tried to cover for it with a rushed smile.

"We've been in touch with them, too," he said.

"Really?" Whitford replied, his eyes wide and his breathing heightening. "What's the news?"

"Son, I wish I could tell you more about the moon," the President said, "but they've been pretty cagey about what information they're willing to share. Musk liked to be his own man before the war, and he likes being his own man even more, now that nobody on Earth can tell him what to do."

"I am sure we can find out about Sheryl," Coombs said to her XO, "but what's *really* gotta be hammered out is: What good is the *Nevada* to you now, Mister President?"

"I like an officer who doesn't small talk," President Wester said. "But now's not the right moment to talk about *Nevada's* new mission. Before that happens, there are many details to attend to. I guess you and yours have been fairly isolated since the bombs dropped. I am amazed the *Nevada* is in one piece, frankly, and still operating under her own power! There's plenty of time to talk about your future. Meanwhile, I expect you and your first officer to get my team a complete list of every consumable you need, and every broken part that's gotta be replaced."

"Aye, sir," Whitford replied for both him and his skipper.

"After that, then?" Coombs pressed.

"After that," the President said, still smiling as he always did, "yes, we'll do a full cross-briefing. But I expect you and Lieutenant

Commander Whitford to go do some of that 'leg stretching' your crusty master chief was talking about. Relax. Enjoy civilization for a bit. Just know we're here for you."

Captain Coombs chewed her tongue for a moment as she judged Wester, feeling him out, and not liking what she felt. But then, maybe he was right? What was there, after all, to be unsure of? He was the President, and everything so far seemed completely legit.

"Forgive me, sir," Coombs said, "I think I've just been out to sea too long. You're right. Some bona fide R and R would be good."

Wester clapped both Coombs and Whitford on their backs, and then had the two submarine officers ushered out by a pair of admirals. Mildly dazed, Coombs allowed herself to be led back up to the surface and to the dock, where she was shocked out of her befuddlement by the sight of utter pandemonium. The sub's remaining complement were splashing about on the beach nearby, spraying what appeared to be huge cans of beer all over each other and screaming wildly. On the beach just a few yards up toward the tree line, a massive ice cooler full of the beer cans sat enticingly in the sunshine, and several barbecue pits roared with fresh flame. The popular tunes of the pre-war era blared from a portable Bluetooth stereo someone had placed next to the cooler, and for a brief instant Coombs allowed herself to forget that the world had annihilated itself.

Whitford was hesitant.

"What's the matter, Mike?" Coombs asked.

"Skipper, a minute ago you were cool as an ice cube. Now you're willing to succumb to . . . this—"

"Insanity?" Coombs finished for him.

"You could call it that," Whitford said, watching the cavorting crewmembers with unease.

"I know how you feel, Mike. But what is, and is not, sane, is strictly a matter of majority rule. And in this case"—the commander panned a hand around her, in reference to their screaming, hollering comrades—"you and I are definitely the minority."

Coombs watched Whitford blanch as she popped the Australian-label beer open—foam frothing across her hand and arm as she did so—and tip it in his direction. When he didn't immediately take it, she shrugged, then took a long, grateful tug on the can. And gave off a gasp of approval.

"God, I didn't realize how much I missed this shit," she said, wiping her mouth with her sleeve to clear away the residual wetness.

"I've always thought it tasted more like last year's horse piss, ma'am," Whitford replied with a frown.

Coombs looked at her XO for a moment, deciding whether he had made a joke or not, and then laughed heartily and tossed the open can to a nearby petty officer who thankfully caught it and slurped it down.

"You're right, Mike. Let's let the crew enjoy themselves, while we go draw up the must-have list. As long as the President is offering to buy, I say we take him for all he's got."

"Yes, ma'am!" Whitford agreed heartily.

Once inside the sub, Coombs and Whitford caught up with Kruger, and together they made their rounds of the ship. No problem went ignored. No missing nor damaged nor malfunctioning part was overlooked. Three hours later, they returned to the surface to find their thoroughly smashed crew sitting around the barbecue pits and yodeling God knew what sea songs.

"I love a good liberty," Kruger said approvingly.

"Then why don't you join them?" Evelyn said honestly.

"Naw, ma'am. At my age, a sailor tends to get a little partied out. I killed off too many brain cells when I was a kid. Can't afford losin' the ones I got left. Though, I am amazed to see they've got steaks, burgers, and hot dogs for us. Where in the world did they find the beef?"

The skipper smiled, and then she and her two mates walked back up the dock, savoring the feel of the night breeze as it wafted in again from the sea. Once on land, three clean and properly pressed junior officers met them. Each wore a different US military branch uniform, but they all had respectful smiles on their faces. And each was strikingly attractive.

"The President would like us to show you to your quarters now," the lead female junior officer said.

"Quarters?" Kruger said with surprise.

"Yes, Master Chief," the woman replied. "The President believes that you may appreciate not having to sleep in the confines of your ship after all this time. He offers the use of more...hospitable surroundings?"

"Lead on," Coombs said.

The three junior officers did so, and within a short time had taken the three submariners along a winding path that went some distance around the circumference of the island to a spot that had been cleared and set with row upon row of beach bungalows. Electric lights glowed from each structure, and the three junior officers split, taking the captain, then the XO, and finally the chief of the boat in different directions.

"Wait," Evelyn said, holding up a hand to stop her escort, a pretty young man whose name tag read Ralling, "what about our inspection report on the *Nevada?*"

"The President said it could wait till morning, ma'am," Ralling said with a smile as he ushered her through a sliding door and then touched the electric key to slide it shut. Outside, the sounds of the waves rolling on the sand could still be heard. Inside, all the comforts and luxury of a twenty-first-century high-class hotel could be found. Massive bed, massive bathroom, massive kitchen—at least in comparison to the cramped confines of the *Nevada*—to include a fully stocked fridge and pantry, and an entertainment center that dominated an entire wall of the single living room.

Coombs gawked for a few minutes as she wandered from area to area, and then back to where Ralling waited patiently for her.

"Christ, what is all this?"

"Only the best for the fighting men and women, ma'am," Ralling replied evenly as he clasped his hands behind his back at parade rest.

"But . . . do *all* of you live in such luxury on this island?"

"I'm just an ensign, ma'am, so I don't have quarters like this. But, I am happy to say, what I've got now is a thousand times better than any quarters I'd have ever gotten before the war."

"Amazing," Evelyn said softly as she sat in an overstuffed reading chair. She was in a fairylike wonderland, or so it felt—after so much time wandering the world's oceans, the last of the Ohio-class missile boats, trying to see what few parts of the world remained in the wake of the conflagration.

Coombs sat like that for a good ten minutes, just staring off into nothingness as she metabolized the day. She had not known such pleasurable surroundings in all her life, even before the war. A sizeable fortune must have been invested in her bungalow, and from the looks of it, there were hundreds of such units lining this side of the island.

The president had managed to build *all* this using black-budget money?

"Ma'am, is there anything else I can do for you?" Ralling asked with a warm smile as she continued to sink into her daze. She slowly looked up at him, not understanding what he had said, and then snapped back to awareness.

"Huh? Oh, no. Thank you. Sorry. Wool-gathering. You are dismissed."

Ralling looked about him and then down at the floor. He cleared his throat experimentally.

"Ma'am," he said, stepping close to her and looking into her brown eyes. "Is there anything I can *do* for you?"

Ralling's face held a friendly smile, and his deep blue eyes penetrated hers. Evelyn found that the young man was wearing a mildly fragrant cologne. The smell was almost intoxicating, and she felt her breathing increase as he continued to stare unblinking into her eyes with his own. Evelyn's already pink cheeks turned bright vermilion when she realized there was much more to Ralling's offer than she had assumed.

She tore her eyes away from his.

"Umm, uh, no! No, thank you, Ensign Ralling. I'll be fine," Coombs blurted, smiling nervously and feeling the urge to giggle like she was fourteen again. And she felt incredibly stupid because of it.

Ralling nodded a few times, still smiling, and turned to stride to the door. He pressed the open key, and then stepped into the night air. Before he left, he turned to face her again.

"Ma'am, if you change your mind for any reason at all, just use the communications wand on top of your entertainment center. It gets you most of the channels on the island, and will buzz me first if you use it to get an outside line."

Evelyn waved him off, then allowed a good five minutes to pass before a series of half-crazed giggles ripped across her throat, and then small sobs.

What in the hell was this place, anyway? What was it doing to her? For the briefest of moments she had actually considered taking the strong young guy up on his subtle offer. Despite the fact she outranked him. That was a huge no-no for any field-grade officer, to indulge herself with a junior one. But it had been forever since she'd tumbled with any man. And there was no question at all that she sorely missed such recreation.

Further thoughts on these matters only yielded further confusion and more sobbing.

"Too fucking much," she finally sniffed, wiping at her nose. "I should just get some damned sleep and figure this all out tomorrow."

Morning brought with it soft light, the sound of gently breaking waves, and a small buzzing sound that refused to go away. Evelyn swam in her unconscious for a moment, then decided that the noise was too annoying to let continue. She roused herself from her bed and stumbled to the front room. The noise was coming from beyond the front door. She tapped a hand idly on the lock panel, and the door slid open to reveal the young Ralling, still as handsome as the night before.

Evelyn stared at him for a moment, eyes blinking, and then she stood up straight as he snapped her a salute.

"Ma'am, the President is ready to hear your wish list," Ralling said crisply.

Evelyn returned the salute and was about to proceed out the door with the young aide when she realized that she hadn't changed before going to bed. She'd slept the whole night in her blue digital-camo working uniform.

"Oh Christ," Evelyn muttered.

"No worries, ma'am. The President is not expecting you until ten-hundred hours. You've got time to get cleaned up and grab a bite with your mates. I also took the liberty of bringing you this."

Ralling produced a shrink-wrapped package from behind his back. Evelyn accepted it and discovered it contained nicely starched khakis. Specifically, a naval officer's uniform.

Evelyn thanked Ralling and tossed the package on the reading chair. The young officer spun on his heel and walked swiftly away while Evelyn leaned against the open doorframe and looked out across the dawn sea as it gently rolled in from the horizon. There was an unreal feeling in the air that had not dissipated from the evening before—a feeling that was alarming, as well as intoxicating. Here, in this place, all the hard reality of the post-nuke Earth was melting away before a wonderland of comforts and luxuries that no one on the *Nevada* had ever seen, nor had expected to ever see.

But, Commander Coombs supposed, rank did have its privileges. Of *course* the President would deck the place out like a resort.

Evelyn let these thoughts continue as she strode back to the bathroom and quickly stripped. Inside, she tapped fingers on the control pad and felt a refreshing burst of hot water spray across her body from the nozzles in the ceiling and walls of the shower stall. Soap came easily from a push dispenser, and very quickly Evelyn was clean as a whistle.

She stepped from the shower, toweled off, then spent a few minutes assembling the packaged uniform and slipping it on. Everything necessary had been provided, including pins, ribbons, rank, and so forth.

She was met on the deck outside by the sight of Kruger clopping toward her. Like Evelyn, he was dressed in brand new khaki, but he was frowning as he approached her.

"Good night?" she asked, wondering what might have happened. "Where's the XO?"

"Haven't seen him yet, ma'am," Kruger said. "And his place was empty when I got there, before coming here. He must have gone ahead of us, Skipper."

"And there's something else, isn't there?" Evelyn said, growing uneasy.

Kruger's face turned pink.

"The young female lieutenant who escorted you last night?" Coombs guessed.

"Hell, ma'am, is it that obvious?"

"She's young enough to be your *granddaughter,* Ben," Coombs scolded. "And besides which, she's commissioned. Jesus, what were you thinking?"

"She was very smooth when she came onto me," Kruger admitted. "Very smooth. And she talked like she knew the old days. Like she knew the Navy from when *I* was a young man. We talked about the old times, practically like she'd been there. Well, one thing led to another, and . . . shit, I'm still a man, aren't I? And it's been a long, long time."

Coombs thought about Ralling and his tacit offer.

The uneasy sensation inside her, intensified.

"How about the rest of the crew?" she asked.

"Sawing logs, most of them. Sleeping off those hangovers."

"Did you take roll?"

"No," the master chief admitted. "But where could they hope to go?"

"Nowhere I guess," Coombs said. "Come on, let's go find Whitford. Something's truly strange here. I mean, we ought to be overjoyed at the discovery of this place. But I can't shake a subtle, bad vibe. And I really want to talk to the President some more."

The pair walked back toward the center of the island following signs as they went. They eventually bumped into several more officers. These officers directed them on the path back to the main door to the innards of the island, and soon they found themselves back in the computerized cavern where they had been just the afternoon before. An aide met them there and directed them through a series of corridors to a large conference room where they were offered seats and full plates of breakfast.

The President joined them.

"So, Commander, do you have that list for me?" Wester asked with a smile as he tore into his bacon, eggs, and manhole-cover-sized pancakes.

Evelyn passed the President a small thumb drive across the table, and he promptly dropped it into a slot near his knee. The list appeared in the center of the table on a pop-up digital display.

Several brass joined the group at that point, entering from side doors, and the two crewmembers of the *Nevada* quickly found themselves engaged in a running discussion on what worked aboard the *Nevada*, what didn't, and the items in between. Many of the generals and admirals were amazed to hear that the ship had survived as well as she had over the many months at sea, without proper refit or refurbishment. Coombs was quick to point out the outstanding efforts of her XO in these areas—despite the fact he was conspicuously elsewhere. She made a mental note to really find out why as all the brass made their own notes on their personal computer pads while she spoke.

When the report had been made in full, the President and his staff vanished into an adjoining office and left the two submariners to pick at the remains of their meals.

"You think we'll get half of what we asked for?" Kruger asked.

"I don't know *what* we're going to get," Coombs replied. "This place is a little like Santa's workshop at the North Pole. I wouldn't be surprised if we got nothing, or if we got a whole new ship. It's just so hard to say. We have no idea what kind of spare parts the president has holed up in this place."

"Well, Commander," President Wester said with a smile as he and the brass walked back into the conference room, "you will be pleased to know that we can help you with *all* these problems. We're fully equipped to make the repairs necessary to the *Nevada*, and will gladly supply the necessary staff to get your ship back to a full complement, too."

Commander Coombs sat back in her chair and placed a hand over her mouth, eyes wide.

"Thank you, Mister President. We could not have hoped for this much. It's almost a miracle, really."

"I know," the President replied, still smiling. "I know."

"So, when can we get to work?" Kruger asked one of the admirals who flanked the President. The flag officer simply darted his eyes in Wester's direction, and then looked back to Kruger.

"Nonsense, Master Chief Kruger!" the President said. "You people haven't even been on liberty for a full day, and you're ready to go back to work? At least have the sense to enjoy our hospitality! The work can wait."

More handshakes followed, then Coombs and Kruger were shuffled out of the conference room and back to the surface where they found their entire boat empty of personnel, save for a tiny handful of petty officers whom Whitford had posted dockside as shore patrol.

Day two was a louder, more raucous repeat of the first. All the tension, grief, and mixed emotions of the war—followed by the long loneliness at sea—were all coming out in one great drunken venting. Every sailor had steam to blow off and made the most of his or her time on the President's little Shangri-la, including more than a few pairs splitting off to head back to their quarters—not even trying to hide their intent.

Coombs patrolled the beaches in her bare feet, watching the sky and the surf, and wondering what had happened to her executive officer. Though the bizarre nature of her situation still loomed large in her mind, she forced herself not to worry about it. This was very likely going to be the last taste of the old world that she or any of the other sailors would ever get.

Occasionally she ran across one of the strangers from the island itself. They exchanged friendly banter, talked of the upcoming repair work to the *Nevada*, and the one time she saw Kruger—alone, he made it plain for her to see—she speculated heavily on what it was the President wanted with the sub. Two-thirds of *Nevada's* launch tubes still held missiles, each armed with warheads. Was that what this was all about? The President's ability to exert power—either by threat or through deterrence? As yet, Coombs still had no idea if any of the other world leaders had survived. The few major ports the *Nevada* had visited had all been disasters. She'd had to make call at much smaller ports, bartering for supplies, where the locals ruefully recounted tales of survival, and of scratching a living from what was left.

By comparison, the crew of the *Nevada* now enjoyed heaven.

That evening, food was served by the President himself. He wore a comfortable-looking Hawaiian shirt and a set of flattering cotton slacks. The meal was several grades above beach barbecue.

Evelyn allowed the man in the door, noting that two Marines seemed to want to follow.

"Men, I think I can handle this," Wester said over his shoulder. The Marines reluctantly withdrew and closed the door behind them.

"Nobody from the Secret Service survived the war?" Evelyn said as he placed the tray of scrumptious-smelling food down on the bungalow's single meal table, and began setting out silverware and plates.

"Military formalities, Commander. Mostly to humor my staff of admirals and generals."

Wester finished setting up the table and then motioned at the seat opposite his. Evelyn slowly took that seat, then began serving herself without making a sound. Her eyes held Wester's—expectantly.

"You know, I guess I was foolish to expect you and your people to just fall back in after all this time," he said. "You're wondering where I've been, and what happened to the chain of command when the nukes obliterated the country. Yes, I know things are dire back home. Yes, I know it looks bad for me to be here—with all this sumptuous luxury—when life back in the States is hell for most."

"Yes," Evelyn admitted. "All of that's crossed my mind."

"But I want you to realize I'm pretty different, now. I'm not the kind of president you had at the start of the war. This whole thing has changed me as much as it has changed everyone else. Including yourself."

"Maybe, Mister President," Coombs said. "But have your policies? I have to assume the *Nevada* is going to be part of your plan to reassert yourself in a world that is largely leaderless."

"I don't expect a woman like you to understand the subtler nature of international diplomacy. But whether you like it or not, humans are political animals. Because of this fact, I can only see more destruction in our future if *somebody* doesn't step out there, and lead. We've got the one—and maybe only—chance to unite this damned globe under my government. An opportunity sitting in our palms. If we don't take it, I don't think anything can prevent us from backsliding all the way to the Stone Age."

Evelyn watched Wester calmly as his speech became more and more heated. The fire in his eyes as he spoke told her that he truly believed what he was saying. There was also the matter of his natural charisma, which was starting to go to work on Coombs despite her best effort. She knew that if she wasn't careful, the man could have her all turned around by the end of the night.

"That may be, sir," Evelyn said, "but we tried it once your way, and look what happened."

Wester waited silently, his attitude telling Evelyn that he expected more than that. But she volunteered nothing further. If the deaths of billions weren't evidence enough of the failure of doing business the old way, then she did not know what was.

When Wester could see he would get no more reply, he dug into his food, purposely not watching the commander.

They ate in silence for a good long time. Evelyn wondered why the man had even bothered to come down and see her in the first place.

"Why do you care anymore what I think?" Coombs asked bluntly as she finished off her plate and pushed it away.

"I could stick any one of my brass on your boat, Commander, but I'd rather not have to. I think I'm smart enough to realize that the men and women on your sub will respond poorly to me putting some pencil-pushing admiral in charge. That will dramatically reduce the efficiency of your people, and endanger the goals of this country."

There he went again, referring to the United States as if it were still a real thing. Coombs inwardly groaned.

"You can't convince me to go around threatening people with nukes anymore," she said flatly. "I did that once already. I even had my bluff called. And the millions of dead that I've now got on my conscience refuse to leave me alone. Do you have any idea what I'm talking about?"

Wester stopped in midchew and looked past her shoulder, off to a window where the sun was just starting to wane. His expression held hints of something far away; a distant, serious memory. His brows furrowed slightly and there was the faintest vibration in his eyes.

"Yes, I know. Believe me. I know."

"Then why?"

Wester swallowed his unchewed bite, swabbed his mouth with a napkin, and then stood abruptly.

"You want to know how I survived? How this whole place remained intact despite the war? When Air Force One landed here on two good engines, we were running on fumes, and most of the United States lay under a radioactive pall. The runway was old, and too short. We went off the end, lost the landing gear, and halfway rolled, eventually breaking up into pieces. The fire should have gotten those of us who lived, but there was something strange about the flames. Something strange *in* the flames. I heard voices, as if many crying out together, then coalescing into one voice. It promised us—promised *me*—there would be a future. For a price."

As the man spoke, Commander Coombs watched the skin on his face slowly crinkle then evaporate off the muscle and tissue underneath. Her mouth hung open as she witnessed the formerly handsome man's hair fall out and fluttered to the ground like bird feathers, but disappearing into wisps of gray ether before they reached the floor. His clothes quickly deteriorated until they were but blackened, ragged scraps dangling from the cooked muscle and sinew underneath. A skull's visage now stared at her.

"Join us," the barbecued cadaver said, extending its blackened, skeletal hand. "The nukes woke something up in this part of the world. Something which has slept for a thousand years. Maybe it was all those souls suddenly shuffling off their mortal coils? Maybe it was something else. I can't pretend to understand it, even now. Except to say *I live*. And so do all who serve me. They live as well. After a fashion. And so will you."

Evelyn screamed like she'd not screamed since she was a small child newly woken from a horrible nightmare, jumped up from the table, running to the opposite end of the room, where she slammed her palm repeatedly on the electronic button for the door. When it opened, she pelted out into the gloaming.

Whitford was there to block her way. Or, at least, what passed for Whitford. His skin was sickly white, as were his eyes—no pupils nor irises. His starched khaki uniform was as clean as could be, but there was an unmistakable stench of death to him as he spread his arms to prevent Captain Coombs from passing.

"Don't fight it," he said. "Fighting just makes it harder."

"This isn't real," Evelyn shouted. "None of it can be!"

"I didn't think so, either," Whitford said. "But the wraiths have a way of convincing you."

"Wraiths?" Evelyn said, blinking her eyes, not understanding.

"The President's right," Whitford said. "Something awoke in this part of the world, once the bombs fell. The Chinese are an old people, after all, and once upon a time, they knew an ancient magic. Mostly forgotten, until so much human and animal life perished all at once. Then the magic came out of its slumber. Dark, and hungry."

Again, Evelyn screamed like she was a small girl and spun ninety degrees—leaping off the pavement and onto the sand, then charged out across the beach as the dying light gave way to blackest night. Behind her she could hear the voices of both Whitford and the President—or what had become of them—calling for her. Warning her that she wasn't going to escape. In her mind, Evelyn desperately hoped this *was* a bad dream. That she was still back at her suite, sawing logs, or even in her bunk aboard ship. Anywhere but here, now, running blindly from a sudden, wretched dream.

Commander Coombs ran until she was gasping for air—the sand making it hard to keep up her pace—and then she saw the dock lights where her ship was still moored. The tiny figures of the shore patrol still standing watchfully.

Out of the dark, a body tackled her.

Commander Coombs went down like a sack of oats, and felt a large, warm hand close over her mouth.

"Shhhhh," hissed a voice in her ear. "They might hear you!"

Kruger's hand slowly slipped from her face when she didn't resist him.

"Master Chief!" she hissed back. "What the *hell* is happening here?"

"Hell is too right by half," Kruger said quietly into her ear. "If you're like me, you had some visitors tonight who made you an offer you weren't meant to refuse. Like me, I reckon you said, 'No!' and got out as fast as your legs would take you."

"It can't be real," Evelyn panted. "It can't."

"I was never much for chapel in my adult years," the master chief said, "but if my great-grandmother could see me now, she'd say this was the bona fide Devil's work."

"We've got to get to the sub!" Evelyn said.

"Too late," Kruger said sadly. "I was headin' back *from* the dock, to see if I could find you, when you practically ran over me. The *Nevada* appears taken, ma'am. The shore patrol . . . gone, like Whitman's probably gone. And a lot of others."

Captain Coombs slowly got to her feet, and looked away from shore, back to the land.

"But what about all . . ."

She never finished her thought, as the many lights from the many bungalows and suites began to smear and grow fuzzy, like rain on an automobile windshield during a downpour, until suddenly every single building took on a distorted, not-quite-distinct, and decidedly vaporous quality—the light no longer warmly yellow, but orange, fading to red, which faded into the blackness around them.

An unearthly moan seemed to rise from the land, as if a thousand voices wailed. Then, ten thousand. None distinct in their own right, but all joined in a terrible choir of pain and longing.

"We'll swim for it!" Commander Coombs shouted, and reversed herself, preparing to spring down the sand to the water's edge, and dive in. Except, the waves were alight with ghastly glowing figures that slowly came up out of the water. They didn't hurry. There was no need. With so many—most little more than skeletons, mobilized by some unseen force which compelled them forward—there was nowhere for either Coombs nor Kruger to go. Quickly, the apparitions surrounded the pair of US Navy personnel, who stood back-to-back and glared at the spectral remains of men and women who'd perished and were now seemingly reborn. Albeit in the most awful manner one might conceive. The evil emanated from them, like a palpable wave.

"I wish I could say something other than, it's been an honor serving with you, ma'am," Kruger said over his shoulder. "May the Lord please take mercy on us."

HMS *Defiant* was a Type 45 guided-missile destroyer. Perhaps the last any British shipyard would ever produce. Converted to nuclear just before the onset of the war, she'd sailed much farther from home than any of her siblings. On her bridge, the men and officers of the Royal Navy maintained their alert. It had been a long time since anyone or anything had reached out to them via encrypted satellite communication. At first, Commander Jenkins had suspected someone from Hong Kong might be calling. Hong Kong still having its British roots, not quite killed by the communists since their takeover at the beginning of the new millennium. But instead of Hong Kong—surely destroyed—the satellite messages had aimed the *Defiant* to a tiny bundle of islands off the western coast of Taiwan, which had been badly decimated in the opening moments of the war, and from which all life had been presumed extinguished.

Until now.

"What do you make of it?" the commander asked his XO.

"Bloody peculiar," the XO replied. "But the codes match up. Somehow, there's United Kingdom territory on the horizon. Though I can't rightly say how that's possible. We'd be fools to take the codes at face value."

"And we'd never forgive ourselves if we didn't get in closer and have a look. It's been a long time since any of us saw friendly faces. And while we struggled to find safe ports in Australia and New Zealand—those poor bastards—maybe some little scrap of home remains? Here? Right at the center of where it all started?"

"Aye, sir," the XO said. "Wouldn't that be a miracle?"

The *Defiant* sailed toward the coordinates.

IT TAKES TIME TO GROW

✪

T.C. McCarthy

"In waking a tiger, use a long stick."
—Mao Zedong

We do not speak of the great cold anymore because the story is old, and its words have worn thin, cracking in places and too delicate to unwrap or its edges could crumble. I don't need to remember our history; neebs know it all. The old women do as well, using it on misbehaving children: *do not speak to an elder like that or they will send you to the great cold.*

We learn as children that this was once a real punishment, and also a test given to us by our forefathers because to travel north and return from the ice proved you were a warrior. But nobody travels there now. The ice has retreated a distance so great that none in my generation or my father's have seen it; to travel that far means going into areas that are jars recently uncovered, their contents a new poison to the Earth. My father says that in a time almost as old as the beginnings, there were many more laws and rules, ones that kept anyone from travelling north into ice-lands or east, where the lowland jungles gave birth to wicked flesh-eating tribes. We are lucky, he says, that there is a new test.

Neebs are the wisest in our tribe. They know the ancient words and writings, and when my father once returned from the hunt with a book of words, the neebs took it to one of their huts. For three days they studied. But when they emerged and the people expected them to explain what my father had found, one of the wise ones said *this knowledge is meant for neebs.* But everyone knew the book had filled the old women with dread since several of them emerged from the hut with tears.

Neebs teach us that to point at the moon will get our ears sliced and that when we travel from the village we must call out to our spirit so it doesn't remain behind, lost in the pines and tea plants. Once a bird flew into our dwelling. My father called a neeb who chased after it, explaining that bad luck would come if she didn't kill it. As the tribe's leader, my father's sons had to know all the laws and all the spirits' names, and the oldest neeb made sure we could recite everything in our sleep. My mother was a neeb but I don't remember her. She was, others tell me, the most beautiful woman in the village.

My mother died in the last tribal war but my father is a Kaitong, the one who leads our warriors, and he brings me on hunts—customary for Hmong boys who reach the age. I once killed a rock ape in the mountains near the old city where they have a warren of tunnels, endless mazes of dirt and rock where the creatures hide from sunlight. That was a year ago. My father still tells the story around the fire and since then the men let me take from the servings meant for those who have proved themselves in war. It is a high honor. Rock apes are magical creatures that steal the tribes' babies to drink their blood, and whose long fangs can bite through a tree trunk. It has been over a hundred years since any tribe has killed one, and after my arrows skewered an ape to a tree, none of the monsters have been seen near the village.

Because of this I have my own bow and knife and am permitted to travel short distances into the western and southern jungles, and sometimes I go as far as the dead city near the Eastern Salt Sea. My father learned of this. He was furious that I had broken the law but also proud that his child had the courage to go alone. Everyone saw it in his eyes while one of his warriors whipped my bare back. My father tells me that I am different from my brothers. He says my soul is from the time before, a world destroyer's; it has spent many lives on the Earth and returned from ancient days when men with skin the color of clouds flew in great birds to drop curses from the air. That is why I do not fear the cities, he says: my spirit remembers destroying them.

When my time came, I knew where I would go. Questions he had raised about the men in birds were slivers of fire in my chest and head, with one way to extinguish them. On that day I said to my father, "I'm ready; I must go."

"I wondered when you would come to me."

"And I invoke *lo lus uas peb*."

Father stared for a moment, thinking, before he placed a hand on my shoulder. "Please do not do this. I suspect where you would go, and there is only death in these places."

"I have learned our laws," I said.

"It is your right to choose. But nobody ever does because of the danger, and I am the Kaitong, and it is *my* right to choose whether you take the test alone. If you invoke *lo lus uas peb*, I will send you out with Lig—one of the apprentice neebs."

"A girl?" I asked. "You would insult your own son?"

The words had come out before I had a chance to think, but my father did not get angry. "Not a girl—a *wise one*. Where you are going, a neeb will prove useful, and it will help her learn about the days from before. You have a strong spirit, and it does not surprise me that you would choose your own path; the elders will also not be surprised."

"I will take Lig." I turned before he could see the rage in my eyes, which grew from knowing what others would say when they learned I would not be going alone, and worse: with a girl.

That night the older neebs locked the two of us, me and Lig, in the house of spirits and performed the rites all night long, their voices lifted in song and in chants. This was my first cleansing. I ignored Lig, who sobbed beside me and who had dressed in her ritual clothes, their reds and yellows so bright they were visible even by candle. She was still a child, at least a year beneath me, and part of me felt guilty for having forced my father to send her into the wilds. The old neebs' prayers should have calmed Lig, but they appeared to have no effect, which did not surprise me; the prayers did nothing to calm my excitement either.

The next morning a thick fog lay within the mountains' low meadows, far beneath us while my father and the hunters prepared me for the journey. The neebs attended to Lig, and I could not hear their words.

"This is your grandfather's crossbow," my father said. He slung it over my shoulder along with a hollow bamboo quiver of bolts. Then one of the hunters wrapped a leather belt around my bare stomach. "And this is his sword."

"I did not know grandfather's sword survived the war with the lowlanders."

"It did. And this is his spear. He used it to kill the chieftain, and we have never cleaned the blood from it. Blood is strong magic. The metal is reclaimed from ancient days."

The spear's dark shaft ended with a long steel tip, triangular, razor sharp, and stained with brown-red spots.

"It is weighted well."

Father nodded. "He knew before I did that his grandson would be a great warrior; my father's last command was to keep them safe for you. Only ancient steel can be sharpened to that fine of an edge. Be careful."

When the last warrior finished with my belt, they all left. To say goodbye brought evil spirits and bad luck, so they remained silent, and I watched my father's back to look for signs of sadness but there was nothing. Someone tugged at my shoulder. Lig was there, still dressed in her ritual garment and still crying, so out of sympathy I kept to myself the fact that her clothes and sandals would not hold up in the wilds.

I started down the path most people avoided—the one leading northward—and Lig tugged my shoulder again. "They said you are mad, that you would take us toward the cold."

"We make for the Nam Thi. Then north into the old lands."

"You are insane!"

"This is *my* test," I said, continuing down the path even though she had stopped to stamp a foot. "Stay behind if you wish; tell the elders and the neebs that you refused their direction."

Lig said nothing. She pouted when after a while I stopped to sit cross-legged beneath the shade of a large tea plant, its broad leaves second only to the lotus as the most sacred to our tribe, and we waited. Soon the mountainside became still. Lig once opened her mouth as if to speak but then said nothing, instead sitting next to me. Even though I knew which direction to go, this was the most important step of our journey, and she knew not to interrupt because to do so would insult the mountains. Mountain spirits were not to be ignored, and to venture on a journey without their blessing would have brought evil.

The sun rose to its highest point before a muntjac emerged from the trees alongside the path ahead of us, a long distance away, where it stopped to turn its head. Its stare bored into my chest. The size of this beast would have made it a prized kill for the hunt, and muntjac never came this close to the village, so this was a powerful sign; wherever the thing led we would be obligated to follow. It turned north, headed along the path we had already started down, and then disappeared around a curve with a leap.

"That is the sign," I said.

"The sign that we will die."

"Save your breath, neeb. This will be a long test."

The journey northward took more moons and suns than I could count, and before long I had to cut Lig's ceremonial clothing so she could move more easily, throwing her sandals into the thick bushes that flanked the path. Before long we ran out of dried meat and had to hunt. The spirits provided, and it was another powerful sign: muntjacs appeared along our trail when needed, and we used small cooking fires to avoid attracting predators. Even Lig began to smile. It was as if the way had been prepared long ago, the trees and grassland hills scrubbed clean of dangers from the time before.

After what felt like an entire moon cycle, our path took us lower and out of the mountains where the jungle claimed its rights to the earth and rose up in a wall of green as if a line had been drawn in the clay.

"To the east," I whispered, "and the south and west, the jungles do not appear like this. Here, the trees appear suddenly as if God ordered the jungle to stop in a line."

"Ice," Lig said.

"What?"

"You warriors know nothing. It is because of the great cold. That line is as far as the ice came, before it began the retreat. It means that to our north, there will be newly exposed dwellings of the old ones, the places we have been warned about."

"Do you believe that?" I asked. "It is said that the ice scraped the earth clean wherever it touched, and that even rock could not withstand it. How could the old ones' dwellings survive?"

"You are a fool."

I hadn't been mad at Lig since we first left, but now my chest tightened. "I am a prince, son of the Kaitong and one who has killed a rock ape. You're just a girl."

"And *you* are too stupid to realize that you *should* be terrified!" Lig started into the jungle. She knew it would be an insult to me, since this was my journey and not hers. "I read the writings your father brought back. Did you?"

I pushed in front of her, looking for an animal trail to make the way easier. "A warrior is not to read the old languages."

"I know. We would never allow warriors to have that knowledge. The papers spoke of a great heat that resulted from the weapons used in the ancient war, a heat worse than any cooking fire. This fire lasts forever."

"So?"

"So, *son of a Kaitong,* heat melts ice. The old dwellings were never covered, were never scraped from the earth because the ice never took hold within them as a result of the eternal fires of destruction. Who knows what evils have grown there over all these generations?"

Her words passed through me, cold; where once had been confidence now lay questions and doubt, and I glanced around, whispering for my spirit to draw close and stay with me. *No test is without a trial.* These words rose to the top of my thoughts having been spoken by my father to me and my brothers, and from his father to him. This was the test. The harder the trial, the greater the glory, and the greatest glory always came to those ready to lead the tribe and navigate the dangers of jungle and forest, mountain and lowland. Always.

"I dreamed," I said. "After I spoke of my dream the mother neeb and my father told me that I am returned from the old ones, a warrior. These places will not kill me."

"Death is not always the worst outcome."

The deeper we moved into the jungle, the darker it became. Soon even the insects stopped their droning, and massive trees submerged us within their ocean of greens and blacks, the air still, heavy and warm—so thick it became difficult to breathe. A search for muntjac tracks along the trail we'd found yielded nothing, and soon it was clear that no animals had traveled here in the last few weeks. This was a place of ill magic. Lig's muttered prayers broke the silence, and I joined her, my lips moving without sound at the same time I dropped my spear to draw my crossbow and load it with a bolt. She saw me, and her mouth opened to speak. But Lig stopped when I raised my crossbow, pointing it at a wall of low bushes that had managed to grow within a small patch of sunlight, one that wormed its way through the high canopy.

You could sense it. Whatever force or spirit had quieted the jungle dwelled within the bushes ahead of us, and it occurred to me with a deep sense of dread: a warrior would know what to do, would protect his neeb. I moved forward. A few steps brought me closer to the foliage, and I dropped the crossbow, drawing grandfather's sword in one fluid movement.

Without warning, a storm of vines erupted from the bushes and shot toward me like thousands of green tentacles, their intelligent hunger making my head pound with a pulsing rhythm. My sword moved without thought. Years of training took the place of conscious decision making, a force of will from within my spirit guiding the blade to slice through the vegetation, sending lopped-off sections of intelligent vines to writhe on the jungle floor.

"Strangle vines!" I screamed. "Grab my crossbow and spear."

Lig snatched up my weapons and we ran, sprinting along the first path we could find and without thinking of other dangers that may lie ahead. But we were lucky. Soon the jungle sounds returned, and we hid at the base of a seraya tree, its trunk towering overhead and massive roots forming a pocket that hid us from view. My hands trembled in the wake of having almost killed us both. There was no excuse—having spent so much time in the wilds—for missing the signs of strangle vines, and a deep sense of shame began to replace fear and the exhilaration of escaping death. I was about to apologize when I heard water.

I grabbed Lig's hand and pulled her up so our heads poked over the roots, where the sound was clearer. She heard it too. Ahead of us to the north the jungle grew on a downward slope, and we crept forward, pushing through the brush and tangles until I found a game trail, which we followed until the jungle broke into a shower of sunlight and heat. This was a riverbank. A few meters beneath us the Red River flowed, its water dark with sediment and swirling in eddies so gentle they whispered promises of safety.

"Beyond this river is the ancient world, a place once called China," Lig said.

"And the city I saw in my dreams."

"The city you saw is called Kunming. It was a center of horror and death, where ancient priests created monsters of war that they unleashed upon the earth. Upon our people."

"You have seen these places?" I asked. "How?"

"It is in the old writings. Books and maps. Mother neeb made me study them when she learned of your intentions. We knew you'd come here. On the map there was an ancient road"—Lig paused to stare at the far bank and the hills beyond it, before she pointed—"and if it is still passable, it leads through a valley that should be somewhere in that direction. We are a day from the old city."

"Good. We will refill our water skins and continue. By tomorrow, we will enter this place—Kunming—and you will see I was right to come here."

"And the sixth angel poured out its bowl on the great river." Lig had mumbled the words, but they sounded strange and powerful, resonating with my spirit.

"Is that a prayer?" I asked.

"It is a warning—from a long time ago, for people like you. It came from the men with pink skin, who harbored us in their lands until we could return to our mountain."

"It is late," I said. "We will sleep by the river and make for the city at first light."

No sleep came to me that night, and prayers did nothing to calm my nerves, which refused to relax or ignore the sense of anticipation. I had been to old places before. The cold had not ever reached our village, and so ruins of their small towns in the lowlands rose out of the earth, half covered in dirt. These had been picked clean—the leftovers of life in empty crusts, which animals and man had scavenged again and again. Kunming would be different. Even from this distance you sensed the energy because it flowed like the Red River did, between the steep mountains and hills, seeping between trees and tea plants until it filled the hollow we'd used as our camp.

I did not remember much of the next day. We broke camp and found a shallow place to cross, my spear gripped in both hands in case a massive khej or some other monster had claimed this section of the waters for itself. But we passed with no incident. Then the hills of China enveloped us, their slopes covered with younger trees than the ones we had just left, and Lig said something about *a new jungle being born from the ice* but the words barely registered; everything had gone quiet again. We had entered a new world after the crossing, a place avoided by muntjac, and the farther we traveled the more my excitement grew: What would I find as a prize? To return to the village with a tool or ancient weapon would be seen as a great sign. Lost in those thoughts, my surroundings disappeared, and it surprised me when the hills gave way to another mountain range where we found one of the old paths. It must have been tremendous when new; Lig and I marveled at the width and materials used for its construction, huge blocks of pale rock through which plants now grew to reduce sections of the road to sand. I asked Lig how many people lived here in order to justify such a large path but she didn't answer.

Just before sunset we crested a pass in the mountains where we stopped. I felt my heart beat against my chest, its muscles pumping blood as if readying me for battle. Beneath us in a valley stretched out a massive dwelling of the old ones, its size nothing like I'd seen before and even stories of the old capital near our village made it clear this place was once greater—perhaps the greatest dwelling place that had ever been built. And now that we'd arrived my excitement shifted to fear, a sensation that something was wrong with the silence, which festered in this desolation. I almost didn't feel Lig when she grabbed my hand.

"Listen to me," she said.

"What?"

"We must stay to the edges of the city. You can see where the old weapons were used, in the areas where nothing grows and the tall homes were flattened."

"Those are homes?" I asked. The things rose into the sky for miles, their sides covered in green vines. "How many families lived in them? Wouldn't birds run into their sides, and how did one get all the way to the top? How brave these men must have been, to live next to the cloud spirits."

I had many questions and was about to ask them all but Lig waved me quiet. "Listen. There is a dangerous heat here, even at the edges. You will get your prize, and then we must leave."

"Do you hear that, Lig? No animals or even bugs, just plants."

"Promise me."

"*I promise.* This is why they sent you, because I am a warrior and you are a neeb. It is right that I listen to your council. Besides, something is off with this place, and the sooner we cross back over the Red River, the better. We have an hour or two of sunlight; let's move."

Ice had scavenged the outer edges of the city so that a tall berm of sand and rock, punctuated by massive boulders, encircled like a wall. Lig stumbled but we made it over. Beyond the berm we moved into shadows. The homes stretched so high above us they blocked the sun and the warmth, making me shiver at the same time thousands of rectangular openings stared down with black eyelike voids. Something rustled in one closest to us. I spun toward a door, its wood long since rotted away, and lowered my spear at the same time I crept toward it.

"It was just a breeze," Lig whispered.

"Maybe. What does that writing say, over the door?"

Lig looked away, embarrassed, so I repeated the question.

"It says *Yuxi Adult Store and Entertainment*," she muttered.

"Adult store?"

"They used to sell things in places called stores; they were like inside markets. This one sold ... items."

You could see that her face was still red, but I decided not to press the question further.

My eyes adjusted to the dimness inside and marveled; this was once the market of a wealthy old one, its walls still gleaming with gold and silver despite the place's age. Much of its contents had turned to dust. I asked my spirit to announce my entry, to alert any others that we had come in peace and would not disturb the sleep of those still here. It was a wise thing to do, I thought, for whoever once dwelled here must have been a powerful man and commanded great respect. The rustling sound came again and I relaxed. Lig had been correct; a breeze moved what little remained of old fabric that hung from a nearby window.

"What is that?" I asked, pointing. A long rectangular table stood against a wall near the doorway we had entered, much of it consisting of shattered glass that hung within a metal frame. A dull metal object inside the frame looked different.

"That is a weapon. They called it a pistol. It is like a crossbow but instead of a bowstring it used a small explosion to send metal into an enemy." I grabbed at it and Lig hissed. "Be careful! It could still function, even after all these years."

"I am a warrior, and this is my test," I said, tucking the pistol into my sword belt. "*This* is my prize. Now we can go."

Lig and I both heard the noise—someone's voice, singing—and we hurried outside where we stopped, our mouths open in amazement.

A figure moved toward us, still distant enough that you could not see details but her long dark hair flowed in the breeze, and she wore a gown made from metallic fabric, its weave shimmering whenever she passed through a shaft of sunlight. It looked almost like the woman floated. There was no sense of leg movement, and when she got closer I realized why: the vines, which covered the tall homes around us, also coated parts of the roads where they sent out carpets of small tendrils that lifted the woman off the ground and carried her forward.

"What is she saying?" I asked.

"That is the old tongue, Chinese. She is asking us to stay with her."

"What? Is *she* an old one? How could any have survived the war and the heat?"

"There is something wrong with her," Lig said.

Another rustling sound caught my ear, this time from nearby in the shadows; the vines there had begun sprouting. Smaller vines and tendrils like the ones carrying the woman crept toward us. Not strangle vines—these were something different, and as I watched, one of them grew a small flower that puffed and blew fine white dust into the air, forming a cloud around us.

"She has no eyes," Lig muttered. "Only holes, like the empty windows of these homes. I'm so tired. Maybe I will stay."

"Run!" I screamed.

You could feel it; the dust got everywhere and without warning a sense of fatigue hit, almost forcing me to my knees and blurring my vision. The woman continued forward. Now she was close enough that her dark eyes became visible, their empty sockets dripping black liquid that slid down both cheeks and onto the road.

I grabbed Lig but it was too late; the vines had taken hold of her and wrapped both legs in their thick fibers, sending small tendrils to pierce the skin of her calves, and when I tugged at her she screamed.

"I want to stay," Lig said. "The woman needs us. You can stay too; there is knowledge here, and I can see her thoughts as she sees mine. Through the vines."

"I am not staying. Come, I can save you but it will hurt."

"Leave that one alone," the woman said. Now she spoke in our language, but her booming voice was not that of a human, but of something else. This was a danger I'd never faced. The enormity of it overpowered me with realizations that Lig was becoming more entangled by the second and that at any moment the dust could render me unconscious.

And the woman was almost upon us.

"She is ours."

A vine came closer, forcing me to jump away from Lig where I landed in a patch empty of vegetation, and the movement out of the dust cloud allowed me to shake off some of the strange effects. Part of me wanted to stay; how could I return to the village, even with my prize, and explain that I had abandoned one of our neebs to a monster? That was not the action of a warrior or Kaitong's son. But there was no saving Lig; after retreating a distance, careful to avoid any vines, I watched as the woman reached Lig's side. The vines had grabbed hold of every one of Lig's limbs, and at first I thought the woman bent down to kiss her victim, but instead she ripped Lig's arms off in a single motion.

I ran. The last sounds I heard were Lig's screams and a faint voice that came not from the woman, but from the air itself.

"We will come visit you soon," it said. "This one had much knowledge, and now we know the path. You will see us again in a while. It takes time to grow."

DISPATCHES FROM KREDO

✪

Nadia Bulkin

"US Delegation Visits Kredo," Dennis Zamora, January 16

An American delegation led by Secretary of State Bill Stoakley is visiting Kredo from January 16–17 to discuss shared regional security concerns and opportunities for socioeconomic cooperation, marking the highest-level visit by US officials in the nation's independent history.

At a joint press conference following his closed-door meeting with President John Mark Manalo, Secretary Stoakley praised Kredo's achievements in raising national living standards through the use of biofuel as well as bringing stability to the Pacific by safeguarding the *Armillaria kredensis* organism known as "God's Bounty," commonly dubbed Kredo's most precious natural resource. "The United States reaffirms the deep importance of our friendship and strategic partnership with Kredo," stated Stoakley.

The visit holds special significance for President Manalo, who received his master's degree in political science from Peirce-James University in the United States. At the press conference, Manalo called the United States a "beacon of progress" and a "true inspiration to the world." He stated that he and Stoakley had discussed opportunities to strengthen ties in trade, health, education, and science and technology.

Sources in the Manalo administration have pointed to a US fishery treaty as a likely short-term goal for bilateral cooperation. Earlier this morning, President Manalo and First Lady Julie Manalo met Secretary

Stoakley at St. Philippa Port, where they visited Kredo's historic fish market. Secretary Stoakley inquired about potential side effects that the *Armillaria kredensis* might have on fish caught off the coast of Kredo, and the President assured him that the fungus does not stretch within three kilometers of the coastline. Later, a spokesperson for the US delegation noted that "Secretary Stoakley has no concerns about the safety of Kredo's fish catch given the geographic boundaries of the organism and the neutralizing elements of Kredo's soil."

The visit comes as the United States enters its sixth month of hostilities against China. The Manalo administration and the National Promise Party have pledged to maintain Kredo's historic position of nonalignment in the conflict, making room for continued bilateral relations with both the United States and China.

Other members of the US delegation, including Lieutenant General Dave Seabolt of the US Indo-Pacific Command and Deputy Assistant Secretary for Biological Nonproliferation Policy Elsa Canning, also held meetings with their counterparts today. Tomorrow, Secretary Stoakley will travel to the interior in order to tour a small biofuel facility in Batan village to learn about the energy potential of *Armillaria kredensis* fruit. Batan village is considered a leader in local biofuel production, using mushrooms harvested from "God's Bounty" to generate light and heating for more than fifty households, a school, and a clinic.

"Manalo Faces Criticism Over Base Rumors," Justine Cinco, February 20

Early on Monday morning, a small team of custodians scrubbed fresh graffiti off the exterior walls of the Office of the President. In the latest indication that anger toward President John Mark Manalo over his perceived close ties to the United States is on the rise, unknown vandals had spray-painted "Imperial Stooge" and "No US Base" on the white walls facing Tanjung Boulevard overnight.

When asked for their thoughts on the graffiti, most of the custodians declined to comment. One man said that the President was only doing what he thought was best for Kredo.

The most recent round has been spurred by memos leaked to the press revealing the Manalo administration's intent to proceed with a US proposal to establish a military base on Kredo. The memos, originating from within the Office of the President, suggested that the base could be placed near the villages of Lupa, Batan, or Pasigan.

Revelations about the potential base deal coincide with the announcement of a planned treaty allowing a small number of US fishing vessels to fish in Kredo's exclusive economic zone for a large sum, reported to be as high as 100 billion dollars. The timing has raised concerns that the national government has accepted a quid pro quo with significant implications for Kredo's global positioning without consulting the population.

A spokesman from the People's Front for Development called the deal a "one-way ticket to war." Allowing the United States to stage troops or equipment at Pasigan could additionally pose a state security risk given the village's proximity to the *Armillaria kredensis* restricted zone, where years of open-pit mining have led to open access to subterranean rhizomorph cords.

In a Monday KTV interview, presidential adviser Jericho Caparas acknowledged these concerns while suggesting that a security guarantee from the United States would provide Kredo with stronger insulation from war than nonalignment would. "It is not enough to be an asset that everyone wants to court," Caparas stated in the interview. "We need to also be an asset that someone will protect. Because one person's asset is another's liability."

Still, other critics claim that a base deal will have negative consequences for the population and ecosystem of Kredo. Tito Sayson, the head of Lupa village, shared that many local subsistence farmers were concerned not only about the presence of US troops but also about the possibility that Kredo could be forced to sign a biological disarmament pledge.

Such a pledge might prohibit any harvesting of any fruit of *Armillaria kredensis*, destroying the livelihoods of thousands of villagers who rely on selling its harvested mushrooms to biofuel facilities. "Americans see the [rhizomorph] roots and become scared," Sayson said, "but they don't understand that the roots only protect our land from invaders, they won't hurt anyone off the island."

It is currently unknown whether the rhizomorphs of *Armillaria kredensis* continue to produce mycotoxins when transplanted off the island, nor whether this *Armillaria kredensis* can be transplanted to new soil.

Separately, the Caretakers of the Bounty have called for an environmental impact study to assess the ecological risks of building a military base at each of the three proposed sites. "Our utmost priority must be safeguarding the bounty that God has blessed us with," read a statement released by the clerical group. "The organism God's Bounty, with all its blessings and curses, was entrusted to the people of Kredo and not the soldiers of the United States."

"Manalo: Every Option Is On the Table," Dennis Zamora, March 1

President Manalo sought to clarify his government's stance on foreign obligations at a campaign stop in Pasigan village on Thursday, stating that "Kredo's only enduring commitment, now and forever, is to our nonalignment. Beyond that, every option is on the table."

While he acknowledged that deciding not to host a US military base may result in the loss of the proposed US fishery treaty, he expressed confidence that Kredo would be able to secure an equally valuable contract with another country. "We have plenty of friends," Manalo stated.

When asked about the future of mushroom harvesting for biofuel, Manalo stressed his commitment to ensuring that this traditional pillar of the economy continues to prosper and power the homes of hundreds of Kredo families.

Manalo's primary opponent in the election, PFD-backed Marvin Dizon, has made rejection of any foreign military commitments a central plank of his platform. According to recent opinion polls, as many as 68 percent of Kredo citizens disapprove of the presence of any foreign military on Kredo. As many as 75 percent of Kredo citizens believe that Kredo should retain a policy of total nonalignment. Most citizens who disagreed with these two statements hailed from coastal areas where many fishermen espouse superstitious beliefs about *Armillaria kredensis*.

A separate poll conducted on February 26 showed Manalo and Dizon in a close race. Political commentators have suggested that the ultimate outcome of the race may hinge on whether the Caretakers of the Bounty maintain their historic stance of political neutrality or throw their weight behind a particular candidate.

While the Caretakers have never endorsed a political candidate, they were reportedly shaken by rumors of the Manalo administration's military base agreement. Sources close to PFD leadership have told us that PFD representatives recently traveled to the restricted zone to urge the Caretakers to voice their concerns about President Manalo's leadership. "They are hoping that the Caretakers will see that the President's rashness poses a risk to their God-given responsibility to protect God's Bounty," one source said.

"American Thieves Executed," Dennis Zamora, April 18

Two American men were executed on Friday in accordance with the customs protecting the security of the state and the sanctity of *Armillaria kredensis*. Matt Mulligan and Eric Clark were buried alive in a rhizomorph-exposed pit within the restricted zone by the Caretakers of the Bounty and the Kredo Armed Forces. The Caretakers recited the "Return to Earth" prayer to hasten the prisoners' decomposition.

The Americans were detained near the restricted zone near Pasigan village at 3 A.M. on March 21. The men's bulky personal protective equipment, designed to protect against exposure to mycotoxins, drew the attention of locals and caused the two men to be easily apprehended. During the interrogation, samples of *Armillaria kredensis* mushrooms and rhizomorphs were found in the men's possessions, along with tools designed for subsurface extraction.

Mulligan and Clark were convicted on April 11 of theft jeopardizing the security of the state, unlawful entry, and aggravated assault. Despite evidence that both men had previously worked for a US private security company active in the Philippines, the state ultimately opted not to charge the men with espionage. Mulligan and Clark repeatedly stated during their trial that they were acting in a private capacity, intending to sell mushroom "batteries" and rhizomorph "poisons" on the global black market.

The US government had lobbied Kredo for clemency for the two men, requesting that their sentences be reduced to prison terms that they could serve in the United States out of consideration for their families. However, President Manalo rejected the request due to the grave threat their actions posed to Kredo's sovereignty. "We must set an example to let the world's marauders and pirates know that Kredo and its natural resources are not open for looting."

In response to the executions, the US Department of State issued a statement calling Manalo's decision "inhumane" while continuing to call Mulligan and Clark private citizens who "made a terrible mistake."

Last week, President Manalo conferred medals of honor to the six soldiers and nine civilians who caught and detained the men, declaring them national heroes of the highest order.

"Dizon Wins Presidency, Vows to 'Put Our People First,'" Polo Viray, May 9

Businessman Marvin Dizon has won the presidential election, defeating incumbent President John Mark Manalo after a turbulent race. Dizon, representing the People's Front for Development (PFD), received approximately 53 percent of the vote, while Manalo, representing the New Promise Party (NPP), received approximately 46 percent.

Dizon capitalized on broad support from Kredo's interior region, particularly among populations whose sources of income were disrupted by the ban on mining colloquially known as the God's Bounty Protection Act. Dizon has called on the law to be reformed under his "Put Our People First" policy, including reducing restrictions on mushroom-harvesting and infrastructure development in the interior.

Dizon declared victory shortly after midnight on May 9. "This is the biggest honor of my life," he stated. "My father was a humble miner from Lupa village. He wasn't rich but he cared for us—until they shut down all mining and wiped out his life's work. Just like that, my family went from making ends meet to barely being able to afford food—all because some officials with clean shirts and American accents decided that our land was too fragile to support our people."

He went on: "When I decided to run for president, I had one goal in mind: freeing us of the limits we have imposed on our own potential."

Shortly after official results were announced, PFD social media posted a message suggesting that the current president John Mark

Manalo had fled Kredo for the United States—a claim that this newspaper could not immediately verify.

"Dizon Signs Chinese Investment Deal," Polo Viray, June 4

President Dizon announced that he would sign a 200 billion dollar infrastructure investment deal with Chinese state-owned manufacturer Sinoport aimed at modernizing the nation's interior.

The infrastructure projects—including the construction of an airport near Batan, the modernization of Port Philippa, and the foundations of a national road network—are expected to employ hundreds. In announcing the deal, President Dizon highlighted "infrastructure-led growth" as the wave of the future "that Kredo must not miss out on."

Development in the interior of Kredo has been significantly stalled since the island's energy-dense mushrooms were revealed to be the fruit of a single, ancient specimen of a newly discovered species of a pathogenic fungus, *Armillaria kredensis*, dubbed "God's Bounty" by religious clerics. Advocates of development counter that Kredo's soil has neutralizing elements that prevent the permeation of the rhizomorphs' mycotoxins through soil, citing clean mycotoxin tests of deep-rooted plants and trees grown near the restricted zone.

The Office of the President also announced that in a few areas in western and central Kredo, access to mushrooms will be limited as a result of the new construction projects. The government has pledged economic support for subsistence farmers as compensation.

"PFD on Defense Regarding Sinoport Deal," Justine Cinco, July 22

PFD officials shot back at accusations that the Dizon administration has sold access to the *Armillaria kredensis* fungus, Kredo's God's Bounty, to China.

On July 17, a group of fishermen that has been acting in an unofficial customs capacity claimed to have found samples of God's Bounty mushrooms on a Sinoport vessel that was disembarking from Port Philippa. The vessel's crew claim that they docked on July 15 to deliver construction materials for the Kredo International Airport project and departed on July 17 with a few Sinoport employees returning home to China. The crew attributed the *Armillaria kredensis* samples found on the vessel to "accidental debris" accumulated during construction.

In a separate incident on July 19, the Caretakers of the Bounty found evidence of unauthorized construction taking place within the restricted zone near Lupa village. Sinoport has denied responsibility while also suggesting that the location of the restricted zone makes it difficult to build roads connecting the interior to the coast. However, a source in the Kredo Armed Forces suggested that fishermen had found building materials aboard other Sinoport vessels that appeared designed to withstand exposure to mycotoxins—raising concerns that China is attempting to build permanent access to *Armillaria kredensis*.

Former Manalo adviser Jericho Caparas blasted the Dizon administration for approving the controversial Sinoport deal, stating that "opening up access to the nation's most precious natural resource without a security guarantee is beyond reckless and borderline treasonous."

When asked for comment, presidential Chief of Staff Angelo Brava stated that "there is no need for a security guarantee because we are not a party to any conflict."

The Office of the President has released multiple statements affirming that God's Bounty remains safe, secure, and completely under Kredo's control. But such statements may not be enough to satisfy a population that has been primed to be suspicious of foreign interference.

The investment projects are already unpopular among fishermen, who blame increased ship traffic for disruption to their prime fishing waters. However, signs of discontent appear to be spreading even in the island interior. Earlier this month, a foreman for the Kredo International Airport project was fired when footage surfaced of him suggesting that investment funds were needed to "pay for all those do-nothing Caretakers" at a village meeting, sparking outrage.

"Restorative Movement Takes Power; Dizon Arrested,"
Justine Cinco, August 28

Former President Marvin Dizon was arrested during a military operation to restore internal security late Friday night. Colonel Joseph

Raya of the Kredo Armed Forces announced that Dizon had been detained along with several cabinet members and PFD leaders. "In accordance with the law, Mr. Dizon is no longer President," Colonel Raya stated.

The arrest follows two weeks of violent riots throughout Kredo that saw Dizon's supporters—many of whom had been employed in now-suspended Sinoport projects—clash with large numbers of anti-Dizon protesters. The protesters have largely consisted of members of the isolationist Restorative Movement and the fishing and subsistence farming communities.

As many as fifty buildings were damaged by fire and projectiles on Tanjung Boulevard. On August 17, anti-Dizon protesters made their way to the Office of the President, where they played the Kredo national anthem and wrote "imperial stooge" on the walls. The clashes resulted in fourteen deaths and dozens injured—an unprecedented toll for civilian unrest in Kredo. Colonel Raya stated that the Dizon administration's "failure to secure the peace" contributed to the decision by the Kredo Armed Forces to mobilize.

Colonel Raya confirmed that the former officials will be put before a military tribunal on charges of abetting the unlawful theft of the nation's most precious resource. According to the law, the punishment for this offense is execution by God's Bounty.

While not partaking directly in the protests, the Caretakers of the Bounty welcomed news of the arrest and urged the military to swiftly appoint a new president to "begin the national healing process." Sources say that the Caretakers are likely to back Mary Joy Sanggalang, the long-standing leader of the Restorative Movement, for the presidency.

Early this morning, China strongly condemned what it called a "coup against the legitimate government" and warned that Kredo was now under the control of "nationalists who are a danger to world peace."

"Drop-Off in Foreign Fishing Vessels Sparks Concern,"
Kate Bayani, September 15

Manny Abad, 56, has taken his trawler into the Kredo Sea every year for the past 30 years. He usually sees dozens of foreign fishing vessels in the rich international waters just beyond Kredo's exclusive economic zone, and even chats with some of the "regulars" over the radio. But he's never seen so few foreign vessels as he has in the past month. "Last week, we were alone," he said. "It's like they have been warned away."

The Caretakers of the Bounty released a statement last month applauding the Sanggalang administration's "closed door" foreign policy after a turbulent eight months punctuated by controversial attempts at foreign interference by both the United States and China. But Abad is wary of the possible unforeseen consequences of Kredo being "left alone." Like many fishermen, Manny is more frightened of God's Bounty than thankful for its gift.

"I don't go too far inland anymore because every time I see one of those little mushrooms sprouting up out of the ground I remember that we're sitting on a bomb," he says. I ask him to clarify, and he does: "It's not the bounty that will kill us. It's the people who would rather the bounty not exist than fall into their enemy's hands."

Sof, another fisherman who declined to use his full name, provided an allegorical example of a beautiful woman whose many suitors decide to kill her so that none of them can win her. "Preciousness brings pain," Manny added, a play on the common sobriquet of God's Bounty as the "nation's most precious resource."

For now, Manny and Sof say that they will continue to take advantage of reduced fishing competition—but as I prepare to walk away from the beach, I can see that they are nervous.

The Sanggalang administration did not respond to requests for comment.

DUPLICATE

✪

Freddy Costello and Michael Z. Williamson

Video File 1
"Does anybody around here remember if I did anything this year?"
Lieutenant Colonel, US Army (EUCOM) preparing his Officer
Evaluation Report support form.

★ ★ ★

~~TOP SECRET~~

"To all who see these presents, greetings." I'm Niles Geston. I like old things. I'm an historian, which means I like old, stuffy military documents. I'm also a librarian, data recovery archivist, and a virtual archaeologist. I use the Oxford comma and put two spaces after periods. I'm also now a part-time kelp farmer, by the direction of the government in the current year spirit of survival-of-the-human-species and democracy things.

I spend four days of the week doing what I'm academically and professionally trained to do as an official employee of the Armed Forces Post-War Information Reconstruction Office, operated by what's left of the "Seven Eyes" unitary provisional government. Seven Eyes consists of the United States, the United Kingdom, Australia, Canada, India, Singapore, and New Zealand. Except Singapore doesn't exist anymore, and New Zealand is barely hanging on, but we still call it Seven Eyes. Go figure.

For the remaining three days of the week, I farm kelp out on ~~(REDACTED)~~ Collective. I suck at it.

Shit what was that?

Sorry, I didn't mean to leave you hanging, but one of my pod mates seemed like he was going to barge into my crèche unannounced. The mere act of recording anything remotely like this is enough to get me reeducated, but what the hell, I hate kelp farming, I'm not on the authorized bio-eugenic marriage wait list, and I don't think I'm making Collective Farming Supervisor or Leading Historian anytime soon.

So that you and all future generations (assuming there are any) all know the truth behind the great big mess you've inherited from us, World War Three started over whale dong. Counterfeit whale dong. I'm not joking, the global superpowers, you know, the ones led by the "adults in the room," blew up the world because of whale dick. Whale dick, whale dick, whale dick. Ground up, powdered ten-foot-long blue whale penis.

I'll give you the short-short version. The People's Republic of China faced extreme demographic and socio-economic crises, brought on by its own complex internal contradictions of policy and culture. Let's just say that official state communism, that is the post-geriatric kleptocracy of the Chinese Communist Party, had to incentivize a population that, just like the pandas they supposedly loved so much, couldn't or wouldn't fuck to save itself from population implosion due to an enormous gender imbalance, aging, and the resulting economic contraction. One might be tempted to compare them to pre-war Japan, minus the cartoons, live dolls, and tentacle porn.

The Chinese Communist Party's inner circle made a desperate appeal to the population via promotion of weaponized traditional animistic medicinal solutions, hoping for a baby boom. Large swaths of the population, as educated and bourgeois as it had become, had bought into it. Whether from fear, lack of unfiltered information, or a tacit acknowledgment that state atheistic materialism had really lacked something in the whole "meaning of life" department. Maybe they just needed a baculum to bone.

Now comes the fun part. What do you do when you've poached or farmed most of your traditional animal remedies for marital problems to extinction? When there is no more seahorse or tiger-penis extract? Well, no pun intended, you rise to the occasion. You create disinformation. You invent alternatives. You put an entire society's effort into promoting these. All of a sudden, the official Party line is "Whale dong was always a treatment for impotence!" News flash. It wasn't. "Platypus spleen is an aperitif, according to our glorious ancestors!" *(The ones we completely made up five minutes ago).*

What do you do when other countries, especially the Anglophone allies, won't allow you to harvest those things? You do it anyway and make the United States and its tagalongs in NATO quite upset with you. Especially when said harvesting comes with human trafficking, drugs, counterfeit currency, intellectual-property piracy, and organized crime to exploit your still-enormous diaspora population. Now add a dash of neocolonialism all over Africa, and Central America. Belt and Road foreign policy with a side of sex tourism.

What happens if all that poaching and smuggling isn't enough?

You start selling fake whale dick and hope people don't notice it's fake. And you harvest Australian platypus spleen, maybe even make fake musk deer extract for cosmetics too, since you already harvested that to near extinction.

If you really think you're clever, you steal highly advanced prototype rapid-growth cloning technology and DNA samples of the original animals.

You make a duplicate. Duplicates made from cloned animals can be a little, well, "off," just so you know. I believe that is what was called a "spoiler alert."

Then things start to get interesting.

★ ★ ★

Email Exhibit #3506

"Between us girls, would it help to clarify the issue if you knew that Hungary is landlocked?" US Navy CDR to US Army MAJ (EUCOM) on why a deployment from Hungary is likely to proceed by air versus sea.

★ ★ ★

FROM: COMMANDER, SEVENTH FLEET (C7F)
TO: CDR FRASIER D. COPELAND, hey/ho/letsgo, CO GDDG-17
USS Occasio-Occasio
SUBJECT: WARNING ORDER
~~SECRET~~

Frasier,

Thanks for moving quick on SECNAV's Decolonization Directive. Everyone jokes quietly that she's the "secretary so nice she named herself twice," but she wanted to make a point about giving back to the indigenous community of Aztlán. By the way you should fix your pronouns in your signature block before someone complains.

Sorry decolonization kept you tied up an extra two weeks on the shakedown. These Green Propulsion Guided Missile Destroyers are proving to be a lot more... problematic than expected. And it's not just the smell, even though the biomass plant tends to smell worse underway. SECNAV won't admit it, but she fired the last CNO for highlighting how much nausea and diarrhea degrade medical readiness. The new bacterial scrubbers are delayed until next FYDP.

I want to give you a heads-up on the WARNO that's about to drop from PACFLT. You're getting tapped for Freedom of Navigation in the South China Sea. I know the new missiles deployed on those little Chinese artificial reefs make FON trips a little sporty, but there's no intel indicating any intent to actively interfere. There's too much domestic tension on the Chinese mainland, and the insurgency in occupied Taiwan is sucking up all their bandwidth for the moment, so we might as well take advantage of it. I'm not a fan of the O-O going solo, so we'll have a sub shadowing you.

Now here's the fun part. White House wants Commander USINDOPACOM to make a point about Chinese smuggling. It's the usual: endangered species animal parts. Add in illegal over-fishing, drug precursors, fake electronics, environmentally unfriendly fossil fuel burning equipment, the works. State fears this might escalate tensions, so they're not so happy about this, but there you have it.

So, by the time you get to the South China Sea, this certain Chinese supertanker, the *Luck Dragon,* will be ready to leave port from Macao and head to Tonga, with a few stops along the way. Pick up and drop off stops. I've attached an intel brief for you and your command team.

When she reaches international waters, you will rendezvous with one of the new Coastie cutters.

Both of you are to shadow the supertanker and then... ... *DATA LOST*

(NOTE: I've been trying to reconstruct this for two years now, still no luck —NILES)

★ ★ ★

Air Force One Recording, Entry #706

"*So, what do you wanna do?*"...

"*I dunno, what do YOU wanna do?*"...

"I dunno, what do YOU wanna do?" etc. COL, US Army, (DIA) describing the way OUSD(S) (Undersecretary of Defense for Strategy) develops and implements their strategies.

★ ★ ★

~~TOP SECRET~~

POTUS: "...no honey, I won't be home this weekend."

VOICE 1: *(Military Assistant? - UNK —NILES):* "Madam President, we have an emerg—"

POTUS: "Can't you see I'm busy?"

VOICE 1: "Ma'am, the Chinese sank the *Occasio-Occasio*."

POTUS: "DON'T CALL ME MA— I'm sorry what?"

VOICE 2: *(SECDEF most likely —NILES):* "It's true. The O-O, along with one of our Coast Guard Green Environmental Enforcement Cutters intercepted that illicit supertanker we discussed at the PDB *(Presidential Daily Brief)* a month ago. We boarded the supertanker and found a jackpot. Broadcast some of it live too. You should see the ratings."

POTUS: "What about the O-O? SECNAV must be beside herself."

SECDEF: "The Chinese must have had a sub escorting it. Torpedoed the O-O. Left the cutter to pick up the survivors. They scuttled the supertanker. We picked up the Chinese sub only after it fired."

POTUS: "I can't even begin to count the norms they just violated!"

SECDEF: "Well, you know I've got just the thing."

★ ★ ★

Audio File #7

"I'll be right back. I have to go pound my nuts flat..." Lt Col, USAF, (EUCOM) after being assigned a difficult tasker.

★ ★ ★

Hello, Niles again. It's been about three weeks since I touched this. Picked up some upper respiratory thing while cleaning the algae separators. The Level II Public Servant Clinic said it was a new coronavirus variant. I'll add that one to the list. It hit me bad for about two weeks. Cricket paste doesn't taste so bad when you can't taste anything. I burned through a lot of social credits for food, fuel, and water while I couldn't work. The good news is the pod is no longer a mess, I had plenty of time to clean it while my pod mates were temporarily relocated for quarantine.

Apparently, Counterintelligence interviewed them while I was on the mend. I think someone might suspect my little history side project. If it's who I think it is, I'll see them later this week. We might have a little "chat."

That's not what this entry is for though. For my hypothetical future reader, I want to set up what comes next on the road to ruin.

So, we're not at the "and then they fired all the missiles" part yet. First, there were a lot of diplomatic démarches. Everybody got a démarche. And there were sternly worded letters read by stern-looking diplomats at the United Nations.

The New European Union strongly condemned the *Luck Dragon* Incident. Just the incident, they didn't come out on one side or the other. Since reestablishment, they tended to keep their mouths shut on anything important, and member states were locked into Chinese mercantilism. Their recovery from the previous bout of wars and environmental tragedy was still in a precarious state. Rocking the boat could have proved disastrous for them and their large populations of displaced refugees. Tensions between those groups and NEU native populations were always high.

Poland-Lithuania (it was an odd year, during even years it was Lithuania-Poland), was a bit more belligerent. They chastised China for a whole raft of wrongdoing. The P-L/L-P Commonwealth had a long history of Russian, and now Chinese economic exploitation they wanted payback for, especially when it came to disastrous deforestation, Chinese guest workers who were very poor guests, and with flooding their markets with cheap electronics made with some nasty carcinogens.

Russia pretended it was still important, but they were on their third president and government-in-exile in as many years, so it was all rather confusing, since the other two Russias also issued statements. Russia is a big enough landmass, even with rising seas and the year-round lack of Arctic ice, that it fits three Russias. They don't much care for each other, let alone anyone else.

The Japanese and Koreans mined their ports, but their rather muted responses had a bit of the "well here we go again, again" feel to it, and seriously, who could blame them?

The American response? Things escalated quickly. First, the President was caught on a hot mic referring to mainland China as "West Taiwan" after a press briefing, and then . . .

★ ★ ★

White Presidential House Situation Room, National Security Council Transcript, Artifact #15

"*Let's face it: Africa sucks...*" *Department of State representative (Bureau of African Affairs) at a conference on Africa.*

★ ★ ★

~~TOP SECRET~~

POTUS: "Well, I think I made them mad. How much damage are we looking at?"

SECSTATE: "Oh yeah, it's sanctions and embargoes all the way down. Rare earths, they know they got us there. And they sank our destroyer 'in self-defense' of course, and we 'committed an act of war,' yadda yadda. So far, the only ones supporting them in the UN are Russia and Nicaragua, and the New EU is abstaining."

POTUS: "Wait, which Russia?"

SECSTATE: "All of them."

DIRECTOR OF NATIONAL INTELLIGENCE (DNI): "We did get one of their subs too, lost with all hands, but they won't admit to it, and I think we should keep that under wraps for now as well. The wrecks of both the sub and the supertanker are extraordinarily deep, but there may be a chance we can recover some intelligence before the Chinese can mount a recovery."

NATIONAL SECURITY ADVISER (NATSEC): "We're backed into a corner, Madam President. We must hit the Chinese where it hurts them the most, and it must be in a way the American people can feel satisfied after the tragic loss of the *O-O*. They're out for blood."

POTUS: "Must be sweeps week."

SECDEF: "I think we go public with the rest of the videos the boarding party and drones transmitted from that ship! It will give us all the justification we need."

DNI: "I disagree. We do that, and someone will expose what *we've* been working on these last few years as well, and that'll bury us."

POTUS: "Where's VPOTUS?"

P-HOUSE Chief of Staff: "In Australia. At a Greenpeace 'Save the Platypus' event."

POTUS: "Yeah, those things are getting poached left and right, and the Aussies are getting pissed about it. Have zim hold tight. We might need zim to work some shuttle diplomacy between us and the Aussies, the Kiwis, the Indians, and the Sings."

274 *Weird World War: China*

SECDEF: "If you're ready for the briefing?"

POTUS: "You'd better have options for us. Why not one of the standing plans?"

SECDEF: "Madam President, since the last administration left office twelve years ago, the interagency and the Department have been working on some controlled escalation plans. The concept worked well enough with the Russians. Ukraine and Belarus will be habitable again by the end of the century, so we think the risks with China are acceptable."

SECSTATE: "You know that's why the most powerful country in Europe is now freaking Ultra-Catholic Poland-Lithuania, or are we on a Lithuania-Poland year?"

POTUS: "It's an odd year."

SECSTATE: "Got it. Those 'phobes can go to their make-believe hell!"

CHAIR OF THE JOINT CHIEFS (CJCS): "Mz. Secretary, I think we should move forward with the briefing. Depending on what the Boss chooses, we'll need to backbrief the service chiefs and the combatant commanders immediately...Excuse, me, I'll be right back, I need to check on something."

(CJCS LEAVES THE ROOM.)

SECDEF: "Ma'am... dam, Madam President—sorry about that, shall we continue?"

POTUS: "Hurry up, this is a real election year, and I've got a full plate."

SECDEF: "First, we need a robust naval and air flexible deterrence package in Asia and the Pacific, immediately. If VPOTUS can work the allies and partners, we'll be good to go. I recommend we show them the entire boarding videos, the ones we haven't shown to the public yet."

DNI: "I still think that's a bad idea!"

SECDEF: *(Either didn't hear the objection or didn't care —NILES):* "Here's where things get tricky. We boost our deterrence in Asia. This messages to the Chinese that we can very quickly pivot and put a real hurtin' on them. But the real name of this game is Africa. We're going to do a little supply chain disruption of our own. We deploy a large counter-poaching and counter-economic exploitation peacekeeping force, at the invitation of the Organization of African Economies."

POTUS: "Africa? We're going to hit the Chinese by going to Africa.

What the hell does Africa have to do with this? Africa sucks. For an NGO, the OAE is one hell of an organized crime ring. They only cut off the right arms. What, exactly, is your theory of success here?"

SECDEF: "Both us and the Chinese are dependent on rare earth elements for electric vehicles and military products, and they're always trying to cut us out of the action. We need to cut them out instead. And we do that by going after their magic dick medicine."

POTUS: "I'm sorry, what?"

SECSTATE: "I'm confused, there are no rhinos left in Africa. The Chinese stole, bought, or poached them by proxy years ago."

NATSEC: "Actually rhino horn isn't used to treat impotence or infertility in Traditional Chinese Medicine, and it's racist to suggest that. But it is used to treat delirium, fever..."

DNI: "Do you really think this is time for this? Anyway, isn't it tiger dick..."

(UNK VOICE): "Yeah, now it's whale dick..."

POTUS: "CUT IT OUT! But if we ramp up deployments to Africa, that's going to pull forces from the Tejas DMZ, and that's leaves us short of Army forces for Asia."

(LOUD INTERRUPTION)

CJCS: "Madam President, the Chief of Naval Operations called to tell me that they've recovered what might be the last of the *O-O's* survivors!"

POTUS: "We got lucky there weren't too many dead or MIA. Who is it?"

CJCS: "The captain, CDR Frasier Copeland."

DNI: "They sure it's him? It's been almost a week."

CJCS: "Positive ID due to ... ummmm."

POTUS: "To what?"

CJCS: "A distinctive tattoo."

DNI: "Distinctive?"

CJCS: "On the captain's penis, Madam President."

POTUS: "Is it a feminine penis?"

(END TRANSCRIPT)

★ ★ ★

Chinese Communist Party Central Military Committee Archive, Item #78-65-01

   "Is that a Navy or a Marine admiral?" MAJ, US Army, (EUCOM)

★ ★ ★

~~TOP SECRET~~

(NILES: *I think my Mandarin holds up well, but I'm too worried about being caught if I use an online translating tool, so this is from memory.*)

PEOPLE'S LIBERATION ARMY (PLA) GENERAL: "The Americans am idiots!"

COMMITTEE MEMBER: "Well yes, our understand this."

GENERAL SECRETARY: "Gentlemen, pleasure calm yourselves. Currently, admiral, would do yours report pleasure continuity." *(Close enough —NILES)*

PEOPLE'S LIBERATION ARMY NAVY (PLAN) ADMIRAL: "Yes, yours most esteemed translucent dental floss." *(Wait—that can't be right —NILES)*

"...we am the monitoring latest American surface active groups beginning to deploy originate our two-hundred-year planned Hawaiian province, and our intelligence also suggests that pending deployment for bomber aircrafts of that 'show for force.' planned is preparing that counterstrategy based in our four principles, six actions, two slogans, and twenty-five warfares doctrine, stemming originate yours benevolent guidance the upon lasted plenary council, and we..."

GENERAL SECRETARY: "Whereour issupercarrier? Why are is it don't deployed?"

PLAN ADMIRAL: "Your excellency, our take deployed our autonomous robotic speedily attacked carriers already, fully embarked taking combat drones the and latest stealth sparkle heaven lit exploding phallus." *(NOTE: "missiles" —NILES)*

"...our intelligent that would do be that suitable deterrent and shown for force, while capable of..."

GENERAL SECRETARY: "Where the is fucking supercarrier?"

PLAN ADMIRAL: "President Cao Cao is currently the touring ship taking several members the for government, our think it inauspicious and impolite to ended he is anytime early."

PEOPLE'S LIBERATION ARMY AIR FORCE (PLAAF) GENERAL: "I the believable right honorable admiral means to said the this supreme president is praying the to lucky golden cat."

GENERAL SECRETARY: "Gambling? Why are will himself be gambling?"

PLAN ADMIRAL: "Well due to budget shortfalls the for lasted few years, while then highly go to quarantine enforcement and sterilization, our come upon below of woman of overdue refit. Then, the while supercarrier were on drydock, some... arrangements... were make taking local businesses, to helped the fund worked and improved morale the for sailors and workers."

PLAAF GENERAL: "He means an onboard casino, whorehouse, and opium lounge."

GENERAL SECRETARY: "The president is late in he is a party dues anyway, and this is unacceptable. Sent that team to arrest himself and those for he is a cabinet engaged on such salacious and decadent imperialist counter-revolutionary actively. Have this ship ready to sailed immediately!"

PLAN ADMIRAL: "Yes, Yours Excellency, we'll cleaned outward this den for iniquity, whores and junkies immediately!"

GENERAL SECRETARY: "Who say anything around cleaning it outward? cao cao go off to enjoyed himself and didn't even cut my on the in active. Fuck himself prevent the kept casino!"

PLAN ADMIRAL: "Of course, Yours Excellency. Prevent should our waited until those finish the filming president's episode for 'Boats and Hoes'?"

★ ★ ★

Video File 14 (FRAGMENTARY)

"Things are looking up for us here. In fact, Papua-New Guinea is thinking of offering two platoons: one of infantry (headhunters) and one of engineers (hut builders). They want to eat any Iraqis they kill. We've got no issues with that, but State is being anal about it." LTC, US Army (Joint Staff) on coalition building.

★ ★ ★

Niles here. Okay, my pod mates just left for their shift, so I have some time to myself. Things have taken an interesting turn over the last few weeks.

Wait one second...

Sorry, I thought one of them was coming back inside.

So, last week at the farm, I ran into a colleague of mine from Archival Sanitation. He's a professional Disinformation Reducer. That means "censor," but that word has been unremembered. He redacts sources, and marks documents and multimedia files for future classification review. Which means they disappear into a black hole forever. He hates it, and we got to talking about a few things. The point is, I think I can trust him.

★ ★ ★

Recording, United Nations General Assembly, New York, New York, Video File #15

"*If we wait until the last minute to do it, it'll only take a minute.*" *MAJ, US Army (EUCOM)*

★ ★ ★

UNCLASSIFIED

CHINESE AMBASSADOR: "We absolutely and unconditionally condemn this vagrant act of American piracy and imperialism, of course that's to be expected by the criminal regime in Washin—"

US AMBASSADOR: "Criminal? Oh, you want to talk about 'criminal'? Check out these awesome selfies our Coast Guardsmen took onboard your smuggling vessel! Those cloned rhinos are what's criminal! That skin color isn't natural!"

CHINESE AMBASSADOR: "How dare you! You attacked a simple commercial vessel; you had no right to board and attack the crew! Your thugs fired the first shots!"

US AMBASSADOR: "MX. Secretary-General, may I draw your attention to the video I'll now play."

★ ★ ★

~~TOP SECRET~~

BREACHER: "GET DOWN ON THE DECK, NOW!"

(Incoherent shouting in Mandarin and English, and **BREACHER's** *camera shows multiple Chinese crewmen dropping tools, slowly lowering themselves to the ground.)*

COAST GUARD 2: "Holy shit, dude, are those rhinos? They don't look too good!"

*(**BREACHER's** camera briefly swivels to look at the rhino pens, just cheap chain link fences with linked concrete filled drums for barriers.)*

COAST GUARD 3: "They don't sound too good either, they're not moving much. Look out!"

BREACHER quickly swivels back to the crewmen.

BREACHER: "I SAID STAY ON THE GROUND!"

CREWMAN 1 stops in his tracks, postured as if he was about to rush the

BREACHER.

BREACHER: "PUT DOWN THAT PIPE RIGHT NOW, DO NOT COME CLOSER, OR I WILL USE DEADLY FORCE!"

COAST GUARD 2: "I got the crew, dude, put that camera on this other stuff. This is insane."

(23 seconds of white noise and static)

(BREACHER's POV shows crates stacked up and spread around the cargo hold.)

BREACHER: "Let's see, we got crates full of packets of ground-up powders, and they don't look like booger sugar. Peculiar, but very interesting."

COAST GUARD 3: "You? You speak English?

CREWMAN 2: "Little. Little."

COAST GUARDS 3: "What is this? WHAT IS THIS?"

CREWMAN 2: (Mandarin, then broken English.) "It whale, whale! Muck deer!"

COAST GUARD 3: "What the fuck?"

(BREACHER, watching exchange, adjusts his radio.)

UNK VOICE through RADIO: "...this isn't industrial tooling; these look like some sort of medical hazard tanks. And there's a big... aquarium in here, I think those are seahorses."

COAST GUARD 2: "Watch out, dude, same asshole with the pipe from before!"

(Loud shouting in Mandarin. CREWMAN 1 attempts to slowly walk toward the BREACHER, but stumbles. The BREACHER opens fire. More shouting. The bright flash floods out the camera for several seconds, along with more shouting.)

COAST GUARD 3: "I think that really woke up the rhinos... oh shit!"

(BREACHER turns to see a large indistinct mass, and the feed cuts out.)

(NOTE: Further reconstruction with other artifacts from the boarding action corroborates the fact that the rhinos became agitated following the shooting of the Chinese crewman. It is unclear whether they were released, possibly by another crewmember when the boarding party was distracted, or the rhinos beat their way out of their confinement. Information from later in the war period indicates the rhino clones possessed a flaw of some kind. Engineered

to be docile, these had some sort of defect that caused them to become even more dangerous than their natural forbearers, especially the females, but I'm not a biologist. —NILES)

★ ★ ★

Recovered *UN* Security Council Archive Transcript #16.1-*Annex A*

"The chance of success in these talks is the same as the number of R's in 'fat chance...'" GS-15 Civilian, Supreme Headquarters, Allied Powers Europe (SHAPE)

★ ★ ★

US AMBASSADOR TO THE UNITED NATIONS: "The United States demands full and immediate compensation to the nation and especially the families of those lost aboard the USS *Occasio-Occasio*, and a full accounting of illegal PRC activities in Africa and around the globe."

PRC AMBASSADOR TO THE UNITED NATIONS: "The Chinese People's Republic categorically rejects these boundless and shameless accusations by the imperialist thugs of Washington. Continued abuse and false words uttered in this esteemed assembly will be met with severe consequences. The People's Republic has never engaged in illicit activities whatsoever, and we renounce this—"

EMPIRE OF KENYA AMBASSADOR TO THE UNITED NATIONS: "Horse shit! Those weren't simple rhinos you reconstructed, you created unstable armored battle unicorns! You did this to destabilize Africa and create a biological weapon! They're already killing people by the hundreds, since apparently, they don't have any problem reproducing, unlike those stupid pandas..."

PRC AMBASSADOR: "Outrage! We have been nothing but the providers of economic justice and goodwill to the peoples of Africa and Southeast Asia, unlike the perfidious Americans. Surely, Mr. Secretary-General, surely you will restore or..."

SECRETARY-GENERAL OF THE UNITED NATIONS: "It's MX! Everyone will observe proper pronoun usage in this forum! My pronouns are mx/mxz! How dare you misgender me!"

(NOTE: no pronunciation guides extant —NILES)

"...By overwhelming vote via the General Assembly, the United Nations universally condemns the actions of both the United

States of America and the People's Republic of China in this unfortunate event, as both countries displayed a blatant disregard for international norms and rules, hereby zhe all..."

US AMBASSADOR: "I don't know what 'zhe' means Mrrr-whatever Secretary-General, but the United States will today put before the Security Council this resolution requesting authorization for the use of force against the Chinese government for multiple, continued, and flagrant violations of environmental laws resulting in crimes against humanity, to include weaponizing harmless animals!"

KENYAN AMBASSADOR: "At no point in history has a rhino ever been 'harmless.'"

SECRETARY-GENERAL: "We will ignore America's offensive mockery of pronoun justice, but rest assured, the Council on Human Rights will not! *Both* the United States and China have committed grotesque acts of pollution and contamination against the Earth, with purposefully sunken warships and unauthorized disposal of human remains! Therefore—Wait, what?"

(Sounds of chaos ensue—random gunfire, shouts, and crowd noises)

VOICE ON MEGAPHONE: "WE ARE THE ANIMAL LIBERATION MOVEMENT, and WE WILL NOT BE SILENCED, AND... wait, what are you trash doing here?"

OTHER VOICE ON MEGAPHONE: "WHAT ARE WE DOING HERE? Oh, um, sorry one sec, WHAT ARE YOU DOING HERE? WE ARE THE MOVEMENT FOR THE LIBERATION OF ANIMALS, AND WE WILL NOT BE SILENCED! And did we double-book?"

★ ★ ★

American Nightly News Broadcast, Satellite Television, Archive File #897345
"I'm planning on taking the weekend off... notionally..." LT, US Navy (EUCOM) midway through a huge, simulated command exercise.

★ ★ ★

FEMALE ANCHOR: "The United Nations building in New York City was the scene of absolute chaos earlier today as the US and China continue to blame each other for the incident in the South China Sea which led to the loss of an American warship and a Chinese submarine, but not before the world caught a glimpse of what some are calling hard proof of Chinese genetic experimentation and illegal trafficking in rare animal parts. This was before two different groups of animal rights protesters stormed the building, overwhelming security. Over to our on-scene reporter for more."

ON-SCENE REPORTER: "We're live from the police barricade outside the UN building where things got briefly out of control earlier today, resulting in a huge surge of protesters who temporarily overwhelmed security, before the NYPD and National Guard troops responded in force..."

RANDOM STREET GUY: "Conspiracy! They were let in!"

ON-SCENE REPORTER: "Yeah, so they overwhelmed security, but were quickly subdued. Quite possibly because this wasn't a coordinated event, and two rival groups of protesters..."

RANDOM STREET GUY: "False flag crisis actors!"

ON-SCENE REPORTER: "...But..."

FEMALE ANCHOR: "I'm sorry, Kelsey, we have late breaking news. We take you live to a press briefing from the Presidential House in Washington, where the President is about to make a statement about American troop deployments as tensions with the Chinese seem to be getting worse."

★ ★ ★

Battlefield History Detachment #10, Debriefing File #4477

"'Leaning forward' is really just the first phase of 'falling on your face.'" Col, USMC

★ ★ ★

~~TOP SECRET~~

US ARMY HISTORIAN: "So Captain Crane, can you please restate your account, and let's leave out the unprofessional commentary and profanity this time?"

CAPT CRANE: "Okay, okay. Sorry. So, my ODA team was deployed for foreign internal defense training and special reconnaissance with the Vietnamese Army, up along the Chinese border. We'd been there for a few months already before things got crazy out in the open-source world, but since we'd had a, call it a 'feeling,' that things were going to take a turn for the worst, SOCOM wanted us in there early. The Vietnamese have no love for the PRC, and the Chinese are still mad since their two little wars didn't go so well for them. That's to say nothing of the historical animosity there. Higher saw this as a fantastic opportunity to prepare a land domain flank against China if things really got out of hand in Africa or elsewhere."

USA HISTORIAN: "And that's when your mixed force encountered a Chinese patrol conducting a cross-border reconnaissance?"

CRANE: "I don't know if you could call a force that size a 'patrol.' Reconnaissance-in-force was more like it. They looked like they were planning on staying awhile.

USA HISTORIAN: "Did you make the call to remain in place and observe?"

CRANE: "Based on my orders and on the capabilities I had on hand, both my team's and the Vietnamese, yes. We knew something was up, but we'd been offline for several days on purpose to avoid detection, so I hadn't gotten the latest intel."

USA HISTORIAN: "So, who ran into whom?"

CRANE: "Well, that's where things get funny you see, and why we're redoing this damned interview, again!"

HISTORIAN: "Now hold on!"

CRANE: "So, again, one of our indigenous force types decides he's going to take out a sentry. Honestly, I think his bros put him up to it, or he had some sort of personal score to settle, maybe for his family, I don't know. You'd think the way they do things they would have beaten this kind of sh—sorry, behavior, out of them. So, his squad leader breaks radio silence to warn me, and that's when somebody just opens up. Pretty soon, there's a firefight between us and the Chinese pickets, and that turns into a fighting retreat by us. This gets the Chinese all enthused, and they start a hasty attack. It's just so badly executed; I mean it's a clusterfuck."

HISTORIAN: "We'll just beep that out."

CRANE: "Yeah. Anyway, they execute so poorly, we're able to rally and send the Vietnamese forces and flank the bastards. I'm getting ready to launch a counterattack here, I mean, we're outnumbered at least three-to-one, but these assholes suck shit and crap incompetence, so I think we can take 'em and let the politicians sort it out later."

HISTORIAN: "How did you learn about the noncombatants?"

CRANE: "So, get this! We're ready to hammer them, I mean we're about to overrun some positions through this thicket, and we hear shouting in English!"

HISTORIAN: "Continue."

CRANE: "Not good English either, that snotty European 'Ztop vhat you are do-eeeng' English. And, then these fucking hippies, uh, these noncombatant civilians, are coming out of the trees and wave banners and shit between us and the Chinese. They have some reporter with them too, you see her all the time on streaming news. Kinda hot in that crazy dumbass college chick way, suck the paint off a new truck."

HISTORIAN: "Captain Crane, please stay focused!"

CRANE: "Anyway, so we all just kind of stand there and we're looking at each other. Civilians, PRC, us. I can see this PRC officer, the look he has on his face, I think he mouthed 'What the f—?' to me, and I just shake my head back. So, the whiny, nasally skinny civilian dude starts yelling at us all. He says, 'Ve are zee Ecologeests Without Bor-dares, and ziss is ze 'abitat of zee Southeast Azheen Climbing Tree Octopus!' Then these fuckers all start chanting and waving signs at us."

HISTORIAN: "So, who shot them first?"

CRANE: "Well, somebody beat me to it."

★ ★ ★

USAFRICOM, Audio File #75

"I've become the master of nodding my head and acting like I give a shit, and then instantly forgetting what the hell a person was saying the moment they walk away." General / Flag Officer Executive Assistant

★ ★ ★

TOP SECRET

US ARMY BRIGADIER GENERAL, JTF-RHINO: "I should have retired last year."

US AIR FORCE COLONEL: "Sir, Intel's ready to go for the Commander's Update Brief."

BG: "Let me hear it first."

INTEL BRIEFER: "US, Coalition, and African partners and allies, and co-combatants, and . . ."

BG: "Yes, all the good guys, got it, speed this up."

INTEL BRIEFER: "Forces all over the AOR are reporting hostile encounters with PRC-produced clone animals. If you'll direct your attention to the screen."

(NOTE: I can't find the actual video files, but I do have the briefing slide

deck. Rabid mutant Chinese clone tigers, rhinos, gazelles. Ripping people to shreds. Ripping both Chinese and American forces to shreds. Real disturbing stuff. —NILES)

COLONEL: "Oh that's just wrong."

INTEL BRIEFER: "This has led to a strategic pause in the Chinese offensive, as the Chinese seem to be attempting to deploy chemical or biological countermeasures against these animals. This has caused significant defections in their African allies, most of whom are declaring neutrality, or declaring hostilities against both Coalition and Chinese forces and vowing to fight to expel both."

BG: "Yeesh, this is a mess. What's that mean for us, Chief of Ops?"

COLONEL: "Well, we have reinforcements on the way from CONUS and they'll arrive in less than 30 days but expect the Chinese Navy to harass the convoys. They probably won't shoot, unless they can prove their new torpedoes are green enough to get around the UN sanctions."

BG: "Well, that doesn't leave much for the fight in Asia. That puts most of the Army here and on the southwest border. What's home plate doing about that?"

COLONEL: "Seems like it's boom time for private military contractors. These are just straight up mercs."

BG: "Where'd we get them all?"

COLONEL: "China, it looks like."

★ ★ ★

Video File #56

"Who are you talking to? . . . Hang up the phone!" Lt Col, USAF, mentoring MAJ, USA (EUCOM) on how to stay in his own lane.

★ ★ ★

I am Niles Geston, and the last few months have been extremely productive, and I'm not talking about the damn kelp farm! The more of my oppressed fellows who see the truth about the War, the truth about our world and the nightmare it's become, the more our only course of action seems clear to us. Soon. We continue to build our network. We've found that surveillance is neither total, nor persistent. We've found that a regime that survives on falsifying records and destroying memory is easy to also steal from. Someday, we'll hang them with their own hemp rope.

★ ★ ★

China-Burma Theater of Operations, Joint Task Force Tree Octopus, Excerpts from US Situation Report (SITREP) #83

"Let's just call Lessons Learned what they really are: institutionalized scab picking." Anonymous

★ ★ ★

~~SECRET~~

OBSERVATIONS AND LESSONS LEARNED:

– PARA 3.A.1. Green tanks carry fewer rounds and need generators to recharge.

– ***

– PARA 4.1. The role of the newly appointed Environmental Officers is to discuss designations of protected terrain under a "green flag," per UNSC Resolution 80452/12.88.4 Sub-Para 18, which introduces the green flag as an internationally recognized symbol of rules-based environmental order and the new norms of conduct between nations.

   – 4.1.1. All tread-damaged terrain since H+0 is declared environmentally contaminated and designated protected wetlands.

   – 4.1.2. Terrain damaged as such is off-limits for armored and mechanized operations of any kind. PRC compliance observance reported at less than fifty percent.

   – ***

– PARA 5.1.1.B.17. During periods of environmental temperatures over 38C, all forces are only authorized to run fossil fuel engines 45 minutes of each hour.

– PARA 5.1.1.B.18. Remaining 15 minutes of each hour monitored and tracked as mandatory carbon footprint pauses.

– ***

– PARA 13.8.1.A.3. All personnel are hereby limited in their further use of tungsten ammunition to no more than 5 rounds per combat load. Ammo status AMBER.

– PARA 13.8.1.A.4. It was discovered that all tungsten ammunition stocks are sourced from the People's Republic of China and must be destroyed. No amnesty authorized. Ammo status RED.

– PARA 13.8.1.A.5. Joint Staff has ordered return to AR-15-based issue long-arm platforms.

– PARA 13.8.1.A.6. Significant problems with reissuing AR-15-style weapons. Large numbers of personnel refuse to train with and use the "black plastic scary gun."

★ ★ ★

Cheyenne Mountain Complex, Audio File #62

"I just realized that this War on Terror might take a little longer than we thought, so I am developing a new system of hanging charts on walls to solve our problem and win the war." LTC (EUCOM) after a review of long-range Counter Terrorism plans.

★ ★ ★

~~TOP SECRET~~

POTUS: "So how do we break the stalemates, people? What are our options to get us back on the move in Africa and in Southeast Asia, and control escalation? The Russias, all three of them, are making a lot of ugly noises, and the NEUs are getting more skittish by the day!"

NATIONAL SECURITY ADVISOR: "Madam President, fortunately, all parties to this conflict are keeping nuclear weapons off the table, for now, and I think we can keep it that way."

DIRECTOR, NATIONAL INTELLIGENCE: The CIA has a recommendation, if you're willing to hear it, Madam President, it will require your authorization for a clandestine operation."

CJCS: "Tony, if this is what I think it is, I want to lodge my formal protest of this course of action. There's no way to guarantee just what will happen once the asset is deployed!"

POTUS: "It's a good thing the VPOTUS is still in Australia and the Speaker is in a continuity of government site, this is a real gamble here you're asking me to make. I hope you're right."

★ ★ ★

New European Union Premium Streaming News Content, #45

"Even if Al-Qaeda nuked this place, the Chief of Staff would approve a 4-star visitor the very next day!" GS-12 Civilian (EUCOM)

★ ★ ★

MALE ANCHOR: "We now take you live to a special report from Hainan Island, China and to our special correspondent, Christina Shrubs."

SHRUBS: "Thank you, Tom. Can you hear me?"

MALE ANCHOR: "That's a 'lima charlie' as our brave service members like to say, Christina!"

SHRUBS: "Yeah, got it. Thanks, Tom. As you can see here, I'm embedded with Greenpeace and the UN observers' contingent assigned to encourage and document compliance with international law regarding environmental damage during war time, and it seems there's a peculiar predicament here. You can see there is a large group of pandas in this area, and the Chinese forces have been forced to suspend their combat operations against American special forces who are believed to be in this area of Hainan."

MALE ANCHOR: "Wow, that's got to be making them upset, Christina!"

SHRUBS: "That's correct, Tom. And as you can see, a Chinese PLA officer seems to be arguing with the Greenpeace representative and the leader of the UN observers. But there doesn't seem to be any sign of the Americans."

(The group of pandas continue to slowly work their way closer and closer to the tree line. Rolling, walking on all fours, and then suddenly, several of them stand upright and take off running.)

MALE ANCHOR: "Wow, Christina, those pandas appear to be the American special forces... and they appear to be... dressed as pandas?"

SHRUBS: "Truly brilliant observation, Tom, but who knows what the special forces are doing here? This could be a major turning point in the war."

MALE ANCHOR: "Christina, do you think you could get me a couple of challenge coins? My son really loves those!"

SHRUBS: "I'm going to try and get a statement from the UN or Greenpeace here!"

UN OBSERVER: *(Speaking to the PRC troop leader)* "Well, technically, they're not in an illegal fake uniform, just one that's well camouflaged. It's not our fault your troops couldn't see through that, but good on you for your caution in the defense of a truly special rare species!"

PLA OFFICER: "Damn it! Come on out, guys!"

(A small team of Chinese special forces, dressed as cranes, stands up and walks out of the other side of the tree line.)

PLA OFFICER: "You find them?"

CHINESE SPECIAL FORCES OPERATOR: "We ain't found shit!"

FILE #770

THIS PAGE INTENTIONALLY LEFT BLANK

People's Liberation Army Supreme Command, File #7

"We are now past the good idea cutoff point . . ." MAJ (JS) on the fact that somebody always tries to "fine tune" a COA with more "good ideas."

★ ★ ★

CCP GENERAL SECRETARY: "The tea crop is blighted! Next will be grain! That's what those American SOF bastards were doing in Hainan! And you incompetents let them!"

PLA GENERAL: "We can prove the Americans used a bioweapon! This will make them a pariah like they deserve!"

PLAN ADMIRAL: "Well, it's not like our track record in this area has made us a lot of friends at the UN, or anywhere else. There are still new viral outbreaks every few months, and they hit us too!"

PLA GENERAL #2: "Korean forces have advanced beyond Pyongyang. With the majority of our forces committed in Africa, the island chains and Indochina, we're at a loss to stop them should they push beyond the Yalu."

GENERAL SECRETARY: "What about the Russians?"

PLA GENERAL: "Which ones?"

GENERAL SECRETARY: "The Siberian ones, you dolt!"

PLA GENERAL: "Yes, we asked them to intervene. Their response was rather curt."

PLAN ADMIRAL: "The other two are just itching to go back into Europe though."

GENERAL SECRETARY: "Can we get them to go after the P-Ls?"

PLA GENERAL: "It's the L-Ps this year, but yes, I think we can engineer something. The L-Ps have a crane exhibit at the national zoo in Vilnius. We could infiltrate our SOF and create a—"

GENERAL SECRETARY: "No more cranes!"

PLA SPACE STRATEGIC FORCES: "Mr. Chairman, now might be time to consider our space orbital-to-ground options."

(Silence for several moments)

GENERAL SECRETARY: "You realize that once we do that, there is no going back for the world, none!"

PLA SPACE STRATEGIC FORCES: "If we don't strike now, with everything we've got, space kinetics, cyber, the works, we're done."

PLAN ADMIRAL: "The Japanese blockade of Taiwan, China, is nearly completed."

GENERAL SECRETARY: "Time to get into the bunkers. Strategic Forces are authorized to launch. Nukes only as a retaliatory strike, if the Americans survive long enough to launch theirs!"

★ ★ ★

US Embassy Canberra, Australian Capital Territory: Vice President of the USA and Australian Foreign Minister Discussing Impact of US-China War on Australia, Transcript File #77:

"Never pet a burning dog." *LTC (Tennessee Army National Guard)*

★ ★ ★

~~TOP SECRET~~

VICE PRESIDENT OF THE UNITED STATES (VPOTUS): "Mr. Foreign Minister, thank you for meeting with me today. I understand the Prime Minister is indisposed, but the President asked me to make one more final appeal regarding additional Australian forces being committed to the joint area of operations on the mainland. I trust our security on the compound is reassuring, given unfortunate recent events?"

FOREIGN MINISTER: "It is, considering if by 'unfortunate recent events' you mean launching a bioweapon on my country's national territory. Oh, by the way, you won't be leaving this compound any time soon, not if you want to stay treaty allies, until reparations are made."

VPOTUS: "The platypuses? Yes, well, you see…"

FOREIGN MINISTER: "I personally watched one of these things rip apart a dingo and mount its corpse! Can you imagine if that was a baby?"

VPOTUS: "That might have just been a clump of cells, let's not get carried away here!"

FOREIGN MINISTER: "The baby wasn't real; it was a reductio absurdum!"

VPOTUS: "The President has assured me that our best scientists are rapidly approaching an antidote vaccine that will adjust the aggression in the surviving mutated platypuses. Now, this will sterilize them, but we think there are enough untainted specimens in zoos that can rebuild the population once the war is over and the new norms established. This was all done in the name of helping to reduce China's increasing grip on your nation's politics, which has been negatively affecting our alliance, I might add, and put a dent in the illicit revenues they've gained through smuggling endangered species and animal products."

FOREIGN MINISTER: "Helping? 'Defeat Chinese smuggling.' Do you honestly believe this has 'helped' the situation at all? Your crank mad scientists deployed a fucking bioweapon on the sovereign territory of a treaty ally, killing off most of a healthy native species beloved all over the world and a national symbol, and turned the survivors into bloodthirsty baby-eating, dingo-fucking mutant attack-platypi in a country where most of the native flora and fauna are already trying to kill everyone, and that's just called 'Tuesday' around here!"

VPOTUS: "Well, Minister, you see..."

FOREIGN MINISTER: "What do you have to say for yourselves, hmmm?"

VPOTUS: "We had to destroy the species in order to save it."

★ ★ ★

Audio File #138-X

"If you want to take down a country, gimme a call. We'll get it done." General/Flag Officer, (EUCOM) to a gathering of US Ambassadors.

★ ★ ★

This is Niles. The time for revolution is at hand! We will never get a better opportunity than this! I've been in touch with fellow travelers throughout the Collectives, and our network has grown strong. The regime is powerful, but wobbly and precarious. Its power is much less assured than they want us all to believe. There are some internal disagreements between our revolutionary factions, but those will be sorted out once the revolution has begun in earnest. We'll overthrow those who would lie to us and make us liars in the process. We were never meant to live like this. The usurper provisional government carries on the legacy of the United States and its Commonwealth allies in name only, and even then, just barely. This travesty must be stopped!

★ ★ ★

National Command Authority (Location and Date Unknown), Transcript #100

"Ya know, in this Command, if the world were supposed to end tomorrow, it would still happen behind schedule." CWO4 (Chief Warrant Officer) (ret) (EUCOM)

★ ★ ★

The Chinese KEW strike crippled US and coalition forces, and struck at the homelands, killing millions and devastating essential industries and critical infrastructure. Moments later, two of the three Russias launched an invasion of the P-L Commonwealth, the eastern flank of the New European Union.

The President asked for and received a formal declaration of war against China and two out of three Russias, and did the formerly unthinkable, committing surviving US strategic nuclear forces to the attack. Fortunately, since the outbreak of the police actions in Africa, those forces had been on high alert so many more survived than the Chinese had hoped to kill.

It is not known how much of the American government has survived, nor how viable the United States is currently. We are struggling to restore communications to US forces overseas as well as our European allies and partners.

The French responded at last, several hours later. After a short midday break, they fired their missiles, providing a second-strike capability after the initial American and European strike.

It is currently unknown how much of the Russian and Chinese governments, populations, or forces have survived either.

★ ★ ★

Audio File #451

"We the willing, led by the unknowing, are doing the impossible for the ungrateful. We have done so much for so long with so little, that we are now qualified to do anything with nothing." Anonymous.

★ ★ ★

NILES: "I, Niles Geston, *(white noise)*... And this will probably be my final entry."

BOOM! (*Muffled explosions in the background, and the staccato of automatic weapons, shouts in the distance and indecipherable loudspeaker announcements.*)

NILES: "The ones I trusted, precious disciples of knowledge of a world soon to be lost forever, all dead or dying."

BASH BASH! (*Beating upon metal, following by an electronically distorted, amplified voice.*)

VOICE 1: "OPEN UP IN THERE, OPEN THIS POD IMMEDIATELY, AND BE BOUND BY THE LAW OF THE REUNITED STATES OF AMERICA!"

NILES: "I commend these data records to the future, because I know they'll find the books, they'll find the magnetic tapes, hard drives, DVDs. There's more now, scattered throughout the world, hidden. Deep—"

BASH BASH! (*Beating upon metal, followed by an electronically masked, amplified voice.*)

VOICE 1: "NILES GESTON! YOU ARE ACCUSED OF UNAUTHORIZED RESEARCH, MURDER, SABOTAGE, CONSPIRACY, AND TREASON! OPEN UP IMMEDIATELY AND YOU WILL RECEIVE A FAIR TRIAL!"

NILES: "They are coming. I cannot get out. They are coming. God, if you're there, don't let them find this audio. Forgive us our sins…"

BASH BASH!

VOICE 1: "THIS IS YOUR FINAL WARNING! WE WILL USE DEADLY FORCE!"

NILES: "I saved some whiskey for a moment like this, just in case. A friend in Pod Block 1138 traded it for a book."

BOOM! (*A much louder explosion, the sound of gas escaping under high pressure, and a burst of automatic gunfire.*)

VOICE 1: "That him?"

VOICE 2: "Gonna need DNA, his face is gone."

VOICE 1: "Does it matter?"

VOICE 3: "Don't bother searching. Orders are 'Once we get him, dead or alive, burn everything. Then clear out the pod blocks, no prisoners. Burn the rest.'"

VOICE 1 & 2: "Copy."

VOICE 3: "Where's Montag? Get him in here. Burn all of it."

VOICE 1: "You hear that?"

RECORDED AUDIO, UNKNOWN VOICE: "…but a whimper."

BOOM!

THE END? *(Naahhh)*

ABOUT THE AUTHORS
✪

Nadia Bulkin is the author of the short story collection *She Said Destroy* (Word Horde, 2017). She has been nominated for the Shirley Jackson Award five times. She grew up in Jakarta, Indonesia, with her Javanese father and American mother, before relocating to Lincoln, Nebraska. She has two political science degrees and lives in Washington, D.C.

D.J. (Dave) Butler has been a lawyer, a consultant, an editor, a corporate trainer, and a registered investment banking representative. His novels published by Baen Books include *Witchy Eye, Witchy Winter*, and *Witchy Kingdom, In the Palace of Shadow and Joy, Between Princesses and Other Jobs*, and *Among the Gray Lords*, as well as *The Cunning Man* and *The Jupiter Knife*, co-written with Aaron Michael Ritchey. He also writes for children: the steampunk fantasy adventure tales *The Kidnap Plot, The Giant's Seat*, and *The Library Machine* are published by Knopf. Other novels include *City of the Saints* from WordFire Press and *The Wilding Probate* from Immortal Works. Dave also organizes writing retreats and anarcho-libertarian writers' events, and travels the country to sell books. He plays guitar and banjo whenever he can, and likes to hang out in Utah with his wife and children.

Julian Michael Carver is the pen name for film editor Joey Kelly. A science fiction and media tie-in writer, Carver is a member of the International Association of Media Tie-In Writers. In 2021, Carver wrote the official film novelization for the movie *Freshwater*. In 2022, the novelization was nominated for the Scribe Award for Best Adapted Novel. Carver has also written several novels for Severed Press and has written licensed tie-in fiction for the franchise BattleTech through Catalyst Game Labs. He edited the 2022 film *Alien Abduction: Answers* starring world famous author Whitley Strieber. He is also a video content creator. Some of his content has been featured on *Ancient Aliens, Forensic Files 2, Roseanne,* and *The Sinner.*

Brenda W. Clough is the first female Asian-American SF writer, first appearing in print in 1984. Her novella *May Be Some Time* was a finalist for both the Hugo and the Nebula awards and became the novel *Revise the World*. Her latest time travel trilogy is *Edge to Center*, available at Book View Café. Marian Halcombe, a series of eleven neo-Victorian thrillers appeared in 2021. Her complete bibliography is up on her web page, brendaclough.net.

Larry Correia is the Dragon Award-winning, *New York Times* best-selling author of the Monster Hunter International series, the Grimnoir Chronicles alternate history trilogy, the Saga of the Forgotten Warrior epic fantasy, the *Dead Six* thrillers (with Mike Kupari), the *Gun Runner* sci-fi novel (with John D. Brown), and the Monster Hunter Memoirs novels (with John Ringo). His most recent novel is the dark fantasy *Servants of War* (with Steve Diamond).

Freddie Costello graduated Harvard with a degree in administrative documentation forensics. After school, he commissioned as a Coast Guard officer and served first aboard an icebreaker as the ship's Beverage Accounting Officer, and in the Pentagon's Planning Management Supervision office. He medically retired after receiving an eye injury from a binder clip battle, for which he earned a Meritorious Service Medal. He now works in the VA as a patient benefits analyst.

Steve Diamond is a horror, fantasy, and science fiction author who writes for Baen, WordFire Press, and a number of small publishers and game companies. He is known his dark military fantasy/horror novel, *Servants of War* (with Larry Correia), his YA supernatural thriller, *Residue*, and his collection of horror short fiction, *What Hellhounds Dream & Other Stories*.

Kevin Ikenberry is a life-long space geek and retired Army officer. As an adult, he managed the US Space Camp program and served in space operations before Space Force was a thing. He's an international best-selling author, award finalist, and a core author in the wildly successful Four Horsemen Universe. His novels include *Sleeper Protocol, Vendetta Protocol, Runs in the Family, Peacemaker, Honor the Threat, Stand or*

Fall, Deathangel, Fields of Fire, and *Harbinger*. He is also the author of the alternate history novel *The Crossing* from Baen Books. Kevin is an Active Member of SFWA, the International Association of Science Fiction and Fantasy Authors, International Thriller Writers, and SIGMA—the science fiction think tank. He lives in Colorado with his family and continues to work with space every day.

Stephen Lawson served on three deployments with the US Navy and is currently a helicopter pilot and commissioned officer in the Kentucky National Guard. He earned a Masters of Business Administration from Indiana University Southeast in 2018, and currently lives in Louisville, Kentucky with his wife. Stephen's writing has appeared in *Writers of the Future Volume 33, Orson Scott Card's InterGalactic Medicine Show, Galaxy's Edge, Daily Science Fiction, The Jim Baen Memorial Short Story Award, The Year's Best Military and Adventure Science Fiction,* and *Weird World War III*. His blog can be found at stephenlawsonstories.wordpress.com.

Nick Mamatas is the author of several novels, including *I Am Providence* and *The Second Shooter*, and the novella *The Planetbreaker's Son*. His short fiction has appeared in *Best American Mystery Stories, Year's Best Science Fiction and Fantasy, Asimov's SF,* Tor.com, and many other venues—much of it was recently collected in *The People's Republic of Everything*. Nick is also an editor; his anthologies include the Bram Stoker Award-winning *Haunted Legends* (with Ellen Datlow), and *Wonder and Glory Forever: Awe-Inspiring Lovecraftian Fiction*.

Dr. Theodore C. McCarthy ("T.C.") is an award-winning and critically acclaimed author and technology development strategist. A former CIA weapons expert, T.C. is a recognized authority on the impact of technology on military strategy and his debut novel, *Germline*, won the Compton Crook Award. T.C.'s latest books, *Tyger Burning* and *Tyger Bright*, were recently published by Baen Books. Find out more at tcmccarthy.com.

Rob McMonigal's fiction has previously appeared solo in *Fireside Magazine* and, with co-writer Erica Satifka, in the Broken Eye Books anthology, *It Came from Miskatonic University*. He's also the editor-in-chief of the long-running comics review site, www.panelpatter.com. His Twitter handle is @rob_mcmonigal.

Kevin Andrew Murphy grew up in California, earning degrees from UCSC in anthropology/folklore and literature/creative writing, and a masters of professional writing from USC. Over the years he's written role-playing games, short stories, novels, plays, and poems, and created the popular character Penny Dreadful for White Wolf, including writing the novel of the same name. Kevin's also a veteran contributor to George R.R. Martin's Wild Cards series. His Wild Cards story "Find the Lady" for *Mississippi Roll* won the Darrell Award for Best Novella for 2019, and he has a graphic novel featuring his character Rosa Loteria currently being illustrated, plus other projects in the works he can't announce just yet. He brews mead, plays games, and now resides in Reno, Nevada.

Blaine L. Pardoe is an award-winning and best-selling author of military science fiction, true crime, alternate history, military history and political thrillers. He has been a featured speaker at the US National Archives, the Smithsonian, and has spoken at the US Naval Academy on his works. He was awarded the State History Award by the Historical Society of Michigan and is a silver medal winner from the Military Writers Society of America. Mr. Pardoe won the Harriet Quimby Award from the Michigan Aviation Hall of Fame for his contributions to aviation history. His books have been mentioned on the floor of the US Congress. While he is probably best known for his thirty-seven years of contribution to the BattleTech series, he is now focused on other projects. His latest works include the Blue Dawn series of alternate history novels and the upcoming Land & Sea military science fiction series. He can be reached at bpardoe870@aol.com, and on Facebook and Twitter.

Erica L. Satifka's short fiction has appeared previously in the Weird World War series, as well as in places like *Clarkesworld* and *Interzone*. Her 2021 collection *How to Get to Apocalypse and Other Disasters* (Fairwood Press) has received praise from the *Washington Post*, *Tor.com*, and *Locus*, and she is the recipient of the 2017 British Fantasy Award for Best Newcomer. Visit her online at ericasatifka.com.

Martin L. Shoemaker is a programmer who writes on the side... or maybe it's the other way around. Programming pays the bills, but a second-place story in the Jim Baen Memorial Writing Contest earned him lunch with Buzz Aldrin. Programming never did that! His work has appeared in *Analog Science Fiction & Fact*, *Galaxy's Edge*, *Digital Science Fiction*, *Forever Magazine*, *Writers of the Future*, and numerous anthologies including *Weird World War III*, *Weird World War IV*, *Robosoldiers: Thank You for Your Servos*, *Year's Best Military and Adventure SF 4*, *Man-Kzin Wars XV*, *The Jim Baen Memorial Award: The First Decade*, and *Avatar Dreams* from WordFire Press. His *Clarkesworld* story "Today I Am Paul" appeared in four different year's-best anthologies and eight international editions. His follow-on novel, *Today I Am Carey*, was published by Baen Books in March 2019. His novel *The Last Dance* was published by 47North in November 2019, and the sequel *The Last Campaign* was published in October 2020.

Brad R. Torgersen is a multi-award-winning science fiction and fantasy writer whose book *A Star-Wheeled Sky* won the 2019 Dragon Award for Best Science Fiction Novel at the 33rd annual Dragon Con fan convention in Atlanta, Georgia. A prolific short fiction author, Torgersen has published stories in numerous anthologies and magazines, including several Best of Year editions. Brad is named in *Analog* magazine's who's who of top *Analog* authors, alongside venerable writers like Larry Niven, Lois McMaster Bujold, Orson Scott Card, and Robert A. Heinlein. Married for over twenty-five years, Brad is also a United States Army Reserve Chief Warrant Officer—with multiple deployments to his credit—and currently lives with his wife and daughter in the Mountain West, where they keep a small menagerie of dogs and cats.

Brian Trent's work regularly appears in *Analog Science Fiction and Fact*, *The Magazine of Fantasy & Science Fiction*, *The Year's Best Military and Adventure SF*, *Terraform*, *Daily Science Fiction*, *Apex*, *Pseudopod*, *Escape Pod*, *Galaxy's Edge*, *Nature*, and numerous year's-best anthologies. The author of the sci-fi novels *Redspace Rising* and *Ten Thousand Thunders*, Trent is a winner of the 2019 Year's Best Military and Adventure SF Readers' Choice Award from Baen Books and a Writers of the Future winner. He is also a contributor to Baen anthologies *Weird World War III, Weird World War IV, Worlds Long Lost, Cosmic Corsairs,* and the Black Tide Rising anthology *We Shall Rise.* Trent lives in New England. His website and blog are at www.briantrent.com.

Michael Z. Williamson is, variously, an immigrant from the UK and Canada, a retired veteran of the USAF and US Army with service in the Middle East, the Mississippi Flood, and several cornfields and deserts. He's an award-winning and best-selling author and editor of science fiction, and a #1 Amazon bestseller in political humor. His favorite administrative tool is a flamethrower.

David J. West writes dark fantasy and weird westerns because the voices in his head won't quiet until someone else can hear them. Passionate about many interests he has written historical novels, *Heroes of the Fallen, Bless the Child,* and *Blood of Our Fathers*, and western horror in the Dark Trails Saga and the Cowboys & Cthulhu series. David also writes under the not-so-secret pen name of James Alderdice for his fantasy books in the Brutal Sword Saga. He is a great fan of sword & sorcery, ghosts and lost ruins, so of course he lives in Utah.

Deborah A. Wolf was born in a barn and raised on wildlife refuges, which explains rather a lot. She has worked as an underwater photographer, Arabic linguist, and grumbling wage slave, but never wanted to be anything other than an author. Deborah's first trilogy, The Dragon's Legacy, has been acclaimed as outstanding literary fantasy and shortlisted for such notable honors as the Gemmell Award. This debut was followed by *Split Feather*, a contemporary work of speculative fiction which explores the wildest side of Alaska. Deborah currently lives in northern Michigan. She has four kids (three of whom are grown and all of whom are exceptional), an assortment of dogs and horses, and two cats, one of whom she suspects is possessed by a demon. Deborah is represented by Mark Gottlieb of Trident Media Group.

ABOUT THE EDITOR

★

Sean Patrick Hazlett is an Army veteran, speculative fiction writer and editor, and finance executive in the San Francisco Bay area. He holds an AB in history and BS in electrical engineering from Stanford University, and a Master in Public Policy from the Harvard Kennedy School of Government where he won the 2006 Policy Analysis Exercise Award for his work on policy solutions to Iran's nuclear weapons program under the guidance of future secretary of defense Ashton B. Carter. He also holds an MBA from the Harvard Business School, where he graduated with Second Year Honors. As a cavalry officer in the elite 11th Armored Cavalry Regiment, he trained various units for war in Iraq and Afghanistan. While at the National Training Center, he became an expert in Soviet doctrine and tactics. He has also published a Harvard Business School case study on the 11th Armored Cavalry Regiment and how it exemplified a learning organization. Sean is a 2017 winner of the Writers of the Future Contest. Nearly fifty of his short stories have appeared in publications such as *The Year's Best Military and Adventure SF, Year's Best Hardcore Horror, Robosoldiers: Thank You for Your Servos, Worlds Long Lost, Terraform, Galaxy's Edge, Writers of the Future, Grimdark Magazine, Vastarien,* and *Abyss & Apex*, among others. He is the editor of the *Weird World War III* and *Weird World War IV* anthologies. Sean also teaches strategy, finance, and communications as a course facilitator at the Stanford Graduate School of Business's Executive Education Program. He also hosts the *Through a Glass Darkly* podcast. He is an active member of the Horror Writers Association.